Good Girls
Don't
Die

Isabelle Grey began her career as a non-fiction author and feature writer for national newspapers and magazines before turning to television, contributing episodes to numerous drama series from *Midsomer Murders* to Jimmy McGovern's *Accused*. Her novels *Out of Sight* and *The Bad Mother* are also published by Quercus.

Also by Isabelle Grey

Out of Sight
The Bad Mother

ISABELLE
GREY

Good Girls
Don't
Die

Quercus

First published in Great Britain in 2014 by

Quercus Editions Ltd
55 Baker Street
7th Floor, South Block
London W1U 8EW

PB ISBN 978 1 78206 766 5
EBOOK ISBN 978 1 78206 767 2

10 9 8 7 6 5 4 3 2 1

Printed and bound in Great Britain by Clays Ltd, St Ives plc

Typeset by Hewer Text UK Ltd, Edinburgh

For Jackie Malton

PROLOGUE

She could hear him moving around on the other side of the closed door. She must have blacked out because she didn't remember him leaving her here alone. She put out a hand to steady herself against the wall as she shifted to relieve the pressure on her bruised hip bone, but the shooting pain in her ribs took her breath away, and she only just stopped herself from crying out. She forced herself to keep breathing as the clammy terror returned. She didn't dare try to call out, even if she'd felt capable of drawing enough breath to yell and scream for help.

Beyond the closed door, she heard a clink, a tap run and then the unmistakable chunk of a kettle being placed back on its plate and the sound of the switch being flicked on. Maybe if she lay here silently while he made himself a tea or coffee, if she waited for him to drink it, then maybe he'd calm down and, when he came back through the door, he'd let her go. Or at least not hurt her any more. Or not so badly.

Gingerly she wiped her face with the back of her hand, and felt the stickiness of blood mixed in with mucus and tears. She tried again to ease herself into a better position on the hard floor, ready to make an attempt at standing up, but every movement was agony and she was afraid of making a sound that would bring him back out of the kitchen, so she gave up and lay where he'd left her. Enough light from the darkened street outside came in through the glass panels in the front door for her to make out the outlines of the narrow hallway. She wondered what time it was, if anyone might have reason to miss her yet.

She'd watched earlier as he'd locked the front door and pocketed the keys. It was when she'd attempted to escape that he'd grabbed her by the hair, spun her round and slammed her so hard against the wall that her knees had given way and she'd slid downwards, no longer a person, just physical matter sliding down a wall. Then he'd seemed to tower over her, slapping and punching again, kicking and yanking her up by the hair so he could hit her some more, until she'd cowered as tight as she could into the meagre shelter of the wall. His fury had been determined, rhythmic, almost impersonal.

She heard the kettle switch off and for a heart-stopping second panicked that he might be intending to use the boiling water as a new weapon. Then she heard the rattle of a teaspoon against china, the scrape of a chair as presumably he sat down, and her heart pumped back into action with a sickening jolt. She didn't want to think of him, to picture him, but right now her life depended on remaining hyper-aware of his every movement and intention.

She was mortally afraid. He'd done some real damage. Whatever primitive part of her brain was supposed to sense these things told her he'd broken several ribs. She shivered with shock and from the cold of the tiled floor. She mustn't pass out. She must stay awake, vigilant. She must concentrate, focus on something, anything. She knew what to think about: that no one else was going to help her. No one. Only one person could possibly help her now. Her.

ONE

The white laminate front door opened straight off the narrow pavement into a small living room. It was a sunny Monday morning, and Detective Sergeant Grace Fisher was responding to a call from parents concerned about their twenty-year-old student daughter. It was only today, they'd said, that their daughter's housemate had thought to let them know that Polly hadn't been home for three nights and wasn't answering her phone or responding to messages. Grace's call to the university Student Services had confirmed that Polly Sinclair had no reason to panic over her second-year exams, and her tutors had flagged up no other concerns, but her parents, now on their way to Colchester from Lincolnshire, had anxiously insisted it was totally out of character for Polly to remain out of touch like this.

Grace was new to the Essex force, and she wanted her first day to kick off well. A tiny success would be nice, like finding Polly squirrelled away under a duvet somewhere with a new boyfriend. A bit of optimism, a chance to bond with her colleagues, an opportunity to walk back into the unfamiliar office with a job well done, all these things would help her believe that this could be fresh start. But uniform, who routinely dealt with missing person cases, had already escalated the case to the Major Investigation Team. Although Grace could think of many reasons why a perhaps overwrought twenty-something might seek a bit of time out before having to pack up and switch lives for the summer vacation, attempts to 'ping' and locate Polly's phone showed that the battery was dead or had been removed, and they could find no trace of any electronic footprint since last Friday night. It didn't bode well.

The clutter of shoes, magazines, coffee mugs and phone and laptop chargers in the cramped living room instantly took Grace back a decade to her own student days, before she'd joined the police, before this Monday morning in an unfamiliar town. Those faraway days at uni already felt like someone else's life, but the reminder might be useful in making sense of why they were here.

Polly Sinclair's housemate, Jessica, stood before them, barefoot, in a pink vest and cut-off denim shorts. Grace could see that she was trying hard not to betray her eagerness at playing her part in this potential drama. 'It's the end of exams,' she explained. 'We were all out getting caned, celebrating. I just thought . . .' She pulled a penitent face. 'You know, maybe Polly spent the weekend with some guy she liked? I never thought she might, you know . . .'

Grace nodded but kept quiet; she'd noticed right away how Jessica had eyes only for DS Lance Cooper. He was thirtyish, maybe a year or so younger than Grace, and not bad-looking; if his angular features, dark hair and faithful brown eyes were all it took for Jessica to unburden herself, then fine by her! Stepping unobtrusively into his shadow, Grace took the opportunity to survey the room. A fine layer of dust and a couple of empty wine bottles showed there'd been no attempt to clear away any incriminating evidence. Whatever had happened to Polly, it didn't look like it had started here.

'You told her mother that you last saw Polly at a bar in town?' asked Lance.

'Yes, the Blue Bar.'

Lance responded with an engaging smile. 'Yeah, I've been there. Who were you with?'

'No one in particular. It's where everyone goes. I left early, went back to my boyfriend's. Polly was fine when I left.'

Grace detected a strain in Jessica's voice, like the whine of a tired child. With their high-tech toys and party drinks, most students weren't much more than kids, after all. She certainly hadn't been anywhere near as grown-up as she'd optimistically imagined she'd been at that age.

'You saw Polly?' Lance pursued. 'She was still at the Blue Bar when you left on Friday night?'

'Yes, I said goodbye.'

'Was she with anyone?'

'Just friends. I spoke to a couple of them this morning. They said they left her in the centre of Colchester, calling for a cab. She wasn't with anyone else.'

'Any idea what time that was?'

Jessica shrugged. 'After midnight?'

'Anyone hassling her during the evening?'

'No. She was having fun. We all were.'

'Does Polly have a boyfriend?'

'No, not really.'

'She wasn't into anyone special that night?'

'No.'

'But you weren't too worried about her because you thought she might have gone home with someone?'

Lance reached out and lightly touched Jessica's arm, a brotherly gesture that Grace liked.

'None of our business what she gets up to,' he told her, 'except that we need to know what's in character, and what's not.'

Jessica, still unhappy, nodded. 'It's the end of exams. She's worked like fury.'

'So, letting off a bit of steam?'

'We were all a bit hammered. That's why I didn't think to call her parents. If she hooked up with some guy after I left and liked him enough not to come home, then . . .'

'But you've no idea what guy?'

Before Jessica could answer, the doorbell rang. Jessica's face opened up joyfully, but Grace knew better than to hope it would be Polly with some simple story about a hangover and lost keys. 'It'll probably be your landlord,' she said, anticipating Jessica's disappointment as she went to open the door. 'We asked him to be here while we search the house.'

'Search it?' Jessica was alarmed. 'Why?'

Leaving Lance to soothe her, Grace shook the hand offered by Pawel Zawodny, a stocky, sandy-haired, blue-eyed man in his mid-thirties wearing faded jeans, clean white T-shirt and work boots.

'Hi,' he said, meeting her eyes cleanly before letting go of her hand. 'I was asked to attend. Has there been a break-in?' He looked past Grace at Jessica. 'You girls OK?' His English was accented, but confident and correct.

'Thanks for coming so quickly, Mr Zawodny,' said Grace, hoping she'd pronounced his name correctly. He didn't flinch, so she assumed either she had or he had long ago stopped bothering when people got it wrong. 'I'm DS Fisher, this is DS Cooper. It's just routine. Polly's parents are upset that she's not been in touch, so we need to check the house.'

'Will you have to go in my bedroom?' asked Jessica, making for the narrow staircase.

'Don't worry, we're only here to make sure that Polly's safe,' Lance said with a reassuring smile. 'We're not inter-ested in anything else. So please wait down here until we're finished.' He turned to Pawel. 'Shall we start outside?'

As Grace, too, turned towards the landlord, she thought she caught a flicker of alarm in his face but, if it had been there at all, it was quickly gone.

The enclosed courtyard behind the kitchen was a sun-trap. The brick walls had been painted pale blue, and a little slatted table on metal legs and two folding chairs had been set up on the gravel. The kitchen had been cleverly planned to maximise the space, and appeared well maintained, despite the mound of dirty crockery in the sink and the overflowing waste bin. The landlord kept out of the way while Lance opened cupboards, looked behind the shower curtain in the downstairs bathroom, and then went upstairs to check inside wardrobes and under beds in the two bedrooms. Grace followed, trying to paint a picture for herself of the two girls' life here. Jessica's room at the front was stuffy and untidy; Polly's was smaller but relatively clean and neat. It contained the usual complement of possessions; if she'd meant to leave, she'd not taken deodorant, moisturiser or mascara. Nor, Grace noted, the half-finished blister pack of contraceptive pills from her bedside table.

When Lance asked Pawel to hoist him up for a look through the hatch into the insulated loft space, Grace went back downstairs to Jessica. The girl was fiddling with her phone, and Grace waited for her to finish.

'If Polly did go home with someone on Friday,' Grace asked, 'do you have any idea who it might be?'

'I already called everyone I can think of.'

'We're not here to judge. I got myself in scrapes at uni I wouldn't want people at home to know about. Once we know she's safe, we don't have to say where she was.'

Jessica returned Grace's smile. 'I know. But Polly's generally pretty well behaved. That's why I'm worried about her.'

'OK.' Grace touched Jessica's arm. 'Be great if you could give us list of everyone you've spoken to, everyone you can remember who was in the bar on Friday night. Could you email me any contact details you have?' She handed Jessica her newly printed card: *DS Grace Fisher, Major Investigation Team, Essex Police.*

Jessica took the card from her just as, upstairs, Lance landed back on his feet with a thump, causing the girl to move swiftly to the bottom of the stairs. She looked back at Grace in distress. 'Has something awful happened? Is there something you're not telling me?'

'No, nothing.'

'I should have done something sooner!'

'I'm sure there's no cause for alarm. Polly will probably turn up and have some completely trivial reason why she's been not been in touch. If we can just have that list of names?'

Pawel and Lance joined them in the small living room. 'The washing machine, it's working OK now?' Pawel asked.

'Oh, yes, thanks. That was so sweet of you to come over.'

'No problem,' he said, opening the front door. 'You call if you need anything, OK? Let me know once Polly comes home safe.'

'Thanks, Pawel. I will.'

Grace stored away the fact that Jessica pronounced the 'w' in his name as a hard 'v'. Then Lance, too, gave Jessica his card, they said goodbye and followed the landlord out into the sunshine.

Pawel had walked a little way up the road, away from the window that fronted the pavement, and, as he stood waiting for them, looked Grace frankly up and down. In response, she straightened her shoulders, not letting him own the view, glad now that she'd worn a new fitted summer dress to make a good impression on her first day. She'd chosen it to show off the tan on her bare arms, acquired over the five days she'd spent in Barcelona before moving her car-load of boxes to Essex. She was curious to see how Pawel Zawodny would react when his eyes rose to meet her level gaze. He raised his eyebrows, as if amused by the candour of her challenge, and she struggled not to smile.

'When did you last see Polly?' she asked, feeling Lance step in behind her, as she had done for him, encouraging Pawel to engage primarily with her.

'Friday,' he answered. 'I came to fix the washing machine. The door catch had broken. Not a big job. But girls, they have to wash their clothes every day. Friday morning, I came. Early.'

He had watched without comment as they searched the house, and had still not asked for more information than they had offered, yet Grace now sensed some slight unease in him. 'Did you speak to Polly?' she asked.

He shook his head. 'She was upstairs. With some boy. I used my key to come in.'

'Did you see him? Would you recognise him?'

'No. They were . . .' He waggled his hand. 'Having fun. I let myself out.'

'Had you seen her with anyone before?'

'So long as no boyfriend lives in my house rent-free, I pay no attention.'

'Thank you. Here's my card in case you think of anything else that might be helpful.'

Pawel took the card from her hand, touching her fingers, but did not immediately look up to meet her gaze. 'When did she go missing?' he asked.

'We're still making enquiries.'

He nodded, then shrugged, gave a wave and walked over to a bright red Toyota pick-up parked across the road.

'Did Jessica mention Polly's overnight guest while I was upstairs?' asked Lance.

'No.'

'Well, we'd better ask her.' He turned back to the house, but Grace put a warning hand on his arm.

'If she knew, we need to think first about *why* she might not have told us,' she said.

'We still need a name.'

'Yes, but what if she was worried about getting someone else into trouble? In which case it might be counterproductive to march straight back in and call her on it.'

'Maybe.' Lance glanced over to Pawel's Toyota just as the engine fired up. 'But I'd also like to check he's telling the truth.'

'OK, but –' The noise of the pick-up passing them in the narrow roadway drowned her out. 'Look,' she continued, 'I've never been to Wivenhoe. I wouldn't mind getting my bearings. How about you give me a quick local tour first? Then we can come back to Jessica.'

'Yeah, fine.' He glanced at his watch. 'There's a cafe on the quay. We could grab an early lunch if you like.'

Grace hesitated. It was a friendly gesture, but she was reluctant to get involved in too much personal chat on her first day. Over the weekend, as she'd made a start on unpacking her boxes in the anonymous rented flat, she'd promised herself that she'd begin slowly: watch and learn what people were like, who was who, how and where she might best fit in.

'Not sure I'm really hungry yet,' she replied, and was both relieved and mildly disappointed when Lance didn't seem to mind being turned down.

She let him lead the way, turning right into the High Street and walking down towards the river. Grace paused to peer along side turnings that became prettier as the water came into view. More redbrick terraces similar to Polly and Jessica's rented house were interspersed with older and more charming pink, white or blue-painted facades with rounded bay windows and pointed dormers set into pitched roofs. One or two that had higgledy-piggledy half-timbering looked older still. Some boasted railings in front but most opened straight off the quiet streets.

Two girls – they looked Chinese – jogged past in expensive running gear. Grace found them incongruous in such a very English setting, but supposed that Wivenhoe, only two miles from the university campus, must be a pleasant place for students to find accommodation. On the way here, Lance had explained the transport links Polly might have used: there was a bus to the university and regular trains to Colchester – and on to London – from the station at the end of Polly's street. A few students would presumably own cars, and Grace had also noticed half a dozen men in helmets and Lycra shorts speeding along on bikes.

Several people sat with drinks outside the pub on the quay, and a variety of boats were moored along the riverbank. Wivenhoe lay at the neck of an estuary that opened out into the North Sea – she had consulted an OS map before they left the office – and was surrounded by miles of mudflats, creeks, woods and gravel pits. Rationalising any kind of search for Polly would be a strategic and logistical nightmare.

'Uniform were right to prioritise this one, don't you think?' she asked Lance.

'Dunno. She's over eighteen, fit, healthy, solvent, no apparent mental health problems. The weather's been good, no accidents reported. If she wants to go AWOL after exams, no reason we shouldn't let her.'

'But not using her phone for more than forty-eight hours – for someone Polly's age that's like severing an artery.'

'She'll probably get some cash out today, and we can all stand down.'

Grace frowned at him, perplexed by his tone. 'Is that what you think?'

'Nope, just keeping an open mind.' Lance looked coolly at her, and she felt somehow put in her place. She reminded herself that she was no longer a detective inspector, just a sergeant again, the same as him. And, with a sinking heart, she hoped she wasn't supposed to take any other meaning from his remark.

'Seen enough of the neighbourhood?' he asked.

'Yes.'

'Right. Let's go back and speak to Jessica. See if she does know who the mysterious lover-boy is.'

Grace followed Lance back up the High Street, hoping irrationally that this time Polly herself would be there to open the front door.

TWO

Dr Matt Beeston's office was situated above one of the first 'squares' they came to after walking from the car park across a wide expanse of rolling green parkland that included two large ornamental lakes. Like the concrete and plate glass of the university Grace had attended, these buildings, too, had failed to blend into their setting in the way the architects must have hoped, and, fifty years on, the campus still looked like a stage set for some futuristic Sixties movie.

Dr Beeston, too, looked ill-suited to his box-like office, where broken vertical blinds failed to shield him from the bright sunlight. He peered at them from behind his unkempt desk and, before asking who they were, apologised that he was running late for a meeting. Although Jessica had told them he'd only just completed his Ph.D., he seemed more boyish than Grace had expected. He was physically slight but undeniably attractive in a cute sort of way and, despite his preppie clothes and the Arsenal pennant he'd hung on the wall behind his desk, it wasn't a stretch for her to imagine Polly inviting him home and into bed.

Jessica had admitted that some of her reluctance to tell them that Polly's overnight guest was a law lecturer had been down to the fear that she'd get him into trouble. And certainly the stressed way Dr Beeston was attempting to stuff a bundle of files into an expensive leather satchel made Grace wonder if maybe he was slightly out of his depth. Lance explained that they were detectives and would need five minutes of his time, and he gave them his full attention.

Matt's first response was that he didn't know a student named Polly Sinclair, but when Lance suggested he might have accompanied her home last Thursday night, he blushed furiously.

'Oh yes, of course,' he said. 'Her name had slipped my mind. Not very chivalrous of me.'

'So you did spend Thursday night with her in Wivenhoe?' asked Lance.

'Yes. Why?' His voice sharpened in alarm. 'She's not one of my students. And she invited me back.' He seemed glad of the shelter of his desk, and busied himself again gathering up his papers. 'I've never taught her.'

'We're the police,' Lance explained patiently. 'We're not interested in university regulations.'

'Right, right.' Matt took a deep breath and sat down, the colour fading from his cheeks. 'So why are you here? How can I help? What is it you want to know?'

'Have you seen or heard from Polly since Friday morning?'

It took another moment for him to take on board how carefully he was being observed, but when he did, Grace was curious to note that his reaction seemed to be a mixture of discomposure and aloofness. He still hadn't asked if Polly was all right.

'We were both pretty hammered,' Matt explained. 'It was only, you know . . . I left the next morning with a hangover, and that was that. Isn't that what she says?'

'Did you contact her?' asked Lance. 'Arrange to see her again?'

'No.'

'Or try to?'

'No. Look, she was sweet, but we both agreed it wasn't the start of anything. She was no more keen than I was.' His nervous attempt to sneak a look at his watch made Grace wonder how long it would take him to focus on anything other than himself.

'We're sorry to delay you, Dr Beeston,' she said, speaking for the first time. 'And we have no wish to embarrass you unnecessarily, but we have to ask: did you and Polly have sex that Friday morning?'

Now he looked well and truly scared. 'Look, am I being accused of something here, because, if so –'

Grace continued to gaze coolly at him. 'We need to corroborate other statements.'

He gazed back, apparently trying to work out what they really wanted. Then his face cleared. 'It's that foreign builder guy, isn't it? The one who was spying on us.'

'Who was spying on you?'

'He had a foreign name. Russian-sounding. He came to fix something downstairs.'

'While you were in the bedroom?'

'Yes. He was creeping around outside the door. A real peeping Tom.' He let out a breath of relief and sat back in his chair. 'Has he done something to her?'

'Polly hasn't been in contact with anyone since Friday night,' Grace explained, watching him carefully. 'Her family are concerned about her. You've no idea where she might be?'

Comprehension was followed by a look of calculation, reminding Grace that he had a Ph.D. in law.

'I spent *Thursday* night with her,' he said. 'I'd never met her before then, and left her house about nine o'clock on the Friday morning. I was here teaching by ten.' He spoke with fresh confidence, though Grace had a hard time imagining him dominating a lecture hall. 'So I'm sorry,' he went on, 'but I have no idea what might have happened to her since then.' He picked up his satchel again. 'Have you spoken to Student Services?'

'Yes.'

'Then, as I say, I really can't help.' Matt looked from one to the other of them with an apologetic smile. 'If that's all you wanted, I hope you don't mind, but I really am very late.'

Grace and Lance accompanied him out, and he hurried off with a departing flutter of his hand.

'Well, he was a charmer, wasn't he?' Lance observed as they emerged onto hot concrete.

'He liked a student enough to sleep with her, but couldn't care less where she is now,' said Grace. 'So much for pastoral care.'

The windless air, heated by sunlight reflected off the surrounding expanses of glass, lay heavily along the walkways and within the engineered social spaces. It would soon be the end of term, the end of the academic year, and Grace imagined there was already a feeling of winding down, of lassitude, about the place. She wondered if Polly was happy here.

Earlier, as they'd walked across the park, Lance had pointed out a group of tower blocks and said they provided student accommodation. Grace thought that if the architecture felt so unyielding even with today's blue sky and greenery, then it must be pretty bleak in winter. It certainly explained why Wivenhoe was a popular place to find digs. Maybe she, too, should have looked there for a place to live, even though it would have meant a longer journey to work.

'Fancy something to eat?' Lance interrupted her thoughts.

She followed his gaze and saw there were several cafes and a couple of shops – a mini-market and a bookshop – amongst the more office-like buildings. 'Sure,' she replied, realising that she was now both hungry and thirsty.

They bought sandwiches, water and coffee and found a place where they could sit in the shade. The surrounding picnic tables and fixed concrete benches were filling up. The students in their colourful shorts, dresses and T-shirts were like an excitable flock of exotic birds, and Grace listened dreamily to the rising chatter. She allowed herself to give in for a moment to her tiredness, reminding herself that she was here now: she'd made it, and could afford to relax a little, unclench her shoulders and breathe more freely.

'So Pawel Zawodny's a peeping Tom,' said Lance.

'He was perfectly open about saying he'd heard them having sex.'

'But what was he doing sneaking around upstairs? The washing machine's in the kitchen.'

'True,' Grace agreed. 'But Dr Beeston is the one who appears to feel compromised, not Polly's landlord.'

Her attention was caught by a young man standing in the open doorway of the bookshop. He seemed a bit too neatly dressed, and somehow too *poor*, to be a student. He had that same undernourished look as the procession of thin, pale-skinned, restless youths she'd watched come and go in custody over the years. But, just as she was thinking how odd a figure he cut in this setting, the young man caught her eye. He gave her a pleasant smile before disappearing after some customers into the gloom of the shop. That explained it, she thought: he must work there.

'But what if Pawel's a voyeur?' Lance stole back her attention.

'More likely just opportunistic.'

'Except sometimes voyeurism is a preparation for sexual violence,' he said, munching on his baguette.

Grace smiled. 'You've been reading the FBI studies.'

'Yeah, I went to a lecture by an expert from Quantico,' Lance told her. 'Why, you think they're wrong?'

'No, but they're working backwards from known serial killers. Doesn't mean that all voyeurs are planning to abduct people.'

Lance put down his half-eaten baguette and wiped his mouth with his paper napkin. Grace feared she'd sounded patronising and cursed herself. 'Pawel was in the house, heard them having sex. Wouldn't you have been tempted to take a peep?' she asked lightly. 'Been just a little bit turned on?'

Lance looked at her in surprise, and she grinned, hoping to disarm him. It seemed to work, for he picked up his sandwich again. 'I guess so.' He took a bite and chewed thoughtfully. 'Like being in a cheap hotel and hearing people through the wall. You can either turn the TV up as loud as it will go or join in.'

'Too much information!' She laughed, and was glad when he laughed with her.

As they walked across the square to bin their rubbish, Grace glanced up at the row of windows where Matt Beeston's office was. Her overall impression was that he was self-centred and immature. Those qualities didn't rule him out as someone who could have harmed Polly in some way, yet – though the idea of an accusation of sexual misconduct had occurred to him a little too readily for her liking – she doubted his ability to lie convincingly enough to cover up more serious crimes.

She waited for Lance to knock back the last of his water, ready to throw away the plastic bottle, and noticed the young man back in position, looking out from his bookshop doorway. If he had looked in her direction she would have returned his earlier smile. She considered running her reasoning about Matt past Lance, but knew her thoughts were really just gut reactions. Not that gut feelings about people didn't count, but they counted less than facts. Instinct and intuition weren't evidence. She should have learned that by now.

THREE

Detective Superintendent Keith Stalgood's ingrained habit of sighing gave the impression of an impatient, irritable man, yet it hadn't stopped Grace warming to him when he'd interviewed her a month ago for the job on his team. She'd sensed straight away that this tall, well-built man, with a sharp face and a fine head of short, iron-grey hair, would be a good boss. Not that it would have mattered: after quitting her job and remaining unemployed for nearly four months, Grace had had little choice but to accept whatever was on offer and be grateful.

Her stepmother's friend, Hilary Burnett, communications director for the Essex force, had fixed up the interview for her and then sweetly invited her to stay the night before. Over a microwaved lasagne, Hilary had shared what she knew about the man who led the Major Investigation Team. Formerly a DCI in the Met's murder squad, Keith had elected to leave London in return for a promotion to superintendent. He and his wife lived in Upminster, so the commute to Colchester was no worse than before, though Hilary reckoned that, really, he was easing down into early retirement and wanted a quieter life.

But this morning, at Grace's second meeting with him, she'd already decided that Hilary was wrong, that Keith's impatience was due to a vigorous, practical mind. He certainly seemed happy that she and Lance had acted on their own initiative and gone in search of Matt Beeston after Polly's housemate had reluctantly identified him as the missing girl's overnight guest.

'So why didn't the housemate volunteer the information?' asked Keith, rolling up his shirtsleeves as he came out of his office to join the team in their open-plan area.

'She thought it would get Dr Beeston into trouble, because of sleeping with a student, but I think it was mainly to protect Polly,' Grace told him. 'She didn't want us knowing that Polly had shagged one guy on Thursday, then possibly gone off with another on Friday. She insisted Polly wasn't usually like that.'

'Which matches what the parents say,' said Keith. He glanced at his watch. 'They'll be arriving any moment. Everything they've said so far confirms that this is totally out of character. I know how naive parents can be about what their kids get up to, but Polly sounds like a nice girl.'

'Jessica said Polly told her Matt had been a mistake,' said Grace. 'That by the morning she was hung-over and couldn't wait to get rid of him.'

'Matt Beeston is a member of the academic staff,' said Lance. 'Polly's a modern languages student, wouldn't be taught by him, but officially it probably shouldn't have happened.'

'No,' Keith commented drily. 'How old is he?'

'Twenty-six.'

'He claims he didn't see her after leaving her house on Friday,' said Grace. 'And we confirmed that by ten o'clock he was teaching.'

'Right. Though I'm not sure the fact that he went home with her on Thursday night takes us any closer right now to what happened to Polly twenty-four hours later. We've got no live data, no sightings, no leads.' He turned to DC Duncan Gregg, a balding, overweight man who seemed, Grace thought, kind and unflappable. 'Anything from the CCTV around the Blue Bar yet?'

'Just this so far.' Duncan tapped at his keyboard, then swung his screen around so Keith could view the brief sequence of grainy black-and-white footage. The camera angle remained static as three young women stumbled across the screen, laughing and clutching drunkenly onto one another. The one in the middle – Polly Sinclair – clearly had trouble staying upright on her high heels.

Grace snuck a quick look at her new colleagues: none of them spoke, their faces showing that they were all equally moved by the fleeting glimpse of a ghostly apparition.

'I've spoken to these two.' Duncan pointed at the screen. 'They went home on their bikes.'

'On bikes?' asked Keith.

'They claim they weren't as drunk as they look.' Duncan spoke without irony. 'When they left Polly, about a quarter to one, she was about to call a minicab. We're still talking to the cab companies, but none so far took a call from Polly's phone on Friday night. We're running checks on the regular drivers.'

'Her friends confirmed she had her phone with her?'

'Yes. We tried pinging it again. It's still dead. Reverse billing shows no incoming calls or messages after ten o'clock. The last transmitted signal was from the town centre just before one a.m.'

'The town centre was busy,' said Keith. 'If she was taken against her will, it was done quietly, without fuss.'

'So she bumped into someone she knew?' suggested Grace.

'Someone could've offered her a lift,' agreed Lance. 'Or she may have been a passenger in a taxi booked in someone else's name.'

'We're checking all minicabs that went to Wivenhoe that night,' said Duncan.

'And compiling a list of her friends,' said Grace. 'Matt Beeston doesn't drive, but, though he denies seeing her, his flat is walking distance from the Blue Bar.'

'Alibi him for Friday night,' instructed Keith.

'The Blue Bar was packed,' said Duncan. 'It'll take a while, but we're working our way through everyone who paid by debit or credit card.' Grace caught the rest of her new colleagues hiding smiles, but had no idea why. 'So far no one recalls Polly hanging out with anyone in particular,' he concluded.

'Polly's landlord, Pawel Zawodny, may be of interest, too,'

said Lance. 'He told us he was aware of Polly and Matt Beeston having sex. If that's because he was spying on them, then he's a voyeur. Plus he has a key to the house.' He gave Grace an encouraging nod.

'Jessica spent Friday night at her boyfriend's place, so, if Polly made it home, she was there alone,' she told Keith. 'We ran checks on Zawodny.' She consulted her notebook. 'Thirty-four, a carpenter from Szczecin in Poland. Been in the UK twelve years. No criminal record. He bought the house in Station Road six years ago, did it up himself. Owns two others in Wivenhoe, also renovated by him and rented out to students. Only to women, though that may be coincidence. He drives a red Toyota pick-up, lives in a rented flat on the edge of Colchester and shares a yard off the main Harwich road.'

She was about to add that the challenge in the cool way the Polish builder had looked her up and down had flagged up something about his attitude to women – maybe just that he enjoyed a challenge – but, constrained by Keith's neutral gaze, decided it was simpler to keep quiet on her first day.

'Find out where he was Friday night,' ordered Keith. 'See if his truck was picked up on any cameras.'

'Yes, boss.' Lance smiled at Grace, making a tiny clenched-fist gesture of triumph.

'Do we release the CCTV footage to the media?' asked Duncan.

'Not yet,' said Keith. 'Let's see it again.'

'We may pick her up elsewhere,' said Duncan as he turned to the keyboard to replay the clip. 'We're still on it.'

'Hard on the parents if this is their final sight of her,' Keith observed.

Grace didn't have to imagine how many times, in the superintendent's years with the murder squad, he would have had to break bad news. She couldn't blame him for wanting to offer Polly's family a happy ending. 'Her housemate said they'd been celebrating the end of exams,' she reminded him, as if trying to make excuses for the missing girl. 'She looks happy enough, doesn't she?'

Keith sighed. 'Yeah, I suppose so. OK. Anything we've missed?'

Everyone looked around the room. They all knew better than to ask the obvious question: Where the hell is she?

Hilary Burnett put her head around the door. Her lipstick was freshly applied, her lightened hair brushed to frame her face, her navy linen dress had no creases and her two-inch heels appeared to give her no discomfort at all. She awarded Grace a swift smile before addressing Keith. 'Quick word?'

She advanced into the room before he could refuse. Grace sensed a ripple of exasperation as several members of the team looked away or started to move back to their desks, but couldn't be sure whether it was at the intrusion or at Hilary herself. Although Grace had yet to meet any communications director whose role was popular with the troops, she hoped it was not a sign of personal dislike. If so, and Hilary's role in bringing her to Essex was going to complicate her acceptance, then she'd just have to live with it: Hilary had shown her both kindness and generosity, and Grace was all too aware how rare those qualities could be.

'Polly Sinclair,' Hilary began briskly. 'Can we offer something to the local paper? The editor complains we don't engage them enough. We could ask them to jog memories of any sightings. We'd need to give them photos. Might be helpful.'

Keith stared at her as if she were speaking a foreign language, but then nodded. 'Let me find out first how the parents feel about going public,' he said slowly. 'It's early days.'

He made for his own office, but Hilary dogged his footsteps.

'They're coming in, aren't they?' she asked. 'Maybe I could set up an interview with them and Roxanne Carson, and then with the local BBC people?'

'Roxanne Carson?' Grace spoke without thinking, and felt abashed when everyone turned to look at her. 'Sorry, it's just that at uni I knew a Roxanne Carson who went into journalism.'

Hilary smiled at Grace. 'She's the crime reporter on the local paper, the *Mercury*. About your age, so she probably is the same person. That's nice!' Hilary turned back to Keith. 'She'd do a sensitive piece.'

Keith rolled down his shirtsleeves, retrieved his jacket from the back of his chair and, shrugging it on, herded Hilary before him out of the office. 'Plenty of work for you all to get on with,' he called over his shoulder as the door shut behind them.

The closing door was a signal for people to settle back into familiar places, and, as Grace observed a kind of a smoothing out across the room, she was made physically aware of being the new girl. She'd been allocated a desk that morning, and moved over to it now with an unexpected pang of homesickness for the incident room in Maidstone where, until last year, she'd been a comfortable part of the gang. She'd known some of those people – Colin, Jeff, Margie – for years, worked alongside them, been through one or two pretty traumatic cases with them. And for what? It only went to show that you didn't necessarily know people at all. Still, she couldn't help missing being an organic part of something, even if a lot of the time it had just been mundane chat about cars, sport and holidays.

Meanwhile she barely knew the names or even roles of half the people in this room. The clean, tidy surface of her own desk contrasted with the files and papers cascading across everyone else's. Lance, leaning over Duncan's shoulder, was occupied with something on his computer screen. She wasn't sure quite what she should be getting on with, but it felt too conspicuous to sit here idle. For something to do, she opened up Twitter and began searching for Polly Sinclair. She wondered how many friends Polly had, what they were like, how far Polly had really been able to trust them.

FOUR

It was Roxanne who suggested they meet at the Blue Bar. The imposing exterior showed that the premises had once belonged to some venerable Victorian institution, a bank or corn exchange, but the revamped interior, with big wooden ceiling fans and giant potted palms, had been designed to resemble either a New Orleans jazz club or the lobby of a Thirties colonial hotel. Grace, standing in the doorway scanning for the friend she hadn't seen in several years, couldn't help thinking of Polly Sinclair who, six days ago, had sat over there by the window with a group of fellow language students. A few of them had been drinking shots and become quite rowdy; now, at seven o'clock, it was too early for a big crowd of serious drinkers, and Grace easily spotted Roxanne Carson seated at the bar. She called out to her friend, and Roxanne slid down from the tall bentwood chair and held out her arms. 'Grace Fisher! It is so good to see you again!'

'And you! Been far too long.'

'Of all the gin joints in all the towns . . .'

They laughed and hugged, then levered themselves up onto the bar stools. 'So how long has it been?' asked Roxanne. 'Not that it matters, you look just the same! Hair a bit shorter, but slim as ever, damn you!'

'You look good, too.'

Grace knew that, trim and tall, with straight brown hair, regular features and grey eyes, she'd never be the one to draw attention from anyone glancing in their direction. Roxanne, on the other hand, was petite and curvy, with a mane of dark curls that she said came from her Sicilian grandmother. At uni she'd never had any trouble attracting either friends or lovers, yet on Grace's first evening in the hall of residence she'd heard Roxanne sobbing through the wall of the neighbouring room. She'd made her get up and take the bus with her into Brighton, where they'd sat on the beach, eating fish and chips and throwing stones at the reflection of the harvest moon in the water. Although never best friends, after that they'd remained close enough to stay in touch for a year or two after graduation.

A barman, good-looking in white shirt and narrow black tie, came up and greeted Roxanne by name; if he recognised Grace as one of the detectives who'd come to speak to his manager two days before, he gave no sign. 'It's two for the price of one on shorts before eight o'clock,' he said. 'Special midweek promotion, just for the ladies.'

'We're fine with the house red, thanks,' replied Roxanne with a flirtatious smile. She turned to Grace. 'OK with you?'

'Sure.'

'So, the last I heard, you'd got married,' she said.

'Yes, and now I'm waiting for my divorce!' Grace achieved the light-hearted tone she aimed for whenever the subject arose.

'Quick work,' observed Roxanne. 'What happened?'

'Oh, the usual. Bad idea to live with a man you work with, I guess.' Two glasses of wine were placed in front of them, and she raised hers in a toast. 'Cheers!'

'So what happened?' repeated Roxanne with a mischievous grin. 'You're not getting off the hook that easily.'

'Oh, we didn't agree on stuff at work. Trev was happy to remain a constable, but I reckon he never forgave me for being fast-tracked.'

'That's a bit lame.'

'Well, he was in the police national cycling team, and that was always his main priority.' Grace knew it sounded like an excuse but, even though she could see that Roxanne was waiting to hear more, she took a swig of wine and looked away around the bar.

'How long were you married?' asked Roxanne.

'Two years,' she answered curtly. 'So what about you? How long have you been in Colchester?'

'I've been at the *Mercury* four years. Too long! I'm desperate to move on, but all the nationals are downsizing, buying stuff in and putting even their regular journalists on shifts. Too much is online these days.' She reached across to touch Grace's arm. 'Didn't mean to pry. Sorry. Sounds like it still hurts?'

'It's OK. It got complicated. I'll tell you another time.'

'Oh, here.' Roxanne dug in her battered trophy handbag

and drew out a folded newspaper. 'I brought you a copy. We ran my interview with Polly Sinclair's parents today.'

Grace heard the pride in her friend's voice and responded with appropriate enthusiasm. 'Great, thanks. I've only seen the office copy.'

'I love having my name in print that big,' Roxanne said with shameless delight. Grace grinned, then cleared aside their glasses so she could spread the newspaper out on the bar.

A photograph of a smiling Polly – blue-eyed with blonde curls, sweetly plump – took up nearly a third of the tabloid's front page. *Student missing for four days*: the headline was in large, bold type. In a box at the side was a smaller image of Phil and Beverley Sinclair – the decent, apologetic couple who now haunted the police station – with the heading *Desperate parents appeal for help*. Phil, a burly man in a short-sleeved white shirt, had his hand over his wife's clenched knuckles. Beverley must once have shared her daughter's fair-haired prettiness, but it was clear that the lines running across her brow and down beside her mouth would now deepen into permanence. Grace had only met them briefly, a sharp reminder that, while their journey to Essex heralded an agony of uncertainty and dread, she could think herself lucky enough to have arrived just as a potentially intriguing case kicked off.

Roxanne caught her eye and gave an awkward laugh. 'We're ghouls, aren't we? Feasting off misery and misfortune. Or I am, anyway. At least you're *doing* something.'

'Not true,' Grace said. 'Your article's already had a good

response. A lot more people who were in here last Friday night and remembered seeing her have been in touch. Gives us a far better timeline.'

'Good,' said Roxanne. 'So what's the theory?'

Grace saw the glitter of a reporter's eye, and her own heart sank. 'You know I can't discuss it. You have to go through Hilary Burnett, or I'm in big trouble.'

'Like Hilary knows what's really going on!'

Grace shrugged helplessly.

'I had a call from the crime reporter on the *Daily Courier* just before I came out,' said Roxanne. 'If this turns into a decent story, it could be my chance to get a foot in the door in London, so if there's any way you think you can help –'

'I can't. I'd love to, but I really can't. And you realise that if it does turn into a major inquiry, then I may not be allowed to speak to you at all.'

'Yeah, I guessed as much,' Roxanne acknowledged with a sigh. 'Still, maybe Hilary will make sure the local paper gets the edge. I know she's really hot on networking, helping women give the old-boy clubs a run for their money.'

'Yes,' Grace agreed, glad that Roxanne wasn't going to push too hard. 'It's thanks to her that I landed up here. She used to work in corporate PR with my stepmum.'

'So you're alongside Lance Cooper?' Roxanne asked with a sly grin.

'I am.'

'Hot, isn't he?'

Grace laughed and held up her hands. 'I am not even going to go there!'

'I forgot, love and work don't mix.'

'No.'

'Shame! But you must've found out whether he's spoken for?'

'I only got here on Monday!'

'Huh, call yourself a detective! Will you find out and let me know?' Roxanne finished her drink and signalled to the bartender. 'Shall we get a bottle this time?' she asked.

'Yeah, why not?' Grace had been afraid Roxanne would hold the necessity for professional discretion against her, but her friend seemed to understand that it wasn't personal. She began to relax, and heard a Black-Eyed Peas track start to play. Recognising the music of their years at uni together, she felt whisked back to a time when she'd still been carefree and confident that life would go her way.

'It really is good to see you again,' Roxanne voiced Grace's own thoughts with unexpected sincerity. 'The local reporter may know everyone in town, but I haven't actually made many friends here. So if you'd like to meet up and do stuff, whatever, just give me a shout.'

'I will! I was rather dreading the weekends myself, not knowing a soul.'

'Good. Look, shall we grab a table and get something to eat? The tapas here isn't too bad.'

'Great.'

The Blue Bar was beginning to fill up, raising the noise level to a din. Grace and Roxanne were older than most of the crowd. Even the barman, Grace recalled from his statement, was a student doing part-time work. As they moved to a table, she looked again around the high-ceilinged chamber; on the night she disappeared, Polly, bare-legged, had worn a short pale blue dress, blue high-heeled shoes and a small green bag with an across-the-body strap. The last signal transmitted by her mobile had been close by at about one o'clock in the morning. Then the phone, like Polly herself, had simply vanished. There had been no sightings, her parents had her passport, and she'd not used bank, credit or travel cards, nor accessed any of her digital networks.

From everything they now knew about her, it seemed unlikely that she'd chosen to cut herself off from friends and family. Even when she'd gone to Australia and Thailand on her gap year, and had gone hiking, ridden elephants and got a tattoo, she'd kept in constant touch and complained if her mum failed to send regular news bulletins from home, asking specially for photos of the family dog, a golden retriever. Now that she had been missing for nearly five days, the chances that Polly would be found safe and well were diminishing rapidly.

Was whoever was responsible for her fate here tonight, Grace asked herself. Was the perpetrator – if there was one – amongst these loud, red-faced, excited young men? They were little more than teenagers. Would one of them be capable of abduction, rape or perhaps even murder? Was one of them some kind of obsessive stalker who had Polly locked away somewhere? But if so, where?

The day before, she and Lance had gone to take a look at Pawel Zawodny's yard, pretending it was a casual courtesy to call on him, not to waste his time, and found it kept in good order on a busy industrial park with security monitored by CCTV. If he'd taken Polly by force, he'd hardly imprison her there.

They'd also checked into Matt Beeston's background: second son of two barristers, he'd gone to a private north London day school, had no criminal record, and the university had no record of any complaint against him.

Unlucky Polly; a split-second's misjudgement and she may have put herself in the power of someone out to do her harm. Grace felt her adrenaline pump at the memory of being out on the beat as an inexperienced constable, of the demand for constant vigilance, the endless monitoring of one's environment, the need to assert and maintain control. Fail to notice a tiny mood shift, or trust the wrong person at the wrong time, and it could all go catastrophically wrong. Was that what had happened to Polly?

Grace shook herself. Wrong to identify with the victim: that way you missed things, jumped to inaccurate conclusions. Wrong to think about the past: she was here to move on. She picked up the menu and turned back to Roxanne, willing herself to recapture that earlier lovely moment when she'd remembered being naive, wide-eyed and careless.

The air was still warm when they finally left the bar. They made for the High Street as Roxanne phoned for a taxi. People from other clubs and bars had spilled out onto the noisy streets, making the most of the balmy June night, and there was much drunken laughter and banter outside a popular kebab shop. One girl, misguidedly attempting a somersault on a bike rail, slipped and lay giggling on the ground while her girlfriends shouted their glee and tried to haul her up. A group of buff young men – Grace had the impression they might be paratroopers from the local barracks – gathered round, all clutching beer cans and cheering and jeering in equal measure. Fired up by the attention, the girl tried to repeat her clumsy performance with equally dismal results. When Grace had shadowed uniformed beat officers as part of her graduate-entry training, she had accompanied her share of revellers to A & E after they'd got into brawls, fallen over or vomited themselves into unconsciousness. It was both distasteful and a shocking waste of police time. Her colleagues – many of them legendary boozers themselves – were probably right to despise members of the great British public who couldn't hold their drink. Yet Grace had remained aware of how vulnerable inebriated youngsters of both sexes could be to robbery, violence or sexual aggression.

Roxanne must have seen the serious expression on her face, for she gave her a playful push, nearly overbalancing herself in the process. Laughing, Roxanne grabbed on to her friend in just the same way that Grace had watched Polly's grainy avatar cling on to her mates to keep herself upright.

'Polly was as caned as we are now when she disappeared,' she told Roxanne. 'It's on the CCTV footage.'

'What d'you think has happened to her?'

Grace shrugged, aware of the shadowy doorways and

silent alleyways around them. 'No idea. But look at us – she'd have been pretty easy prey for someone who was sober and determined, wouldn't she?'

The cab Roxanne had ordered drew up, and as they identified themselves and clambered in, Grace looked back at all the young women innocently enjoying a boisterous summer night in this old market town, and wished them well.

FIVE

She lay awkwardly on top of the jagged debris that covered the half-cleared site where a Sixties office block in the centre of Colchester had been torn down. The body had been arranged with feet apart, legs straight and covered demurely by the smoothed-down, patterned skirt. The arms rested to the sides, and the head was pillowed on some red fabric that looked, from where Grace stood, like a neatly folded item of clothing. Trying to peer past the crime scene investigators, who were carefully laying plastic stepping boards over the rubble, Grace saw but did not immediately account for the dead woman's short dark hair, startling herself with the realisation that this was not Polly Sinclair.

Despite the surrounding activity, and the undeniable thrill of privileged access to the epicentre of this event, Grace's brain was sluggish this early in the morning. It had been such fun to gossip all night with Roxanne, but now she was regretting the amount she'd had to drink and her short, fitful sleep. She tried some deep breathing to boost her oxygen level.

'Not seen a corpse before?' Lance's quiet enquiry was sympathetic, but Grace, caught off-guard, replied more snappily than she intended.

'Of course I have. I'm fine.'

Lance stepped back, and Grace saw his face go blank.

'Do we know who she is?' she asked, trying to retrieve his goodwill.

'Not yet. The super's talking to Wendy now. The crime scene manager,' explained Lance, nodding in the direction of the forensic van where Keith Stalgood stood engrossed in serious discussion with a woman about Grace's age. With her shapely figure and white-blonde hair, Wendy looked like she'd be more at home on a country and western stage than amid the gruesome buzz of a crime scene.

Distracted by the purr of a powerful engine, Lance turned to watch a gold Porsche Panamera slide in behind the forensic van. He smiled. 'Good, here's Samit. Now we can get started.'

'Samit?'

'The pathologist, Dr Tripathi.'

The driver's door opened and a middle-aged man got out. He wore chinos and a check shirt, and had a pleasant, unassuming face with watchful eyes behind rimless glasses. Seeing them stare in his direction, he nodded politely, then went over to greet Keith.

'Nice car,' Grace observed.

'Last case we were on, he had an E-type Jag.'

Grace was relieved to see the friendliness had returned to Lance's eyes. The CSIs finished laying the walkway and, after instruction from Wendy, disappeared into the van. They soon returned with the kit for a portable tent, which they expertly slotted together to hide the body from prying eyes and protect it from contamination.

'Don't know if we'll get to suit up nor not,' said Lance glumly. 'Keith won't want any more of this rubble dislodged than necessary.'

'Sure. Do you reckon this is linked to –?'

'Don't say it!' Lance cut her off. 'Because if our guy has gone and left us a second victim, then this is one serious "oh shit" moment.'

She nodded, understanding perfectly what he meant: they hadn't a single lead on Polly's disappearance, and here another woman was dead.

Looking around, Grace realised that the street on which Samit's Porsche and the forensic van were parked led up towards the Blue Bar. Over the past couple of days every nearby alleyway, garden, yard and unoccupied or neglected building had been searched for any clue to Polly's fate, but nothing had been found. Now this.

Keith beckoned them over, and they went eagerly. Wendy and Samit had already ducked under the inner cordon of tape and were pulling pristine forensic suits up over their clothes.

'I want you as exhibits officers,' Keith informed them brusquely.

Grace and Lance grinned at each other and dived for the forensic van. Moments later they joined the others inside the tent. In the filtered light, with only their eyes visible, their white-suited figures seemed unearthly. Samit concluded his initial description of the young woman; while he concentrated on posture, body weight and identifying marks, Grace saw a slim young woman with expensively cut short dark hair and good-quality clothes. Last night's eye make-up now appeared clown-like against the dead pallor of her face.

Squatting down, Dr Tripathi began the process of taking surface swabs and tapings, each of which he handed to them to be bagged and marked. 'I'm now going to lift the skirt,' he informed Keith, who gave a nod of agreement. Delicately, he folded the patterned skirt back up to the dead woman's waist. 'Well,' he exclaimed softly. 'That's a new one even on me.'

Grace looked over his shoulder: the victim had no underwear, and a clear glass bottle glistened between her pale thighs. Grace instinctively turned away, but then made herself drag her eyes back, to look with her mind, not her emotions. The neck of the bottle had been neatly inserted in the dead woman's vagina.

Samit continued his narrative. 'There is a bottle between the subject's upper thighs that appears to be intact and contains a clear liquid.'

Grace could see that the bottle had been aligned so the label faced neatly upwards. The gaudy design of red and silver illustrated the name, Fire'n'Ice, and some of the letters had been written backwards in an attempt to suggest Cyrillic script. She glanced at Lance, who mouthed 'vodka' at her.

Samit stood up to make room for the photographer and turned to Keith. 'What's your strategy?'

'I'd like to remove the bottle now so we can get started on any fingerprints or DNA it might provide,' Keith told him.

Samit nodded. 'Be better to remove the clothes in the mortuary, too, rather than on this rough ground.' He crouched back down, examining the position of the bottle more closely. 'I'm unable to see any blood or obvious wounds around the vagina. There are no visible marks to suggest a violent struggle, nor that she was dragged here.'

'There's no clear route in or out,' said Wendy. 'There's no way of knowing whether this is the murder scene or whether she was dumped here.'

'Nor how many people might have been involved,' added Keith.

Grace stared out at the jagged, uneven surface of broken bricks, tiles, glass, concrete and rubbish, heard in the near distance the build-up of morning rush-hour traffic, thought of the young woman she'd seen last night, attempting her drunken somersaults. She'd witnessed how easy it would have been to lead such a lamb to slaughter.

'Sooner we get a starter for ten, the better,' said Keith.

Taking out a torch, Samit shone it into the eyes of the corpse, raising his chin to focus through the bottom of his varifocals. 'Possible petechial haemorrhage suggests strangulation. Though it's anyone's guess what we'll find beneath her.' He straightened up. 'She could have a bloody great knife stuck in her back for all I know,' he commented drolly.

As Samit stepped back, Grace was able to look straight down into the dead woman's face. Her features were rounded, soft, childlike, jarring against the dark hair of her brutally exposed genitals. Grace could see now that the red garment placed carefully under her head was a folded-up woman's jacket. Beneath her right ear something bulged under the fabric. Grace pointed to it. 'That looks like a pocketbook.'

Keith nodded approvingly. 'Might give us an ID. As soon as you're ready, Samit, I think we should move her.'

'Right. Then I can do the PM immediately,' said Samit.

'Good.' Keith turned to face them as best he could in the confined space of the tent. 'The bottle goes to forensics, but what you've all seen here stays under wraps until I say otherwise, understand? Not a word of this leaks out to the media. No one outside the investigation is to know any-thing about it. No one. Right?'

'Right, boss.'

He waved Lance and Grace out of the tent, and they made their way to the edge of the inner cordon, where a CSI came to take their evidence bags from them.

'This place is a going to be total nightmare,' grumbled the CSI, surveying the rubble. 'God knows how much mate-rial we're going to have to take and preserve.'

Grace and Lance stared at one another as they snapped off their disposable gloves and peeled the protective covers from their shoes. Despite the shock of what they had seen, the excitement of being handed a secret to keep had turned the investigation into an adventure.

As Grace hopped about on one foot, pulling off her suit, she noticed Roxanne watching from the far side of the road. The reporter beckoned urgently, in defiance of the uniformed officers tasked with encouraging the few pedestrians out so early in the morning not to rubberneck. Handing her suit to the waiting CSI, Grace walked reluctantly as far as the blue-and-white tape where, certain it was not a good idea to be seen speaking to a journalist, she remained safely inside the cordon where the uniformed officers could hear every word.

'Hey, Roxanne.'

'Is it Polly?' Roxanne's eyes shone, her pen already poised over her open notebook ready to take down a quote.

'You have to go through Hilary.'

'Oh, come on! The whole national media pack's going to be here by lunchtime. Give me a head start, at least!'

Grace shook her head. 'Ask Hilary.' She turned away and, aware of Roxanne's hungry eyes boring into her back, walked the few yards back to where Lance waited. He looked at her with raised eyebrows. 'Did she know you were going to be here?' he asked.

'No!'

Over his shoulder she saw Keith, exiting the tent with Samit, notice Roxanne and then direct a sharp, questioning look at her.

'Shit!'

'Come on,' said Lance. 'Work to do.'

Grace saw that he was rescuing her, and was relieved to let him shield her from their boss's displeasure.

Suddenly she was desperate to know just how much Keith had been told about why she'd really left Kent. She'd given the breakdown of her marriage as the reason for quitting her job, and very much doubted that Colin, her old DCI, would have had the balls to deviate from that version of events in his reference. Grace imagined that her stepmother had probably told her old friend Hilary most of what she knew, which thankfully wasn't everything, and Hilary had asked no direct questions. But news travelled fast: had Hilary gossiped with anyone here about the obvious gaps in Grace's story? Grace hadn't picked up any signals that she had, and now told herself firmly there was no point speculating on what Lance and the others did or didn't know. Best just to keep her head down and get on with the job.

Once they had finished signing over the evidence bags, they began the short walk back to the police station, weaving their way through quiet, narrow lanes where the shops were only just opening for the day. Although they did not immediately speak, Grace could sense Lance's bubbling excitement.

'Do you think the bottle was an afterthought,' he said eventually. 'A last-minute impulse? Or was it the whole point of the exercise?'

'It must have been arranged like that postmortem. Which means he didn't use it as a weapon.'

'If I'm allowed to reference the FBI' – he shot her a teasing look – 'there's a difference between "staging" and "posing".'

Grace nodded encouragingly. She was already familiar with the distinction but, pleased that they were evidently on good terms, didn't want to steal his thunder.

'Posing is what he likes to do for himself, his signature,' he explained. 'Staging is for our benefit, a message.'

'So which is this?' she prompted him.

'I reckon she's been staged.' Lance checked over his shoulder to make sure they were not overheard; Grace was thankful that there was no sign of Roxanne trailing them. 'Laid out all neat and tidy to taunt us because we haven't found Polly yet.'

'And the bottle?'

'Has to be a sick joke, surely? No one in their right mind would –' He shook his head in disbelief.

'Who says he *is* in his right mind?'

'True. But there was no other obvious violence; it wasn't a sadistic attack.'

Grace considered the grammar of the crime scene. Her immediate reaction had been that the almost gentle pose and delicately inserted bottle contained an eloquence she couldn't yet decipher. 'Her head was cushioned. He made her comfortable before he left her.'

Lance shook his head stubbornly. 'It's a message for us. Some game he's playing.'

'He's trying to communicate something,' agreed Grace. 'But I don't think it's a game.' She wanted to say that the message, whatever it was, had seemed to her to be *sincere*, but now clearly wasn't the time to change Lance's mind about what they'd seen. Besides, she was more interested in hearing his thoughts than in putting forward her own. She could bide her time.

'Maybe he's pissed off because we *haven't* found Polly,' he said, 'and this is his way of letting us know.'

'That there'll be a price to pay if we don't play his game, you mean?'

'Yeah. It'll all be about him keeping control, won't it?'

'If you're right,' she said, 'then you're saying this poor girl's death is supposed to steer us to something we've missed.'

'Exactly!'

'So what is it?' she asked. '*Why* haven't we found Polly? Where is she? What point are we missing?'

SIX

Photo ID recovered from the pocketbook in the jacket folded beneath the victim's head suggested that the dead woman was a twenty-one-year-old final-year law student named Rachel Moston. Her parents were on their way to the mortuary to make a formal identification. Keith meanwhile had sent Grace and Lance over to the law faculty to build up as full a picture of her as possible.

They walked once more from the car park across the green sward to the raised concrete structures of the campus. The morning sun reflected harshly from the windowed expanse of walls, exacerbating Grace's dull headache and tempting her to suggest they grab a cold drink before locating the faculty office.

Heading for the mini-market, Grace spotted Roxanne coming out of the campus bookshop. The reporter, slipping her pen and notebook back into her bag as she ducked into the cafe next door, did not notice them.

'What's she doing here?' asked Lance, annoyed.

In answer, Grace pointed to the bookshop door, where

a page of newsprint from the local paper had been taped to the glass: Roxanne's interview with Polly Sinclair's parents, headlined with their appeal for help in finding their daughter.

'If people are talking to the *Mercury*, we need to hear what they're saying,' said Lance, changing course and pushing open the bookshop door.

They entered the hush of a near-empty shop. At the far end, a man with a lank ponytail and a plaid shirt with rolled-up sleeves appeared to be doing a stock check. Nearer the door, the neatly dressed young man Grace had observed on Monday was straightening piles of books on a display table. He had short, fine hair and wore the kind of grey trousers and white shirt that supermarkets sell as generic school uniform. Once they had shown their warrant cards and given their names, he introduced himself politely as Danny Tooley, the assistant manager, and asked how he could help. Lance pointed back towards the entrance. 'You've displayed that piece about Polly Sinclair.'

'Yes. I put it there.'

'Is Polly Sinclair a customer?'

'Yes. Have you found her?' he asked eagerly.

'Not yet.'

Danny frowned. 'But Roxanne said a body had been found.' He nodded towards the door through which the reporter had departed, betraying a kind of nervous excitement Grace had observed many times in people on the periphery of a major enquiry. 'That's really terrible. But it's not Polly?' he asked. 'You've not found her?'

'We'll be releasing an official statement later,' Grace told him.

'What was the reporter talking to you about, Danny?' asked Lance.

'She said a girl had been murdered but she didn't know who it was. She wanted to know if I'd heard anything.'

'And had you?'

'No. Do you know who it is?'

Lance ignored the question. 'So why did Roxanne think you might know?'

Danny looked at them as if they were a bit slow. 'Because everyone comes in here. And Polly's a friend. I mean, we're friendly.'

When Grace had noticed the young man standing in the shop doorway and watching the students eat lunch the other day, she'd assumed he'd be all but invisible to them, but she reminded herself that that might not be the case at all. 'How well do you know Polly?' she asked.

'She comes in regularly, and we bump into each other in Wivenhoe occasionally.'

'Is that where you live?' asked Grace.

'Yes.'

'When did you last see her?' asked Lance.

Danny thought for a moment, as if the question were unexpected. 'The end of last week. She came in to talk to me.'

'Friday? Saturday?' pressed Lance.

'Friday probably.'

'What did you talk about?'

'Nothing much. I seem to remember she needed some books for the summer vacation.'

'Did you ever meet outside the bookshop? Apart from bumping into each other, I mean.'

Danny shook his head.

'And that's all you've told Roxanne Carson?'

'Yes.'

Grace saw that Lance's questions were making Danny anxious, and tried to lighten the tone. 'Do you like working here?' she asked. 'You must be right in the hub of things on campus.'

'I love books.'

'So are you studying for a degree?'

He seemed pleased by the question, but shook his head. 'My mum was ill and I had to look after her, couldn't stay on at school. But I've been working here nearly two years now.'

'How old are you, Danny?' asked Lance.

'Twenty-three. This is like having my own personal library.'

'And you get to know your customers?'

Danny nodded, his eyes wide and serious. 'I see their names on the student discount cards. Not everyone's as nice as Polly, though.'

'And what is she like?'

'Lovely. Bubbly. A bit disorganised.' Danny smiled, a sweet smile, as if he liked talking about her. 'She left her phone here on the counter once. That's how we got chatting.'

'Does she have a boyfriend?' Grace asked, more interested in his reaction than the reply. 'Did you see her around with anyone in particular?'

Danny shrugged with what looked like genuine unconcern. 'Sometimes. No one steady, though. Not that I noticed, anyway.'

'But you must notice all kinds of stuff,' she said. 'Perfect observation post here!'

Danny peered at her as if uncertain whether or not she was mocking him. 'I usually read when it's quiet.' He made his reply sound like a rebuke. He nodded towards the pony-tailed man at the back of the shop. 'The manager likes all the assistants to be well-read.'

'But you'd notice if anyone was bothering one of the women on campus, if someone was having problems or disagreements? Anything we should know about?'

He shrugged. 'I haven't seen anything like that. Sorry.'

'OK.' Grace handed him a card and gave him a friendly smile. 'In case anything occurs to you later.'

He accepted the card and placed it carefully into a wallet he took from his back pocket.

'Did Roxanne speak to your manager as well?' asked Lance.

Danny shook his head, his eyes on Grace as he put away his wallet. The door opened and a group of students entered, milling out to different sections of the shop. Danny's attention moved to them, and Grace nodded to Lance: they were done here.

'Thanks, mate,' said Lance.

'You're welcome. Anything I can do to help.'

Lance made as if to leave, then turned back. 'There is, actually. We'd really appreciate it if you didn't talk too much to the media. Sometimes that can really get in the way of an investigation, and I know you wouldn't want that. I can tell that you want Polly to come home safely just as much as we do, right?'

'Right!'

'Great. See you around.'

'Bye!' Danny smiled and gave a little wave.

Outside, Grace looked back, but the young man was walking away with one of his customers.

'Do you think he was holding out on us?' asked Lance.

'What about?'

'About how much he really told your friend Roxanne. Do you think she'd have slipped him some cash?'

'I thought the opposite, that maybe he was bigging up the little he did know.'

'Why?'

'However he likes to tell it, he's always going to be an outsider, isn't he?' she said. 'I wonder how well he and Polly really knew each other.'

'She's a pretty girl. I doubt he'd stand much of a chance with her.'

'No.'

'Oh well, just so long as he hasn't sold some kind of story to the tabloids,' said Lance. 'We don't want to get caught out.'

Grace didn't care to imagine what Keith's reaction would

be were he to learn some vital piece of evidence from a newspaper headline rather than from his own troops. As they passed the cafe they'd seen Roxanne go into, Grace glanced inside, but there was no sign of her.

'Can you ask Roxanne? Find out what people are telling her?' asked Lance.

Grace shook her head. 'No way. I can't be seen talking to her. You saw the look Keith gave me this morning. Besides,' she teased, 'you'd probably have greater powers of persuasion!'

'How come?'

'She's been asking me whether or not you're single!'

'You're kidding, right?'

She laughed with him, but the illusion of intimacy was fleeting, a sad reminder that access to the only old and familiar friend she had here in Essex was now barred, if only temporarily. If Roxanne *had* paid Danny for any kind of exclusive, then of course she was only doing her job, but it increased the distance between them.

Grace and Lance had to ask for directions before success-fully locating the dean's airy and well-maintained corner office. They had asked to speak to a student co-ordinator in Dr Beeston's department, but their request had been passed further up the chain and they'd been given an appointment with the dean of faculty. Simon Bradford was a pleasant man in his early fifties, dressed in the kind of classy lightweight suit that suggested a few semesters spent at an American university. He quickly introduced the ele-gant, bird-like woman beside him as Fiona Johnson, the director of communications. It was clear that the university was not taking lightly the likelihood that one of their students had been murdered, despite the somewhat lackadaisical reaction to Polly's disappearance earlier in the week.

Lance explained that because they were still awaiting both formal identification and cause of death, the information they were about to divulge must remain highly confidential. Nevertheless, they were currently investigating the murder of Rachel Moston. The dean was well prepared and quickly pulled up her student profile on his computer while Ms Johnson expressed appropriate sentiments of regret.

'Where did this take place?' was her first question, and Grace could see her instant relief when Lance told them that the body had been discovered early this morning not on campus but five miles away in Colchester town centre.

Dr Bradford, scanning his screen, shook his head sadly. 'No problems this end,' he said. 'Rachel Moston had consistently good grades throughout her three years here, good attendance record and no academic warnings. Such a waste, a real tragedy. I can only feel for her family.'

'What about her relationships with fellow students? Any close friends we might speak to?'

'You'd have to ask one of her tutors.'

'If you could you let us have a list of her year group,' said Lance.

While Dr Bradford tapped at his keyboard, ready to print the document, Grace smiled at Fiona Johnson. 'I just wanted to say how helpful Student Services have been over Polly Sinclair,' she said lightly.

'Has she still not turned up?' Ms Johnson matched her conversational tone, but Grace found it impossible to believe that the presence here of the university's director of communications was unrelated to the fact that now the fate of two students would be front-page news.

'No. Her parents are extremely concerned, as are we.' She turned to the dean. 'Might we have a list of all Rachel Moston's tutors as well, please? Who would it be best to speak to about her?'

A printer at the side of the room hummed into life, and Dr Bradford let Fiona Johnson be the one to rise and fetch the year group list, which she handed to Lance. Seconds later another sheet rolled through, which Ms Johnson handed to Grace. There were seven names, amongst them that of Dr Matt Beeston. Silently Grace passed it on to Lance.

'I'm afraid we have to ask, but is there anyone on this list we ought to be paying attention to?' Grace made the question sound entirely routine. 'Any issues over pastoral care, or any complaints against any of these tutors?'

She nearly missed the hint of warning in Dr Bradford's glance at Ms Johnson. It was little more than a raised eyebrow and a dip of the chin, but it was there, and Grace wondered what they were hiding. It made her think of Colin, her old DCI, and how desperately he'd hated being put on the spot like this, how much virtually any large institution resented its boat being rocked, its self-serving procedures being forcibly picked apart.

'Had there been any formal complaints made in relation to the conduct of university staff,' Ms Johnson answered, 'we would have taken appropriate action and it would be a matter of record.' She turned and locked the dean into a moment of silent accord before turning back to the detectives. 'There is no record of any formal complaint made against any of these faculty staff.'

So why, wondered Grace, are you at such pains to spell it out? And why had Matt Beeston been so jolly keen to remind them that Polly wasn't one of his students? She met Ms Johnson's level gaze. 'Anything off the record we should know about?' she asked in as friendly a tone as she could manage. 'This *is* a murder enquiry.'

'I really wish we could offer more help.' Ms Johnson rose to her feet, smoothing her skirt and avoiding eye contact. 'Don't hesitate to contact me if there's anything else we can do.' She extended her hand: the interview was over.

SEVEN

The entire team, including the civilian support staff, had crowded into the main Major Investigation Team office for the first briefing when Keith returned in the afternoon with the post-mortem results. Everyone was keen to get the investigation fully launched, and Grace, too, relished the heady adrenaline surge, all too aware of the long days of hard work, little sleep and badly digested sandwiches, coffee and pizza that probably lay ahead.

Duncan added a photograph of a bottle of Fire'n'Ice vodka to the board, then perched on the nearest desk, waiting for Keith to begin. Everyone had been told about the existence of the bottle, but no one other than those who'd been in the forensic tent at six o'clock that morning knew about its intimate connection to the victim, nor had been shown the relevant crime scene photographs, which Keith had locked away in his office.

'Right,' Keith began. 'Rachel Moston. Twenty-one. Just finished her final-year exams and, according to her parents, had a good placement fixed up with a London law firm.

Regular boyfriend who we've confirmed was in Nottingham last night, taking part in a university judo competition. According to him, she planned to go with friends to the Blue Bar last night.'

Mention of the Blue Bar sent a ripple of anticipation around the room, though no one yet had the balls to ask if they were officially linking Rachel's murder to Polly Sinclair's disappearance.

Accurately reading their minds, Keith sighed. 'Rachel Moston's debit card transactions confirm she *was* there. She settled a fairly hefty bar bill a little before midnight.'

Grace was all too uncomfortably aware that her own name would show up in the list of electronic purchases from last night, but swiftly decided she could inform Keith of that later. Meanwhile she did her best to hide a ripple of shock: had she and Roxanne rubbed shoulders with the dead girl hours – minutes, even – before she was killed?

'Preliminary autopsy results suggest death was caused by ligature strangulation,' Keith continued. 'No indication of recent sexual activity. We're fast-tracking material from her fingernails, but she has no obviously defensive bruising or wounds. We're also waiting for toxicology. Stomach contents, supported by her bar bill, suggest she'd had a fair amount of white wine. Impossible to say if she'd added any vodka to the mix.' Keith looked up from his notes. 'So, last movements. Does anyone know where she was heading when she left the bar? Where did she go between leaving the bar and the discovery of her body on the demolition site just before six a.m.?'

Wendy raised a hand, and Keith gave way to the crime scene manager. 'We can't say for certain that's where she was killed,' she said. 'Nor what time the body was left there. But the perpetrator obviously had time to arrange the body without being disturbed. Either the streets were quiet by then, or he's a pretty cool customer.'

Keith nodded. 'From the moment Rachel left the bar, I want to know where she went, when and with whom.'

'We're compiling lists of her friends and of everyone who was at the bar last night,' Lance told him.

'What about the bottle?' Keith asked.

'It was half empty, still capped. The remaining contents were vodka,' said Wendy. 'No prints, which suggests it was wiped clean. We've fast-tracked swabs for DNA. We also recovered some fibres from her clothing.'

'Fire'n'Ice has been on special offer at Tesco since last Friday,' said Duncan. 'Their superstore has shifted over two hundred bottles of the stuff this week alone.'

'We'll have to check out every purchase,' sighed Keith. 'And then tie them up to any available in-store CCTV. Start with the previous twenty-four hours.'

'Yes, boss,' Duncan said happily.

Grace had noticed on her first day how her colleagues had smiled at one another, and she had now discovered the reason why: while Duncan undoubtedly enjoyed focusing on this kind of data-gathering for its own sake, it also meant he had to work closely with the team's civilian case manager, Joan, for whom he apparently yearned silently and painfully. Catching Lance's eye, Grace took his covert wink to mean they were all rooting for this office romance.

'There's also a mini-market on campus that stocks the brand,' Duncan added, oblivious. 'They're sending us their data.'

'Rachel could have bought the vodka herself,' Grace pointed out.

'Unlikely she'd take it with her to a bar,' said Lance.

'Find out if anyone saw her carrying something that could've been a bottle,' ordered Keith. 'And, if we assume it was our matey, the killer, who brought it to the party, did anyone notice someone with a bottle?'

'Was it organised or a chance encounter?' Grace asked. 'And if it was planned, then was Rachel the intended victim?'

Keith nodded. 'Where and when did they meet? Was matey in the bar? Hanging about outside? If so, did anyone notice him there? How did he know where she'd be?'

'He wiped the bottle, took time to stage the body,' observed Lance. 'That suggests confidence. Has he done this before?'

'He may have just got lucky,' warned Duncan. Grace knew he was right: they'd all been told often enough how easily an investigating officer, seduced by a narrative that slotted evidence together too neatly, could make fatal mistakes.

'We can't rule it out,' said Keith. 'So check the National Injuries Database, and with Interpol.'

Lance, pleased, made a note.

'There's still her underwear,' said Wendy. 'We haven't found her knickers yet.'

'He's kept them as a trophy!' said Lance, and was treated to a withering glance from his boss.

'Finally, I want to know how he left the scene, and where he went then,' ended Keith.

Aware that Lance had been fizzing with impatience to share their discoveries, Grace glanced at him; he nodded back encouragingly.

'Boss?' she began.

'Yes?'

'One of Rachel's law lecturers was Matt Beeston.' She didn't need to spell out the connection to Polly Sinclair. 'She was in his seminar group.'

'Find out where he was last night,' Keith ordered. He turned to Duncan. 'See if he ever bought a bottle of Fire'n'Ice.'

'There's no record of any formal complaint against him from a student,' Grace continued. 'But it seemed to us like the university authorities were going to a lot of trouble to spell that out to us.'

'Well, that's only to be expected, isn't it?' asked Keith, frowning impatiently.

Grace feared she was wasting his time: it wasn't enough to say she'd had a strong feeling there was something Ms Johnson and the dean weren't saying, especially when it might not even be about Dr Beeston. 'Sure,' she said, letting it go.

'There's one more angle to look at,' Lance jumped in. 'Polly and Rachel had the same landlord.'

'Pawel Zawodny?' exclaimed Keith.

'He owns three properties in Wivenhoe, and two are rented out to dead or missing girls!'

'OK. See if you can place him in town last night.'

'That's not all,' Lance went on. 'The university Accommodation Office told me that two past tenants made unsubstantiated complaints against him. Accused him of creepy, vaguely stalking behaviour.'

'What about the night Polly disappeared?' asked Keith. 'Was he in town then?'

'We still don't know,' admitted Lance. 'He says he was alone at home, but we've no corroboration.'

'Well, keep working on it,' ordered Keith. 'You and Grace go talk to Rachel's housemates.'

'So we are making the link between Rachel and Polly, then, boss?' Lance asked, braving the hush that immediately fell over the crowded room.

'I think we have to, yes,' Keith answered curtly. 'But only in this room, and most definitely not in front of Polly's parents.'

As Keith retreated to his own office, Lance punched the air and turned to Grace with a grin. 'Voyeur who's well organised and precise. And Fire'n'Ice is a Polish import. You wait and see!'

Grace returned his smile and touched his arm lightly. 'I'll be ready in a moment. Just need a quick word with the super.'

She knocked on Keith's door and went in without waiting for permission, closing it behind her.

'Sir, I need to tell you something.' She realised that, unconsciously, she'd clasped her hands behind her back and was standing with feet parallel and apart, as if she were a trainee on parade. She swallowed and unclasped her hands. 'I was at the Blue Bar last night.'

Keith raised his eyebrows, clearly both surprised and annoyed. 'There's no room in this team for anyone who thinks they can fly better solo, DS Fisher.'

'No, sir. That's not why I was there.'

'So what were you doing?'

'I met a friend for a drink. It was her suggestion that we meet there.'

'Who's the friend?'

Grace hung her head. 'Roxanne Carson.'

She expected anger – he'd have every right – and tasted a familiar bitterness at the back of her mouth as she waited for the inevitable rejection and disbelief.

Keith regarded her steadily. 'She was also at the crime scene at six o'clock this morning.'

'Not through me, sir, I promise.'

'You knew her at university, right?'

'Yes. We'd lost touch but Hilary gave me her number.'

He gave her a long, hard look, then sighed. 'OK. But I want all future contact with her logged. You can go.'

'Sir?' Grace stood her ground. 'I noticed a group of young men near the High Street. It was late and they were drinking and joshing some girls. They looked liked they might be paras. Should we check them out?'

Keith nodded, a glint of amusement in his eye. 'Knock

yourself out,' he said. 'The army is seldom keen on having to answer to outsiders, and there are two or three thousand soldiers in Colchester. Even if you wait until you've a more specific request, I still wouldn't hold your breath.'

Feeling a little foolish, Grace was at the door before he called her back. 'Tell Lance to keep himself busy for an hour. Since you're already on such good terms with the media, you can sit in on the press conference. Hilary likes to present a bit of diversity.'

He gave her a kindly look; Grace, expecting suspicion and condemnation, felt light-headed and she realised she wasn't sure how to respond, that she had all but forgotten what it was like to be made welcome.

EIGHT

Ivo Sweatman picked up the story from his news feed. A strangled young woman wasn't much in itself, but she'd been identified as Rachel Moston, a twenty-one-year-old law student, due to graduate this summer from the University of Essex: the perfect kind of senseless tragedy to arouse the wrath and sorrow of the hard-working, family-minded readers of the *Courier*. Then he noticed that she'd been murdered in Colchester, which was where he'd toyed with the idea of doing a piece the day before about a missing student. He had no plans for the weekend, it was a sunny day, and maybe a trip out to Essex on expenses would liven things up. Didn't matter whether the two incidents were related; they were now. If something bigger came along, he could easily dash back to London before the Young Ferret had a chance to sharpen his elbows.

The media conference was the usual affair. He didn't recognise Hilary Burnett, and had the impression that she was relatively new, not only to Essex but to police culture. That could go either way, but he'd make sure to be extra friendly in case her inexperience left her unguarded. He scanned the room. Not many people here: a local BBC news crew, a couple of stringers; didn't look like any of his esteemed London colleagues were on to it yet. He'd left a message for Roxanne Carson at the Colchester *Mercury*, but she'd not got back to him. In any case, he guessed she might be the elfin-looking girl with a mass of dark curly hair in the second row. He'd noticed that women seldom sat right at the front: too afraid of being thought ball-breakers. He waited for her to catch his eye, then smiled and shifted along so he could sit behind her. He leaned over the gilt and red plush chairs – why were these places always furnished like second-rate bingo halls? – and held out his hand.

'Ivo Sweatman, chief crime correspondent on the *Courier*. I think we spoke the other day?'

She looked thrilled, bless her. 'Hi, yes. Roxanne.'

Her hand was dainty, but he recognised a kind of gluttony in her eyes that he approved of. He was satisfied now that he'd been right to abandon his desk, even if it did mean leaving the Young Ferret to dream he was king of the castle in the interim.

'So what's the latest?' he asked.

'They've not added to the previous statement.'

'Are they linking it to Polly Sinclair?'

'Keeping an open mind. Still hoping Polly will turn up.'

'What do Polly's parents say?'

Her face fell, and he guessed she was ticking herself off for not having thought to make the call.

'If they're going to talk to anyone, it'll be you, won't it?' he cooed. 'After that lovely interview you did.'

She blushed; she actually blushed! This was almost too easy: like shooting fish in a barrel.

'I'll call them as soon as this finishes.'

He was about to say 'Do it now', but a hush fell as Keith led the way to the long table set up facing the sparse audience. Behind him was a huge image of the red, white and blue Essex Police crest, topped by *Taking a lead in making Essex safer* – a brand motto the force might live to regret. Ivo had worked a lot of cases with Keith when he'd been a DCI in the Met, and his old pal now gave him a businesslike nod. Hilary Burnett spotted it, and Ivo rather suspected she would be none too keen on them getting together to rehash old times. Next to Keith was a slender, rather lovely young woman who reminded Ivo of his first wife. Probably his daughter as well, except it was at least ten years since he'd set eyes on her.

Hilary opened with a feeble joke that nobody had come to listen to her, and lost no time introducing the senior investigating officer, Detective Superintendent Stalgood, who was accompanied by Detective Sergeant Fisher, a member of the enquiry team for Rachel Moston's murder.

After the usual platitudes about liaising with the university authorities to offer reassurance and advice, concerns for student safety and stepping up patrols, the SIO got down to the nitty-gritty, which didn't amount to much. Apart from confirming that the cause of death was strangulation, making this officially a murder enquiry, and a bland catch-all that they were vigorously pursuing several possible leads, it was obvious they had nothing – or nothing they wished to share.

'This is an incredibly difficult time for Rachel's family and we are keeping them informed of every step of our investigation,' said Keith, wrapping up his spiel. 'I and my officers are committed to bringing her killer to justice as quickly as possible.'

Hilary indicated that they'd now take questions from the floor and Ivo shot to his feet, notebook ostentatiously in hand. 'Ivo Sweatman, *Daily Courier*. Do you currently have anyone under arrest?'

'Not at this time. As I say, we're pursuing a number of leads.'

'Is there a link between Rachel's murder and the missing student Polly Sinclair?' Ivo asked. He was gratified that a couple of heads swivelled in his direction: the other pillocks either didn't know about Polly or had been too slow to make the connection. He was almost sorry he'd done their job for them, but he was more interested in poking Keith to see what reaction he got.

Disappointingly, it was Hilary who took the question. 'Only one in seven thousand, four hundred missing people are victims of homicide. This force alone handles over two thousand missing person reports per year, ninety-nine per cent of which are resolved. Despite our ongoing concern for Polly Sinclair's well-being, we have no reason at this stage not to believe she will yet be found safe and well.'

Ivo could tell from the way Keith's lips narrowed that he

was annoyed by this pointless attempt at deflection, which only went to confirm Ivo's surmise that Hilary was out of her depth. Ivo caught Keith's eye, raised a provocatively ironic eyebrow and, sure enough, Keith rose to the bait.

'We have not so far been able to locate Polly, and her disappearance is entirely out of character. Her parents are naturally extremely anxious, and our concern for her welfare grows with each passing day.' Keith spoke with what sounded like genuine passion. 'We are keen to hear from anyone who has seen Polly, or has any information about her whereabouts or movements since late Friday night. I'd also like to make a direct appeal to Polly herself to get in touch with us.' He turned to face the TV camera directly. 'If you're watching this, Polly, please contact us. You're not in any trouble. We simply wish to make sure that you're safe and well, and we will completely respect your privacy.'

'Two girls apparently victimised in a matter of days,' pressed Ivo.' You're sure you're not on the lookout for a serial killer?'

Well used to this game, Keith gave him a look of weary forbearance and answered with a terse 'No'.

Seated behind Roxanne, Ivo couldn't help but catch some covert eye contact between DS Fisher and the cub reporter. DS Fisher caught him looking, and immediately tried unsuccessfully to camouflage the direction of her gaze, confirming Ivo's feeling that this story was definitely a runner.

'I'd urge you not to get ahead of yourself, Ivo,' Keith continued. 'And not to alarm the public unnecessarily.' He deliberately swept his gaze around the room, away from Ivo. 'I reiterate, we have made a thorough search of the surrounding area near to where Polly Sinclair was last seen, and we remain gravely concerned about her disappearance.'

'Polly was last seen after she left the Blue Bar, is that correct?' Ivo allowed his pen to hover innocently over his notebook. 'Where was Rachel Moston last seen?'

'My officers are continuing their enquiries to establish the circumstances surrounding Rachel's tragic death, and we will of course keep you all informed. We urge anyone with any information to come forward as soon as they can.' Keith nodded briskly to Hilary and rose to his feet.

'Thank you, everybody,' Hilary called over the immediate buzz of voices. She waved a folder above her head. 'I have spare media packs if anyone wants one.'

Ivo leaned over to speak in Roxanne's ear. 'Who's the Ice Maiden?'

She turned to look at him and then followed his gaze. 'Old friend of mine,' she whispered eagerly. 'Grace Fisher. Only arrived this week.'

'Where was she before?' he asked casually, as they edged out together along the row of chairs.

'Major Investigation Team at Maidstone.'

'And how come you know her?' he asked, prompting her to go ahead of him towards the exit.

'We were at uni together. Sussex.'

'Why did she make the move here?' Ivo expected Roxanne to get wise and clam up, but she was either greedier or greener than he thought. Or both.

'Her marriage broke up, I think,' she told him. 'She was married to another copper.'

They paused at the street entrance. 'Don't suppose you can recommend the best place to stay?'

'Sure. The Queen's is central, and it's just been modernised.'

'Look,' Ivo gave his most disarming smile, 'I really could do with some help. Makes all the difference, working with someone local. Don't suppose there's the slightest chance I could buy you dinner?'

This time she at least attempted to dissemble. 'Sure,' she said nonchalantly. 'I don't think I've anything much else on tonight. Nothing I can't shift.'

'Great. Thanks so much.' He hoped he wasn't laying it on too thick. 'See you in the bar at the Queen's about seven?'

'Perfect.' She walked away, a spring in her step, already scrolling down the screen of her mobile.

By the time he'd checked in, rearranged his room the way he liked it and connected his laptop to the hotel wi-fi, tomorrow's story was already written in his head. *Six days in hell . . . Parents' anguish as police sources deny that a manhunt has begun for a serial killer who may already have slain blonde-haired Polly Sinclair . . .* He still had plenty of time to file his copy. He'd rather not have to run with the photos of Rachel and Polly available on the police media website; it would be better to get exclusive pictures. He could probably scrape something off Rachel's social media pages, but he'd head out later to see what else he could pick up. Meanwhile he'd do a little digging into Hilary Burnett, discover the best way to curry favour there. Later on he could set Roxanne the task of extracting exclusive material out of Polly's parents.

He thought back to when he'd first started in Fleet Street, back in the days when it really *was* Fleet Street; he'd had a night editor who insisted that any journalist worth his salt always carried a letter of resignation in his back pocket. Times had changed, and these days Ivo preferred simply to make sure he always had some kind of advantage over anyone even remotely connected with a story, or enough anyway to give him an edge over any opposition.

He poured himself some fizzy water from the minibar. If he was going to stay in town for more than a few days, he might track down a local meeting: you never knew who you might run into in the fellowship. Then he kicked off his shoes and settled himself comfortably on his bed with his laptop. Everybody knew that Keith Stalgood kept a whacking great skeleton in an unlocked cupboard, but while he was at it, he might as well check out the Ice Maiden, too: shouldn't take more than a couple of calls to Sussex University and Kent Police to get to know DS Fisher a whole lot better.

NINE

As Grace watched the young woman cry, the adrenaline that, since today's dawn start, had so far overcome her combined hangover and lack of sleep began to ebb away. She, too, would have liked to sit with her head in her hands and shut out the world for a moment. Caitlin and Amber were Rachel Moston's housemates, and, like the murder victim, also third-year law students about to graduate. It was Caitlin who was weeping, tears of helplessness and disbelief that made her look like she must have done as a child. Amber, shocked into silence, had backed off to one side of the room as if needing the wall for support.

Upstairs in Rachel's bedroom fellow officers were working their way through her belongings; on the kitchen table her laptop lay already bagged up with an evidence seal.

'Are you really sure it's her?' asked Caitlin.

Grace nodded. She did not give details of Rachel's parents' visit to the mortuary, nor the anguished phone call they had subsequently received from Rachel's boyfriend.

'Were you with her last night?' Grace asked instead.

'No. We were at a gig on campus,' explained Caitlin. 'That's why we weren't really sure where she was. I'd texted her, but she didn't reply.'

Grace nodded: they'd already read Caitlin's text on the mobile also found in the jacket that had cushioned Rachel's head.

'How would she normally have got home after a night out?'

'Train. If it's late, then a taxi. There's usually other people heading back to Wivenhoe so we can split the fare.'

'Your landlord is Pawel Zawodny?' asked Lance. Caitlin nodded. Grace also saw Amber pay attention for the first time.

They had learned that this three-bedroom house on Alma Street, one of the prettier roads in Wivenhoe, was the most recent of Pawel's student lets. Grace could see how he had extended the ground floor into a small conservatory to create a single, light living area. The walls were painted a similar blue to Polly and Jessica's tiny courtyard, with dark-grey built-in shelves. The floor was an inexpensive wood-effect, but nicely done and in a tone that matched the slatted blinds. It was obvious that he took trouble over his projects, that he was, just as Lance had said, organised and precise.

'Do you know his other tenants?' Lance asked. 'He has a couple of other student houses in Wivenhoe.'

Caitlin shook her head.

'Might Rachel have known Polly Sinclair?'

'Don't think so. I only know the name because people are talking about her.'

'Is she the one who's gone missing?' Amber spoke for the first time since introducing herself.

'Yes,' said Lance. 'Rents a house in Station Road. Drinks at the Blue Bar.'

'Second-year modern languages,' added Grace, but both girls shook their heads. Caitlin began to cry again, and Amber came to sit beside her, tucking her knees up under her chin and placing an arm around Caitlin's shoulders while looking up at the two detectives with big frightened eyes that reminded Grace of the exaggerated animation of Puss in *Shrek*.

'Did Rachel often go to the Blue Bar?' asked Lance.

'I guess. We all do if we're in Colchester. It's a good place to meet up.'

'One of your tutors, Dr Beeston, drinks there, too,' said Grace. 'Was he friendly with Rachel?'

'Matt? No!'

Grace smiled. 'You seem pretty sure.'

'We try to avoid him, that's all. He fancies himself too much as a player.'

'Rachel wouldn't have been meeting him there?'

'No way.'

'Have you ever felt threatened by him?'

'Nah. I mean, he's a nice enough guy, I suppose.' Caitlin paused. 'He's fine as a teacher.'

'But you wouldn't socialise?'

'No.'

'So what do you mean, then, when you say he's a player?'

'He hits on the newbies, before they wise up. He's a bit lame, that's all.'

'Bad enough for anyone to complain to the faculty?'

Caitlin merely shrugged, so Grace moved on. 'Can you think of anyone Rachel might have felt threatened by?' she asked. 'Anyone hassling her or giving her unwanted attention? A rejected boyfriend, or someone from home?'

Caitlin looked to Amber, who dragged her gaze away from Grace only to shake her head.

'Rachel's really straight, you know?' Grace had to strain to hear Amber's quiet voice. 'Easy. Kind. Her life is just friends, family, boyfriend, work. *Was*,' Amber corrected herself, reaching for Caitlin's hand. '*Was* kind and easy. This can't be happening! She had such a good job lined up and everything. She can't be dead! It's not fair!'

'I'm really sorry.' Grace spoke as calmly as she could. 'Just a couple more questions, then we'll leave you in peace. Firstly, did Rachel have a red jacket, cut like a bomber jacket, with button-down breast pockets?'

Caitlin nodded miserably.

'Was vodka a drink she liked?'

'I don't know. Not particularly.'

Grace knew that the officers upstairs had already checked for any vodka bottles in the house, and that the rubbish had been bagged up and would be taken away for examination. She gave Lance a slight nod, indicating he should take over the questions.

'Do you see much of your landlord?'

'He was here yesterday, to mend the shower,' said Caitlin.

Lance looked triumphantly at Grace. 'What time was that?'

'About six. He came over specially, because we wanted showers before we went out.'

'And Rachel was here then?'

'Yes.' Caitlin's eyes filled once more with tears.

'How long was he here?'

'Not long. It just needed a new fixing in the wall.'

'How do you get on with him?' Lance asked.

'Fine. Pawel's a good landlord. Makes a real effort.'

Grace noticed that Amber, staring at her hands in her lap, was picking at her nails. 'Would you say the same, Amber?' she asked gently.

Amber looked as though she'd been caught out at something. 'Oh, yeah, he's fine,' she said dismissively, hiding her hands.

'All his tenants are women,' Grace observed, as if the thought had only just stuck her. 'No issues there?'

'No,' Amber answered, with the kind of moody shrug a teenager might give. Grace wondered what she wasn't saying, and why. She looked at Lance, but he appeared not to have noticed anything amiss.

'OK, thanks,' Grace said. 'We may have further questions, and we must ask you not to touch any of Rachel's belongings.'

'You'll probably get the press banging on your door,' Lance warned them. 'Or trying to make contact with you through your social media. We can't tell you what to do, but we'd very much prefer you not to talk to them or engage with them in any way as it can complicate the enquiry. They can be very persistent, so let us know if it gets too much.'

'You may be better going to stay with friends tonight.'

'I just want to go home,' said Caitlin. 'Is that all right?'

Grace nodded. 'You've got our cards. Just send us your contact details.'

She and Lance let themselves out and walked back to the car.

The midsummer solstice was approaching and it wouldn't be dark for several hours yet, but as Lance drove, Grace watched the trees already casting flickering shadows across the road. The way out of Wivenhoe led past small post-war council estates and then a ribbon of bungalows. She could see stretches of woodland beyond and it was not long before they reached agricultural land. Where was Polly, she asked herself. What vital lead were they missing?

She summoned to mind the image of Rachel's body early this morning lying on the sharp-edged broken bricks, roof tiles and lumps of plaster of the demolition site. Grace had seen other crime scenes, other bodies that sprawled on the ground as they had fallen or been thrown down, dumped or pushed aside, bruised, bloodied and bloated corpses with splayed legs, ungainly arms, faces pushed into mud and dirt – or worse. Never had she seen a murder victim left the way Rachel Moston's killer had left her.

There had been no attempt to conceal the body. As soon as it was light, Rachel had been spotted by someone walking past. She'd been laid down decently, the violating bottle hidden modestly beneath her skirt, so much so that the office cleaner who called the emergency services had thought at first it was someone playing a prank, lying down there deliberately as some kind of practical joke.

Had Rachel been carrying her jacket, Grace conjectured, or had her killer removed it in order to fold it beneath her head? For, despite the crude indignity of the vodka bottle, Grace was sure there was something genuinely tender and regretful, an air almost of sorrow or contrition, about the way Rachel had been so delicately laid down on the rough ground.

She thought back to when they'd spoken to Matt Beeston. Despite his obvious alarm that Polly might have made some kind of complaint against him, he hadn't been in the least regretful. There had been no hint of apology, either, in the direct way Pawel Zawodny had eyed Grace up and down in her summer dress that first day. She hoped they weren't looking in entirely the wrong direction by concentrating on what connected Polly and Rachel.

She became conscious of Lance glancing at her from time to time as he drove. 'Sorry,' she said, smiling. 'Too tired for small talk. D'you mind?'

'No. But –'

'What?'

'Another time.'

'No, go on.'

'You know there's talk about why you left Kent?'

She felt clammy and sick. All the old tension and broiling injustice and hurt came flooding back. She looked angrily out of the side window, waiting for the rush to subside: it wasn't Lance's fault, after all.

'I thought you ought to know.' He sounded half apologetic, half aggrieved.

'Thanks,' Grace said, turning to look at him. 'Really, I appreciate it. Better to know.' She took a deep breath, bracing herself for the worst. 'So what are people saying?'

'Why don't you tell me first what happened?'

'What, I'm a suspect?' She laughed bitterly.

'If you don't want to talk about it –'

'No. It's fine.' She tried to work out how little she could get away with. 'A guy called Lee Roberts, a very popular uniformed constable and star of the police national cycling team, got busted red-handed along with the dealer who was selling him banned steroids and amphetamines.'

'Word is you fitted him up.'

'It was a clean bust,' she told Lance sharply, and hoped her burning face wouldn't give her away. 'But I had been concerned about him. He'd always had a short fuse and was starting to get paranoid, showing signs of amphetamine psychosis. There was an incident with a prisoner. I didn't think it should've been hushed up and I said so. Spoke up about him needing help, too. No one did anything, but then when he got caught, he blamed it all on me.'

'And you left Kent because –?'

'I quit.' All over again, she tasted the bitter disappointment of her DCI's silent relief when she'd handed him her letter of resignation. 'Like I say, Lee Roberts was a very popular guy.'

'And you weren't?'

'Obviously not.'

'And that's it?'

'Pretty much. Does that fit with what you've heard?'

'I guess so.'

Grace could see from the tight set of Lance's mouth that he wasn't entirely satisfied, but this would have to do, for now, at any rate. She wasn't going to start telling him about the hate mail, the dog turds in her desk drawer or how Lee's girlfriend spat in her face one weekend in a crowded supermarket aisle. She had no evidence to prove her fellow officers had waged such a war of attrition against her: after all, who could she go to? Not the police, that was for sure.

To her relief, her mobile rang, and she thanked whatever stars were looking out for her. Duncan's name appeared on screen, and she put him on speaker. 'Hey?'

Duncan's excitement filled the car. 'Transactions on Matt Beeston's credit card show he was buying drinks at the Blue Bar last night. Same time Rachel Moston was there. Not only that, he was there the night Polly disappeared, too.'

'He never mentioned that,' said Grace.

'Correct.'

'Rachel's housemate just told us that he's a player, hits on the new students.'

'Even better. The super wants him picked up right away. Plus the clothes he was wearing last night.'

Lance pushed back against the steering wheel and pressed his foot down on the accelerator.

'Thought you'd be disappointed,' she teased.

'Why?'

'You placed your bets on the Polish landlord.'

'Ah well, you know what they say: he'll come again!' His eyes on the road, Lance didn't seem too bothered by the investigation's swift change of focus.

Grace settled back in her seat, reflecting that if only this had been an entirely fresh start, without any of the rotten stuff from the past still hanging over her, she'd have been well satisfied by the progress they were making.

TEN

Ivo was happy. This was the moment he loved best, when all the cowboys were gathered around the campfire watching sparks fly in the dark and telling tall tales about past adventures. This first evening – before the death knocks and doors slammed in your face, before the news editors started demanding more, bigger, better, before the lethal rivalry and betrayals got properly saddled up – was always the sweetest. Even without a drink in his hand, he was happy. Most of the old faces had now turned up. Funny how they always nosed their way to the same hotel. Few newspapers these days ran more than a couple of foreign desks, and they let fresh-faced kids who thought they were immortal run around in war zones, but crime would sell for all eternity, allowing him and his colleagues to keep tight hold of their expense accounts. His little ferret chum back in the office would have to go on yearning for Ivo's job for a good while yet.

Beside him, in the bar of the Queen's Hotel, sat Roxanne Carson. She was a good girl, the kind who would no doubt also be setting her cap at his job. She'd called right away to tip him off that a member of the public had rung her paper with the news that the police had made an arrest. This public-spirited informant was soon encouraged to divulge that she lived in the flat next door to Dr Matt Beeston, a university lecturer, who'd been taken away by police late that afternoon. Moreover, the informant wasn't surprised: when pressed, she'd volunteered that her neighbour didn't put his rubbish out on the correct days, and when he did, none of it was in the proper recycling bags.

Despite a barrage of calls to Hilary's mobile, all she would say when Ivo finally got through was that a twenty-six-year-old man was helping them with their enquiries. Which was fine and dandy so far as he was concerned. He'd impressed on Roxanne the first rule of journalism: you don't share. Or only with him, anyway. So, with any luck, the *Courier* would be the only national to lead tomorrow with the man's identity. And a little more besides.

It was the work of moments to rummage around on Facebook and Instagram and then follow up with a few cold calls, enabling Ivo to put together a new and unexpectedly juicy story on Dr Beeston. Tomorrow's edition would carry photos of Matt partying, captioned with quotes from female students about the randy lecturer's 'relaxed' and 'unstuffy' style of teaching.

The academic's frolics had been so accessible that Ivo had still had time to spare for a bit of digging into the Ice Maiden. A few more calls and emails had thrown up some unexpected background, and when Roxanne had arrived promptly at the hotel, he had probed gently to see how much she knew about her friend. She was either the soul of discretion (which he doubted) or DS Fisher had understandably chosen not to divulge the full story (which made his research all the more valuable).

Accepting the first of several drinks, Roxanne had been keen to offer further tributes to the power she hoped to impress and from which she hoped to extract favours in return. One nugget – that Polly's father had recently had treatment for cancer – he filed away: it wasn't news but would make a good inside follow-on in the absence of harder copy. The other – that in Polly's final CCTV images she'd been too pissed to walk straight – was pure gold. There'd already been talk at the *Courier* about running a summer campaign on the shame of Britain's underage drinking culture, and this would play straight into it. What was the statistic? That British girls were the hardest-drinking teenagers in the western world. What with the different health angles, demands for action from MPs and local councils, haranguing the drinks industry, and a few first-person celebrity tragedies, they could spin it along for weeks – right through the August silly season when news stories could be hard to find. Odds were that Rachel Moston, too, had been drinking, in which case her murder would keep Ivo right at the heart of a crusade claiming to protect these young women from themselves. Result!

And while Ivo had already scanned both Polly and Rachel's social media sites, Roxanne had been able to insinuate herself into some of the conversations the girls' friends were having on Twitter and Facebook. Nothing usable yet, but at least she'd wormed her way in there. She'd also befriended some kid who worked in the campus bookshop, who was in a good position to keep watch and listen. According to him, the university authorities had already instructed people not to speak to the press except through the vice principal's office, but this kid had known Polly, wanted to help find her, and promised to keep Roxanne informed. The fact that he'd turned down Roxanne's offer of a hundred quid was only to the good; it meant he wasn't likely to ditch them for a higher offer from elsewhere.

Roxanne had also finally – what on earth did they teach 'em on these fancy journalism courses? – checked in with Polly's parents, who'd been too shocked by the murder of one of their daughter's fellow students to give more than a brief statement, but at least Roxanne had not blabbed it to every other reporter in the bar, and it had beefed up his story very nicely.

He observed her now, leaning forward in her chair, drinking in the banter and scurrilous gossip. Her eyes shone and her mouth hung open a little. She was a ripe little thing. Not that he fancied her himself. He no longer had the energy to take on someone nearly half his age, and two ex-wives were quite enough, thank you very much. He wasn't sure whether she realised how hard these beer guts around the table were trying to impress a pretty girl. She caught him watching her and gave a tiny smile: she knew, all right. Good. He needed her to be clever, just not so clever that he had to worry about her loyalty. Before she left tonight he'd dangle some catnip to keep her keen. He could surely wangle her a few shifts on the paper, maybe even let her feast her lusting eyes on the Young Ferret's job.

Now Fleet Street's finest were bragging about the goriest stories they'd each covered and speculating on where Polly Sinclair might be found. Manacled in a cellar? Chopped up into little pieces and fed to the pigs? Abducted by aliens? You could be sure the police had already had at least ten calls from eyewitnesses who'd seen the spacecraft land and take off, and would receive a dozen more. As the gang got louder and more raucous, the bar staff began to look anxiously in their direction as other guests, picking up the gist of their laughter, shot pointedly disgusted glances towards them. But this lot didn't give a toss. It just egged them on. If what they wrote was so repugnant, how come circulation figures inevitably rose whenever the papers led with a particularly brutal or salacious crime? Punters loved it.

Ivo polished off his mineral water and sat back, letting his mind wander. It would soon be time for the ten o'clock news on the telly, and he'd have to watch to see if they fitted in coverage of the murder. That would probably depend on whether the current British hopeful had got knocked out of the latest tennis. Meanwhile, he thought about the twenty-six-year-old man helping police with their enquiries. If they had him bang to rights, then he'd likely be charged tomorrow and the whole thing would be *sub judice*, so they might as well all shut up shop and go home. Just as well he'd got his story in when he did. But he hoped Keith hadn't bagged his man this easily. If there *was* a serial killer on the loose, then finding a couple more bodies first would be much more fun. Ivo hated the summer air conditioning back in the office, and would far rather hang around Colchester for a while yet.

The police had not picked up Dr Beeston until the end of the day, so would more than likely hang on to him overnight to soften him up a bit. Ivo thought about being locked up in a cell. It had only happened to him once – which was a miracle when you thought about it – but he'd never forgotten it. The twenty-six-year-old would have eight hours for it to sink deep into his bone marrow that he'd lost control. He'd have to piss four feet from where he laid his head. They'd have taken away his phone. No one was going to bring him a cup of coffee or a clean shirt just because he wanted one.

If he's not guilty, Ivo figured that he'd start off thinking it'll be all right; he's innocent, it's just a stupid mistake. All he has to do is explain and they'll shake his hand, thank him for his time and let him go. After all, he's got a Ph.D. and clean fingernails. Miscarriages of justice don't happen to people like him. But ever so slowly he'll come to understand that, in the cells, there are no 'people like him'; there are just those waiting to be locked up and those waiting to do it. It'll finally dawn on him that no one's going to let him out until they decide it's what *they* want to do.

Ivo thought about the many versions of the story he'd heard at meetings. *My last drink was when I woke up in a cell. My last drink was once I realised I'd lost control of my life.* It was a good lesson and he wished he'd learned it a whole lot earlier than he had. He thought again of what Roxanne had told him about the last images of Polly Sinclair stumbling drunkenly away from the Blue Bar. Poor kid. It was shame that she'd make the front page only to become yesterday's fish and chip paper. As for Dr Beeston, little did he know but, regardless of whether or not he was guilty of Rachel Moston's murder, the poor sod's nightmare at the hands of Ivo and his esteemed drinking colleagues around the table here was only just beginning.

ELEVEN

Grace let herself in, slung her keys and bag on the kitchen worktop and looked around the new-build flat on the edge of Colchester that was now her home. All the rooms were just that bit too small. Varnished wood, beige twill carpet and cream walls. She hadn't yet found anywhere to store a suitcase, ironing board or vacuum cleaner; the doors of the fitted cupboards barely closed over a coat hanger, and even the dishwasher was pint-size. Not that Grace had had the chance to spend much time here since she moved in six days ago. Wearily she surveyed the unpacked boxes that lined one wall of the compact living room, but they could wait: it was nearly midnight and she'd have to be back at work for six, ready for the strategy meeting for Matt Beeston's interview.

There'd been a real buzz in the station as she'd left. Having someone in the cells, even if few were yet fully convinced of his unquestionable guilt, was energising, and there was an elated, purposeful air to the place that felt good to be a part of. More than a part: she and Lance had gone to Matt's equally compact modern Colchester flat to make the arrest. He'd answered his door wearing a football shirt and baggy shorts. Although they'd bagged up some of his other clothes and shoes, they hadn't let him change, so he'd had to sit in the back of the car in his shorts and flip-flops, looking every inch the nervous teenager. She and Lance might not be that much older, but they intended by their manner to impress upon him that they were already a world apart in terms of their authority.

They'd taken a quick look around Matt's flat. It was sparsely furnished, with little in the way of proper furniture; he'd made do with piling stuff on the floor or cramming random possessions into tattered cardboard boxes. Nevertheless, it was spotlessly clean: he either had a regular cleaner or a good reason to apply the bleach.

Bringing him in through the back entrance, Grace knew that the sudden bustle in the corridors was due to people curious to catch a first glimpse of the suspect, and she wasn't immune to a little vanity in being seen to be the DS escorting the prisoner into custody. Most murders were messy domestics, tragic but hardly glamorous; this killing was different. Even without knowledge of the carefully positioned vodka bottle, it had snagged the imagination of those within the station. And, with Polly yet to be found, there was still everything to play for.

Matt was booked in and passed fit to detain. He wanted his own solicitor, which caused a delay, by which time, under the rules of the Police and Criminal Evidence Act, he had to be given food and then eight hours of uninterrupted rest. Duncan had no need to spell out to the custody sergeant that they wouldn't be too fussed at any further delay that might leave the ex-private schoolboy helplessly kicking his heels in a stale cell overnight while they gained more time to chase forensic results, check facts and follow up the list of Dr Beeston's past and present students.

Simon Bradford, the law faculty dean, had now admitted that the young lecturer had received an *unofficial* warning from his departmental head over lack of judgement and inappropriate socialising with female students. The dean had nevertheless vigorously defended his own earlier lack of transparency, citing confidentiality issues and university protocols. It was a smokescreen, and both sides knew it; furthermore, in the interests of damage limitation, he had then solicited a public acknowledgement – to which Grace refused to agree – that the university had, from the start, been fully supportive of the police investigation.

Grace had tried not to let her anger at the dean's hypocrisy consume her – she knew it was fuelled by baggage from her past – but now she felt the silent walls of her flat close in on her, echoing the bitter hours she'd spent trying to make sense of the malice she'd faced in Kent. Her persecutors, too, had justified their lack of mercy by an appeal to loyalty and comradeship, by fealty to uniform. Had the university, in protecting its reputation, shielded a killer?

Trying to shake off these bad thoughts, she went to open the fridge. There was nothing much in there, and it was too late to start ordering takeaway, even if she fancied it: by the time it arrived, she'd be too tired to eat. She had a couple of bottles of wine, but, after this morning's hangover, she wanted to keep her head clear. She took out a bottle of fizzy water and leaned against the counter, glad of its reviving freshness. She made herself focus on what would happen tomorrow. It was unlikely that Keith would put her, untested and new to the team, in the interview room with Matt, even though she'd done the Tier 3 training and successfully led several key interviews in Maidstone. More likely it'd be Duncan and Lance who'd question him, while she watched the feed with Keith, ready to double-check Matt's statements and follow up any new information he let drop.

She liked interviewing, had even been commended for it in past cases, but she also liked being able to observe. She couldn't always put her finger on exactly what it was she reacted to, but she trusted herself to pick up on little gestures, silences, glimpses of fear, guilt or shame. Putting into words what her jumble of subliminal insights might mean for an investigation wasn't always easy, either. Colin used to tease her about it in those early, honeymoon days at Maidstone. Just spell it out, he used to say. And Jeff and Margie once left a set of those wooden nursery-school blocks, with a letter of the alphabet on each face of the cube, on her desk. The latest high-tech aid, ma'am, they told her: she might find them useful when she wrote up her case files. And until everyone tired of the joke, she had used them a few times to spell out obscenities which she left on their desks.

The happy memory was painful, but it seemed like she

just couldn't shake herself free of the past tonight. She gave in, letting herself recall the laughter they all used to share in the pub: her, Trev, Margie and Jeff each taking turns to buy a round, Trev on tomato juice if he was in training for a big race; or she'd watch him relax and mellow over a double Scotch if the pressure was off, giving her that special look that suggested they wouldn't stay too late tonight . . . Quite often Lee was there, too, Trev's cycling teammate, the hero, the champion. She still didn't understand how she could've been the only one to notice how jittery and short-fused Lee had become. Trev had refused to listen, claimed she simply didn't get that the man was busting his arse in order to win; told her that riding at Lee's level wasn't fun, it hurt, it stressed him out, to leave the guy alone. And so she'd backed off, willing to trust her husband rather than her own instinct.

And where had that got her? Alone here now in this anonymous flat, weary and tired of this endless state of delayed shock and hurt and disbelief. She promised herself that one day she would expunge the memory of them jeering as she'd come down the steps from the magistrates' court. Only a narrow path had been shovelled through the filthy snow, leaving her little choice but to walk past the group huddled around Trev. He had his back to her and did not look round. His neck was slightly reddened where the unfamiliar collar of his new suit had rubbed against his buzz cut. Only two of them had actually jeered; no prizes for guessing which clowns they were. Margie, pulling at her scarf, had glanced in Grace's direction and given an apologetic shrug: it was easier to stick with the others. Jeff had stared at her belligerently but made no sound, and even Colin, her boss, just gazed expressionlessly over her left shoulder into the leafless branches of a tree across the road. The minicab she'd ordered was waiting and she'd dived into the overheated sanctuary of the frayed back seat. As it had pulled away, she recalled the phrase that had come to mind: if you're walking on thin ice, you might as well dance.

Well, she was trying her damnedest but she'd never been that much of a dancer. She felt too angry, though whether at herself, or at Trev, or Lee, or her former colleagues – or right now, at the dean of the law faculty – she wasn't entirely sure. She was alone now because she had done what she believed to be right. Wasn't that why they'd all joined the police in the first place? If only she could convince herself that telling the truth, trying to do the right thing, hadn't been the worst mistake of her life.

Grace turned off the light in the paltry kitchen. Maybe it was just as well that Keith wasn't likely to put her in the interview room in the morning: she was in no fit state to attempt to read Matt Beeston's mind.

She undressed in the box-like bedroom and went to take a shower. As the hot water poured over her shoulders, she thought of Matt in his cell, lying alone on a thin plastic mattress with the choice of facing a graffiti-covered wall or a metal toilet bowl. Would she be able to tell from his face tomorrow morning whether or not he'd spent the night thinking about what he'd done to Rachel Moston, about how he had laid her out so carefully on the inhospitable ground and then violated her with a half-empty bottle of cheap Polish vodka?

She turned off the water and stepped out of the shower. Wrapping herself in a towel, she faced the steamed-up mirror and wiped away a patch of condensation above the sink, ready to brush her teeth. Meeting her reflected eyes, she caught a glimpse of how she felt others must see her: a plain face, serious, wary and tired. She spat out the toothpaste, dried herself off and went through to the bedroom, put out the light and settled down to listen to the unfamiliar night noises.

Even with the window open, the building felt stuffy. She'd watched similar blocks of flats being built, and there never seemed to be any natural materials on site: no bricks, wood, stone or slate. It was as though this whole place was constructed of plasterboard, metal, plastic, cables, glue, grout and mastic, while she longed for shelter, for something solid and enduring. The blue-painted brick and gravel of the little suntrap yard of Polly and Jessica's house came to mind. Perhaps she should look for something like that to rent once this short lease expired. Though whether she'd want Pawel Zawodny as a landlord was another matter.

Grace realised she wasn't ready to sleep. Her mind was churning, and all thoughts led back to the investigation. Or to Trev, which was worse. She settled herself comfortably, stared up at the ceiling and gave herself permission to review the week properly, day by day. It seemed as though every piece of the investigative jigsaw had already been considered; one or two slotted together, but it was far from clear where they fitted into a bigger picture. As she waited for a distant car alarm to fall silent again, a connection she'd missed earlier suddenly jumped into her head: when the young man in the campus bookshop this afternoon had given his name – Danny Tooley – she'd failed to recall that she'd come across it before.

She got out of bed and padded through to the living room to fetch her laptop. Back in bed, she piled up her pillows behind her, crossed her legs and settled it open on her lap. The screen gave out all the light she needed. She'd already trawled through Polly Sinclair's Twitter account on Monday and, though she hadn't checked out everyone, she had found that Polly was linked to over two hundred people. And, yes, she was correct: the list of followers included Danny Tooley. Now she clicked onto his account and found he followed seventeen women and six men. Rachel Moston was not amongst them, but nearly all of them also appeared in Polly's lists. Polly was the first person he'd followed and he had favourited several of her tweets. He had never sent a single message to anyone and, apart from Polly, who'd followed him back, his only followers appeared to be automated bots, except for the last person on the list – Roxanne Carson. Grace was about to follow Roxanne herself, so she could keep tabs on her, but remembered that she'd have to log it with Keith as the senior investigating officer and decided it was too much trouble.

Grace checked out Facebook. Danny had opened an account, but never posted to it and had no friends. It was enough, however, to allow him limited access to other accounts.

She wasn't sure what it all meant. There was certainly nothing to connect him to Rachel Moston, the murder victim. And it didn't really give Grace anything new: Danny hadn't hesitated to tell them that he and Polly had been friendly. All the same, his activity on social media sites made it clear he rather liked Polly, and that it would appear to be pretty one-sided, which meant he might well know more about her life than he'd been willing to let on. She hoped he hadn't decided to trust Roxanne with what he knew rather than the police.

She wished she could talk to Roxanne, find out what Danny had said to her, what Roxanne had made of him, but she'd have to clear that with Keith first, too, and he'd almost certainly say no.

She closed her laptop and slid it onto the floor. Maybe she could sleep now. It was late and she had to be up and alert in – shit! – less than five hours. There was no breeze, but at least a few distant traffic sounds drifted in through the open window. They were all double-glazed, and she didn't want to think about what it would be like to sleep here in the winter when they were shut and she was sealed in. She listened to the building noises, sure there was an inaudible background hum that made the air reverberate uncannily. Her thoughts drifted. Did Danny Tooley have a crush on Polly, or was he maybe even stalking her? But then why was Rachel Moston dead? With that thought bouncing around her skull, Grace finally fell asleep.

TWELVE

In the interview room bright and early the next morning, Matt Beeston was doing his best to be helpful. Monitoring the interview remotely with Keith, Grace could see that the presence of his solicitor, who appeared to be an old friend of his parents, gave him heart. All the same, he couldn't hide his unease at being unshaven and unshowered, nor at how poorly his football shirt and baggy shorts contrasted with the others' formal clothes. While Lance and Duncan were open, encouraging and respectful, they made no acknowledgement of the fact that they were responsible for his being plucked from his home and offered a disturbed night in a dirty cell. Grace wondered if his solicitor had yet chosen to inform his client of his exposure in this morning's *Courier* as the 'randy lecturer helping police with their enquiries'.

She watched his body language carefully. So far, his manner suggested confidence that it wouldn't take long to clear things up so that he'd then be free to go. It's what any innocent man would believe. Yet she could also detect an underlying tension, an almost reckless anxiety. She'd seen it before: the panicked hope that what lay in plain sight would be somehow overlooked.

Thanks to their hard work last night – not all of which, thankfully, had been splashed across the front page of the *Courier* – they already knew quite a lot of what Dr Beeston had to hide. Grace was eager to find out how long it would take him to give it up – and to learn whether or not other, darker secrets waited to be uncovered.

Lance and Duncan waltzed him through the usual openers, letting him think this would be pretty much a normal conversation. How did he usually spend his weekends? What did he do last weekend? What did he do after he left Polly Sinclair's house last Friday morning? What's the Blue Bar like? How often does he go there? What does he generally drink? Which nights had he been there since last Thursday, when he'd hooked up with Polly?

Keith leaned forward towards the screen, waiting for Matt to answer this last question. Grace watched alongside him as Matt hesitated, making a silent calculation before he replied. 'I was there a couple of times,' he said. Lance and Duncan smiled encouragingly, but kept quiet. Matt glanced quickly at his solicitor. 'Saturday and Tuesday, I think it was. Had a few beers.'

'Saturday and Tuesday,' echoed Duncan. 'Great, thanks.' He paused to watch Lance make a note on the pad of paper before him. 'So beer is what you usually drink?'

Watching the tension drop out of Matt's shoulders, Grace looked at her boss.

'He thinks we don't know,' Keith said, never taking his eyes off the screen. 'That he's off the hook.'

As agreed at the strategy briefing, Duncan led Matt through various other fairly pointless questions before circling back to the real issue. 'So you didn't run into Polly again at the Blue Bar?'

This time Matt leaned over and whispered to his solicitor, who eventually nodded, and Matt clasped his hands together on the table in front of him. 'I didn't tell you before,' he said, looking at Lance, 'but I did see Polly the following night, after we – you know –'

Lance nodded expressionlessly, as if this was precisely what he'd expected Matt to say, but made no comment.

'So that would be Friday night, not Saturday, correct?' asked Duncan, as if the detail were unimportant to him.

'Yeah, I suppose so.'

'Had you arranged to meet?'

'No. We just bumped into one another.'

'Did you speak to her?' Duncan pressed.

'Yeah, but, you know –' Matt shrugged. 'Like I told DS Cooper before, we'd both been pretty hammered before when we . . . Neither of us was interested in a repeat performance.'

Duncan shuffled some papers and appeared to consult one of them before speaking. 'You were drinking beer all evening, is that right?'

'Yes, probably.'

'You're not a vodka drinker?'

'No, not really. Look, I've just remembered something.'

'Did you buy vodka recently? Maybe for someone else?'

Grace knew that no purchase of Fire'n'Ice had shown up in Matt's debit or credit card history, but that didn't mean he hadn't paid cash.

'What?' Matt asked. 'No. Look, the night I went home with Polly, there was this guy –'

'Pawel Zawodny, her landlord. You told us.'

'No, not that. That was the next morning. I'm talking about the night before, when we hooked up.'

'We'd like to talk first about the following night. Friday, the night Polly disappeared.'

'Nothing happened! I spoke to her as I was leaving. We were both cool with the way things were. I left before her. I was with friends. They'll tell you.'

Duncan took names and contact details for Matt's friends before resuming his questioning. 'And where did you go then?'

'I don't remember. Home, probably.'

'Very well. So what was it you wanted to tell us about the previous night? That would be Thursday.'

Matt sagged with relief. 'I'd completely forgotten. Polly asked some guy she knew for a lift home. He refused and she really mouthed off at him.'

'Do you know who it was?'

Matt shook his head. Grace watched him struggle to retrieve a clear memory, to picture the scene. 'I don't know. I didn't pay much attention. And I'd had a fair bit to drink. He seemed familiar, but God knows where from.'

'Can you describe him?'

Matt blew out some air. 'Young, white, just a guy.'

'A student?' suggested Duncan.

'Probably.'

'Can you remember if Polly used a name?'

Again, Matt thought hard. Suddenly Danny Tooley jumped into Grace's mind. Danny had said he lived in Wivenhoe, so might Polly have asked him for a lift? Did he own a car? She dimly recalled that, as she'd waited for the kettle to boil at five o'clock that morning, she'd had the impression that some vital idea had come to her just before she'd fallen asleep. What was it? Something to do with Danny and Twitter? No, that wasn't it. She'd have to work back to it later.

She leaned forward to the microphone that fed into Duncan's earpiece. 'Ask if he could've seen the man any-where on campus.'

Duncan relayed the question without any indication that he'd been fed it. But Matt was shaking his head. 'Maybe,' he replied. 'I've no idea. Sorry. She got stroppy with him, I do remember that. I was surprised, didn't expect her to talk like that.'

'Didn't stop you going home with her,' Keith muttered to himself. Grace liked his spikiness, and speculated that perhaps he had a daughter of his own at university.

'And you're sure it wasn't her landlord?' asked Lance, betraying just a little too much interest, causing Keith to tsk-tsk in disapproval.

Matt once more shook his head. 'No. Well, I never really saw his face. It was only that Polly said it was him, leering through the bedroom door the next morning. But no, I'm pretty sure it wasn't him.'

'So how did you get back to Polly's place on Thursday night?' Lance asked.

'Took a cab.'

'And the other nights you've been at the Blue Bar, how do you get home?'

'Walk, usually. It's not far.'

'So you don't drive?' asked Lance, with a faint and deliberate trace of mockery.

Matt coloured. 'No.'

'Never passed your test?'

'No.'

'How many times did you fail it?'

'What's that got to do with anything?'

'You've held a provisional licence. You can drive?'

'I'm dyspraxic,' Matt admitted resentfully.

'Have you ever driven without a licence?'

'No!'

Lance held Matt's indignant gaze but sat back, letting Duncan resume the lead. 'Let's move on to Rachel Moston. She was one of your students, is that correct?'

'She was in my third-year seminar group, yes.' He glanced involuntarily at his solicitor, who, Grace guessed, had probably coached him. 'I'm really sorry to hear that she's dead.'

'How often did you see her?' continued Duncan.

'It was a weekly seminar. She was a hard worker, a promising student.'

'Did you ever see her outside of class?'

'No. Why would I?'

'Did you ever sleep with her?'

'No! I don't sleep with my students.'

'May I remind you, Dr Beeston, that you're under caution and this interview is being recorded.'

The solicitor leaned closer and whispered something in Matt's ear. He reddened. 'I never saw Rachel outside of my teaching duties,' he said stiffly.

'You never met her at the Blue Bar?'

'No.'

'Never got drunk with her?

'No!'

'But you do socialise with students you teach?'

'Socialise occasionally, maybe, but I keep proper boundaries.'

Duncan nodded and, opening his laptop, frowned at the screen as he tapped at the keys, allowing Matt to watch in frustrated silence.

'They must occasionally want to hang out with you, though, right?' asked Lance. 'Have a bit of a flirt with the teacher?'

Matt, failing to respond to Lance's bantering tone, looked scared as Duncan pushed the computer around so both he and his solicitor could see the screen.

'For the record, I'm showing Dr Beeston a Facebook page with a photograph of him with Emma Hodges,' said Duncan. 'You taught her last year, is that correct?'

Matt looked anxious. 'Yes.'

'Can you confirm that's you in the photograph?'

Grace had already seen the image. Duncan had spent much of the night trawling through the unrestricted social media sites of several of Matt's past and present students. His reward had been to come across a group of photographs taken at a party in what appeared to be someone's parental home. The image he was now showing the young lecturer – and several others like it – showed a flushed, laughing Matt sprawled on an upholstered armchair, a wine glass in one hand and the other cupping the breast of the giggling girl who sat on his lap.

'Maybe you'd like to reconsider your earlier answer, Dr Beeston.'

Matt hung his head while his solicitor whispered in his ear. Eventually he nodded and looked Duncan in the eye. 'It was unwise of me to accept a party invitation in London, and I had a little too much to drink.'

'How many times did you sleep with Emma Hodges while you were teaching her?'

When Matt still hesitated, Duncan sighed deeply. 'We can easily get a statement from Emma if we have to.'

'Shit!' Matt rubbed his face and, feeling his stubble, also suddenly seemed to take note again of the ludicrous clothes he was wearing.

Duncan waited, and Grace watched Matt's face as it finally sank in how dangerously off course this was veering. She saw the panic come into his eyes. 'Please,' he began. 'I just –'

Duncan held up a hand, cutting him short. 'You'll have an opportunity to explain in a moment. First, I want to put an earlier question to you again. Which nights this past week did you go to the Blue Bar?'

Matt looked shamefaced. 'Friday and Wednesday.'

'Why did you lie to us earlier?'

'I didn't lie! I just didn't want the hassle. Look, I told you right from the start that I had a one-night stand with Polly Sinclair, but the rest – I'm very sorry about Rachel, but her death has nothing to do with me.'

'But you did see Polly Sinclair at the Blue Bar the night she disappeared, and you also saw Rachel Moston there on Wednesday night?'

'No!' Matt looked terrified. 'No, I never saw Rachel!'

'So why did you lie about which nights you were there?'

'I didn't lie. I just didn't want to get involved!'

Duncan and Lance observed him calmly, waiting for him to fill the silence.

'It was an error of judgement. I admit that. But, honestly, you have to believe me,' Matt pleaded. 'I never saw Rachel. Ask the people I was with.'

'We will.'

In the privacy of the viewing room, Grace turned to Keith. 'It is possible he never saw her.'

'Really?' Keith looked sceptical.

'The Blue Bar was pretty packed that night,' she told him. 'I was there, and I never caught sight of him. They could easily both have been there yet never bumped into one another.'

'We'll see.' Keith's eyes never left the screen.

'What time did you leave the bar that night?' Duncan asked.

'Not that late. Half-eleven, maybe.'

'And where did you go?'

'Home!'

'Time to rattle his cage,' Keith instructed Grace. They'd agreed in advance they might use this tactic, and she immediately left the room, walked along the corridor to where a red light showed 'interview in progress' and knocked on the door. When Lance opened it, they stood whispering together. While Lance nodded, miming a pantomime of receiving new and serious information, she stared unsmilingly over his shoulder at Matt. As soon as Lance closed the door on her, she scooted back to Keith and the monitor screen.

'Is there anything else you'd like to tell us, Matt?' Duncan was asking, leaving a long and deliberate pause during which Matt's mind clearly scrambled to second-guess their thinking. 'It'll go much better for you if you tell us everything,' the detective continued. 'And tell us the truth. The more you keep changing your story, the more lies you tell, the harder it'll be later in court to convince a jury that you're an honest man.'

'Do you have evidence to charge my client?' the solicitor asked sharply, but Duncan ignored him.

'Is there anything more you want to say?'

'I promise you I don't have a clue where Polly is. You have to believe me. And I swear I never saw Rachel at the Blue Bar. The place was heaving. I had no idea she was there.'

'So why did you lie to us?'

'I was afraid my job would be on the line,' admitted Matt. 'That it would come out that I'd crossed a line with one or two of the women I was teaching.'

Keith snorted in contempt.

'But not with Rachel. I know I'm not supposed to take liberties, and OK, it was stupid to ignore university regulations, but it's not like I'm twice their age or anything, and they can't expect me not have a social life. I'd never hurt anyone. Please, I promise I have no idea what happened to those girls.'

Grace felt a momentary disgust, though whether at Matt's excuses or at their power to reduce him to such abjection she wasn't entirely sure.

THIRTEEN

Half an hour later, Grace dried her hands under the feeble stream of warm air, then approved her appearance in the mirror: neat and tidy; she'd do. She was still partly submerged in how the interview had gone, the way it had reshaped the kind of things she felt they needed to consider. Though she hadn't yet quite nailed what she thought about Matt Beeston, she had recovered from her brief revulsion and felt charged and optimistic again. This was when she always knew without question, despite everything, that she was in the right job. Maybe, she told her reflection in the mirror, she might yet find a way to dance on thin ice after all.

Checking her mobile she saw a missed call from a number she didn't immediately recognise. Aware that it might be from one of the many people to whom she'd handed her card, she returned the call. It took her a moment to place the voice: Min, still technically her mother-in-law. Grace's sunny mood was instantly punctured and replaced by a slush of nausea and regret. She caught her own gaze again in the mirror and recognised the old anxiety in her eyes, the misery of being caught wrong-footed and out in the open.

'Min,' she breathed.

'Thank you for calling back,' Min's voice said crisply. 'I didn't think you would. But I need to talk to you about selling the house.'

'The lawyers are dealing with that.'

'Isn't it enough for you that my son has lost the career he loved? Do you really have to take his home away from him as well?'

'Our home,' said Grace, knowing she shouldn't say anything, shouldn't engage. 'I paid most of the deposit, and I need my share of the money.'

'You know he's had to sell his racing bikes?'

'Min, I have to go.'

'He can't even train with the team any more.'

'No, well, that's down to him.'

'At least leave him his home, some dignity. Do you have to take everything from him?'

'Please, Min. This isn't your fight. And I have to go.'

'You let him down when he needed you. My son would never have done what you said he did.' Min's voice became shrill. 'Are you honestly accusing me of raising a son who could behave like that?'

Grace took a deep breath. Remember your training, she told herself. Treat her as you would a suspect. 'Yes, Min, unfortunately I guess that is what I'd have to say to you. Goodbye.'

She touched the mirror – had her skin really gone so pale? – and watched her fingers tremble against the reflection of her cheek. How could she have said that to Min, a woman she had liked and always got on well with? It was hardly Min's fault that Trev had acted the way he had. The woman must be upset enough without Grace adding insult to injury.

The old panic rose and she fought to beat it down. Had she been wrong? Had she ruined everything for – what? Some uptight, jobsworth morality? Sheer vanity that she knew better than everyone else? She'd learned the hard way that trying to do right didn't get you loved: even her own husband had seen fit to punish her for being a grass.

She took some deep breaths, swung her arms, tried to raise her heart rate to match the adrenaline coursing through her veins. She must go. Everyone would be waiting to get started. She'd left Kent, hadn't she? She was here now. A fresh start. She'd acted in good faith, and she mustn't let her own dark thoughts drag her back to what had happened before. She was a good cop. All she had to do was concentrate on the present, pull her weight and earn her place in the team. Surely she could do that? Surely no one would attempt to stop her doing that?

As she climbed the stairs, trying to refocus her thoughts on Matt's interview, her mind was flooded by the image of Rachel Moston, her skin pale and grey against the rubble. She wondered if there had been a final moment when Rachel had understood what was happening to her. Forensics had now confirmed there was no one else's DNA under her fingernails, no bruises on her wrists or arms to show she'd struggled to free herself. Had she been taken completely by surprise? Or had she known and perhaps trusted her killer and so been paralysed at that moment of terrifying comprehension when she realised what he was about to do? For the young woman's sake, Grace hoped not.

Keith, waiting in his office with obvious impatience, began to speak the moment Grace closed the door behind her. 'So what do we think? Do we believe him?'

'We've established he's a liar,' said Lance.

'Not a very clever one,' Duncan observed. 'Just assumes he's entitled to evade responsibility for his actions.'

'So busy saving his own skin that he could scarcely express even the most conventional regrets for the death of a young woman he's taught once a week for the past year,' said Keith.

'He's narcissistic, sociopathic,' Lance agreed. 'No concern for anyone but himself.'

'Which doesn't fit with the way Rachel was displayed,' said Grace.

'The bottle?' asked Keith, confused.

'No, I was thinking of the jacket under her head,' she replied. 'That shows someone capable of tenderness, someone with a conscience. Not a sociopath.'

'Maybe,' said Keith, leaning back in his black leather desk chair. 'But we're not judging a beauty contest. We need to work out what significance the crime scene had for him, something that we can actually use.'

'Control,' said Lance decisively. 'That's why Matt sleeps

with his students, women who are subordinate to him, who make him feel powerful.'

'And Polly?' asked Grace. 'Are we saying she ran into Matt again the night after they slept together? And what, she belittled him or something, so he killed her?' She heard the doubt in her own voice. 'So where is she? Why didn't he leave her body like Rachel's?'

'And why kill again five nights later?' asked Duncan.

'Polly might've been an accident,' said Lance. 'But he enjoyed it, got a kick out of it, a taste for it. So the next time was controlled, planned, highly organised.'

'So he'll do it again?' asked Grace.

'Slow down!' warned Keith. 'Let's stick to what we know, which is that Dr Beeston is a bit of a party animal, was at the Blue Bar at the relevant times but tried to lie about it, and lives nearby. What's our next step? Do we take his flat apart?'

'It had been recently cleaned,' Grace observed. 'But he didn't seem particularly nervous about letting us in when we picked him up. Or about us bagging up his clothes.'

'He doesn't drive,' Duncan pointed out. 'If his flat is a murder scene, how did he get Rachel's body back into town, and what did he do with Polly?'

'We still don't know that Rachel and Polly *are* connected,' said Grace.

'In which case,' Keith said bitterly, 'we're tying ourselves up in pointless knots. The main reason we've put Dr Beeston in the frame is his connection to both women.'

'There's nothing so far in Rachel's background to point

us in any other direction,' said Duncan neutrally. 'Nothing out of the ordinary on her phone or laptop.'

'Right.' Keith snapped forward in his chair. 'What about this man Matt claims Polly asked for a lift? Do we believe Matt on that?'

'Polly's friends said that on the night she disappeared she was about to get a cab home,' said Duncan. 'We can be fairly certain now that she didn't. Trains had stopped and she wasn't on the night bus. Gone, just like that!' He snapped his fingers like a magician. 'Matey's the only one who knows where she is.'

'Hilary thinks it looks bad that we haven't got teams out searching,' said Keith. 'But without some indication of where to start, the search advisor's advice remains that a helicopter, underwater or ground search of such a wide area would be pointless. The budget simply won't stretch.'

'But if Polly did ask someone for a lift that Thursday with Matt, maybe she bumped into that same person again the next night?' Grace was about to suggest the young man in the bookshop who obviously liked Polly, but Lance cut in before she could continue.

'Could've been Pawel Zawodny,' he said. 'Plus Rachel would've felt comfortable accepting a ride with him. Matt can't possibly have got a good enough look at him at Polly's house the next morning to rule him out as the guy Polly had spoken to the night before.'

'Have you managed to put Pawel or his truck in town on either night?' asked Keith.

'Not yet. But he could have use of another car.'

Keith's sceptical look at Lance made Grace decide not to mention Danny Tooley after all, at least not until she'd checked whether he even had a car.

'Any joy from sales of Fire'n'Ice?'

'The analysts have run the name of every purchaser through the police database. No matches.'

Keith sighed. 'Well, we've got Matt for a few hours yet. Duncan, can you chase Wendy again on whether we can match anything from the demolition site or any of the fibres lifted from Rachel's body to Matt's clothes?' He looked at his watch. 'If there's nothing else, Hilary's waiting to draft a press release. And before that I need to update Rachel's parents.'

They all filed silently out and, back in the main office, immediately encountered a host of upturned, hopeful faces eager for some indication of positive developments. It was clear to Grace that Duncan, if not Lance, shared her sense of deflation. Despite the buzz in the station when they'd brought Matt in, the clock was ticking and they had nothing solid with which to hold him. Once their twenty-four hours was up, they'd have to let him go.

FOURTEEN

While Duncan made the call to Wendy, Grace carried out a basic check on Danny Tooley and was disappointed to discover from the Police National Computer system that there was no car registered to his name and that he did not hold any kind of driver's licence. He had no criminal convictions, either. Nevertheless, she'd still have to write up her justification for the check in the case policy file. She was considering her words carefully when Lance came to lean against the edge of her desk.

'I don't back him as being the one, do you?' he asked quietly.

'Who, Matt?' She shook her head. 'I honestly don't know. If he did it, he's putting up one hell of a front. But then whoever the killer is, he's shown a pretty cool head so far, hasn't he?'

'You saw Matt's office, and how disorganised his flat is. Not exactly efficient and precise, is he?'

'No.' She smiled at him. 'So you still have the hots for the landlord?'

He laughed. 'I do. His yard, his rental properties, they all show he's methodical, pays attention to detail, is good at planning. And he's a voyeur.'

'If we believe Matt.'

'The psychology fits,' he said stubbornly. 'I need something nothing new to convince the super.'

'What about the university Accommodation Office?' Grace asked. 'You said they'd had complaints about Pawel from past tenants.'

'Yeah, I already followed up. They said it's not uncommon for tenants to make these kinds of complaints after landlords retain their deposits to cover disputed damage or breakages, which is why the Accommodation Office didn't remove Pawel's properties from their list. They think there's a fair chance it was just sour grapes.'

Grace fell silent for a moment, letting something rise to the surface of her mind. 'Rachel's housemate Amber went a bit quiet when we asked if Pawel was a good landlord,' she told him. 'I suspect she could have said more than she did.'

'So why didn't you ask her?'

'Because she would've clammed up even more.'

'Or because you don't buy my theory about Pawel?'

'Of course not!' Her sharp tone attracted attention, and she became aware of curious faces turning to them from surrounding desks. Their bland scrutiny alarmed her, and she softened her voice, assuring herself that he hadn't meant it as an accusation, that it was she who'd spoken hotly, not him. 'Whatever it was, I don't think she wanted Caitlin to hear it,' she ended lamely.

'Caitlin's gone home to her parents. Maybe we should take another pop at Amber while the coast is clear,' said Lance.

Grace saw that his eyes were not unfriendly, but nevertheless she felt shaken: Min's call had agitated her more than she'd allowed, so that a single glimpse of impassive faces idly watching her with Lance had triggered searing memories of exclusion and hostility, a rejection that had been out of all proportion to her alleged offence. For a while in Kent her sky had fallen in, but that was no reason to assume it would happen again here.

Lance, oblivious, was already lifting his jacket from his chair. 'Coming?'

He waited impatiently for her to grab her bag. She took a deep breath and managed a genuinely grateful smile. 'Sure.'

It didn't take them long to reach Wivenhoe. On the pavement beside Amber's front door in Alma Street was a small pile of wilting flowers, the kind of mixed pink and yellow bunches sold at petrol stations. They had handwritten notelets stapled to the patterned cellophane. Duncan had reported similar tributes left near where Rachel's body had been found, and had routinely dispatched someone to photograph all the notes: some killers had been known to send flowers or even turn up at their victim's funeral, as if they couldn't stay away. Grace doubted their current suspect was that type.

Amber opened the door a mere crack and peered at them apprehensively before letting them in. Inside, the slatted blinds were closed, making the living space feel dim and subdued despite the bright sunlight streaming through the open conservatory doors beyond the kitchen.

'There've been so many journalists banging on the door,' Amber explained. 'Hassling me whenever I step outside.'

'I'm sorry to hear that,' said Grace.

'One offered money for a photograph of Rachel. I saw the horrible things they wrote about Dr Beeston. Is there nothing you can do to make them go away? Caitlin's gone home, and I'm here on my own.'

Hearing the plaintive tone in Amber's voice, Grace wondered how she would've coped at that age if a close friend had been murdered. She stepped closer and reached out to touch the young woman's arm. 'I'm afraid there's very little we can do to move them on unless they trespass, but do please give us a call if it gets too much and we'll send someone along to have a word with them.'

'They've been in all the local shops and pubs, too, asking about Rachel.'

'Freedom of the press, I'm afraid. Maybe you should think about going home? At least for the weekend.'

Amber shook her head. 'It's difficult,' she said. 'Mum's moved in with her boyfriend, and Dad has no room for me. Besides, our lease here runs 'til the end of the month, so I might as well make the best of it.'

'Pawel wouldn't make it difficult for you, though, would he, if you wanted to go early?' asked Grace. It was a silly question, but she wanted to get to the point of their visit. 'Not given the circumstances.'

The wariness Grace had noticed before was instantly back in Amber's eyes, confirming that there was indeed some kind of story here. 'No, I guess not.' Amber turned away, hiding her face and pretending to straighten a cushion on the settee. 'Why did you arrest Dr Beeston? Do you really think he did it?'

'He's helping us with our enquiries. I can't really say more at this time.' Grace sensed Lance growing impatient at her side and, while Amber had her back to them, gave him a warning hand gesture: slow down. 'But Matt has said something about Pawel that we'd like to run by you, if you don't mind.'

Amber turned and looked sharply at her.

'I think we mentioned before,' said Grace gently, 'that Pawel is also Polly Sinclair's landlord.' She paused a moment for that to sink in. Seeing a little colour rise in Amber's cheeks, she continued. 'We have reason to think he might have been spying on Polly in bed with a boyfriend.'

Amber hung her head, and Grace waited for her to speak. 'Rachel and Caitlin's parents help out with the fees,' she said at last. 'Mine are skint. All they do since they split up is argue about money.'

'Is Pawel understanding about the rent?' prompted Grace, when Amber fell silent.

The young woman nodded. She seemed close to tears, but then raised her head and stared defiantly at each of them in turn. 'Is this going to get him into trouble?'

'We just need to know the truth,' said Grace gently. 'We

need to know anything that might help us find Polly Sinclair. We don't know where she is, and she may need our help.'

Amber collapsed onto the settee, hugging the cushion to her chest and raising her knees up under her chin. 'He said he'd let me off the rent,' she said, her voice muffled by the cushion. 'I'd've had to drop out of my course otherwise. I couldn't afford to increase my debt, and . . . He's a nice guy, really. He offered to take me out on his boat one weekend. Bought me some perfume. And when I was able to pay the rent again, he backed right off. I don't believe he'd hurt anyone.'

'So he helped you out in return for sex?' Grace spoke as neutrally as she could.

'I guess, kind of.'

'When was this?'

'Beginning of term. April.' Amber spoke so softly Grace barely heard her.

'Might he have had the same arrangement with Rachel?'

Amber shook her head. 'No,' she said decisively. 'Her folks are loaded. She'd never need to. You won't tell anyone, will you?' Her eyes filled with tears and she clutched at the cushion like it was a teddy bear.

'Did Rachel or Caitlin know?'

Amber shook her head. 'You won't tell Caitlin?' she asked in alarm.

Grace sat down beside her and lightly touched her arm again. 'No, but we will have to speak to Pawel about this,' she said. 'I'm sorry, but I'm sure you understand. This is a

murder enquiry. He knew both women. We have to elimi-
nate him from our investigation.'

Amber looked around the room. 'He's kind. This place
is way nicer than most student lets. He cares about how we
live. And he let me off three months' rent. He didn't have
to. He could've made things really difficult for me.'

'Did he mention if he'd ever had an arrangement like
this before?'

'No.' Amber thought for a moment and hung her head
again. 'But he acted, you know, like it wasn't an odd idea
to put to me. He wasn't that surprised when I went along
with it.' She looked directly now at Lance, who was trying
his best to be inconspicuous. 'I suppose there's a name for
what I did?'

'You did your best,' he answered kindly. 'Maybe he
wanted to go out with you and thought he'd be rejected
otherwise. Men can be pretty thin-skinned.'

Amber sniffed back her tears.

'So did you go out on his boat when he invited you?'
Lance asked the question as if he was just being friendly
and trying to distract her.

Amber shook her head.

'Do you know where he keeps it?'

'No, sorry.'

'Not to worry. You've been fantastic. Thanks for your
help.'

Grace let Lance wrap things up and get them out of the
house.

'So our friend's got a boat, has he?' Lance rubbed his

hands gleefully. 'Let's get back and see if it's listed on the Ship Register. Find out where it's moored.'

As they hurried back to the car park, Grace imagined having to break the news to Polly Sinclair's parents that their daughter's body might have been dumped at sea. She didn't envy Keith his job. They'd seen a couple of outside broadcast vans parked near the creek, satellite dishes mounted on the roof, no doubt here to record background footage of the sleepy, picturesque little town. She wondered how its inhabitants felt about being in the eye of the media, about being pushed into close association with the tawdry glamour of other people's pain.

'That was a really good catch, by the way,' Lance said, breaking into her thoughts. 'I'd never have picked any of that up. Well done.'

'Thanks,' she said, touched. She'd been surprised at his tact, his effortless ability to win Amber's trust, and gave him a warm smile as they got into the car.

'So how's this?' began Lance, starting up the engine. 'What if Polly turned Pawel down at some point? That would rankle. Then he watched her having sex with Matt, had a day to fantasise, to plan, to wait until he saw how helplessly drunk she was. She knew him, so if he offered a lift home, she'd go with him willingly. Easy pickings.'

'And Rachel?'

'Another one who said no, didn't need him, had to be taught a lesson.'

'She wasn't raped, though.'

'No, he used the bottle instead. Punished the stuck-up bitch for turning him down.'

Grace recalled the cool way Pawel had looked her up and down; was that arrogance, entitlement or just old-fashioned sexism? His attention hadn't immediately struck her as predatory.

'And the vodka was Polish, don't forget!' said Lance.

'You've got it all worked out.'

'You don't seem very excited.'

'I dunno, there just seemed something decent about him. Even Amber didn't really badmouth him. He bought her perfume.'

'It was you who cracked this!'

'We've got enough to bring him in,' she conceded, buoyed, despite herself, by Lance's confidence. Maybe, she thought, the perfume was the same sort of gesture as the red jacket under Rachel's head.

As they approached the outskirts of Wivenhoe, she noticed thick yellow ribbons fluttering from a succession of lamp posts, the same colour as those worn in support of the campaign to find Madeleine McCann and other missing children. Then suddenly she recognised the name of a side road from her PNC check on Danny. 'Can you take a left?' she asked quickly.

Lance indicated and turned sharply down the next road before asking where they were going.

'Just around the block,' she told him.

He did as she requested without comment, cruising slowly past a uniform row of semi-detached post-war council houses with neat pocket-handkerchief front gardens.

'Turn left again at the bottom.'

On their right now was the leafy canopy of Wivenhoe Woods, a council-run nature reserve that, she knew from the maps, ran down to the railway line, with a creek beyond that fed into the river. As they turned once more, into Rosemead Avenue, she peered at number twenty-seven, a nondescript, shabby little house facing an unattractive line of lock-up garages, where a man was tinkering with a motorbike on the cracked concrete driveway.

'Seen enough?' asked Lance.

'Yes, thanks.'

As he waited at the junction, looking to see he was clear before pulling back out onto the main road, he gave her a questioning glance.

'You know the kid we spoke to in the campus bookshop?' Grace explained. 'Danny Tooley. This is where he lives.'

'Did Roxanne tell you something?'

'No! I've not spoken to her.'

'So, what then?'

'I did some digging. I figure he has a crush on Polly. I thought at first perhaps he might have been the guy who offered her a lift, but he doesn't have a car,' she added hurriedly. 'It's as well to rule him out.' She knew how fixed Lance had become on the idea that it'd had been Pawel in town that night.

'So why the detour?'

She shrugged. 'Just curious. He'd like to have been a

student, I think. Wants to be in their gang. He might have followed their movements in far more detail than he was happy to let on.'

'If you think he might've seen something, then we should take another crack at him.'

Grace could hear in Lance's voice that he was just being polite, but she appreciated it all the same. 'Let's bring Pawel in first,' she assured him.

Lance smiled and speeded up, eager to share their news with the team.

When they entered the station, the first person they encountered was Joan, the civilian case manager. 'Good, you're back,' she greeted Grace. 'Two of Matt's former students have come in. They've seen the story in this morning's *Courier* and want to speak to a female officer.'

FIFTEEN

One of the young women had dyed emo-like black hair and an intricate cluster of stars tattooed on her neck beneath one ear. The other, a local girl, sported the fake tan and heavy make-up of her chosen tribe. In other circumstances Kim was probably loud and confident, but here in the moderately comfortable surroundings of the rape suite her voice sank almost to a whisper. Grace interviewed them separately, and it did not take long to establish that they had strikingly similar tales to tell.

Grace knew enough of Matt Beeston's behaviour not to be surprised by either of their shamefaced accounts of a charm offensive followed by drink-induced persuasion, jovial persistence and then indifference. Both young women had been only weeks into their courses, their first time away from home. Flattered by the attention of their boyish law lecturer, each had agreed to go out for a drink, and discovered that one cocktail had rapidly turned into five or six. Kim had sobered up quickly in a Colchester alleyway as Matt humped her against her wall, while the emo girl had been 'walked home' by him where, unable to get rid of him, she'd submitted to his ruthless pestering and let him have brief and unsatisfactory sex with her on her couch. He had left immediately afterwards.

They had then had no choice but to turn up to his seminars, where he'd made belittling comments and bantering jokes at their expense yet blanked any acknowledgement that they'd been on a 'date'. When, separately, they'd appealed to him to treat them with more respect, their grades had suffered. The university authorities had apparently shown no interest in why Kim, who was clearly very bright, had dropped out altogether, nor why the emo girl asked to change to a different subject at the end of her first term. She told Grace that, although she had told the departmental head the true reason she wanted to abandon law, the moment she'd hesitated over making her complaint official the issue had been swiftly dropped, and she'd been too demoralised to pursue it further. She was now predicted to get a first in history, but would have to spend extra time and money to take a law conversion course.

It was only when the *Courier*'s story had begun to attract attention on Facebook this morning that the two women had connected and shared their experiences. Neither had known Rachel Moston more than fleetingly, but they were deeply shocked by her murder. What made Grace burn with indignation was how each independently wanted to know if Rachel's death was their fault; whether, if they'd spoken out more forcefully, she might still be alive.

Grace hated that they should have been left so unfairly

burdened. She could admit to herself now that when she'd first seen the *Courier*'s racy front page she'd almost felt sorry for Matt: the police were only doing their job, but it had been obvious that such coverage of his arrest, even if he were subsequently cleared of any involvement in Polly's disappearance or Rachel's murder, must spell the end of his academic career. Now she was pleased. Kim and the emo girl's stories resonated with her own experience of bureaucratic failure; she knew she was being a bit self-righteous, but she couldn't help hoping that the media would go on to expose how the authorities – whose duty it was to protect students from an abusive and predatory teacher – had so wilfully ignored these two young women.

She took time to thank both young women for their courage in coming forward and to assure them that if either decided after all to make a formal statement then she would do everything in her power to pursue rape charges against Matt. He might have used alcohol to subdue them rather than threats of violence, but neither had wanted sex, and his subsequent abuse of power had only compounded the violation. Watching them leave together, she felt glad that they had at least found one another.

The corridor was quiet as she made her way upstairs, and she stopped to lean against the wall for a moment, as all her rows with her husband came flooding back. She'd argued that Lee had nearly killed that prisoner in the van, was out of control, might do worse next time. For Lee's own sake, never mind the next guy in the next van, the truth had to come out. But Trev would have none of it: no matter what Lee had done, it could be sorted. Lee was a good bloke, a mate, his best mate. Bottom line, always, is that you don't grass up a mate. Do that and you deserve what you get.

Off the record, she'd had a quiet word with Colin Pitman, her DCI, just like the emo girl had with her departmental head. Colin had made his distaste for the van assault pretty plain and assured her she could leave it with him. But Lee's aggression had got worse, while any complaint that might have become official was shuffled around until it died of suffocation; no one was put in a position where they had to take responsibility. Is that what had happened with Matt? Was that why Polly was missing and Rachel was dead? Grace wondered if the university authorities would ever blame themselves? If Colin ever had?

Or had Trev been right all along, and it was Grace who'd had a skewed idea of loyalty, Grace who had deserved to be bullied and excluded?

She'd joined the Job straight from university, fascinated by the courses in criminology and forensic psychology that had been part of her degree. She'd wanted a career where she would need to understand offenders, could simultaneously protect victims and hope to turn around the lives of those who acted out their chaotic, deprived childhoods through crime. Her few short weeks shadowing the uniformed beat officers had soon blown away such misty-eyed idealism, yet also served to strengthen her conviction that the criminal justice system must protect both victim and offender alike. Abandon that duty, and all was lost. Yet not one of her colleagues – not Jeff,

Margie or Colin – had offered her a shred of support, not even at the very end.

At that thought, she pushed herself away from the wall and wearily climbed the stairs to MIT. Keith saw her come in and beckoned her straight into his office.

He listened patiently to Grace's summary of the two young women's accounts of non-consensual sex, then sighed thoughtfully.

'So what do you think?' he asked at last. 'Is there an argument here to completely rethink Polly's disappearance?'

'How?'

'What if Matt Beeston treated her like he did these two, and now she's gone AWOL to escape the humiliation?'

Such an idea had not occurred to Grace. She thought it over. 'Her housemate said she was out drinking perfectly happily the following night,' she pointed out. 'And presumably she wasn't too drunk to consent to sex when she woke up with Matt on the Friday morning.'

'All the same, we don't really know what happened between them. And hurt feelings and fear of embarrassment can both loom very large at that age,' said Keith.

Grace nodded. 'All the publicity about her disappearance isn't going to make it any easier to reappear and have to explain why she ran off, either.'

Keith rubbed his hands back and forth through his short grey hair, then stared belligerently at Grace. 'Is Matt Beeston our man or not?'

'He rendered both these students helpless by getting them very drunk. Given that alcohol is part of his modus operandi, then the half-empty vodka bottle might well carry significance for him.'

'And, from what you say, humiliating his women afterwards seems to be part of the kick.'

'Yes. Except –' Grace still baulked at the folded jacket placed under Rachel Moston's head.

'Go on.'

'The killer took unnecessary time and trouble to straighten Rachel's clothes, make her appear comfortable. Matt doesn't strike me as the compassionate type.'

'Maybe those actions have other significance. Maybe he didn't like the idea of being judged, and tried to make what he'd done look less bad.' Keith saw the scepticism in Grace's eyes and laughed. 'You wouldn't believe what I've heard from perpetrators over the years, the crazy logic that sets in once everything's gone quiet and matey finds himself all alone with a dead body.'

Grace nodded. She knew she must guard against having too fixed a view of incomplete evidence, yet couldn't help fearing that the investigation was getting lost in an over-complicated maze. She looked up to find Keith regarding her shrewdly.

'Are we getting this all wrong?' he asked.

'I don't know, boss.'

He didn't seem to mind her candour, and nodded towards the outer office. 'What do the others think?'

Grace shrugged. 'Lance is tracking down Pawel Zawodny's boat. That may give us the break we need.'

By way of response, Keith got to his feet, went to the

door of his office and beckoned for Duncan and Lance to join them.

'Matt Beeston denies any direct contact with Rachel Moston outside of his teaching duties, right?' Keith asked, as soon as the others had come through the door.

'Yes, boss,' Duncan confirmed.

'And says Polly Sinclair never visited his flat?'

'Correct.'

'OK. Have a word with his solicitor. Put it to him that we're going to take his client's flat apart. A full forensic sweep. If he thinks Beeston might have even the slightest worry about us finding evidence that places either woman in his flat, then perhaps his client could be encouraged to reconsider his statement sooner rather than later.'

'Yes, boss.'

'Meanwhile re-arrest and interview Beeston on suspicion of rape.'

'Right.' Duncan left the room, closing the door behind him. Keith turned to Lance. 'Where are you up to with the landlord's boat?'

'It's listed on the Ship Register,' Lance told him. 'A twenty-four-foot cabin cruiser called *Daisy Chain*. Haven't found out yet where it's moored.'

'Make that the priority,' ordered Keith.

'Pawel Zawodny's home town is Szczecin,' Lance continued. 'It's a big port up on the Baltic coast. He could well be an experienced sailor.'

'Find the boat and get it secured. See if anyone knows when he last used it, if he had anyone with him. Once you've done that, bring him in.' Keith turned to Grace. 'Get on to the criminal service in Szczecin. Find out if Zawodny is known to them, or was ever flagged up in connection with any other dead or missing girls.'

'Yes, boss,' Grace and Lance replied in unison.

'And the tenants who complained about him to the Accommodation Office: talk to them, find out what was going on.'

Keith began tapping at his keyboard but looked back up as they reached the door. 'Nice work by the way, DS Fisher, getting Rachel's housemate to open up like that.'

Surprised, Grace looked over at Lance, who, deadpan, made a show of pretending the SIO's commendation had nothing to do with him. Grace smiled to herself: despite the frustrations of the case, it was wonderful to be accepted as part of a team again.

SIXTEEN

Ivo hadn't had a drink in four years, but attending meetings had become as much a part of his routine as going to the pub had been. Besides, you never knew who you'd bump into. You *really* never knew. So far, he'd never actually taken advantage of what he'd seen and heard in meetings, although once or twice he'd been sorely tempted. If his editor only knew the twenty-four-carat scandals Ivo had self-spiked, he'd go ape-shit. Mind you, Ivo figured it might not be so very long before his editor began showing up at AA, too, so then he could decide for himself whether or not to keep the faith.

He arrived at the Quaker Meeting House just before the eight o'clock start. It was a pretty building, one of countless church halls or chapels Ivo had visited in countless small towns. He thought about his personal map of the UK: where other people remembered places by meals out, family attractions, civic monuments, he could only place a location in relation to child killings, multiple rapes, care home scandals or gangland executions. Maybe when he retired he should take an interest in church architecture or something instead. Amazing how much history you could learn from headstones and memorial plaques.

Despite the charm of the exterior and the pretty entrance hall, the modernised room in which fifteen or so people had already gathered was depressingly bland, with chunky institutional lighting and uncomfortable folding chairs. Ivo had to confess that his choice of venue had been influenced by the stray hope of seeing Keith Stalgood – always nice to see a familiar face, especially if the face felt inclined to give an unofficial lead on how a murder enquiry was progressing – but caught no sight of him. Accordingly, he selected a place at the back where he'd be near the door in case the detective superintendent did manage to slip in late.

When Ivo first started attending meetings, his choice of a group close by Scotland Yard had stemmed from a genuine desire to avoid fellow journalists yet still be amongst people who could understand the stress of day-in, day-out proximity to violent crime. Not that he waved that around as an excuse any more. He used to. Drove his first wife mad. Especially after Emily was born, when he'd come home sozzled and sit with a glass of whisky in his hand railing about the cruelties of the world while his wife sang lullabies upstairs – or whatever it was mothers did with their babies these days. Fucked if he ever paid enough attention to have a clue.

Emily must be old enough for university by now. For all Ivo knew she could be here at Essex. That would be a story.

Or not. His AA sponsor thought he ought to contact Emily and make amends, but Ivo reckoned her mum would've done a good enough job of bringing her up and the best thing he could do for them both was to steer well clear.

The last few occasions he'd seen his daughter were muddled up in his mind. It was around when his drinking first hit rock-bottom, and Emily's mum told him to get lost and stay lost. Couldn't blame her. After the divorce he'd straightened out long enough to marry a second time, before going seriously on the skids. Ah well, that was then and this was now. No question, every so often he still missed those hazy days when the rest of the world seemed one drink behind, but at some point about four years ago he'd decided, to his surprise, that he wanted to live. There seemed to be only one thing left in which he could take pride – being a crime reporter – and he discovered that it truly mattered to him to do it well, which meant beating every other piss-pot on what was left of Fleet Street to the scoop.

Christ, he told himself, better not let the Young Ferret ever catch him out in such rank sentimentality. Better stop thinking about himself and pay attention to what people in the room were saying. But he found his thoughts sliding towards the interview Roxanne had wangled for him earlier today with Polly Sinclair's parents. Did Ivo feel guilty that he'd shafted Keith Stalgood? Nah, he wasn't going to lose sleep over that. It was already out there in the public domain. Everyone knew Keith had been disciplined a couple of years ago over a botched enquiry that went tits up in court, and if Ivo hadn't put the question to Phil and

Beverley Sinclair when he had the chance, some bastard at the *Mail* or the *Sun* bloody would, and then his editor would be all over him like a rash.

Phil and Beverley had known nothing about Keith's background, and the pain in their eyes when Ivo told them had made even him shift uncomfortably in his chair. Damn it, he'd thought, they were still hoping their daughter would turn up safe, and meanwhile their faith in the police investigation was about all they had to cling to. Never mind – their pain was precisely what his readers wanted, raw and bleeding on the page.

So he'd twisted the knife. 'Jayden Chalmers was fourteen,' he'd told them. 'Reported missing by his mother. Keith Stalgood was a DCI in the Met back then. He thought the kid was a runaway and by the time they found the body vital evidence had been contaminated, jeopardising his killer's trial. They only managed to get a manslaughter conviction.' Ivo had thought better of telling them that Jayden's well-wrapped body was eventually found in the loft where his murderous stepfather had placed it and two police searches had managed to overlook it. They could Google that information for themselves, and he wanted them to focus on Keith.

Ivo had been impressed by the way Beverley Sinclair had raised her chin, speaking clearly and looking directly into his eyes. 'We're not ready yet to believe that our daughter's gone,' she'd said. 'God would never be so cruel.'

Bingo! Ivo had thought. Tomorrow's headline! He'd nodded sagely, knowing his face wouldn't give him away, unlike Roxanne's naive expression of shock. She'd have to toughen up if she wanted to play with the big boys.

It was after the Chalmers case that Keith had started coming to meetings. Not that his drinking had had any bearing on the way the enquiry had been handled. The cock-up hadn't even really been Keith's fault, though that hadn't stopped his superiors expecting him to carry the can so they could avoid an official review and move on without too much very public soul-searching over restricted budgets and cuts to manpower. They had enough on their plates, dealing with the utter cock-up of the Stockwell tube shooting. So good old Keith had fallen on his sword, and presumably been rewarded with the pension-boosting promotion of this backwater job here in Colchester.

The detective turned up just as the coffee urn was wheeled in. Ivo watched him approach: an upright, soldierly man with a careworn face, he'd never looked like a boozer. The secret ones never did.

'Biscuit?' Ivo offered him the plate. Christ, the man looked like he could do with something sweet to wipe the grim expression off his face. It was a shame, but Ivo could feel in his waters that this case wasn't going to end well for him, either.

Keith shook his head. 'No, thanks. Thought I might catch you here.'

The back of Ivo's neck prickled. He fucking loved it when it got all cloak and dagger. They each took a regulation green cup and saucer and moved slightly apart from the rest of the group.

'Provincial life suiting you?' Ivo asked. 'Golf handicap improving?'

'Doing about as well as your unfinished novel, I imagine,' Keith replied drily.

'So, is there something you want to share tonight?' Ivo was itching to hear what the SIO had to say but, knowing not to push too hard, waited as Keith lifted his cup, became aware of the unpalatable liquid it contained and replaced it in the saucer. What in heaven did the man expect? The kind of artisanal, single-origin shit served by rock-star baristas that the Young Ferret favoured? Whatever he'd come to say, Ivo wished he'd just spit it out!

'The murder inquiry still has a long way to go,' Keith began at last. 'But the story you ran this morning proved helpful in bringing forward new information.'

'Glad to hear it.'

'With a little more information, we might be looking at separate charges.'

'Anything new to add?'

'You might try getting a comment out of the dean of the law faculty. Any students reporting problems with academic staff? What's the policy on staff–student relationships? That sort of thing.'

'Consider it done.' It wasn't urgent enough to update tomorrow's edition, and besides, Ivo already had his plaintive, attention-grabbing lead, but it would make a good page five filler for Monday. He'd certainly run something: bad idea to spurn inside information in case it went elsewhere next time.

'Otherwise, I wouldn't get too ahead of yourself on the present suspect in the Moston case, if I were you,' Keith warned.

'I appreciate the tip.' Ivo gloated at the thought of spreading a little disinformation around the campfire back at the Queen's Hotel, where he could encourage the opposition to sprint off the blocks with the wrong story. Not that it would ultimately matter a bean to his competitors if they raced away with the idea that Matt Beeston was the likeliest suspect: journos had proverbially short memories and an uncanny ability to manoeuvre 180-degree handbrake turns when yesterday's screaming headlines turned out to be 110 per cent wrong.

'Good.' Keith relaxed slightly, taking a look around the room, greeting one or two others with familiar nods.

'I see you have a new face on the team.' Ivo guessed Keith would be wise to him, but it was worth dangling a line all the same to see what he might catch.

'DS Fisher?'

'Thought she was a DI?' Ivo still wasn't entirely sure why he'd got quite so hooked by the Ice Maiden's misfortunes, but he was sure there'd come a time when his instinct would be rewarded.

Keith gave him a piercing look. 'Don't fuck with my team, Ivo.'

Ivo hunched his shoulders, head to one side, and spread his hands in a timeless gesture of wronged innocence. 'Me?'

But he must have given something away, for Keith moved closer, his voice hard. 'Have a think about where you are.

Recovery is about more than not drinking. You're supposed to keep your side of the street clean, remember?'

'I've also got circulation targets to beat,' Ivo said archly, though in truth he didn't feel very playful right now.

'Fine, whatever,' said Keith. 'But I won't stand for any mischief. I don't know what you're after, but I'm hunting a killer.'

Ivo was an inch shorter than the superintendent but he stood his ground, maintaining eye contact, until Keith shook his head in contempt and walked away. Don't patronise me, Ivo thought to himself. It's not rocket science. You've got your job, and I've got mine.

SEVENTEEN

It was late when Grace left the station on Friday evening. Everyone was tired and knew they'd probably be working much of the weekend, so no one had suggested a swift half before heading home. As she turned the corner and crossed the road towards her block of flats, she barely noticed the man leaning against a car until he pushed himself upright and she recognised the lithe figure of her husband.

'Trev!'

He smiled the smile that used to melt her heart. 'Hello, Grace.'

'What the hell do you want?'

'Nice to see you, too.'

He spoke lightly, ruefully, but she fumbled in her bag for her key. 'You can't come in,' she told him, striving to keep her voice strong.

'I came to see you're all right, that's all.'

'I'm fine. So you can go now.' She got hold of her key but, loath to turn her back on him in the shallow doorway, found it awkwardly impossible to insert it cleanly into the lock.

'Don't be like that,' he said. 'My mum said she spoke to you, that you didn't sound yourself. I was worried about you.'

'Really?' Grace couldn't help herself. She whirled around to face him head on, her eyes blazing. 'Min had no right to call me. And she wasn't the least bit worried. She just wanted to tell me I was ruining your life!'

Trev spread his hands in a gesture of appeasement. 'Come on, love. She's my mum!' He looked at his watch. 'Look, I bet you've not eaten. Treat you to a pizza? I noticed a decent-looking place around the corner.'

'No.'

He looked at her steadily before he responded. 'OK. Fair enough.' He used the patient tone a parent might use to a tired child. 'I guess I knew it was a long shot. I didn't mean to make you uncomfortable. I'm sorry. Bye.' He walked away, leaving Grace in turmoil.

She opened the street door to the building, then stood watching as he returned to his car. He opened the driver's door and looked back at her: the man she had married, laughed with, loved, and had believed she'd be with for ever. He gave a half smile, then dipped his head ready to climb inside. How often had she fallen for that look when it had been only a matter of who did the washing-up or went out for milk? He had come a long way to see her; maybe, after all, he really meant to set things straight at last?

'Trev!' she called quickly, half hoping he wouldn't hear. And that she wouldn't live to regret it.

He looked up immediately and, though he didn't yet shut the car door, she saw hope soften his face. She noticed, too, that he had let his hair grow longer; he knew she'd never liked his buzz cut.

'I *am* hungry,' she told him, cursing herself for giving in. 'Pizza would be good, but I need an early night.'

They fell into step together. Confused, she couldn't decide whether his height and athlete's tension so close beside her felt comfortingly familiar or like a threat.

'You must be on the Rachel Moston case?' he asked.

'Yes.'

'How's it going?'

'Oh, you know. Early days.'

Understanding her professional discretion, he fell silent until they reached the pizza place. He held the door open, reminding her that he'd always had perfect manners. The place was busy, and they were forced to stand close together for a minute or two while a waitress cleared a table and found menus. They ordered quickly, and Trev waited until they were alone before reaching across to touch her hand. Involuntarily Grace jerked back and tucked both hands beneath the table. She asked herself what on earth she thought she was doing here.

'Sorry,' said Trev. 'I miss you, that's all. Can't blame a man for that.'

'I'm not discussing the financial settlement,' she told him.

He looked hurt. 'No, we have lawyers.'

'So what do you want?'

'Look, we've both learned hard lessons. But I thought maybe it was time for us to move on.'

'OK.' Grace wondered what lesson he thought she had learned.

'I've got a new job,' he said. 'Not much. But it's a start.'

'That's good. I'm glad for you,' she said carefully.

'I realise what you've been through since you quit your job. That's why I'm here. I worry about you. I want to look after you. For us to do better.'

She regarded her husband across the table. His candid blue eyes, silky dark-blonde hair, kissable lips. He must have looked like this as a mischievous kid, cadging an extra helping of ice-cream. No wonder his mother found it impossible to believe what he'd done. She still found it hard sometimes herself.

'We can sort it out now,' he went on. 'Come back, Grace. Come home.'

She felt tears prick the back of her eyes. What kind of woman, of lover, would she be if she refused?

'I don't know, Trev,' she began, but was interrupted by the waitress bringing their drinks.

'Let's try again,' he said eagerly, once the waitress had gone. 'At least give me a chance, and see where things go.'

'I can't, Trev. Not after what happened,' Grace said softly.

'I've finished my community service,' he told her, reaching out again for her hand. She did not snatch it away, but neither did she let him take possession of it. 'Had to redecorate an old folks' home. And I told you I'm working, managing a bike shop. I'd like a fresh start.'

Grace said nothing, remembering the night she had spent in a modern budget hotel, lying alone in a bed that never got warm, savouring the bitter irony of craving the sound of his voice while nursing the wounds he'd inflicted. All she'd wanted then, as she hid from the world, was to talk to him, to have his smooth, sinewy arms around her once again to shield her from the panic and mend the unbearable sense of loss his actions had inspired.

'What about you?' he asked.

She shrugged. 'I'm here. It's fine. Nice to be busy.'

'No, I mean the past. What you did.'

'What I did?'

'Look, I know I was out of order, but so were you.' He paused, but clearly found no comprehension in Grace's reaction. 'Lee was my best mate long before I ever met you,' he went on. 'We worked together, rode together. What was I supposed to do?'

'Get him off the junk he was taking before he killed someone?'

'By grassing him up?'

Grace hung her head. Deep down, a part of her knew he had some right on his side: however much she split hairs over exactly what she'd done, she had transgressed an unwritten code of loyalty.

'Deny it all you like,' said Trev, 'but I know you made that call.'

'I gave the dealer's name. Said when he'd be on the plot. I never meant for Lee to be picked up, too.'

'So it *was* you.' Trev sat back, folding his arms, looking at her with fresh pain in his eyes.

Shit, she thought, he'd never known for sure. And I'd always been so careful never to tell him. Why did I open my big mouth?

'So the others were right.' He looked hurt and bewildered. 'It really was you who grassed him up.'

A fresh thought struck her. 'Jesus, Trev! You mean you really weren't even sure when you –?'

The waitress brought their food and fussed around with a pepper mill and questions about salad and more drinks. When she had gone, Grace still hadn't worked out what else there was left to say.

'You do understand, don't you?' he pleaded. 'I had to do something. What kind of mate would I have been if I'd stood by when Lee's life was totally falling apart, and all thanks to you? I couldn't be some pussy-whipped dork of a husband. I couldn't do nothing.'

'No.' Grace understood only too well: mates first and last, always. Wives weren't mates, and everyone else – plonks like her, top brass, scrotes, whatever – could go hang. What else had she expected?

'And I held my hands up in court,' Trev reminded her. 'I paid the price.'

Yes, she thought bitterly, remembering the jeers from Jeff and the others as she'd left the magistrates' court. Your badge of honour.

Trev appeared to take her silence as acceptance. 'So really

we're quits, aren't we?' he asked, starting to dig into his pepperoni pizza.

'Is that really what you think?' She shivered with cold, though the crowded restaurant was cosily warm.

'Yes. We were both wrong.' He reached across the table and this time she let him touch her. 'But I still love you, Grace. Look, let's just forget this divorce thing. Come home. At least postpone selling the house?'

Grace shook her head. 'I can't. I need the money. I've been unemployed, remember?'

'But why sell?' he persisted. 'By the time we've paid all the costs of moving and stuff, it's hardly worth it.'

'It is to me.'

'We could redecorate, if you like.'

'I'm not going back there.'

'Look, I'll do the bathroom the way you always wanted.'

'That's kind of you.'

'Don't be like that.'

'Like what?'

'We can have a fresh start without wasting money we haven't got any more, can't we?'

'Not in that house.'

'I'm trying to meet you half-way here.' His fork stabbed into his pizza.

'But I don't get to decide where I live?' Grace asked quietly. 'I paid the deposit after all.'

'Yeah, well, you earned more. I heard you're not a DI any more, by the way. How are you managing on a sergeant's pay? Seems like we're all playing snakes and ladders!' Trev laughed, but it wasn't a nice laugh. Recognising the old resentment, Grace suddenly realised that it betrayed a much deeper anger. The punishment he'd meted out that night hadn't only been about Lee.

'This isn't going to work, Trev.' She pushed away her plate and reached for her bag.

'Finish your pizza,' he replied. 'Come on, I even bought you extra topping.' He pointed his dirty knife at her food.

'Go to hell!' Grace stood up, her hands shaking as she managed to retrieve a twenty-pound note from her purse and drop it onto the congealing cheese and mushroom on her untouched plate. She walked away without looking back.

EIGHTEEN

Safe in her flat, Grace couldn't stop shaking. For a little while she worried that Trev would follow her, lean on the buzzer and give her no peace, but, though usually he hated to lose in any kind of situation, he didn't. She thought about calling her sister: it would be good to chat about mundane stuff, catch up on the week. But then she remembered this was Friday, Alison's regular girls' night out when her husband looked after Grace's two boisterous nephews. And anyway, it wasn't fair to dump on Alison, especially when she only knew half the story. Nevertheless, the thought of her brother-in-law loyally putting the boys to bed soothed Grace a little, reminding her that some relationships worked, that not everyone's world was as dark as Trev had once made hers.

She was shivering again, though her flat was as stuffy and warm as the restaurant. Seeking distraction, she opened her 'favourites' playlist, then went around putting on lights and throwing open windows. She didn't care if she disturbed the neighbours. She'd yet to set eyes on a single one of them anyway. Her fridge was empty, but she had milk, and poured herself a bowl of cereal: it was better than nothing.

By the time Beyoncé's inspirational 'I Was Here' had ended, Grace had stopped shaking, but she acknowledged that she couldn't stave off the flood of scary thoughts that would surely overwhelm her if she tried to lie down and sleep. Right now she wanted to run back to the pizza joint and somehow pulverise Trev, to magically erase his very existence, reduce him to a little pile of dust. She was suddenly angry at him in a way she'd never been before, when shock and grief had overwhelmed her more than anger; now, ashamed of the little stab of hope that had made her call out to him as he stood by his car, she felt a murderous rage towards him for his ability to revive such tender feelings only to snatch them away and leave her exposed as stupid and deluded.

But this new wrath frightened her. She had to get out of here. Had to find someone to talk to. She immediately dismissed the crazy idea of calling Lance Cooper – he might take it the wrong way – but couldn't shake off the temptation to sit in a noisy bar and get sloshed with her old friend Roxanne. As she tapped out the message, she knew this text was a serious professional error, but to hell with it! She'd just have to hope it didn't come back to haunt her later.

Roxanne texted back seconds later: *Blue Bar in twenty*.

C U there, Grace replied, heaving a sigh of relief that she wouldn't have to sit out the long hours of the night alone.

Throwing off her neat, well-cut work clothes, she went to search her wardrobe for something frivolous and summery.

Perhaps it was walking in high heels that reminded her of Polly Sinclair, sending a chill over her bare arms. She hoped Polly wasn't lying broken somewhere on someone's hard floor. It was a week ago tonight that she'd disappeared, which was a very long time to be at the mercy of someone who bore her ill will. That's if she was still alive.

She hoped that if Polly was a captive somewhere she'd be able to find ways to survive. Would she be able to picture some place where she'd been happy, and escape into it? Or maybe imagine hugging the golden retriever she'd missed so much on her gap-year travels? Or was her plight so bad that she'd lost all faith in such simple, everyday balm?

That's what Trev had taken from her: the simple ability to believe in everyday magic. She'd loved him! He was the one to whom she'd turned for advice, support, distraction, sex. He was the last person on earth she'd have believed capable of making her so unhappy. Could he really expect her to return to him as if the world were still the same place, when it wasn't, it just wasn't!

Still, she had survived: at a price, but she *had* survived. That renewed her hope that Polly was still alive. It was an unrealistic hope, but that was better than darkness.

Drinkers had spilled out of the Blue Bar to fill the nearby pavements. As Grace approached, a minicab was attempting to inch past them and was treated to drunken cheers and an impromptu screen-wash. The driver switched on his wipers, flicking warm beer back at the jostling, laughing revellers. The mood was good-natured; they were apparently oblivious of recent events.

Inside, the place was heaving but Grace spotted Roxanne's dark curls over by the bar and weaved through the crowd to join her. Roxanne must have read her mind, for she already had the shots lined up, and Grace gratefully knocked back two tequilas before grabbing a nicely chilled bottle of Corona. Unable to hear themselves speak, they found a spot at the edge of the throng outdoors where they could perch on a high-sided concrete planter. A low, heavy summer moon hung between the buildings and a light breeze seemed to carry a whisper of distant fields and trees. The alcohol hit the right spot and Grace let herself sink into its warm embrace.

'So is Matt Beeston still in custody?' Roxanne asked.

Grace found herself laughing: right now, Matt's predicament felt so far away and long ago that Roxanne's eagerness seemed comical. 'Yes,' she answered, judging that giving away such information could hardly matter now that Matt's name was plastered all over the tabloids.

'Did he do it?'

'We'll know more tomorrow.'

'Why, what's happening tomorrow?'

Grace was tempted to tell her friend that Matt had consented to a search of his flat. No doubt word of that would get out soon enough and it would be so pleasant just to speak freely and give Roxanne what she wanted. But she was also weary of the enquiry and preferred to remain off duty tonight. 'I can't say.'

'So what questions should I be asking?' Roxanne asked eagerly. 'Come on, Grace, you've got to give me something. If you find Polly and this starts ramping up, it could be huge!'

'You know I can't.'

'Then why did you call me?' she asked, clearly exasperated.

'My ex turned up.'

'Oh my gosh. So what was that like?'

'Difficult. He wants to call off the divorce, keep the house.'

'And?'

'Just for a second, some stupid part of me whispered that I still love him, and what if I wake up and it's all been some horrible nightmare and nothing happened?'

'So why not give it a try?'

'Do you really want to hear all this?'

'Sure!' Roxanne put a hand on her friend's arm and squeezed. 'Anyway, good men are hard to find. I should know.'

'Sounds like you've a story to tell, too.'

'More than one! You can have the gory details of my love life another time. But really, why not give it another try?'

'Because he beat the crap out of me, that's why.'

'Jesus, Grace!' Roxanne leaned back, her eyes wide. 'Why didn't you tell me? What did you do?'

'Had him arrested. Watched the guys he worked with every day walk him out of the marital home and lock him in a van. Took him to court. Watched him lose his job. Told him I never wanted to see him again.'

'Too bloody right! Had he done it before?'

'Never. I never saw him lift a finger against anyone. It's why he was such a good copper; he could talk even the angriest drunk into coming quietly. I learned a lot from him.'

'Jesus! This calls for more drinks. Stay there! Don't move!'

Roxanne wormed her way through the packed doorway of the Blue Bar, leaving Grace to savour the novel feeling of having finally shared her secret with someone. Outside of work, she'd kept it to herself, hadn't even told her sister the full story. She realised how, over the past few months, she'd become too used to being by herself, confiding in no one, alone with her own dark thoughts, but hadn't seemed able to make the necessary shift. What was it her grandmother used to say? *A man wrapped up in himself makes a very small parcel.* Time to move on. It had to be a good sign that she finally felt ready to unburden herself about what had really happened to her marriage. And what a vast relief it was to find that all it took to rediscover her old self was a few drinks with an old friend!

NINETEEN

As Grace dressed for work early the next day, she only half regretted buying a third round of tequila. Or was it a fourth? Whatever, by the time her head had hit the pillow, her anger at Trev had begun to feel hazy and insubstantial. Even her airless flat had seemed merely boring rather than unfriendly. Roxanne had been a good listener, and they'd ended the night in giggles, making plans for an autumn holiday together somewhere hot. Grace had fallen into bed daring to hope that maybe more had changed than merely the stale air in her flat.

In the still empty office her positive mood plummeted as she leafed through the pile of Saturday morning newspapers. All now had a line on Dr Beeston's 'frolics', and many of them sported photographs of the suspect, none of them flattering. The *Courier*, which had broken the story of his arrest the previous day, now led instead with a large colour photograph of Polly's distraught parents. Below it, a banner caption read *God would never be so cruel!* In a black-edged box in the top right corner was the number 'seven' in heavy type: the number of days Polly had been missing. Above the photo, in even blacker type, Grace read *£50,000 reward*! Below was an appeal to the *Courier*'s readers to help snare the elusive killer stalking the streets of Colchester. As she read, she became aware of Keith's voice raised in heated discussion behind his office door.

Through the half-closed screen of blinds she could make out that he was speaking to Hilary Burnett. It was unusual for the communications director to come in on a Saturday, but the reason swiftly became clear.

'I don't have time for this!' Keith was exclaiming. 'The media are supposed to consult with us before they issue a reward. How the hell did you let this happen?'

'I can't control what the *Courier* does, you know that.'

'No, but you could have warned me in advance! Ivo Sweatman and I go way back. I could've had a word.'

'I'm in constant touch with Mr and Mrs Sinclair. They said nothing about it.'

'Ivo probably told them we'd be pleased. Fuck!'

'There's no need to use that language.'

'You're worried about political correctness? I'm about to have clocks ticking on two separate suspects, yet now I'm going to have to make time to set up extra switchboards to deal with every crank and idiot who thinks this is some kind of lottery prize? "Call this number and win fifty grand"? Jesus! Do you even have any idea what it's all going to cost?'

Hilary persevered as the voice of calm. 'My proposal, which the chief constable has approved, is that we offer an alternative story for tomorrow's news cycle.'

'Fine, whatever, that's your job. Just tell the chief con I want this pantomime kept off my desk.'

'We also have to look ahead. It's Polly Sinclair's birthday on Tuesday, and she'll have been missing for ten days. Is that a headline you want to see?'

'I have other priorities.'

'The *Courier*'s not the only paper counting the days. And the chief constable is eager to avoid any presentational errors,' she urged.

Hearing Keith's muffled exasperation, Grace stepped further back against the row of filing cabinets, well out of their line of sight but still within earshot.

'I'm sure I don't have to tell you how the media will twist things if we don't keep control.'

'Then don't!'

'Ivo Sweatman told the Sinclairs what happened in the Chalmers case.'

'He would, the fucking rat!'

'Keith, please. Let's stay calm.'

'I don't care what they print about me, but that poor couple are going to hell and back. For heaven's sake, would it really hurt Ivo and his pals to show them a little mercy?'

'I do understand.'

'Then get a grip on this, Hilary. And fast. This isn't a glossy magazine awarding stars to a new sunscreen. These are people's lives.'

'Pawel Zawodny.' Hilary changed tack, but Grace could hear the increased tightness in her voice: Keith's jibe about her previous job with a global cosmetics company had plainly got to her. 'Do I release news of his arrest?'

'At least wait until we've brought him in!' But Keith, too, must have regretted his irritation, for his voice dropped a little. 'Maybe after we've interviewed him.'

'And Matt Beeston? Are you still looking at him in connection with either Polly's disappearance or the Moston murder?'

Grace heard Keith sigh heavily. She knew that the search of Matt's flat was already underway, but he'd been happy to cooperate and, although he'd been re-arrested on suspicion of rape, no one was really now expecting to find evidence linking him to an abduction or murder.

'Just buy us some time, Hilary,' Keith said wearily. 'Keep the media off our backs for a few more hours.'

'Might there be any positive developments by this afternoon?'

'We've located Zawodny's boat. Got the search warrant. Forensics are on it now. If we find any trace of Polly, we'll seek charges. But I can't give you a timetable.'

This was good news, but Grace also knew what the SIO wasn't telling Hilary: that, whatever evidence was found on board the *Daisy Chain*, without a body, or a confession, the CPS might not play ball on charging Zawodny.

'So we need to plan for failure. I mean,' Hilary quickly revised, 'for if no charges can be brought.'

'I understand precisely what you mean.' Keith opened his office door for Hilary to leave. 'If we don't have the right man in custody, then we may be looking at further killings.'

If Hilary gave any reply, Grace didn't catch it. Failing, too, to hear the communication director's high heels on the worn carpet, she was taken by surprise as the older woman suddenly appeared beside her. But Hilary did not seem in the least put out to discover her lurking there, and beckoned for Grace to follow her out into the corridor.

'Try and get him to understand,' she pleaded in a whisper. 'I *am* on his side, but I can only formulate a proper strategy if he keeps me in the loop.'

'I'll do my best.'

Hilary patted her arm. 'Good girl.'

Grace might have forgiven the patronising words had not Lance appeared at the other end of the corridor in time to hear them and to witness Hilary's gesture. He nodded to Hilary as she walked past him, then raised a questioning eyebrow at Grace as he headed for the office.

'Hang on,' she told him quietly. 'I think Keith might appreciate a moment to himself.'

Lance seemed about to ignore her advice, but then nodded and leaned against the doorway.

'What was the Chalmers case?' she asked.

Lance's surprised stare was openly hostile. 'It was before Keith came here.' He spoke reluctantly. 'You can look up the details, but he took a right beating in the press. Fair enough, he was SIO, but he wasn't directly responsible for what happened. The Met hung him out to dry. Called it strategic presentation.'

'I see.'

'Do you? I don't know what Hilary wanted from you, but –'

'I like him, too, Lance,' said Grace, cutting him off. 'I think he's a good SIO.'

But Lance wasn't to be placated. 'Hilary's management,' he said curtly.

'She's a friend of my stepmother's.' Grace seized the chance to explain. 'She tipped me off there was a job going here, and then put me up for the night when I came for the interview, otherwise I barely know her. But she means well.'

'She's not one of us.'

Lance's words evoked a leaden feeling that was all too familiar, making her mouth suddenly dry. 'OK, I'll remember that,' she said, turning from him to lead the way into the office.

He pulled her back with a hand on her arm. 'Hilary's not one of us,' he repeated. 'And we don't speak out of turn.'

'Grass each other up, you mean?'

'If you like.'

She lifted his hand deliberately from her arm and then let it go. 'Then why don't you come straight out and say it?' she asked, giving him a level look. 'Say that no one trusts me.'

He looked taken aback, almost hurt, but made no reply. Grace stalked past him into the office.

TWENTY

Two hours later Grace and Duncan faced Pawel Zawodny across the interview room table. Although he had asked for the duty solicitor, he now appeared to take little notice of the nervous young man seated at his elbow. Zawodny, dressed in worn but freshly laundered jeans and a spotless white T-shirt, sat comfortably, feet apart, on a moulded plastic chair that seemed a little too small for him, his calloused hands resting calmly on his muscular thighs. He met Grace's gaze calmly, and she found it impossible to decipher the look in his eyes – angry, resentful, mocking, perhaps even curious? Time would tell.

Wishing now that she hadn't knocked back quite so much tequila, she hoped that her face did not betray how rattled she still felt at Lance's unexpected hostility. It hadn't helped that Keith had then paired Duncan with her instead of Lance for this interview. She appreciated why Lance should feel put out – he considered Zawodny to be his collar – but surely he wouldn't hold it against her that Keith wanted to gauge the suspect's responses to a female officer?

And it wasn't as if she'd tried to influence the SIO's decision. She couldn't bear it if she had, yet again, to be doing her job while constantly walking on eggshells.

As she'd made her way to the interview room, a couple of people had appeared from nowhere to clap her and Duncan on the back and wish them luck. Although only those close to the investigation would know what they had on him – that Zawodny liked to sleep with his exclusively female tenants and then invite them out to sea on his cabin cruiser – word had gone out that everyone in MIT was hoping this would be it, that by the end of the day they'd not only have Rachel's killer banged up but be well on their way to finding Polly, too. Or at least being able to tell her parents what had happened to her.

No pressure, then. Time to get her shit together, and fast, so that Pawel could find no chink in her armour.

Grace was glad of Duncan's calm, solid presence beside her, though it had been agreed at the strategy meeting that she would control the situation right from the very start, with Duncan exaggerating his non-participation in order to observe how Zawodny might be provoked by such male passivity. Not the best time for a hangover.

But Pawel answered Grace's opening questions politely, confirming the facts about his rental properties and their current tenants. His manner seemed entirely natural and indeed confident, though in Grace's experience an innocent person wouldn't mind showing how spooked they were to find themselves in such a situation.

'I note that you've only ever had female tenants in any

of your houses,' she said, pretending to consult separate sheets of paper, not wanting yet to challenge him more than she needed.

'They take better care of things,' Pawel answered matter-of-factly. 'Boys trash the place.'

'But you've never rented to men?'

'No.'

'Why not?'

He shrugged. 'I hear too many stories. It's fine if a house is anyway a wreck, but I put in a lot of work to make mine nice.'

'Do you earn your money back?'

'So long as property values keep rising.' His blue eyes showed what looked almost like amusement. 'I'm here to discuss house prices?'

Grace smiled back; two could play at this game. 'I'm interested in value for money, whether you feel adequately compensated for your hard work.' She pretended again to consult her notes. 'A couple of times you had to retain tenants' deposits, is that right?'

'It's why they pay a deposit.'

'Can you tell me what happened?'

'A whole year, they don't clean the oven. Said their mothers never taught them. A tile blew off the roof. Instead of calling me so I can fix it, they watch the stain spread until the ceiling nearly collapse.'

'That tenant claimed you used to hang around watching them undress.'

'No need to hang around!' Pawel laughed, showing no

embarrassment. 'They walk about in their underwear as if I'm invisible. So yes, I look.' He turned to Duncan. 'Wouldn't you?'

The detective blanked him, calmly writing something on his notepad. Grace couldn't figure out how much significance to place on Pawel's unusual coolness under pressure. After all, she had tracked down the second tenant to a London ad agency where she now worked: the young woman had evidently done a bit of growing up in the last two years and expressed awkward regret at the stroppy retaliation she'd made against her landlord, agreeing now that he'd had every right to retain her deposit to cover extensive damage to the neglected ceiling. She admitted that she just hadn't wanted the hassle of moving all her stuff out of the room so decided it could wait until she moved out.

'And the other complaint?' Grace asked.

Pawel's lips curled in contempt. 'Her boyfriend moved in. I said he had to pay rent. She refused, said her sex life was nothing to do with me. I kept the deposit. She wanted her money, didn't want to have to pay the other tenant back her share, so made up a story that I'd harassed her.'

'And had you?'

'She was a little bitch.'

Grace had spoken to this young woman, too. Now a teacher, she had made no mention of any issue over a live-in boyfriend but had stuck vehemently to her story, including her original allegation that Pawel had stolen items of her underwear. If Grace had to go on a gut reaction, then the teacher wasn't someone she'd rush to spend time with. But being rude and spoiled didn't automatically make her a liar.

Grace pressed on. 'Your houses are much higher spec than the average student let. But these girls are careless, they do what they like. If they don't appreciate all your hard work, maybe it's not enough just to keep the deposit? Maybe you don't think that's fair?'

'They're spoiled kids, some of them,' Pawel agreed. 'Everything paid for by mummy and daddy. They should show more respect.'

'How should they do that?'

'Keep the houses clean and in good order, that's all.' He smiled at her again. 'But they're good business. These princesses are about to pay the mortgage on my fourth house. Not bad for a carpenter from Szczecin.'

Grace could see that his pride was real. Duncan had established that the landlord kept impeccable accounts: mortgages paid on time, hardly any other debt apart from the finance on his truck. Enquiries in Poland had shown the same.

'And *you* live where?' Grace asked.

He gave her a cynical look. 'You already know. A box on the edge of town. It's all I need. Another few years and I sell up everything and go home.'

'No family, no girlfriends?'

He shrugged again. 'Anything serious will have to wait.'

'Really? A good-looking man like you?' Grace smiled to show that she was in earnest. 'What do you do for fun?'

His fingers rose as if in search of something hidden beneath the neckline of his T-shirt. Grace wondered if he normally wore a cross that had been taken from him in custody. She must remember to check.

'I work hard,' he replied. 'I have the occasional beer, go fishing. The electrician I work with, his wife cooks dinner once in a while. Sometimes a movie. What do you want to know?'

Grace glanced sideways at Duncan, who took the cue. 'Ah, fishing!' he said. 'Now you're talking! Do you get out to sea at all?'

'Most weekends.'

'Lucky man! What do you catch?'

'Cod, plaice.'

'You go with friends?' Duncan maintained his chatty style.

'Depends. Sometimes.'

'You get to sea last weekend?'

'Yes.'

Grace observed Pawel grow more watchful as he realised the direction of Duncan's questions.

'Take anyone with you?'

'No.' Pawel drew back slightly, looking at them suspiciously.

Duncan turned to Grace and gave a slight nod for her to resume.

'Ever take any of your tenants out on your boat?'

He paused before giving his answer. 'Polly Sinclair came

on board once. Just at the mooring, when she happened to walk past. We didn't go out to sea.'

'So Polly Sinclair has been on your boat.'

'Briefly.'

Grace tried her best to remain impassive: had Pawel given such a careful reply because he'd calculated that they might find trace evidence of Polly on board the *Daisy Chain* and wanted to cover himself? If so, this was the clearest indication yet that he might be involved in her disappearance. And that he was clever.

'What about nights out?' she asked, deliberately moving on. 'Ever go to the Blue Bar?'

He shook his head. 'Too full of noisy kids.'

'So you know it?'

'Everyone knows it.' Pawel's blue eyes blazed, showing he understood the significance of her questions.

'So where do you drink?'

'At home. A beer sometimes. I don't drink much.'

Grace glanced at the camera that was feeding images to Keith and Lance: if Pawel wasn't a drinker himself, then maybe he disapproved of girls who got plastered.

'The evening you fixed the shower at your house in Alma Street,' she continued. 'Where did you go afterwards?'

Pawel shook his head. 'Home? Maybe the supermarket. I don't remember.'

'Which supermarket?'

'The big Tesco.'

'And the Friday night after you mended the washing machine in Station Road?'

'I don't know. Much the same probably. I'm working on the costing for a new house.'

'You weren't in the centre of town?'

'No.'

'You told us that Polly Sinclair was in bed with someone when you went to the house.' Grace paused, giving him time to recall the memory accurately.

'Sure, I told you, I heard them.'

For the first time, Pawel looked discomfited and uneasy.

'Did you go upstairs?'

He hesitated, gave her an injured look, then raised his chin. 'Sure, why not? It made me horny.'

'Did you masturbate?'

Pawel appeared genuinely appalled and then paled with fury, his lips drawing into a thin line. He turned to appeal to the solicitor, as if he ought to disbar such questions; when the lawyer merely shrugged uncomfortably, Pawel snorted in contempt.

'Please answer DS Fisher's question,' Duncan told him.

'No, I did not.'

'Had *you* ever had sex with Polly Sinclair?'

'No.'

'Ever ask her for sex?'

'No.'

'So what was your relationship? Were you friendly?'

'She made me a cup of tea once in a while. We'd chat. The girls are always on the phone with problems. I get to know them.'

'Did Polly ever ask you for a lift?'

'No.'

'What about your other tenants? Were you friendly with Amber, for instance?'

Pawel turned angrily to Duncan. 'Why do you let her keep asking questions when she already knows the answers?'

Duncan made no reaction, allowing Grace to continue pleasantly. 'I'd like to hear what you have to say.'

'I slept with her a few times.'

'Because you liked her?'

'Yes, I liked her.'

'Not to get value for money when she couldn't pay the rent?'

'It was her suggestion and I accepted. I liked her. She respected my hard work.'

'Have other tenants shown respect by offering you sex?'

Pawel looked from her to Duncan and back again. He fixed his now icy blue eyes on hers and shook his head.

'Did you demand sex from the girl who accused you of harassing her?'

'I see these girls in town giving it away for free,' he replied. 'They expect everything for nothing. I don't give my hard work away for free. Do you?'

'One tenant alleged that you stole her underwear? Did you?'

'No.'

'What about Rachel Moston, was she friendly?'

'No. She acted like I should use the tradesman's entrance in my own house! Then goes out looking like a tart. Sorry,

sorry!' Pawel held up his hands. 'I forget. She's dead. I forget.'

Grace, acutely aware of Keith and Lance watching remotely on the monitor, remembered not only Lance's suggestion that Rachel's killer had used the vodka bottle to humiliate his victim, but also that Rachel's underwear had not been found. She studied Pawel's face, attempting to evaluate whether his contrition was a pretence but, for the first time, he looked down at the floor, keeping his eyes veiled. Until this point he had sat with an easy composure, but now he began to rub the palms of his hands slowly up and down his thighs.

'Rachel's parents gave her a generous allowance,' she said. 'She had a job lined up with a prestigious law firm. Everything handed to her on a plate.' It was hateful to collude in speaking of the victim in this way, but Grace could all but hear Lance urging her to push as hard as she could to provoke another outburst.

'No matter.' Pawel crossed himself quickly. 'I shouldn't speak ill.'

Catching Pawel's gesture, everything fell into place in Grace's mind: angry enough to kill a young woman who refused to show respect for his hard work, he'd nevertheless been sufficiently repentant to rest her head on her folded jacket. 'So you don't like the way the students behave in town at night?' she asked.

'Do you?' he countered angrily.

'Please answer the question, Mr Zawodny.' Duncan's tone verged on offensive.

'They get drunk, ask for trouble.'

'What sort of trouble?'

'I liked Polly. You want to know why I went upstairs?'

'Please. Tell us.'

Pawel began again to run his palms up and down his thighs. He seemed undecided about whether or not to speak. 'I thought I heard her –' He stopped and took a deep breath. 'I worried she was in trouble.'

'You thought she was being assaulted?'

He nodded. 'Maybe I should have gone in. Asked if she was OK.'

'What stopped you?' Grace found that she really wanted to know.

'She saw me at the door. Turned away. She knew I was there, and she didn't care that I was watching. She was a slut.'

'A slut?'

'No one is going to marry such girls.'

'So what does happen to them? To Polly? To Rachel?'

Pawel folded his arms stubbornly across his chest. 'Good girls don't die,' he said.

TWENTY-ONE

'I bet he's our man,' crowed Lance as they joined Keith in his office. 'Has to be! He admits Polly was on his boat. Why else have we found absolutely no trace of her?' His excitement made Grace hope that perhaps he had forgotten their earlier antagonism.

'It's possible,' said Keith. 'But right now it's stalemate. He can't alibi himself, and we can't prove he's actually done anything.'

'How are forensics doing on the boat?' asked Duncan.

'Nothing yet, but it's early days. He admits he took it out last weekend, so find out if anyone saw him. Did he depart from any usual habits last weekend? Anyone notice anything different? Get house-to-house down to the moorings and begin asking questions. If we get started today, we'll pick up the some of the same people who were there last Saturday.'

'Yes, boss.'

'We need to focus on putting Zawodny in town on Friday night and again on Wednesday night. Or catching him in a lie about where he says he was. So nail down his precise movements.'

'He deliberately left a lot of big gaps that he knows will be hard to corroborate,' said Grace.

'So find something to crack him open,' Keith ordered. 'His truck's distinctive, and there are one hundred and seventy-five cameras in this town. Unless he's clever, lucky or was never there, he must have been caught on CCTV somewhere along the line.'

'We want footage that shows Polly in the passenger seat!' said Lance.

'Even by narrowing the time frame, it's going to take us days to trawl through it all, boss,' said Duncan. 'Especially since we've had to deploy manpower back to the switch-boards. Since the *Courier*'s reward stunt, we've been fielding a massive torrent of calls.'

'Fuck!' Keith smacked the desk with the palm of his hand, making Grace jump. 'Tell me the calls are at least giving us something useful.'

'It's going to take a while to sift through and follow up.'

'We'll have two dozen false sightings of Polly just when I have to tell her parents it's possible we may never recover a body!' said Keith.

No one said anything for a moment, and then Duncan spoke in comforting tones. 'We've also had plenty of offers from both uniform and civvies to come in and work over the weekend, boss,' he told the superintendent. 'They know the clock's ticking. Everyone wants to help see this job done.'

Keith nodded his appreciation.

'Plus we've had two more women with unhappy stories about Matt Beeston,' said Duncan. 'Plenty for the CPS to take a look at on the other charges.'

'Good.'

'Pawel's boat, boss,' hazarded Grace. 'If he did use it to dispose of Polly, then why not use it to get rid of Rachel, too?'

'Some killers get pissed off when they don't get attention,' said Lance eagerly. 'Some even go back to move the body, like the Yorkshire Ripper did with one of his. That would tie in with the way Rachel was staged, too.'

'So he's refining?' asked Grace, not entirely convinced but wary of challenging Lance too openly. 'Progressing?'

'Don't get carried away,' Keith warned. 'He may just not have fancied his chances on transporting a second body without being seen.'

'Might it be worth asking around the working girls?' asked Duncan. 'See if they're familiar with Zawodny? Might help build up a profile.'

'Good idea.'

'What about putting feelers out with them for any punters who like playing with bottles?' asked Lance, with a glance at Duncan, who had not yet been told the full story behind the bottle of Fire'n'Ice.

Keith sat back in his chair, considering. 'See what you get first,' he told Duncan. 'I'd rather keep all that under wraps a bit longer. Something only matey and we know.'

Duncan nodded, his curiosity kept well under wraps.

'I had an idea about the bottle,' Grace began tentatively.

'Let's hear it.'

'Well, we've assumed it was a weapon. That the girls were easy prey because they were falling-down drunk. But what if it was *because* they were drunk that he preyed on them? Not *while* they were drunk. That would make the vodka more significant than the bottle.'

'I don't get your point.'

'They weren't good girls. He was punishing them.'

Lance shook his head vehemently. 'The bottle was a *coup de grâce*. A signature.'

Duncan nodded, and Grace could see that Keith's thoughts were already elsewhere, searching for hard evidence, not theories. She could hardly blame him.

'Might be worth speaking to more of Pawel's past tenants,' she said, deciding there was nothing to be gained from clashing with Lance over his interpretation of the crime scene. 'And to Polly and Rachel's housemates. Build up a more detailed picture of what he's like around them. It's clear that he expects respect and appreciation, but how far does he go? After all, he bought Amber perfume. He was concerned about Polly.'

'If you believe him,' said Lance.

'We know what Matt's like. If Polly was too hung-over to fight him off, Pawel may well have heard her cry out.'

'So why didn't she holler for help when he came upstairs?'

'Ashamed?' Grace suggested.

'Enough,' said Keith irritably. 'I want evidence, not speculation.'

'Well, what about the man Polly asked for a lift?' Lance asked stubbornly. 'That could have been Pawel. We could show Matt an album? See if he can pick Pawel out?'

'Yes, but that was Thursday,' Duncan pointed out. 'Besides, whoever it was refused to take her.'

'But it shows Polly would've been happy to go off with him on her own the following night,' Lance argued.

'OK, enough,' repeated Keith, clearly annoyed. 'Say we assume that Zawodny *did* give Polly a lift, then where's the murder scene? Is it his boat? Somewhere else? For all we know, she was alive when she went in the water. Why don't we just stick to trying to establish a few facts?'

Grace thought again of Danny Tooley, wondered if he might remember ever seeing Pawel with Polly – or anyone else. But it was clear that Keith didn't need to be offered any more supposition right now. Maybe later she could slip off and speak to Danny without first running it by the SIO. Maybe not tell Lance, either: she didn't want to risk alienating him any more than she had to.

TWENTY-TWO

On the deserted campus, Grace was pleased to notice that several *Missing* posters with a smiling photo of Polly had been put up at the entrances to shops and departmental offices, and that yellow ribbons had been tied to pillars and lamp posts. The raised concrete walkway was eerily quiet at the end of a Saturday afternoon and she was almost surprised to find the bookshop open. Here, too, there was both a poster in the window and ribbons tied to the handles of the glass door. Inside, Danny sat alone on a stool behind the till, his nose in a book. He looked up when she entered and, recognising her, slid it aside and got up to meet her.

'You've arrested Dr Beeston,' he said, emerging from behind the counter.

'You saw it in the papers?'

'Yes. Roxanne Carson came to ask what I could tell her about him.'

'And did you tell her anything?'

Danny gave a tiny shrug. 'Not really. You asked me not to, didn't you? I just said he always seemed to be hanging around, when most of the teaching staff try to avoid spending much time with the students.'

'Did you hear any gossip about him? Hear any of his students talk about him?' she asked.

'He likes chatting up the women, though I never saw him with the same girl twice.'

Grace laughed. 'You notice quite a bit!'

He smiled. 'Part of the job, to watch people. You'd be amazed how many of them try to steal books.'

'I guess.'

'They're not very good at it, though. They're pretty easy to spot.'

Grace laughed, liking his dry delivery, and was glad, for his sake, that he wasn't as naive as he sometimes appeared. 'Did you ever see Dr Beeston with either Polly Sinclair or Rachel Moston?' she asked.

'I never really knew the other one. Will he go to prison?'

'He's not been charged with any offence, but we're still asking him questions.'

Danny nodded, and Grace couldn't quite decipher his reaction. Was he disappointed? If Matt came in here, she doubted he'd have shown much courtesy to a shop assistant, so perhaps Danny might enjoy watching him get some kind of comeuppance.

'Were any of the girls he chatted up unhappy about it, do you think?' she asked. 'Anyone ever come in here upset or crying? Anything like that?'

Danny shook his head, apparently uninterested now.

'What else did Roxanne Carson ask you about?'

ISABELLE GREY | 187

'Just chatting. I like her. She's OK.'

Grace had to agree: Roxanne had been a kind and sympathetic friend last night, and this morning's woozy hangover had been a worthwhile price to pay for her welcome new feeling of release.

'She was interested in which books sell the most,' Danny continued. 'Said she might come back and do a feature on what students are reading.' He gave her a wry look. 'She won't, though, will she?'

'No.' Grace laughed but, all the same, doubted that Roxanne would have wasted time schmoozing him unless she expected to get *some* kind of story out of it. Maybe she should use the same tactic. 'Out of interest, what did Polly like to read?' she asked. 'Do you remember? It really helps to build up a complete picture. You never know what might lead to us finding her.'

'That's what Roxanne said.' He nodded towards the door. 'I put up the poster for her.'

'Yes, I saw,' said Grace. 'That's great, thanks.'

'Polly likes foreign fiction. She was doing Spanish. We talked about which South American writers she liked.'

Grace smiled encouragingly. 'You mentioned she left her phone here once.'

'Yes.'

'Thing is, we can't trace any signal on it. Is she the kind of person who often loses her phone, do you think? Or forgets to charge it?'

Danny smiled back. 'She can be a bit scatty sometimes.'

'Scatty enough to have gone off somewhere and not told anyone?'

He frowned, considering the question, then nodded. 'Maybe.'

'In what other ways was she scatty?'

Danny smiled fondly. 'I ran into her once in Wivenhoe when she'd missed the bus and was late for an important lecture. She gets on at the bus stop before my road,' he added, as if Grace might require an explanation.

'Don't suppose you know her landlord, Pawel Zawodny?' she asked casually. She turned to select a birthday card from a rack near the counter. 'I'll take this while I'm here,' she added. 'For one of my nephews.' Danny took it from her and keyed in the purchase as she busied herself with finding and handing over the correct change. 'He owns several student properties in Wivenhoe. Has a boat on the river, too. You might've seen him about.'

But Danny shook his head. 'No, don't think so. Do you want a bag?'

'Yes, thanks. So you wouldn't recognise him if you'd seen Polly out and about with him?'

'No.' He put the receipt in the bag and handed it to her.

'You said the other day that Polly popped in for a chat on the morning of the day she disappeared. That was the Friday.'

Danny began to shift nervously but said nothing.

'I don't mean to upset you,' she said reassuringly. 'The two of you were obviously friendly. I don't want to pry into your relationship, but I guess you liked her?'

'We always chatted when she came in. She was nice. We're friends.'

Grace was struck by how everyone constantly mixed up their tenses when speaking of Polly, unsure whether to think of her as alive or dead. 'Would you mind telling me what you talked about that Friday morning?'

Danny hung his head. 'I'd seen her in town with Dr Beeston the night before.'

'On the Thursday?' she asked. He nodded, and Grace began to see what had made Roxanne seek him out him again: although the newspapers knew that Matt taught Rachel, so far they hadn't discovered any direct link between Matt and Polly. Had Danny now supplied Roxanne with it by telling her he'd seen them together in town?

And then it suddenly struck her that Polly wouldn't necessarily have known that Danny couldn't drive: why hadn't she thought of that before! 'Did Polly ask you for a lift?' she asked.

'I don't have a driving licence,' he said quickly.

'No, but she might've asked you anyway. Did she?'

He looked perturbed, then nodded. Shit! thought Grace. There goes Lance's hope of tying Pawel tighter into the mix.

'I didn't want her to go home with him,' Danny said regretfully, making Grace recall what Matt had said about Polly mouthing off at the man she spoke to. 'She didn't know what he's like.'

Grace thought how Matt Beeston must have seen Danny a hundred times around campus over the past couple of years but had recalled merely that the man Polly approached had seemed familiar. 'I imagine she'd had a bit to drink?' Grace asked.

Danny nodded. 'She came in here the next day. She was a bit upset. I don't think he'd been very nice to her. I told her not to worry, that he was an idiot and she hadn't done anything wrong.'

'How upset was she?'

'I think I managed to cheer her up a bit. She was OK after we chatted.'

'But you didn't see her again after that?'

Danny shook his head regretfully. 'No.'

'And she wasn't planning to see Matt Beeston again?'

He shrugged. 'Doubt it.'

'So what were you up to in town?' she asked lightly. 'When Polly asked you for a lift. Do you drink at the Blue Bar?'

'Can't afford it. I'd met up with a couple of my brother's mates. Paras,' he added proudly.

'Your brother's in the military?'

Danny nodded. 'Out at Camp Bastion.'

'In Helmand?'

'Yes. Not many of them left there now.'

'Good for him.'

'Do you think Dr Beeston killed that other one?' he asked fiercely.

'Rachel Moston?'

'Yes. Will he go to prison?'

Grace shook her head firmly. 'I can't say. This inquiry is still in its early stages.'

He seemed to accept her evasion. 'He deserves it.'

Grace could hardly say that she was tempted to agree with him, though for different offences. 'Well, if anything else occurs to you, or you hear anyone talking about him, or learn any information we ought to have, you will let us know, won't you?'

'Sure.'

'And you can't remember seeing Polly in town with anyone else on any other night?'

'No, sorry.' The tension in Danny's face had melted away and he gave her the sweet smile she'd seen once before.

Grace's heart went out to the vulnerable young man and his lonely passions, making her all the more sure that he knew more about Polly than he cared to say. 'If you do think of anything, you obviously know about the reward for information, don't you? Fifty thousand pounds. It's a lot of money.'

She knew she was taking a risk: if police appeared to endorse a reward, witnesses who came forward as a result could be challenged in court as having only come forward for the money. Yet she had to try every route to encourage Danny to give up what he knew, especially if it meant he'd have to be disloyal to Polly by painting her in an unflattering light as drunkenly offensive.

But he shook his head vehemently. 'We were friends. She came in here specially the next day,' he said. 'She wanted to apologise because she was afraid she'd been rude to me. She's a lovely person. You mustn't think badly of her.'

'We want to find her just as much as you do,' Grace assured him. He gave her the twisted smile of someone trying not to cry, and she hoped – as much for his sake as for the investigation – that he hadn't described all of this too vividly to Roxanne.

TWENTY-THREE

The house was at the end of a terrace in a back street of Colchester near the old military garrison area. Grace had learned that, as a long-delayed estate sale, it had been empty for nearly a year. Unmodernised for a couple of decades before that, it would need total gutting, which is why Pawel Zawodny had been able to get it cheap. But it was also slightly bigger than its neighbours, with three bedrooms rather than the usual two, which would significantly increase his rental returns. He had only completed on the sale the previous week, gaining possession of the keys the day before Polly's disappearance.

It had been Grace who had drawn Keith's attention to Pawel's passing mention of a new rental property, and at their second interview she had asked him more about it. He had supplied the address and voluntarily instructed his solicitor to surrender the keys; had, indeed, been meticulously helpful throughout, although never offering a word or detail more than necessary. Grace found it increasingly difficult to read him. She guessed his solicitor had told him it was unlikely that he'd be held for more than twenty-four hours, so it was understandable that he'd shown a gritted annoyance when informed that they'd been granted a twelve-hour extension, and that they could apply to hold him for up to four days. But it was impossible to tell whether the clench of his jaw and the glint of steel in his blue eyes was understandable resentment or renewed determination not to give an inch.

When the team had gathered for this morning's briefing, there'd been a definite sense of resignation in the air. Lance had taken it badly the day before when Grace had confirmed it had been Danny, not Pawel, whom Polly had approached for a lift, almost as if she'd gone out of her way to thwart him, and he had remained detached and distant when they'd gone together to ask Jessica and Amber if either could add to the picture of their landlord. Meanwhile, forensics had not so far come up with anything useful either from his boat – certainly nothing to show that Polly had been recently aboard – or his truck. Uniform had begun canvassing local sex workers, but none had recognised Zawodny as a punter. And so far the worst said of him by any of the other past tenants they'd contacted was that sometimes he'd use his key to enter the house without letting them know in advance.

But then house-to-house had called in to say that their early-morning enquiries around the moorings had brought forward a witness who had seen the owner of the *Daisy Chain* carrying heavy and well-wrapped bin bags aboard the previous weekend, the day after Polly's disappearance.

Concealing their jubilation, she and Duncan had immediately put this to Pawel. But he had an answer for everything – seemed almost to be enjoying the cat-and-mouse game between them – and had coolly admitted taking rubbish to dump at sea in order to avoid builders' fees at the recycling centre. But the witness was solid and reliable, just the type that a jury would take note of, and the earlier mood of defeat had lifted.

And now they were here, on the doorstep of Zawodny's fourth property purchase. Keen not to attract unnecessary attention, Grace and Lance now sheltered each another from twitching Sunday-afternoon net curtains as they pulled on gloves before opening the half-glazed front door with its chipped and faded paintwork. Keith had been unwilling to extend the budget to a full forensic sweep until they'd seen inside, but had – unnecessarily it seemed to her – impressed upon them that they could be entering a crime scene. Grace had taken the SIO's over-cautious reminder to be a sign of his heightened anxiety.

The Yale lock was ridiculously loose, and clearly Pawel's first priority had been to secure his investment by adding a shiny new deadlock. Inside, she and Lance slipped protective covers over their shoes and she took care to follow in his footsteps across the litter of defunct post and fliers for pizza deliveries. Two doors on the right led first into a small, square front parlour with a lethal-looking gas fire and filthy unlined curtains drooping from a broken rail, and then into a near-identical room with a window overlooking whatever overgrown backyard lay beyond. Both rooms were otherwise empty, and the detectives did not further disturb the thick dust on the uncovered floorboards that bore the evidence of someone, presumably Pawel, walking around in sturdy ridge-soled boots.

The narrow hallway retained its patterned Edwardian floor tiles. They were smeared and grimy, as was the planking of the under-stairs cupboard, and some of the marks looked recent. Not much light reached the back of the hallway, and there was no bulb in the socket of the overhead light. While Lance shone his torch on the dirty paintwork, Grace squeezed past him to open a third door that led into a musty-smelling scullery kitchen at the back. She could see mouse droppings on the floor and reckoned the decaying beige Melamine cupboards must have been put in years before she was born. A battered kettle tarnished with splatters of old paint and plaster sat on a portion of counter that had been cleared and wiped, and two broken chairs were drawn up to an equally clean Formica-topped table.

Grace called to Lance. 'Look!' She pointed to the table on which sat an opened economy-size box of tea bags, a bag of sugar, two chipped mugs, a stained teaspoon and an unopened bottle of Fire'n'Ice vodka.

Lance laughed in loud disbelief. 'And he told us he only drank beer!'

This was the first lie they'd been able to catch Pawel out over, and Grace was happy to let Lance savour the moment, hoping that maybe this small success might encourage him to forget his frostiness.

'It's not been opened,' she pointed out.

'Could be for future use!'

'Shall we bag it up or leave it for the CSIs?' she asked.

'Leave it. They may want to photograph it. But we ought to get out of here.'

'Check upstairs first?'

'Go ahead,' he said. 'I'll call Keith, let him know.'

Grace knew it was better if only one of them contaminated the area, but she made her way alone up the steep uncarpeted stairs with trepidation. At the top she called out: 'Anyone there?' She did not expect a response, and felt foolish that Lance would have heard her. With her gloved fingertips she pushed open the first door opening off the tiny landing, peered into the front bedroom and only just stopped herself crying out before she realised that what she was looking at was a heap of mouldy carpet that had been clumsily rolled back to expose the floorboards. From the threshold she looked carefully, but could not see how a body could possibly be concealed within its awkward contours.

She cocked her ear, too, for any telltale buzzing: if Polly had been killed here, if she'd been dead for a week, then in this heat there'd be flies – and a really bad smell – but there was nothing.

Swallowing hard, she turned to the next door which opened onto little more than a box room; it was filled with junk, but she'd have to leave that for the CSIs to sift through. The rust-stained bathroom was empty and the door to the back bedroom was locked. Before she could stop herself,

Grace tapped gently with a knuckle. Laughing at her nerviness, she tucked her hand into her armpit, then saw that there was a key below the handle, set into an old-fashioned beaten-metal fingerplate. She turned it, pushing open the door, but closed it again instantly when the movement was met with a scary whoosh and flap of wings that sent a waft of warm, stale air into her face.

Letting her heart rate return to normal, she opened the door again more slowly, looked into the room and guessed at once that it had been locked as a reminder that broken sash cords had left a wide gap at the top of the window through which roosting pigeons had entered. The floor was covered in a mess of dirt, dust and feathers. There were no footprints. No one had been in here for months.

As Grace made her way downstairs, she could see through the banisters the beam of Lance's torch as he inspected the marks on the woodwork and tiled floor of the hallway. He looked up at her happily. 'Anything upstairs?'

'Don't think so. You got anything there?'

'Hard to tell. Keith says the CSIs are on their way. We're to wait here and let them in.'

'OK.' She didn't like it here. She felt suddenly bone tired and wanted to sit down and rest, but knew she couldn't. 'Shall we wait in the car?'

Lance looked as if she'd taken away his favourite toy, but then nodded. 'Yeah, I guess so.'

Grace was relieved to shut the front door behind them. In the car, she wished she'd told Lance everything when she'd had the chance that other day, driving back from

Wivenhoe. Though whether it would really have made much difference now she had no idea. Someone else had clearly given him the version of events that everyone in Kent had stuck to, so that in his eyes she was a grass, a sneak, not to be trusted, to be kept at arm's length, and she'd have to live with that.

But it meant that she couldn't properly explain to him the power of the memories evoked by this little terraced house – the same as in street after street of little terraced houses throughout England, the same as her former home in Maidstone. Up until now, even when the news had come in about Pawel carrying something heavy and well-wrapped aboard his boat, Grace's deep-down, gut instinct had whispered to her that Pawel was not a murderer. But the sight of the familiar patterns of those Edwardian floor tiles had been a sickening reminder that gut instinct was not reliable. She'd have sworn blind when she married Trev that never in a million years would he lay a finger on her. Staked her life on it. How wrong you could be. She hoped that Polly's instincts had served her better.

TWENTY-FOUR

The girl was a little cracker! She'd done everything Ivo had asked, and more – delivered a diamond as big as the bloody Ritz. Roxanne, of course, didn't have a clue what she'd got hold of, but Ivo had lost no time in showing the Young Ferret the rabbit hole. Red in tooth and claw, the nimble little predator shouldn't take too long to report back – ask me no questions, I'll tell you no lies – and then Ivo should be able to see every shining facet of the gem. He might even have to pop back to London tonight, as no doubt the lawyers would be wanting to take a gander at this one.

All the same, he must be going soft: he'd been gratified enough to call his news editor and put Roxanne's name on the list for weekend shifts, and now she was so excited she could hardly sit still. Little Ms Ants-In-Her-Pants. He'd spelled it out to her that he'd go front-page with her big scoop and take sole credit for it. In return all she'd earn would be a few brownie points with Detective Superintendent Stalgood if she ran an inside spread in her own paper on Keith's tip about fat-cat university bureaucrats. Hardly a fair trade, but she hadn't even cared. Oh, to be young!

The room was jam-packed. Even Whatshername from Sky News was here, busy touching up her lipstick while the production assistant with the reflectors got in everyone's way. Ivo already knew what they'd be running with. They needed more interesting pictures than the stills and talking heads that would satisfy the BBC, so they'd had some specialist ex-SAS tracker out along the creeks all day, plugging his latest action thriller while pretending to search for Polly. Poor old Keith would hate that: it could only make the parents think the police weren't trying hard enough. A crying shame, really.

Meanwhile his fellow cowboys had opened a book on how long it would take for Whatshername to bonk the ex-SAS tracker. From what Ivo had heard, he'd need every survival skill he could muster to come out walking upright after that little adventure. Good luck to her!

He could imagine that Hilary Burnett, too, was probably sliding off her chair. He bet she'd never faced this kind of full-on buzz in her previous job over the launch of some new anti-ageing potion. But if she reckoned this mob were going to queue up nicely for their goodie bags and then be grateful, her lifespan here would prove to be brutal and short.

Ivo was looking forward to seeing the Ice Maiden again, too, now that he knew so much more about her. She wore her travails lightly, he'd say that for her. The Young Ferret had managed to get him a copy of the police surgeon's report, and her delight of a husband had done a pretty thorough job. Ivo probably wouldn't use it, but it was dandy back-pocket stuff: always useful to have an angle, something to give a filler a bit of thrust.

Keith, Hilary and the Ice Maiden finally put in an appearance, and the room quickly settled down. Everyone had deadlines and no one wanted to string this out longer than necessary. He caught a quick little smile of greeting from DS Fisher to Roxanne, who sat starry-eyed beside him, but the flash was gone as soon as it came. Ivo waited impatiently for Keith to announce that they had arrested a thirty-four-year-old man on suspicion of murder, then heaved a sigh of relief; with any luck, thanks to Roxanne, the *Courier* would be the only paper to lead with the man's identity: Pawel Zawodny, a Polish carpenter and the girls' landlord.

Ivo loved having the edge over the opposition. He could exclusively reveal not only that Pawel Zawodny would've had keys to both Polly and Rachel's rented houses – and could sneak in and spy on them in the shower whenever he had mind to – but had a boat, too. Ivo had been just in time to organise a shot of the little cabin cruiser before the police got it covered up and sealed off. 'Watery grave' might be a bit premature but it had a certain ring to it as a future headline.

Even though Ivo knew the police had been making themselves busy in Wivenhoe all weekend, Keith was giving nothing away, which made it all the more imperative that Ivo seize ownership of this new suspect before anyone else got wise to him. Give him a moniker, that was the trick. And besides, a good nickname always increased circulation. In his own head, Ivo had already dubbed Zawodny 'the

Ferryman', but he feared the reference might be too classical to play well with his readers. Oh, the perils of a minor public school education.

The detective superintendent went on to say that they'd been granted a thirty-six hour extension for further questioning, and then wisely left it to his communications director to confirm that Dr Matt Beeston remained of interest to them but had been released on police bail. There wasn't much point concealing *his* name any longer, and Keith had made it pretty plain the other night that this was one he *wanted* thrown to the wolves. The 'campus sex pest' had found the media camped out on his doorstep when he got home, and the images of him trying to escape from them, looking furtive and unkempt in his shorts and football shirt, would doubtless dog him for the rest of his life.

Dr Beeston really should've known better than to run and hide. Had no one told him that the worst sin in Fleet Street is to refuse to talk to the press? After all, no one appreciates getting the door slammed in his face. Roxanne had told Ivo that the Internet trolls had already latched on to the lecturer, despite his having deleted all his social media accounts. And he still had the joy of faeces in Jiffy bags and over-elaborate death threats to look forward to.

Keith was now appealing directly to camera for anyone who was in Colchester town centre from midnight onwards on the relevant nights to come forward, regardless of whether or not they thought they'd seen either of the two young women. His team, the superintendent explained, wanted to build as full a picture of events as possible.

Ivo had known Keith long enough to recognise the confidence in his voice, but Ivo was also damn sure that this appeal meant they still didn't have the clincher with which to charge Zawodny. Ivo had seen this kind of 'let's saddle 'em up and ride out' certainty before, and knew just how very wrong it could go. It's a great day, Ivo thought to himself. Now just watch some bastard like me spoil it.

He also spotted that Hilary was at pains not to mention Polly more than necessary, despite the promising lead of her landlord's boat. It would not be long before the number of days Polly had been missing – the number printed every day in heavy black type in the top-right corner of the *Courier*'s front page – reached double figures. That was unlikely to play well with the SIO's lords and masters, especially not with the spin Ivo would put on it. Polly, the golden girl with the golden retriever, whose golden future lay in the balance, 'Our Polly' – Ivo had seen to it that she was no longer merely Phil and Beverly's beloved daughter, but *everyone's* daughter. It was so predictably simple to whip up an entire nation over the fate of a single child, and then to conjure up an urgent need to find someone to blame for all the borrowed outrage and grief. Still, after all, he'd only be doing what his readers wanted.

So who would the target be this time? The university authorities? The Home Secretary? If the police didn't manage to charge this second suspect very soon, then the answer would be horribly easy: 'Clueless Keith'. Even his bosses would take care to distance themselves the moment they saw what was in tomorrow's paper.

TWENTY-FIVE

Her back to the door, Grace stood to attention in front of the conference table. The chief constable had come over from Essex HQ in Chelmsford first thing that Monday morning and immediately turned the most prestigious meeting room into her temporary office. Irene Brown was a petite, sharp-eyed, plain-looking woman with short hair artfully coloured so that it was neither blonde nor grey. She stood in front of her chair wearing full dress uniform, which Grace guessed she had chosen, despite the summer weather, as appropriate to the severity of the occasion. A copy of this morning's *Courier* lay on the table between them.

'Have you seen it?' she asked.

Grace swallowed. 'Only when I got to the station this morning, ma'am.'

'Do you have anything to say?'

There was no way around it. Grace had been told to hand over her mobile phone before she'd even crossed the threshold of the MIT office this morning, so there was no possibility of covering up her text to Roxanne. Any delay would only make matters worse. 'I met Roxanne Carson, chief reporter on the *Colchester Mercury*, for a drink on Friday night. We did not discuss the case.'

Grace prayed to every god she could think of that this was the truth: no matter how many tequila shots she'd had, surely she would never, ever have been such an idiot as to blab this?

'Was the meeting logged with either the SIO or with Hilary Burnett?'

Grace hung her head. 'No, ma'am.'

'Why not, DS Fisher?' The chief con made an elaborate show of seating herself, sending a powerful message that this interrogation would last as long as it took.

Grace was not invited to sit. She considered explaining the true reason why she'd texted Roxanne that night. She knew enough of Irene Brown's background to hope she might be supportive of a fellow female officer: a former firearms and anti-terrorist commander with a fistful of postgraduate degrees, Irene Brown was one of only a small handful of women holding such senior rank, and had taken a fair bit of flak getting there. But the thought of talking about Trev, of raking over all that had happened in Kent, made Grace's stomach churn in protest.

'It slipped my mind, ma'am. I met with Roxanne Carson not because she's a journalist, but because she's an old friend. We were at university together.' There could hardly be a more feeble excuse but it would have to do. Grace's eyes dropped to the tabloid headline – *A killer's cocktail?* –

above the photograph of a half-empty bottle of Fire'n'Ice that the *Courier* reported had been found with Rachel Moston's body, news of which had been concealed by the police.

A darker unease pushed its way into Grace's mind: she knew Roxanne was eager to escape her provincial job but surely she wasn't so ambitious that she'd deliberately set out to work a friend over for information? Grace wasn't ready to believe it, but it had to be a possibility, didn't it? And if so, then might she have been too loaded to resist? Just how idiotically gullible had she been?

'You are aware that Home Office guidance on misconduct states that police officers do not provide information to third parties, and that this includes family and friends?'

Grace nodded, too miserable to speak: was she about to lose her job? Discreditable conduct was enough to warrant instant dismissal.

'Public confidence in the police depends on officers demonstrating the highest standards of personal and professional behaviour. This is a serious breach of confidentiality and I intend to drill down until I find precisely where and how it occurred.'

'Yes, ma'am.'

'Following Operation Elveden, it's essential that all interactions with the media are logged and approved, otherwise we lay ourselves open to accusations of corruption.'

'I understand.' Thanks to Elveden, some Met officers were now serving prison sentences for selling information to News International, and Grace knew that plenty of others were still looking over their shoulders.

'Very well. Did any money change hands between you and Roxanne Carson?'

'No, ma'am!' Grace was terrified: surely the numerous drinks Roxanne had paid for couldn't possibly lead to the even more serious accusation of wilful misconduct?

'Did you tell her about this?' The chief con leaned forward and rapped her knuckles on the grainy newsprint photo of the vodka bottle. The accompanying story made no mention of the second bottle they'd found yesterday, but somehow the *Courier* also knew that the man in custody was the victim's Polish landlord and that police were examining his cabin cruiser, the *Daisy Chain*.

'Absolutely not,' Grace answered robustly, hoping her face wouldn't give her away. 'I have always steadfastly refused to discuss any aspect of the case.' But Grace knew all too well that, even if she had said nothing to Roxanne on Friday night, she had at their first meeting carelessly disclosed the content of the final CCTV images of Polly Sinclair after she'd staggered out of the Blue Bar with her friends.

'So how do you think the *Courier* acquired intelligence that we have been at such pains to suppress?' asked Irene Brown. 'Superintendent Stalgood informs me that the only people who saw the bottle at the crime scene were himself, the Home Office pathologist Dr Tripathi, the CSIs, DS Cooper and you, DS Fisher.'

Grace, transported back to the forensic tent, with white-suited figures gathered around the body in the eerie light, had no answer.

'Is that correct?'

'Yes, ma'am.' It was a relief to be in agreement for once.

'So what's your theory on why I'm reading about it in this morning's newspaper?'

Grace was about to speak when the older woman held up a hand.

'And not just me,' said the chief con, fixing Grace with a particularly hard stare. 'Rachel Moston's parents had not yet been told about this aspect of their daughter's death. I can only imagine their feelings at learning about it from a tabloid headline. They understandably feel very badly let down. Superintendent Stalgood is with them now, but you will appreciate why I intend to pursue this leak aggressively.'

'Of course. It's terrible.' Grace had had to deal with enough bereaved family members to understand why at the back of every SIO's mind in a murder inquiry was the fervent wish to offer those left behind at best justice and at the very least some hope of closure.

'The story doesn't describe precisely how and where the bottle was found,' Grace pointed out. 'If all the *Courier* knows is that a bottle of this brand of vodka is part of the investigation, then the leak could be anywhere along the chain of physical evidence.'

'Just because the newspaper hasn't printed it yet doesn't mean they don't know,' said Irene Brown.

'No, but if they don't, then it widens the number of people who might have leaked the information.'

'Indeed,' she said drily. 'Nor can we rule out the

possibility that the *Courier* employed illegal means.' She tapped the newspaper with an immaculately manicured fingernail. 'In which case, it may be that no one in the police or forensic services is to blame.'

Grace felt a glimmer of relief: perhaps she wasn't about to be sacked after all.

'I don't want a witch hunt.' The chief con spoke with a crispness that suggested that, were such a purge required, she would shine in the role of Witchfinder General. 'But until we know precisely how this information got into the public domain, I will not tolerate any conduct that falls below the standard expected of a police officer, and I will prosecute any such behaviour to the fullest extent of my powers. Do you understand?'

'Yes, ma'am. I can only apologise for my oversight in not logging my meeting with Roxanne Carson. I promise it won't happen again.'

'If you are discovered to have had any other unauthorised contact with any member of the media in the past week, or to have any further such contact in the future, I will treat it as a very serious disciplinary offence, is that clear?'

'Yes, ma'am.'

The older woman nodded a curt dismissal.

More than glad to make her escape, Grace found Lance waiting outside. He looked her up and down with a mixture of reluctant sympathy and suspicion.

'You'll be all right,' she assured him, and didn't hang about for a reply. All she wanted was a few moments on her own to dredge back through her hazy memories of last

Friday night, sitting outside the Blue Bar with Roxanne, looking at the big yellow moon, knocking back shots and talking about everything under the stars. Everything, surely, except the half-full vodka bottle glistening between a dead woman's thighs? Surely she'd never have been that stupid?

TWENTY-SIX

There was an unfamiliar hunch to Duncan's shoulders as Grace accompanied him down to the interview room. Now the whole station had seen the *Courier*'s front page, and there was no one who hadn't heard why the chief con had arrived so early and already swept away again in her gleaming car, leaving this nasty, curdled atmosphere behind. In the MIT office they'd all waited silently for Keith to return from his meeting with Rachel Moston's parents. He looked as if he'd aged ten years during the half hour in which he'd had to explain not only what the killer had done with a vodka bottle to their beautiful twenty-one-year-old daughter, but also why Mr and Mrs Moston had not been told about it.

The two or three people Grace and Duncan passed on the stairs avoided eye contract and slipped discreetly by; gone was the back-slapping excitement of Saturday when they'd first brought Pawel Zawodny in. Gone, too, was the optimism with which Grace had detoured through Castle Park early this morning on the walk from her flat. Over the weekend, forensics had confirmed that the bottle of Fire'n'Ice discovered yesterday in Pawel's derelict Colchester house bore his fingerprints, and the bar code showed it had been purchased in the big Tesco where he'd already said he shopped. Eventually the store's CCTV would reveal which customers had bought bottles, and, if one of them was Zawodny, maybe also whether he'd picked up more than one bottle, and when he'd bought it. The existence of that brand of vodka in his possession was not only too great a coincidence even for him to explain easily away, but – or so it had seemed until this morning's *Courier* hit the stands – would also hand them a compelling opportunity to observe the veracity of his unguarded split-second reactions.

Then, only Rachel Moston's killer could have understood its significance: now, the *Courier*'s splashy front page had alerted Zawodny's solicitor to the true significance of any questions put to his client about a vodka bottle. The tabloid had presented Zawodny with the gift of precious time in which to craft his responses. No wonder Keith had cursed Ivo Sweatman and demanded to see his head raised on a spike outside the front entrance to the police station where live broadcasters could use it as a backdrop.

Pawel's responses were already difficult enough to read without further unnecessary cat-and-mouse games. On her walk to work this morning, Grace had striven to remember her reactions on first meeting Polly's landlord. It had been her first morning, not an immediately urgent call, no reason yet to view the man with any suspicion. But even then he'd said no more than necessary and asked them almost no questions. At the time, if she'd thought about his silence at all, she'd been grateful: garrulous bystanders she could do without. But now she saw a strong, stubborn act of will, a determination not to give them more than he had to.

Trev, too, had that ability to stand back and keep himself in check, to deny the other person the reaction they were trying to provoke. It was part of what had made him an effective street officer. Even his relentless assault had felt precise and psychologically organised, carried out with the same determined, almost impersonal rhythm and tempo as if he'd been chasing a better time in a vital cycling trial. His fury had been contained and driven by a sense of right- eousness: in his eyes she'd crossed a line, threatened his place within the team, and deserved the punishment he was meting out.

The layout of Pawel's Colchester house, the patterned Edwardian floor tiles in the hallway, the glass panels in the door, had all vividly brought back the sensations of that night. It had been January, bleak and icy, and Trev had left her there for an hour or more as he sat in the warm kitchen beyond the closed door. The cold had seeped into her broken bones and threatened to creep deep into her heart. She remembered fighting to stay awake, to imagine open fires, old school radiators, even the woollen cover of the hot-water bottle her grandmother used to slide between the flannelette sheets of the bed she used to sleep in as a child. Then the kitchen door had opened, spilling enough light for him to step over her and walk calmly upstairs. It had been the sound of him in the bathroom brushing his teeth that had finally spurred her into action. The pain had been indescribable, but she'd pulled herself upright, dragged herself into the kitchen and dialled 999.

Was she was dealing with similar psychological traits in Pawel Zawodny? Was he a man who never lost his temper, who remained in control even when his sense of what was right, of what was due to him in terms of respect, was affronted? A man who could lead Rachel Moston to a demolition site, strangle her and then calmly arrange the body to his satisfaction, his Catholic conscience placing her folded jacket beneath her head as a parting gesture?

If so, Grace thought, as she settled herself at the table in the interview room, then the *Courier* had just made their job even harder by giving him yet more reason to feel in control.

And, she had to face it, the *Courier*'s front page had also badly unsettled her. The sour, toxic mood in the office had reminded her forcibly of Maidstone after she'd returned to work following Trev's suspension. Even in the face of the severity of her injuries, everyone had turned against her. Her grilling by the chief con this morning had revived her worst fears: had she brought their scorn on herself, had they had every right to shun her as cowardly, self-righteous and interfering?

She knew she shouldn't face a suspect when she was racked with self-doubt like this: he'd pick it up and use it against her. She'd considered saying as much to the SIO, but Keith had been in no fit state to take further pressure, either, so she'd kept quiet. She'd just have to trust to Duncan's common sense and stability.

Pawel, in contrast, despite his night in the cells, appeared perfectly composed as he took his place opposite them. At the strategy meeting it had been decided that they had little option but to start off by asking him if he was aware of the newspaper report, yet when Grace invited him to comment, he seemed uninterested.

'Do you drink vodka?' she asked.

'No.'

'Have you ever purchased this brand?'

'No.'

'You're sure?'

He looked at her with a glint of ridicule. 'Yes. I am sure.'

She had ready in her file a photograph of the Formica table in the Colchester house, and now slipped it across the table to him. 'I am showing Mr Zawodny a photograph of a bottle of Fire'n'Ice vodka found in a house he recently purchased. Do you recognise this?'

He frowned and took hold of the photograph, examining it closely. It was the first time Grace had seen him betray the slightest sign of being taken by surprise. But then his brow cleared. 'A house-warming present!' he declared, tossing the print back across the table. 'My electrician brought it when he came to quote for the rewiring.'

'But you don't drink vodka.'

'No, but he thinks I'm Polish so I will like it. He meant kindly.'

Duncan slid a pen and a blank sheet of paper across to him. 'Can we please have the name and contact details of your electrician.'

'Sure.' Pawel scribbled a name and part of an address. 'His number is on my phone, but he's easy to find.'

Grace was watching him carefully. He looked up and deliberately caught her eye, then held her gaze and gave a tiny shake of his head, almost as if he wished her to know that she'd let him down and he was disappointed.

'A bottle of Fire'n'Ice was found with Rachel Moston's body,' she reminded him.

'So you tell me.'

'So you know what was done to her?'

'I haven't seen the newspaper.' He turned to the young solicitor sitting beside him, who nodded in confirmation.

Was it the truth, or a clever answer? Did Pawel know that, despite Ivo Sweatman's lurid innuendo, only Rachel's killer could tell them precisely how and where the bottle had been placed?

'But you admit it's a coincidence that it's Polish vodka?'

Pawel gave a tired smile. 'I don't think that I am the only Polish builder in Essex.'

'You got the keys to your house in Colchester the day before Polly Sinclair went missing. Did you take her there?'

'No.'

Some of the dirty smears on the hallway paintwork *had* turned out to be blood, but not human. The CSIs reckoned it might be from a pigeon that had got itself trapped in the house.

Duncan cleared his throat, and Grace wondered if it was a signal to her to move on. They had discussed at the strategy meeting how this interview would be a poker game, a matter of trying to bluff Pawel into revealing what he knew. If Grace was unable to crack his poker face, then Keith had advised shifting him onto ground where he might lose his cool. In an earlier interview Pawel had been outraged when Grace asked if he'd masturbated while spying on Polly and Matt having sex. It had been one of the few times he'd revealed a strong emotion, so Keith had suggested she ask him about the tenant who'd accused him of stealing her underwear. Had he done so?

She put the question now, and read in his hard blue eyes that he knew it for a game and despised her for it. She pressed on, feeling heavy-handed. 'Do you like to masturbate with women's clothing?'

Pawel looked at her as if she was being ridiculous. 'No comment,' he replied.

'Did you want to have sex with either Polly Sinclair or Rachel Moston?'

'No comment.'

'Did you kill Rachel Moston?'

'No comment.'

'Rachel Moston's underwear has not been found. Did you take and keep her underpants?'

'No comment.' Grace could see how angry and resentful her questions were making him: had she succeeded in touching a nerve or was he insulted, as any innocent man would have a right to be, and was unafraid to show it?

It was getting personal, and she had to remember what this was all about. 'Do you know where Polly Sinclair is?'

This time there was a slight change in his voice. 'No comment.'

'Is she still alive?'

'No comment.'

'Can you tell us anything that might help find her?'

This time he paused, then whispered to his solicitor, who nodded. 'She cried out for help. I should have rescued her. Maybe if I'd done something that morning, she wouldn't be missing.'

That was the last thing Pawel would say, other than 'no comment' for the rest of the interview and, with a conforming nod from Duncan, Grace decided there was no point prolonging it. Pawel was returned to his cell, and Grace found Keith and Lance waiting for them in the SIO's office when she and Duncan got back upstairs.

'What did you think?' she asked immediately. 'About rescuing Polly? Is he genuine?'

Keith shook his head. 'We can't afford to give him the benefit of the doubt,' he said. 'Not until he can alibi himself. There are too many gaps he can't corroborate. Until we're able to place him in town, he'll be able to go on putting his own spin on everything we've got.'

'He's always one jump ahead,' said Lance. 'Like dumping suspicious-looking bags at sea. Telling us from the beginning that he spied on Polly having sex. He knew we'd get to Matt soon enough, who'd tell us he was there.'

'It could just be the truth,' said Grace.

'Don't be taken in by him,' warned Lance.

Grace felt herself blushing: was she being a fool? Again?

Keith ran his hands impatiently through his hair as if somehow a fresh solution would release itself. 'We're letting him run rings around us,' he declared. 'Maybe we should give him more rope. See what he does.'

'Let him go?' Lance's tone was sharp.

'I don't see the point of holding on to him any longer right now, do you? We'll put a tracker on his vehicle, listening devices in his flat and his yard, keep watching him. He may have premises we don't know about, a car not registered to him. If he's our man, then sooner or later he'll lead us to something.'

Keith looked at each of them in turn, but no one could come up with any persuasive counter argument. 'Right, then.' He sighed wearily. 'Anyone got a good suggestion for Hilary on how the hell we contain this mess?'

No one did, and, estranged by failure, they went their separate ways. Grace went down to custody, wanting her presence to issue a final reminder to Pawel that it was she who possessed the power to release him. If he was guilty, then the best way to increase the pressure on him was to place him in thrall to a woman.

But Pawel collected his phone, money and other items from the custody sergeant – Grace had already confirmed that amongst his possessions was a gold cross on a chain – and then turned to her with a mild look and a simple question: 'I am free?'

'For now.'

He nodded, giving her a candid, almost sorrowful look, and then headed for the door. At no point since his arrest had he ever once claimed his innocence or denied harming either Polly or Rachel.

TWENTY-SEVEN

The pub was quaint, an old coaching inn popular with eighteenth-century smugglers, according to a framed potted history above the bar, but it was fifteen miles from Colchester – in the opposite direction to Wivenhoe – and, Grace hoped, not a regular watering hole for any of her work colleagues. She had rung Roxanne's mobile from a public call box at the railway station and asked if they could meet. It was all unpleasantly surreptitious, but Grace couldn't rest until she knew precisely what she had or hadn't said the other night at the Blue Bar.

Unfamiliar with the road, Grace had given herself plenty of time and so arrived early. By the time Roxanne was twenty minutes late – and had not texted to say where she was – Grace was beginning to think this was a bad idea. She wouldn't have blamed Roxanne for bailing out: she must have sounded fairly peremptory on the phone, and Grace could only assume that if Roxanne had had anything at all to do with the leak she must be feeling pretty uncomfortable about it by now. For surely, even if she could forgive herself for betraying an old friend, she must recognise how she'd jeopardised the hunt for a killer?

As Grace waited, she thought back to one of her abortive attempts to straighten things out with her old friends back in Maidstone. She'd asked Margie to meet her one Sunday lunchtime in a pretty village pub well away from work. Margie, who'd been a good mate and watched her back at work, was her witness when she married Trev. Their wedding hadn't been a big affair, but he'd insisted on somewhere truly romantic and had wangled a midweek July package at Leeds Castle. After all the food and speeches, Grace had walked arm in arm with Margie beside the moat, admiring the stately swans, and believed she couldn't be happier. Little more than eighteen months later Margie had sat rigidly by a roaring fire in that village pub as Grace tried to remind her of their closeness, to appeal for understanding and forgiveness. It had been a wasted effort and a scornful Margie had departed soon afterwards, leaving Grace even more miserable than when she arrived – something she hadn't imagined possible.

When Roxanne finally turned up, she was unapologetic about her lateness. 'Are you OK?' she asked, before even saying hello. 'Trev's not been back hassling you again, has he?'

'No.' Grace was taken aback by the question.

'Only you sounded a bit desperate on the phone. And what with all the cloak and dagger stuff with the call box, I got worried.'

'No, no, I'm fine, thanks.'

'Oh, thank goodness. Can I get you another? Better go easy as we're both driving.'

'I'm not drinking. I never drink and drive.' Grace saw too late that she sounded prissy, but Roxanne had already gone over to the bar so it was too late to explain that for a police officer it was simply never worth the risk of being pulled over. She frowned into her water and lime juice. She knew it was perverse to be annoyed by Roxanne's concern, but this wasn't the conversation she had planned.

Roxanne soon returned with a glass of white wine and settled cosily in beside Grace on the dark oak settle. 'I wanted to call over the weekend to see how you were,' she said, 'but I didn't dare risk it.'

'Just as well. I nearly got fired this morning as it was.'

'What?' said Roxanne. 'Why?'

'The story in today's *Courier*.'

'How would that get you fired?'

'You tell me.'

'I don't understand.'

'Really? Tell me, did you happen to get the shifts you were after in London?'

Roxanne grinned. 'On the *Courier*? Yeah, not bad, eh?'

'So how did that happen?'

'Ivo Sweatman put in a word for me.'

'The guy who wrote the story in the *Courier*?'

'Right. You'll have seen him at the press conferences.'

'He sits next to you?'

'Yes,' Roxanne agreed. 'Did you see my piece in the *Mercury*?'

'I've been kind of busy today.'

'About the university claiming student confidentiality when it ignored complaints against Matt Beeston and let him continue teaching.'

'You're not big on confidentiality?'

'Grace, what the hell's the matter? Are you pissed off with me?'

'I don't know. Should I be?'

'What am I supposed to have done?'

'Friday night. Is that how Ivo Sweatman got the information about the vodka bottle?'

'Friday night? You know what happened Friday night.'

'I know you made sure I kept knocking back the tequila.'

Roxanne drew back and studied Grace's face before she spoke. 'You mean you think I deliberately got you pissed to get information out of you?'

'Look, I need to know,' said Grace, hearing the unpleasant edge to her voice. 'Was I so pissed that I told you about the bottle?'

'You don't remember?'

'No.'

Roxanne waited for Grace to say more. Grace knew she ought to backtrack, to apologise, but some stupid pride at all the times she'd had to grovel and crawl to people in Maidstone just in order to carry out some semblance of her job made her stubborn.

'But that's what you think happened?' Roxanne asked carefully.

Grace rebelled against being made to feel like she was

in the wrong. 'I got hauled in front of the chief constable first thing this morning. She was all dolled up in full dress uniform like the bloody Gestapo. They took my phone off me, and if the Professional Standards Department get called in they'll want my laptop, too. If they knew I was here with you now, I'd be sacked.'

'Because you might be telling me stuff you shouldn't and I'd pass it all on to the *Courier*?'

'Yes,' Grace insisted, refusing to listen to the small voice in her head warning her to drop it, right now.

Roxanne laughed contemptuously. 'It was a great front page this morning.'

'Don't play games! Please, Roxanne! I took enough of this crap in Kent. You've no idea.' It took all Grace's strength not to wipe her face as the visceral memory of being spat at in the supermarket aisle returned.

But Roxanne merely shrugged, her face pale against the dark curls of her hair. 'You broke their rules. Maybe they felt entitled.'

'They were really bad rules! I was trying to protect people!'

'But you did pass on information knowing there'd be consequences.'

There was a funny twist on Roxanne's face, and finally Grace remembered some of what she and Roxanne *had* talked about on Friday night at the Blue Bar, how gently Roxanne had coaxed the full story out of her, how comforting and reassuring she'd been. Roxanne had been the first person who'd just sat and listened and then hugged her close. And this was how Grace was thanking her!

'I'm sorry, Roxanne. It's been a tough day. I didn't mean to accuse you of anything. But I do need to know what happened in case it comes to some kind of inquiry.'

'You can work it out, can't you?'

'I was tired and drunk. I need to know I didn't say anything.'

'I'm sure it'll all come back to you eventually.' Roxanne got to her feet. 'I'd better be heading back.'

'Forgive me?'

'Sure. Whatever.' Roxanne turned her back, gathering up her bag and jacket. She had barely touched her glass of wine.

Grace reached out and held her by the arm. 'So where did Ivo Sweatman get his story?'

Roxanne responded with a cold stare, shaking free of Grace's grip before she answered. 'I can't reveal my sources.'

'So it did come from you?'

'Like I say –'

Recoiling from Roxanne's hard look, Grace retaliated. 'You blew our best chance with the suspect today.'

Roxanne shrugged. 'It's a free press.'

'And that gives you the right to run our case for us?'

'We answer to our readers.'

'Really? That's your authority?' Grace demanded. 'Well, Rachel Moston's parents are readers. They read the *Courier* today. So I wish you and your pal Ivo Sweatman had been there in the room with them to explain why the freedom of the press is so fucking important!'

'Don't give me that moral bullshit!' Roxanne hit back.

'You do your job because you get a kick out of it, same as I do, so don't get all holier-than-thou about it.'

Grace sat and watched Roxanne march out of the pub. She felt dreadful. Deep down, she was pretty certain she'd been in the wrong from beginning to end, but some little devil in her had pushed and pushed, as if she wanted to prove to herself how unlovable she was, how untrustworthy a friend. She was right back where she started, and this time she really did have only herself to blame.

TWENTY-EIGHT

As Ivo walked from the car park, he was amazed to see quite so many twinkling lights clothing the curving slopes of the parkland around the ornamental lakes. It was all very pretty, a clear June evening with trees casting long shadows, but nevertheless he'd not expected such a huge crowd to gather here to mark Polly Sinclair's twenty-first birthday. Quite a few of the people who, like him, were still making their way towards the grassy hill beyond the nearest lake carried yellow balloons tied with matching streamers, while others wore white T-shirts printed with a photograph of a smiling, fluffy-haired Polly, with her name and *MISSING* in bright red letters. The *Courier* had had them printed and sent people to distribute them, while the photographer had been given instructions to snap the cutest-looking girls he could find wearing them.

Some small groups, camped around clusters of flickering tea lights, hugged each other tearfully, but mainly there was an incongruously expectant atmosphere. Ivo had already spotted picnickers; quite a few of those arriving alongside him carried bottles of wine and from several directions he could hear music being played. Where did they think they were? Glastonbury? Not that he'd write that in tomorrow's edition. No, it would be more along the lines of *Like stars in the sky, Polly's loyal friends lit candles and stifled tears to wish Happy Birthday to the golden girl, now missing for eleven long days.*

He could see at least three camera crews out working the crowd, recording vox pops for the evening news segments. Half the car park had been reserved for their oversized macho broadcast vans, while he'd been forced to bum change for a pay-and-display ticket. When he'd spoken to Fiona Johnson, the university's director of communications, she'd been hard put to hide her disdain for red-top scum like him. But let some rugged, ex-war-zone anchorman turn up and lavish his camera-friendly dentistry on her and she'd no doubt be melting into his arms. Those TV people were so up themselves it wasn't true.

Ivo was in a bad mood. Although he'd been able to quash the idea without too much trouble, it had been irksome that his editor had allowed his arm to be twisted by the Young Ferret into floating the idea past Ivo that his junior should get an 'additional reporting' credit. True, the Young Ferret's sharp nose and special skills had proved more than helpful, but Ivo wasn't having anyone back in the newsroom forgetting that it was he, wearing out his shoe leather here on the ground, who'd got the ball rolling.

Except that wasn't true, either, and, if he was honest, that's what was really pissing him off. Everything Roxanne had told him so far had checked out, but now she'd wised up and was refusing to disclose where she was getting her information. He suspected her source was the Ice Maiden and that it was DS Fisher who'd enforced the blackout for her own protection. It certainly made sense, but it rankled nonetheless, and he devoutly hoped the cub reporter wasn't hot on the scent of some career-making story that would leave him dead in the water. If there was one situation Ivo really and truly hated with a passion, it was finding himself on the back foot and outsmarted by the competition.

He stood on the brow of the slope from where he could survey the massing crowds. Who the fuck were all these people anyway? They couldn't possibly all have known Polly, so what were they doing here, clutching their balloons and soft toys and flowers and swaying to the plaintive sounds of young female singers Ivo had never heard of? How was making a shrine out of cuddly toys or playing Polly's favourite music supposed to bring her back? 'Our Polly.' Well, he could hardly complain: he'd done as much as anyone to encourage this maudlin outpouring of pain-free grief.

He sensed someone behind him and turned to find Keith at his elbow. 'Evening, all,' Ivo joked, but Keith didn't smile. Ivo couldn't blame him. The *Courier*'s headline this morning had been *Back to square one*, and in his lead article Ivo had gleefully pilloried the SIO and his team for their incompetence. *Has a killer been set free?*, his first column heading, had reminded amnesiac readers that Pawel Zawodny was the second suspect to be released without charge. The next column heading – *Burnt out?* – introduced a snappy discussion of whether Superintendent Keith Stalgood was past his prime, rehashing the fiasco of the Chalmers case en route. So no, all in all, Ivo hardly expected a welcoming grin and a slap on the back from his old sparring partner.

'How did you find out about the bottle?' demanded Keith, obviously dispensing with preliminaries.

Ivo raised his eyebrows. 'It's that important, is it?'

'Don't fuck with me. Or when we do charge our man, I'll make damn sure you're the very last to know.'

'I don't scare easy. Besides, my editor just signed up your previous chief constable to front a column at two hundred grand a year plus a ghostwriter to do all the work, so I don't think we'll be begging at your door for news any time soon.'

Keith sighed and abruptly lowered himself to sit on the ground, stretching out his long, lean legs and leaning back on one elbow. With his free hand he patted the grass beside him and looked up at Ivo. 'Let's talk like reasonable human beings.'

Ivo sat down, his old bones creaking; with his belly, he'd probably struggle humiliatingly to get back up again, but he'd worry about that later. 'OK,' he said. 'Shoot.'

'You're right,' Keith admitted. 'I'm on a hiding to nothing. Hilary's only got half a dozen press officers across the whole of Essex to keep hundreds of journalists happy. It can't be done, even if she actually knew what she was doing. And I'm not naive. I'm fully aware that it would be career suicide for my overlords to take on your bosses by championing someone with my track record and telling you lot to piss off and let me get on with my job. So let's just accept that you're going to make me run this investigation with one hand tied behind my back and there's not much I can do about it.'

'The way of the world,' Ivo agreed. There'd always been something about Keith Stalgood that he'd admired, and he felt obscurely flattered that the man had chosen to level with him.

'There's only one thing I care about.'

Ivo waited, but Keith didn't continue. The sun was heading for the horizon, allowing the hundreds of tea lights to glitter more brightly. A hushed, respectful murmur of voices rose up to them from below and even Ivo had to admit there was something moving, almost enchanted, in the scene.

'Do you want to see another of these kids get killed?' Keith asked in a low voice.

Ivo thought of his daughter: she could be down there and he'd be none the wiser. 'No,' he said. 'I don't.'

'Is someone on my team leaking details of the investigation?'

'I don't know.' Ivo hesitated: it went against every atom of professional instinct to say what he was about to say, but he said it anyway. 'The tip-off came from Roxanne Carson on the *Mercury*.' He saw Keith's face harden. 'I don't know who she's talking to. She won't tell me,' he added, wishing, for some unfathomable reason, to shelter the Ice Maiden from blame.

'And it all came from Roxanne Carson?'

Ivo swallowed hard. 'We applied a few dark arts of our own, in house.'

Keith nodded. 'Thanks, Ivo. I owe you one. I won't forget.'

'It's OK,' Ivo mumbled. 'Call it a freebie.'

Keith scrambled to his feet and, with a discreet flutter of his hand in farewell, made off down the slope. Ivo watched him go, wondering what the fuck was happening to himself: if he didn't watch it, he'd turn into a right sentimental old tosser.

TWENTY-NINE

The scene would have been magical, thought Grace, had it not been for its tragic purpose – and for the jarring presence of Lance beside her. They were here to work, to watch and listen and be on hand if the surveillance team on Pawel Zawodny needed backup. Since Lance's interview with the chief con, he had remained so scrupulously polite towards Grace as to be almost deferential; it was wearing her down, and right now she'd prefer open hostilities to this lumbering elephant in the room. She could hardly believe that this tight-lipped creature slowly weaving his way between the candlelit encampments was the same man she'd laughed with only a few days earlier.

At least she felt a little stronger in herself, having decided on the drive back from the old coaching inn that the odds were she probably hadn't made a drunken idiot of herself at the Blue Bar. On her way to work this morning she'd bought a nice card in which to write an apology to Roxanne. It felt ridiculous not simply to call by her flat and speak to her, but they'd have to wait for this case to be over before attempting to salvage the friendship face to face.

She glanced sideways at Lance: what was he thinking? Did he still distrust her? Resent her for not sharing his certainty about Pawel? But it was no good feeling sorry for herself. However unjust the media's relentless scrutiny, they were all now in this together. After the chief con's early morning visit, even Duncan had confessed that he'd told Joan details he should have kept to himself. He hadn't needed to spell it out; everyone understood that he'd done it to impress her, to woo her with privileged access to insider knowledge. Secrets were sexy, and all police officers had probably done the same at some point in their careers. And, besides, everyone also knew that Joan wouldn't breathe a word, so there was no question that Duncan had been dangerously indiscreet. Nonetheless it was humiliating, the way they'd all had to drill down, to use the chief con's charmless phrase, into their intimate, private moments.

They were all of them trying to do their best, yet failing to satisfy anyone – not this gathering tonight, not the massed media, not the higher ranks breathing down the SIO's neck, not each other, and certainly not the friends and family of the two victims whose killer they hunted so ineffectually.

Down beside the lake, dozens of Chinese lanterns began to drift upwards, paper globes glowing with light and heat, the naked flames reflected in the tranquil water below. A girl's lone voice, strong and deep, began to sing 'Happy Birthday' and gradually voices from all around her joined in. Grace looked at Lance, gave a little nod of recognition, and the two of them also began to sing. It soon ended – 'Happy birthday, dear Polly, Happy birthday to you!' – and was followed by silence, a communally held breath, before Grace made out muffled sounds of people weeping.

Dozens more lanterns were released skywards, rising and drifting until their trapped air was used up and the flames extinguished. Silhouetted against the dark water Grace could make out Phil and Beverly Sinclair clinging to one another, surrounded by Polly's student friends, who stood gently patting their arms and shoulders. Off to one side, heads bowed, stood Rachel Moston's parents, Clive and Rosalind.

Grace was keenly moved, and saw that Lance, too, was making no attempt to hide that he felt the power of the moment. His eyes met hers and she felt something between them shift and give way. He must have done so, too, for he nodded and touched her shoulder. 'We should keep moving,' was all he said, but she really hoped that now they might revert to being comrades again.

By unspoken assent, they turned away from the lakeside, threading their way towards the raised concrete platforms of the campus. Sitting alone, not far from the base of the sloping path that cut through the grass, his head and hands resting on his raised knees, was Danny Tooley. For an instant he raised his head in order to wipe his forearm across his face and gazed unseeing into Grace's eyes. She went straight to him, crouching down to put a comforting hand on his shoulder.

'Hey, Danny,' she said. 'It's me, Grace Fisher.'

Lance came up beside her, but remained standing.

'Danny, I'm sorry you lost your friend.'

He looked up with wet eyes. 'I can't bear it!'

'No, I know. But look –' She swept her arm around to encompass the hundreds of twinkling lights. 'You're not alone.'

Danny's gaze searched hers, as if unsure about accepting her sympathy.

'What do you think Polly would make of this?' Grace asked. 'She'd be pleased, wouldn't she?'

'Yes. It's good to see how many people care about her.'

'She sounds lovely,' said Grace, thinking of how Danny had tried to warn Polly against going home with Matt Beeston and had comforted her the day after her unsatisfactory hook-up. 'I'm sorry I never met her.'

'You let that other man go,' he said. 'The one you were asking about the other day.'

'Her landlord, yes. But we want to find her, Danny. Have you thought of anything else you can tell us? Anything at all.'

Grace was puzzled by the long look he gave her, but before she could coax him into saying more he rolled aside and rose quickly to his feet.

'I don't want to talk. I rather be on my own, if you don't mind.'

Grace let him wander away into the growing darkness. All the light was congregated below them now, and she and Lance turned and made their way down amid the different groupings, tuning into the different sounds of music or conversation as they passed. Then a voice called out to them from amongst those sitting on the ground. 'DS Cooper?'

Lance peered into the gloom, then, recognising Polly's housemate, greeted Jessica kindly. Grace saw that Amber and Caitlin were also part of the circle seated around a grassy carpet of tea lights, candles and lanterns, and nodded to them both.

'Do you want to join us?' Jessica asked hopefully.

'For a moment,' Lance replied, fitting himself into the space Jessica made for him beside her. Grace made her way round to sit by Amber. 'How are you doing?' she asked.

'A bit better,' the girl replied. 'Especially now we've found other places to stay. The Accommodation Office was really helpful.'

'That's good.' Grace was glad to hear that the university authorities had been supportive after the police had notified all Pawel's tenants before his release from custody. She'd noticed that the university also had their own security patrols out in force tonight.

'And it's good that Caitlin's back for a couple of days,' said Amber. 'Though we never expected it to be like this tonight. So many people. It's amazing, isn't it?'

'Yes, it is.'

'Have you seen the Facebook pages we started? Thousands of people have liked them or posted comments to show they care.'

Grace was glad that Amber had found comfort in the curiosity of so many strangers. She held up her phone. 'Yes, I'm following.' For the past couple of hours there'd been an outpouring of support across Twitter, Facebook and other sites, though Grace saw no reason to reveal that the police monitored them all for possible intelligence or signs of suspicious activity.

'I didn't think you knew Jessica?' Grace asked.

'She came to see me. It's like, we're the only ones who really know how this feels.'

Grace chided herself for hearing the slight boast behind Amber's words. No one was immune to the glamour that attached itself to newsworthy crimes, the specialness bestowed by proximity to the victim. Why else had so many people turned out tonight except for the spectacle and the crowd-surge of borrowed emotion? She and Lance had just felt it themselves as they joined in singing 'Happy Birthday'.

Across the circle she saw Lance pat Jessica's hand and then stand up. 'Better keep moving,' she told Amber. 'You look after yourself.'

Grace and Lance walked in thoughtful silence around the perimeter of the lake until they found an empty bench on which they could sit and survey the scene.

'Our friend must be here somewhere, don't you think?' asked Lance.

'Pawel?'

'Still not convinced?'

Tired of conflict, Grace wished for some simple human interaction that wasn't about grief and death. She didn't want to get into an argument. Not tonight. 'I don't know. You and I diverge on what the display was about, but in the end all that is for the barristers to argue over, isn't it?' For a few minutes at least she longed simply to pretend they were just here to kick back, enjoy the end of a summer evening in the park. 'So who are you when you're not on duty?' she asked.

Lance took a moment to reply, and Grace began to fear that he'd refuse after all to mend bridges. 'My dad's in the Job,' he said at last. 'Retired last year. A PC. My sister's married to a guy in traffic, also a PC.'

'So you did good, making DS?'

'They think I'm a jumped-up little prick.'

'Oh! I'm sorry. That must be tough.'

'And you?'

'The opposite. I was supposed to marry someone nice, give dinner parties and run an interior design shop.'

He laughed. 'That your mother's dream?'

'Stepmother's. My mother died when my sister was born.'

'Do you get on with her?'

'My stepmother? Yes. Dad died ten years ago, ten years after he married my stepmum. She could've walked away, and she didn't, so I appreciate that. But you should have seen her face when she thought I'd have to wear a uniform. Not what she had in mind.'

'I have to say, I can't quite imagine you in blues and flat black lace-ups, either!'

'No.'

Everyone from the Major Investigation Team here this evening had been instructed to blend in, and Grace had chosen skinny jeans, canvas shoes and a loose blouse. She'd always hated the swagger of a uniform: another significant difference between her and Trev, who loved the identification with the status and authority of the uniform and, though he would always deny it, felt diminished in civilian clothes. His work shirts had to be washed whiter than white, and he used to whistle with contentment as he blackened his shoes to a polished sheen before each and every shift.

'And it's your stepmum who's friends with Hilary?'

Grace came back to the present with a jolt. 'You've a good memory.'

'I thought about what you said.'

Grace waited to see if he'd say more, but he seemed to judge it sufficient. 'They were in corporate PR together,' she told him. 'Beauty products.'

Lance laughed once more, not loudly but it sounded genuine. 'That figures. So Hilary wants you to wear the same shade of lipstick as her?'

Grace smiled. 'More or less. Though she *was* kind to me. I'm not backtracking on that. She gave me a break when I needed one.'

'Fair enough.'

'And there's a big place in this world for beauty products.'

'Sure.'

They sat in silence for a moment, contemplating the diminishing points of light around them. People were starting to make their way home now and the crowd was thinning out. Fewer lights were reflected on the surface of the lake and, despite the warm night, the widening expanse of dark water sent a sudden shiver up Grace's spine.

'Don't worry, we'll get him.' Lance spoke into the darkness.

'So long as we stick together,' Grace agreed quietly.

THIRTY

Ivo was looking for Roxanne. He'd spotted her earlier, all smiles and cleavage, in a short gypsyish skirt, ankle boots and a denim bomber jacket, chatting to the aftershave advert who fronted for ITN. That was another black mark against her: fraternizing with the enemy. Ivo had kept tabs on her all evening, reckoning her source also had to be here tonight. He was determined to discover the identity of whomever it was she was so zealously keeping away from him. He was beginning to doubt after all that it was the Ice Maiden: so far tonight she'd gone nowhere near Roxanne, and anyway she appeared to be glued to the side of some fellow cop. So who else had Roxanne found to exchange billets-doux with?

But then he'd been diverted by the astonishing sight of the prime suspect, Pawel Zawodny, marching bold as brass towards the lakeside where a makeshift shrine had been set up to the two girls, one of whom wasn't even supposed to be dead, for fuck's sake. Zawodny was carrying a huge bouquet of flowers, had to be a hundred quid's worth at least, and Ivo had got straight on the blower to the *Courier*'s photographer, ordering him to get his arse over here yesterday and get the fucking picture.

It wasn't great, but the snapper at least got something before the police moved in and discreetly hustled Zawodny away. Ivo went after them. It had to be worth a punt at trying to persuade Zawodny to tell his side of the story. Ivo calculated he could risk going to at least thirty grand for an exclusive before clearing it with his editor. But the plain-clothes escort didn't seem any too keen on letting that happen, and Ivo had to content himself with sticking his card on the suspect and begging him to call the number, any time.

Then he had to find a quiet spot to phone in an extra two hundred words of new copy to accompany the shot of Zawodny and his flowers. The night editor, uncharacteristically cheerful, agreed it was never too late to make room for a good splash.

But now Ivo had completely lost sight of Roxanne. He circled around the lake, stopping once or twice to exchange pleasantries with fellow hacks, taking a gloating delight in hinting at what a great photo op they'd just missed. One of them mentioned that he'd seen the local reporter not so long ago, mingling with a group of students and no doubt collecting tributes to Polly and Rachel. Ivo had no problem crashing that party so made his way towards where the hack had pointed.

The trees grew more closely here, and he thought it would be safe to nip behind one and take a leak. Enough silvery light from a waning moon filtered down between the branches for him to make out where he was going. As he finished cursing his prostate, and his eyes grew accustomed to the shadow under the summer canopy, he thought he could make out the figure of someone lying further off in the grass. At first he thought perhaps it was a young couple making out, but then realised it was a woman alone. She was lying sedately, presumably looking up at the stars or whatever soppy stuff it was girls liked to do. Then he recognised the thick dark curls. What was she doing? Surely this wasn't some bizarre attempt to hide from him?

'Hey, Roxanne!' he called. She didn't move, so he zipped himself up and moved closer. 'Roxanne!'

He thought perhaps she was asleep and moved gently to her side, not wanting to startle her. Her arms were by her sides and her short skirt lay in a neat fan shape over her bare, straight legs. Her eyes were open and her head seemed turned at a funny angle. Shit! Ivo jumped back, his heart pounding. He looked around wildly but could see no one anywhere near. He was about to shout out, but some ancient war-horse instinct strangled the cry in his throat so that all that came out was a stifled grunt of fear and shock.

He bent down, trying to leave as little imprint in the grass as possible, and looked into her eyes. 'Roxanne!' He gave her shoulder a little shake but her face remained impassive. The girl was dead. Fuck! Oh fuck, no!

He made himself look again at her face. Her cheeks appeared swollen and puffy, but then he realised that something, some kind of fabric, had been stuffed into her mouth. His instinct was to yank it out, but he restrained himself: a reporter never lets himself become part of the story. All the same, he knew what he had to do, even though his hands shook so much that he had trouble holding his phone still enough to take the photos. He doubted the lawyers would ever let the paper print them, but he didn't want a bollocking from his editor for passing up such a golden opportunity. He moved to get a different angle; perhaps if he took the picture here, from her feet, her eyes would be facing away and it would work better. The phone's flash went off, throwing her slim wrists and delicate hands into sharp relief against the grass. Something between her thighs glinted underneath her skirt.

Ivo looked over his shoulder, seeing himself in his mind's eye for what he was – a foul scavenger picking at carrion, then lifted the fabric with two fingers and, with his other hand, pressed the light on his phone. Her hips were bare, her pubes waxed into a neat black line, and the neck of an empty wine bottle had been inserted into the soft embrace of her labia. Swallowing hard, he took the photo, then dropped the skirt, stifling the urge to straighten it again as demurely as he could. There was only so much explaining he was prepared to do later to some nerdy forensics expert.

So *this* was why Keith had got in such a strop over his piece about the bottle! Even the Young Ferret hadn't been able to unearth this half of the story, merely that a vodka bottle had been recovered from the scene and processed for prints and DNA. Now he knew the darker secret and could quite see why Keith would guard it so fiercely. Why the fuck would anybody do a thing like that? *Who* the fuck would?

In the gloom under the trees Ivo could hear his own

laboured breathing. The sound unnerved him. He hoped he wasn't about to have a coronary. But fuck it, he'd taken this kid under his wing, and now she'd been murdered and this vile thing done to her: that made it personal. He was going to have to expose this twisted little bastard before he died! He straightened up and took a deep breath. His pulse was racing and he hadn't felt this invigorated in years.

Ivo checked the time on his phone. If he called it in now, they'd likely be the only paper to get this into the early editions. Which meant that to stay ahead of the game he had to get the story safely tucked up *before* he called the police. Once the plods got here, he'd be stuck at the station all night making a statement while every other cowboy in town was free to ride around collecting background before they filed their copy. He couldn't have that.

The police would check his phone, of course; they'd know what he'd done. But so what? What could they do to him? It wasn't a crime in this country for an honest man to do his job. Not yet, anyway. Ivo looked down at Roxanne and shuddered. The sight of her made him want to weep. No question, it was a crying shame; she was a sweet kid, a good girl, but it wasn't going to make the slightest difference to her now whichever call he made first. Besides, he owed it to her to tell it right. This was her big story, and now it was his crusade. He must do it before his adrenaline crashed and he lost his nerve. If he let that happen, he knew for sure that there'd only be one outcome: he'd have to find a drink. A double. Just to get him started.

He made the call.

THIRTY-ONE

Lance received the urgent summons to make their way down to the trees between the two lakes. The explanation was brief and to the point: a body had been found.

Keith was already there, talking to a shorter, paunchy man whom Grace was now able to recognise as Ivo Sweatman. Keith glanced at her over Ivo's shoulder and told her curtly to stay back. She looked at Lance, wondering if he meant both of them or just her, but Lance remained with her anyway, making room for uniformed officers who came scurrying out of the darkness with crime scene tape that they proceeded to wind around the ring of trees.

'Any idea who it is?' she asked one of them.

'Local journalist, according to the guy who found her.' The young female PC nodded towards Ivo. 'He knows her. He's one of the London press corps, apparently.'

'Roxanne?' Grace started forward, but Lance caught her arm and held her firmly.

'Wait! You'll have to wait.'

'It can't be her! Why would anyone hurt Roxanne?'

'We don't know it is her yet.'

'We can't have been more than a couple of hundred yards away!'

'I know.'

Grace looked into his eyes, willing him to say it wasn't true. 'Oh Jesus. We saw Pawel Zawodny! He was right over there. Why didn't we keep him in custody when we had the chance? We should never have let him go!'

'Look, we don't know anything. Could even be some kind of accident.'

Keith summoned a uniformed officer to escort Ivo away, then came over to where they stood. He gave Grace a hard look. 'Where have you been all evening?' he asked.

'Skirting around the lake, like you told us. Why? I don't understand.'

'Grace has been with me the whole time,' said Lance firmly, and then Grace understood: she was a potential suspect!

'So it is Roxanne?' she said.

'Yes. I'm sorry.'

'Are you sure she's dead?' Grace started to move forward again, propelled by her sheer disbelief, but Keith blocked her way.

'We're waiting for official confirmation. Samit's on his way. But I spoke to the officers who were first on the scene. They're experienced guys.'

'But what's happened?' Grace's brain, still able only to reject this alien reality, looked for some other way out, some escape clause, some other answer to this riddle.

'Looks like the same MO as Rachel Moston,' said Keith.

Lance lowered his voice. 'Is there a bottle?'

Keith nodded. 'So Ivo says. I don't want to contaminate the scene more than necessary, but Wendy's on her way, should be here soon.'

Grace had stood around many times waiting for the crime scene investigators to arrive, but on those occasions the interval had been simply a tedious matter of minutes to be filled with gossip and banter, the anonymous victim largely ignored, merely the opening of a new case file. Now the idea of turning their backs on a lifeless human being filled her with intolerable distress. 'Is there nothing we can do?' she asked.

'Duncan's organising teams to get names and addresses as people leave, so I want you two here,' Keith spoke softly, his businesslike tone deliberately calming. 'Someone's bringing lights over, so if you want to nip back to your car to get jackets or whatever, now's your chance.'

The night breeze coming off the dark water was indeed growing chilly and the ground beneath the trees was damp, but Grace shook her head: she couldn't leave Roxanne friendless.

'I'll go,' said Lance. 'I've got a torch in the boot, too.' He squeezed Grace's arm before slipping away between the tree trunks.

She and Keith stood awkwardly together. 'You don't happen to know the next of kin?' he asked.

Grace felt a rush of sorrow for Roxanne's parents. They were nice people, lived in Haywards Heath, not far from

Brighton, and she'd visited them several times when she and Roxanne were students. Roxanne's father had a little garage and, back then, her mother worked in the Italian cafe-restaurant her grandparents owned. But that was ten years ago, and Roxanne had mentioned that first evening at the Blue Bar that the cafe had closed when her grandfather died. She told Keith all this, and he asked her to relay the essentials to the Sussex police.

Grace was grateful for the distraction, and pleased to end up speaking to someone in the local district force who was calm and sympathetic. Ending the call, she tried not to think too much about Roxanne's parents hearing the doorbell at this time of night and opening up to find uniformed officers on the doorstep.

A generator van lumbered down the slope and across the grass towards them. Technicians jumped out and swiftly began to set up powerful arc lights. Grace stayed well back, reluctant to face the inevitable sight of the corpse. Keith came up behind her. 'You don't have to be here for this. It might be better if you weren't.'

'Thanks, boss. But I'd like to stay, if that's possible.'

She saw him hesitate before he spoke. 'Ivo said the tip about the bottle of Fire'n'Ice came from her. We have to know who told her about it.'

'Not me, boss!' she promised, praying again as she had when facing the chief con that it was the truth. 'I swear I never told her anything about the investigation.'

'Well, we'll never know now, will we?'

Grace's heart sank: it was a selfish thought, but the only

other person who could confirm what she had or hadn't said that night in the Blue Bar was now dead. She stepped closer to the SIO, raising her chin. 'You *can* trust me, sir.' She glanced into the darkness under the trees. 'We were friends. I owe her the truth.'

Keith hesitated before he nodded, though Grace could see some doubt linger in his eyes. 'OK.' He sighed. 'Ivo said people at his paper gave Roxanne's information a further spin. Someone in a lab may have been bribed, they may have hacked a phone or a computer, who knows.'

'Surely he has to tell you now?'

Keith laughed. 'Don't kid yourself! No, I doubt he'll give me any more than he already has.'

There was a loud click and suddenly they were bathed in bright white light. It made Grace blink and threw every leaf and blade of grass into sharp, colourless relief. Without meaning to, she turned her head and immediately saw, beyond the taut blue-and-white tape, Roxanne lying on the grass. Her face was turned away, her legs straight, her pose so restful she could very well have been asleep. It was Roxanne, but not Roxanne. Not any more.

Grace was determined not to break down in front of the SIO: if she showed too much emotion, he might take her off the case. But she yearned to breathe life back into her friend, not to allow her memory of someone once so sweetly and zestfully alive to be overlaid by the image of this scene. She recognised that part of her grief was self-interested, that her remembrance of Roxanne also preserved the hopeful energy of her own youth; this crime stole something precious from every person with whom the victim had ever shared her life.

'Pawel Zawodny was here tonight,' she said.

'I know.'

'Do we pick him up?'

'Be patient, DS Fisher. Wait and see what we can recover from the scene first. Let's hope matey's slipped up this time and left something we can nail him with.'

Grace made a silent vow to thank Roxanne for her friendship in the only way now left to her: she would hunt down her killer.

THIRTY-TWO

Murky clouds muted the moonlight as Grace and Lance made their way back to the car park by the dwindling beam of his torch. The area was deserted now and the familiar glow of the interior light as Grace opened the car door promised a welcome security. Lance drove, allowing Grace time to stare silently out into the blackness.

Once Samit had arrived and they'd suited up, she'd tried her best to examine the body through the pathologist's professional eyes, and for a while she had succeeded. It had helped, too, that she'd been prepared for the intimate sight of the violating wine bottle, though the little cloud of midges that swarmed over Roxanne's bare skin, magnified by the bright white light, was a mental picture she'd probably never manage to obliterate. Apart from what looked like some kind of fabric placed in her mouth, which Samit would wait to extract under sterile mortuary conditions, Roxanne's body had been positioned in a manner strikingly similar to the way Rachel Moston's had been arranged.

Once Keith had decided to remove the body, and Wendy

had secured the scene, there'd been the usual chat around the forensic van as people wound down and agreed deadlines to deliver test results and reports. Just at the moment when it hit Grace hard that she was the only one here who had truly lost someone, Lance had moved unobtrusively to her side and remained there until the undertakers' van had lumbered off across the grass.

Now they were reaching the deserted lamp-lit roundabouts on the outskirts of Colchester, and Lance casually mentioned that, if she'd rather not be alone for the few hours that remained of the night, she was welcome to come back to his place and get some kip on his couch until it was time to report for work. Grace accepted gratefully.

Lance's flat took her by surprise. It was on the ground floor of a large Victorian house near Lexden Park, and had shuttered windows, high ceilings and bare floorboards. The living room contained only a big leather sofa, a frayed Oriental rug, a low wooden table and an upright piano with tarnished candle sconces that looked like it had once belonged in a pub or a music hall. The lid was up and a book of classical music lay open on the stand. She could read pencil notations in the margins written in what she imagined was the firm hand of a music teacher.

'So you're a pianist?' she said.

'Yeah. Another thing my family reckoned was me being jumped-up,' he replied. 'A bit too girly for them. Little did they know.'

Exhaustion made her indiscreet. 'You're gay?'

He gave her a jaded look.

'I simply never clocked it,' she said. 'Sorry. Too preoccupied this past week, I guess.'

'Well, I don't exactly advertise it at work. What can I get you?'

'You know what I'd really like? Some toast.'

'Coming up.'

He disappeared through to the kitchen. Grace considered following him, but she was too tired. She flopped down onto the leather couch and closed her eyes. Immediately she saw a swarm of grainy black insects and raised her lids again, blinking to relieve the dryness that went with being awake for nearly twenty hours. She lay back and focused instead on the scrolling plasterwork around the ceiling, so different to the mean, plain surfaces of her own flat. How blind she'd been not to perceive Lance's sexuality, not to realise how tough it might sometimes be for him in a workplace that was a long way from banishing homophobia. What else had she been blind to? If she'd listened to Roxanne in the pub, really listened and asked questions instead of banging on about her own problems, might she have learned something that could have prevented her friend's death tonight?

Why Roxanne? Why had she been killed? Keith said it was Roxanne who'd told Ivo about the vodka bottle, and now Grace was terrified in case that knowledge had somehow led to her death. Had she, Grace, put Roxanne in danger by telling her? If only she had some way to know for sure whether or not she'd said *anything* on that tequila-fuelled night!

The sheer physical finality of the undertakers carrying the black body bag to the private ambulance hit her, and she tried to control her breathing to overcome her panic. She'd been too young to remember her mother's death, and her dad had died in hospital, rigged up to tubes and monitors. A guy she'd been at school with had written himself off on his motorbike, but this was the first time someone she knew and had been close to had died such a sudden and cruel death.

And all the time she'd been only yards away! That's what she couldn't get over, couldn't get past. She knew her thoughts were illogical, but she felt like she'd just stood by and let it happen. And what if *was* her fault? What if Roxanne had been killed and violated because of dangerous knowledge Grace had given her?

Lance came back in balancing mugs of tea and plates of toast spread with raspberry jam. He looked at her as she sat up. 'I think you're in shock,' he said. He put everything down on the low table, sat down next to her and handed her a mug. 'Drink this. Supposed to be what got everyone through the Blitz.'

'It's my fault.'

'That a confession?'

'No, but –' Grace longed to unburden herself about what she had and hadn't said to Roxanne, but not even the late hour made her forget the chief con's warning: if she had any other unauthorised contact with the media, it would be treated as a very serious disciplinary offence. And she had: she'd deliberately gone against that order and met

Roxanne in the out-of-the-way pub the very same day. With-holding information from an investigation went against every principle Grace had, but she must not get herself sacked! Nor could she risk telling Lance; it wouldn't be fair to expect him to keep her secret.

'Why Roxanne?' she asked instead.

'Could have been random,' he said. 'Sheer bad luck.'

'You don't really think that?'

'No. That would have to mean Rachel Moston was a random victim, too.'

'And cancel out any connection with Pawel Zawodny.'

Lance nodded. 'I still think it's him. I figure he was put-ting himself back at the centre of attention tonight by hijacking the vigil for Polly. Those flowers were yet another performance.' He patted the phone in his shirt pocket. 'Word has spread. Looks like everyone who was there or heard what happened has told everyone else they know. All the social media sites have gone viral. So far as our guy's concerned, this is like the shooting of John Lennon. His big moment.'

'And another scoop for the *Courier*,' she said bitterly.

'Afraid so. Serial murder scores higher as a headline than any celebrity event. Higher than a rock concert, a film premiere, a royal wedding. This second killing puts him right up there.'

'She was my friend.'

Lance nodded. 'I know. Eat your toast.'

Grace did as instructed, and he waited until she'd finished the first slice before speaking again. 'Seriously,' he began, 'this makes him really dangerous. He's got a lot to live up to now. He's unlikely just to drift back into obscurity.'

'So you reckon we'll have more victims?'

'Don't you?' asked Lance.

'Do you think he chose Roxanne because she was a journalist?'

'Maybe. She's the local reporter. The *Mercury* is fairly widely distributed.'

Grace wasn't convinced. 'Did we drive him to this, Lance? I deliberately humiliated Zawodny in interview. You saw how furious he was. Was this his way of retaliating? Of getting at me because she was my friend?'

'How would he know that?'

'She might have told him. She might have been in contact with him for days for all we know.'

'Surveillance didn't pick it up.' Lance handed her a cushion from his end of the couch. 'Here. We're not going to solve it tonight. We should try and catch some sleep.'

Grace took a deep breath and blew it out again very slowly. 'This sounds crazy,' she said, 'but do you know what upsets me most? That he didn't put anything under her head. That he didn't care. He wasn't sorry.' She twisted the empty tea mug around in her hands. 'Like Roxanne wasn't good enough for him to bother. Was that deliberate? A signal to someone? To me?'

'I think we're over-thinking it,' Lance said gently. 'If I fetch a rug and another pillow, will you be OK here?'

'Yes,' she said, trying hard to follow his example and subdue her anxiety. 'Thanks.'

He returned moments later, checked she had everything she needed, turned off the lights and then headed off to his bedroom. Grace lay still, letting her eyes adjust to the pale light that came through above the shutters that covered the tall windows. She was grateful to Lance not only for providing sanctuary but also for offering friendship despite the many reasons he had not to. Yet, try as she might to empty her head of the night's events, she couldn't stop herself shivering at the thought of Roxanne in mortuary storage. She knew enough of the autopsy process, of what Samit would do to the body, for it not to bear thinking about. Then she began to imagine Roxanne's parents preparing themselves for their journey from Sussex to identify her. She must distract herself! To avoid being alone with such meditations, she reached for her phone and searched for Roxanne's name on Twitter. Just as Lance had said, the timeline was packed with dozens – hundreds – of different people wanting to talk about her, to reach out to one another. Grace was evidently not alone in her mourning. Comforted, she fell asleep clasping her phone to her heart.

THIRTY-THREE

Keith looked like he'd had even less sleep than Grace. In fact, thought Grace, right now he looked like a man you ought to worry about: her dad's skin had gone that same pasty grey in the days before his heart attack. She watched the SIO's expression become even grimmer as he handed Duncan a large brown envelope.

'Roxanne Carson, age thirty-one,' he began, as Duncan added the post-mortem photographs to the board. 'Cause of death was ligature strangulation. Time of death estimated at less than an hour before she was found. No reason to think she was killed elsewhere. No indication of a violent struggle, nor of recent sexual activity except that an empty white wine bottle had been inserted into her vagina, probably after death.'

A ripple of voracious interest passed through the packed MIT office: this was the first time the rest of the ever-increasing team had been permitted to learn the full significance of the vodka bottle they'd read about in the newspaper.

Grace was pretty sure that if Roxanne was working she wouldn't have been drinking, but she asked anyway. 'Was Roxanne drunk?'

'We're waiting on the blood alcohol level,' replied Keith. 'But stomach contents suggest not.'

'It's possible that matey may have just picked an empty wine bottle up off the ground,' said Duncan. 'I saw quite a few discarded bottles.'

'There were hundreds of people there last night,' said Keith. 'And they left a lot of litter. Forensics are going to be a nightmare.'

'Same as the demolition site where Rachel Moston was found,' said Lance. 'A deliberate choice?'

'May well be. Which means that matey's organised and prepared. So, as with the first murder, unlikely to have left fingerprints.'

'We might get lucky on DNA this time,' said Duncan.

Keith nodded. 'Possibly. There are certainly enough points of similarity to assume that Rachel Moston and Roxanne Carson were killed by the same person.'

'There was nothing placed under Roxanne's head, though,' Grace pointed out.

Keith ignored the interruption. 'A handbag, which we've identified as belonging to the victim, was recovered nearby and, so far as we're aware, nothing obvious appears to be missing from it. She was found with a pair of knickers inside her mouth, also probably placed there post-mortem. Her own weren't recovered, and we should be able to confirm that this pair was not brought to the scene but belonged to her.'

'So why this further elaboration?' asked Lance. 'He must mean something by it. It's a kind of conversation, isn't it? Either with himself or with us.'

'Let's stick to facts, shall we?' said Keith drily.

'When Ivo Sweatman found the body, he already knew that a vodka bottle had been found with the first victim,' said Duncan.

'So did everyone who read yesterday's *Courier*,' said Lance.

'Yes, but do we need to rule out the idea of a copycat?'

'Ivo told me earlier in the evening that it had been Roxanne Carson who gave him that information,' said Keith. 'But I don't believe either of them knew the precise details of the positioning of the vodka bottle.'

'All the same, she might have been getting information about Rachel's murder directly from the killer,' said Lance eagerly.

'That's certainly a possibility,' agreed Keith, his expression bleaker than Grace thought possible. 'In which case, we have to ask ourselves why a journalist knew more than we did.'

Keith paused as if battling to stop himself uttering the words he really wanted to say. In any case, no one in the room needed telling: this killing had happened on their watch. Everyone had seen the morning TV news bulletins and copies of today's *Courier* had already been passed from hand to hand around the station. Below the battle cry of a single-word headline – *SLAIN* – Ivo Sweatman had excoriated the police for their failure to protect the young local reporter and demanded an official inquiry into what had gone wrong and in particular why two separate suspects had been released by the police. It was the question they were all asking themselves.

Keith sighed heavily. 'We don't yet know exactly what Roxanne knew, or how or when she found it out. Whether or not she knew her killer or had arranged to meet him last night remains speculation.'

'Do we know if she'd had any contact with Pawel Zawodny?' asked Lance. 'He was at the vigil.'

'After he'd been escorted to his vehicle, officers observed him drive out of the campus car park. They then alerted the mobile surveillance unit,' Duncan explained reluctantly. 'But the tracking device shows that his Toyota remained stationary on the exit road for twenty-six minutes. Close enough for him to have made his way down to the murder scene and back.'

'What happened to the surveillance?' Keith asked sharply.

'They had a car waiting to follow him off once he reached the main road. Their brief was not to crowd him.'

Keith's jaw clenched tight. Grace could easily guess what he was thinking: by releasing Zawodny from custody on Monday, had they allowed a killer to strike a second time right under their noses?

'Where did Zawodny's Toyota go once it got moving again?' Keith asked.

'Straight back to his flat,' answered Duncan. 'As soon as the surveillance unit got word of the murder, they knocked him up. It wasn't long after, but he'd already showered and put his clothes in the wash.'

Keith swore under his breath. 'What did he say he'd been doing in those twenty-six minutes he was parked on the exit road?'

'That he was upset at the way he'd been treated, so pulled over to calm himself down.'

'There were still plenty of people about,' said Keith. 'Did anyone see him?'

'Nothing so far,' said Duncan. 'We've still got hundreds of statements to take. But plenty of people saw him with his bouquet of flowers, so at least there's a chance they'd remember if they'd spotted him again later on.'

'The switchboard has been totally jammed all morning,' said Joan. 'We're also working through all the social media postings. It'll take a while, but we should be able to make a pretty accurate timeline of the victim's movements, too.'

'The *Mercury*'s editor was on the phone first thing,' said Duncan. 'He says he'll help in any way he can.'

'Someone's still on our side, then?' Keith said with heavy irony as the room fell silent. This second death was a crisis for the Essex force, and everyone was aware that urgent discussions were already going on upstairs. Discussions that were unlikely to make their jobs any easier.

'Do we re-arrest Zawodny, boss?' asked Duncan.

'Not yet. I don't want the clock ticking until we're ready, and we've a long way to go before we are. But make sure you put the fear of God into the surveillance unit so they've got tabs on him every second.'

'The media know his identity, know he's still on police bail,' said Duncan.

'You think I don't know that?' snapped Keith. He ran a hand to and fro across his head, his grey hair springing vigorously back into place. 'We've applied to a judge for a phone tap. But we need to get him charged, so that anything the media gets becomes *sub judice*. We need evidence, enough evidence to take to the CPS and get Zawodny off the streets and into custody.'

'Then, boss, I still think there's something to be got from why he's staged this differently to the way he displayed Rachel Moston,' Lance said stubbornly. 'Why the knickers in her mouth?'

'Forget the symbolism!'

Lance turned to Grace, enlisting her support. 'We asked Zawodny if he masturbated over women's underwear,' he argued. 'We humiliated him. Now he's humiliated us. And the underwear is to shove that message home. Stuff the way we shamed him right back down our own throats.'

'I think he's right, boss,' said Grace. 'It was the only time in all the interviews that Zawodny showed any real emotion. He was very angry.'

Keith considered for a moment, then nodded. 'It's an attractive argument. But Roxanne Carson was a reporter. She might also have been killed simply because of what she knew.'

'Would Roxanne's editor know who she'd been talking to, what story she was putting together?' Grace turned to Duncan, only too aware of the ways in which the answers to such questions might expose *her*.

'You'd better get down there,' ordered Keith, when

Duncan shook his head. 'Gareth Sullivan is the editor. Ask him if we can see her notes, whatever's on her work computer. Find out if she'd made any kind of approach to Zawodny.'

'I'll get you the data off her phone as well,' said Duncan.

'And talk to Ivo,' Keith said to Grace. 'See if he can add anything to the statement he made last night.'

'Me?' Grace instantly regretted her exclamation but, as every face turned to her, she straightened her spine and held her head high: she owed it to Roxanne.

'Yes,' said Keith, raising his voice slightly so that everyone heard that he wasn't only speaking to her. 'Let's use the fact that you knew the victim to our advantage.'

Grace dared to glance around the office and was relieved to find that the appraising stares were not as universally hostile as she feared.

'Is there any point talking to Sweatman?' asked Lance, surprised. 'After the garbage he wrote about us this morning?'

'What Ivo writes and what Ivo says in private are two very different things,' said Keith, although he must have seen that it was not only Lance who remained unconvinced. 'We're under attack,' he told everyone. 'And it'll probably get a whole lot uglier before we're finished. But that, so they tell us, is the price we pay for our uniquely vigorous press.'

A growl of anger and dissatisfaction rolled around the room, barely quelled by Keith's roving gaze seeking out any final comments or questions. 'OK, let's keep the information flowing,' he said. 'I appreciate how hard you've been working, and I want to thank you, all of you. But now you have to double it. Then double it again. The next arrest we make has to stick.'

The SIO disappeared into his own office and as everyone else dispersed Grace found herself beside Lance. He smiled encouragingly just as her phone vibrated in her pocket. He waited as she read the text: *Hope you're OK. She was your friend, wasn't she? Hope you know you're not alone. Love Trev xx.*

THIRTY-FOUR

Gareth Sullivan, the editor of the *Mercury*, had a neatly trimmed gingery beard and silver-rimmed glasses. He looked shocked and distracted as he led Grace and Lance through the main open space where his staff were hunched intently over keyboards. 'This is terrible,' he said. 'I ought to send people home but instead they're all working overtime putting together tomorrow's special tribute edition.'

Sullivan showed them into his partitioned office. 'No one can take it in,' he continued. 'Colchester only ever has a couple of murders a year at most, and they're generally drug-related. Well, I don't have to tell you that. Please,' he gestured to a couple of faded, utilitarian chairs. 'Sit down.'

He took a seat behind his desk, leaving the detectives to address him through a canyon of newspapers piled up on either side of its cluttered surface. 'So what can you tell me? Do you know yet what happened, who is responsible?'

'We're here to ascertain Ms Carson's movements last night,' Lance replied. 'Was she following any particular angle or story?'

'No, I don't think so. Just general coverage of the event.'

'But she was at the vigil on behalf of the paper?'

'Yes, absolutely. We had a photographer there, as well.'

'Great. It would be really helpful if we could have access to everything he shot.'

Sullivan shook his head. 'I'll gladly help as much as I can. I hope that's obvious. But I hope that you also understand that it's impossible for me simply to hand over unpublished journalistic material.'

'We're hunting a killer, Mr Sullivan,' said Lance.

'I think we're all aware of that here.'

Grace bit back the impulse to tell him she'd been at uni with Roxanne: clear boundaries were important right now.

'She may very possibly have been killed because she knew or suspected the identity of Rachel Moston's murderer,' explained Lance.

'Which is why disclosing any journalist's sources is such a sensitive matter. The betrayal of a reporter's sources puts every journalist at risk.'

'I'm all for a free press, but you may be suppressing vital evidence.' Lance spoke politely but made no attempt to hide his irritation.

'My reporters speak off the record to a wide range of people, from criminals to whistleblowers. If those people believe I'm simply going to hand their names straight over to the police whenever I'm asked to do so, we wouldn't have a free press.'

'What if your reporter was talking to an active paedophile, for instance? Would you still protect a source then?'

'The police would be able to go before a judge and ask for a production order.'

'We need to take whoever murdered Roxanne Carson off the streets as soon as possible!'

'Are you saying there's an immediate and demonstrable direct threat to public safety?' Sullivan asked heatedly, as Lance glared back, infuriated.

Grace decided swiftly that boundaries should be fudged after all. 'Mr Sullivan,' she said gently, 'I was at university with Roxanne. We were old friends.'

Sullivan nodded, accepting the offer of appeasement. Grace had the impression she'd told him something he already knew and was struck by the acutely uncomfortable thought that maybe her own name was amongst those he was fighting to protect.

'I'm sure she'd applaud your defence of journalistic principle, but I'm even more certain that she'd damn well want us to catch her killer,' Grace told him robustly. 'And she'd expect us to make sure no one else comes to harm. So are you really sure there's no way you can help us without compromising confidential material?'

She was relieved to see Sullivan soften. 'I'm sorry,' he said. 'I don't mean to be obstructive. And I'm not going down the *Courier*'s road of blaming the police. But we're all of us here to –' He broke off and stared out of the window at his featureless view of the neighbouring office block. 'She had so much energy,' he said at last. 'Always wanted more out of life.'

He took off his spectacles and made as if to rub some grit

out of his eyes, but she could see he was wiping away the pricking of tears. 'If you're in contact with her family, please let them know we've set up a Facebook page. She was very popular with readers. Her family may like to see that.'

Grace waited for him to replace his glasses. 'So might you be able to help us?' she asked again. 'If you can't let us take away her notebooks, or whatever shots your photographer took, perhaps you could at least let us look at the material here, under your supervision?'

Sullivan considered. 'How about this?' he offered. 'I'll go through everything. You tell me what you're looking for, ask me questions, and I'll do my best to answer.'

'And if we need to follow up ourselves, will you give us names?' asked Lance.

'I'd have to get permission from whoever gave her the information.'

'And what if that turns out to be her killer?' demanded Lance.

'Then I'll have a pretty difficult decision to make, won't I?'

'You're not serious!' exclaimed Lance.

'I'm not enjoying this any more than you are, DS Cooper,' Sullivan responded. 'Roxanne worked for this paper for four years. I can assure you that I care a great deal more about this appalling crime than you do.'

Grace cut in before Lance could escalate the argument. 'Thanks for your offer, Mr Sullivan. We appreciate it. How long do you think it'll take you to go through the material?'

The newspaper editor stared at the partition wall behind which sat a dozen people who would all endlessly be seeking his comments and approval over the next few hours. When he looked back at Grace, his eyes had a hunted expression. 'If you can send over a list of what it is you want me to look out for, I'll try and get back to you by the end of the day.'

Grace stood up and held out her hand. 'Thank you. I realise how busy you are.'

Sullivan shook her hand, went to open the door, then almost immediately closed it again. 'What about her phone?' he asked.

'It was recovered,' Grace told him. 'Along with her handbag.'

'Then I'll need it back,' he said. 'And whatever notebook she had with her.'

'No way!' said Lance before she could stop him.

'The *Mercury* provides reporters with phones, so all stored data counts as unpublished journalistic material.'

'We'll make sure your property is returned to you, Mr Sullivan,' Grace assured him, giving Lance a sharp jab in the ribs with her elbow. Both knew that the phone data had already been downloaded and copied, but that the half-dozen scribbled pages of shorthand in her notebook would take longer to decipher.

She thanked the editor once more and hustled Lance out of the building.

'What the fuck does he think he's doing?' he fumed, as soon as they hit the pavement. 'All this academic bullshit when he's got a serial killer right on his doorstep!'

'He's got a point, Lance. They're not here to do our job for us.'

'I'm not handing back that phone. This isn't *All the President's Men!*'

'You know we have no choice. Any evidence we get from it is protected under PACE, not to mention the European Convention. If Sullivan doesn't want us to have it and then we use it in court, a defence barrister will tear us to shreds.'

'Anyway, at least we've got the information,' said Lance. 'He can't stop us exploiting it, even if we can't produce it as evidence.'

'So long as we're seen to do it right,' said Grace.' And, with any luck, we might find enough on Roxanne's phone to help us frame the right questions for whatever's in her notebooks.'

Although they walked quickly, the short distance back up the hill to the police station gave Grace time to think. Her continuing uncertainty about what she had or hadn't told Roxanne that night outside the Blue Bar left her paralysed and ashamed. And even if she'd been clear in her mind about how much she'd said, it would still cause difficulties if her name were to emerge from Roxanne's notes. Until Gareth Sullivan had talked about press freedom, it had simply not occurred to her that a journalist's sources would be protected, so she'd assumed that she'd be helpless to prevent the investigation exposing their contact. Now, she realised, it was entirely up to her to decide how much to reveal. More than anything, Grace wanted to bring her friend's killer to justice. Yet wouldn't it be reckless and stupid to destroy her career before it became absolutely necessary to do so?

In Maidstone, it had felt easy to pick up the phone and call Crimestoppers about the dealer who was supplying Lee with steroids and amphetamines, and afterwards to tell herself it had been a clear matter of doing what was right. She'd discovered too late that doing the right thing had seemed uncomplicated only because when she made the anonymous call she had envisaged no consequences to herself – apart from the natural glow of self-congratulation.

If she *had* foreseen all that would eventually follow in the wake of that call, would she still have made it? She'd lost everything as a result – friends, job, home, husband and peace of mind. Did she really possess the guts to tell the truth now and risk losing her job and everything that went with it? Especially if the truth did not even assist the investigation. Could she really survive the potentially cat-astrophic consequences of her actions a second time? But equally, could she live with herself if she didn't do what she believed to be right?

She wished she could talk to Lance, ask his advice, but it would be totally wrong to entangle him in her blunders.

THIRTY-FIVE

Ivo was bored with the game now. Of course he didn't have to stay. If he wanted to join the awkward squad, he could walk out any time he liked. But – Keith's doing, he was sure – he'd been specifically told that it would be DS Fisher who'd be coming down to go over the statement he'd given late last night, and he had no objection to trading questions for half an hour alone in an interview room with the Ice Maiden. All the same, he'd now been kicking his heels in here for over an hour, time in which his competitors were out and about looking busy.

He'd had almost no sleep but managed to convince himself he felt alert and vigorous as long as he kept at arm's length the memory of Roxanne's prone young body in the dark, dewy grass. If he let that slip through his defences, then he felt about a thousand years old, like he'd definitely overstayed his welcome on this earth.

He looked again at his watch and wearily supposed he had to expect some kind of payback in response to the front-page hammering he'd given the SIO and his team over a second killing happening while they were looking the wrong way. And of course, in their eyes, the accompanying photograph of the body, appropriately Photoshopped in the name of decency and in accord with the embargo placed on the precise deployment of the wine bottle, would pretty much put him on a par with the kind of paparazzi scum who frequented Paris road tunnels.

Still, there was some consolation to be had from the fact that by the time word of the murder had reached his fellow cowboys it had been too late for them to update their final editions. This morning's *Courier* had been the only paper to carry any kind of story about it, and Ivo's editor had called personally to congratulate him on his considerable presence of mind at the scene. Ivo knew he ought to pat himself on the back, but frankly he felt sick that he'd got a medal pinned on him because of that sweet kid's death. And when Keith was doubtless at this very moment facing a firing squad upstairs courtesy of *his* lords and masters. Oh well, Ivo reckoned Keith was man enough to understand that, given the situation Ivo had found himself in, he could hardly have pulled his punches.

Brothers in arms, that's how he'd always thought of his relationships with various senior detectives over the years; though he had a more than sneaking suspicion it wasn't how they regarded him. And last night, he'd been vouchsafed his first unassailable insight into why that might be. Sure, he'd been shown his fair share of gruesome crime scene photos and had sat through weeks of harrowing evidence while covering the trials of some of the country's most notorious serial killers, but he'd always pictured himself and the police as opposing teams gleefully chasing the same ball. Last night had proved to him that a life extinguished was no sporting matter, and he'd finally grasped what lay behind Keith's occasional flash of contempt. In fact, he now found it incredible that Keith managed to show him any forbearance at all. He wouldn't give himself the time of day, frankly.

The door opened and DS Fisher came in, disappointingly followed by Hilary Burnett. The Ice Maiden's frosty gaze informed him that her opinion of the man who had stood over a woman's body while he filed his story was, like his own, less than charitable. Nevertheless, his reaction to her disdain surprised him: it wasn't often he actually gave a toss what other people thought of him.

'You must think I'm a cold-hearted bastard,' he told her. 'And you'd be right. But I was fond of your friend.'

She blinked, as if taken aback by his soppy sentimentality. 'Please sit down,' she said. 'You know Ms Burnett?'

'Indeed.' He took his seat, giving himself a stern mental shake: pull yourself together, man!

'We have the statement you made to my colleagues last night,' she said. 'What we want to cover now is the nature of the victim's professional enquiries.' She consulted the sheaf of papers she'd brought with her. 'You said you never spoke to Ms Carson at the vigil last night?'

'Roxanne? No. I think she was avoiding me, to be honest.'

'Why?'

Ivo smiled to himself at how easily she'd let herself be

ensnared. 'She'd mastered my first rule of journalism: you don't share,' he explained.

Did the Ice Maiden give the ghost of a smile, or was that wishful thinking on his part?

'So you don't know who she talked to last night?' she asked.

'So far as I could see, she was just working the crowd. Maybe there were a few people she'd already hooked up with through social media. But I daresay you'll have checked that out already.'

'Yes. Do you know if she was pursuing a particular angle on Polly's disappearance?'

Ivo considered. DS Fisher was not exactly giving it away for free, so maybe he had to be the first to roll over. 'I don't know for sure,' he told her, lowering his voice to sound more sincere. 'But the way she'd clammed up on me suggests she was on to something she figured would be worth keeping to herself.' Ivo deliberately acknowledged Hilary before shifting his gaze back to Grace Fisher and raising a questioning eyebrow. 'Or someone?'

But she looked back at him steadily: if DS Fisher *was* Roxanne's source, then she clearly didn't intend to let herself be spooked by any threat to reveal her identity. Good for her!

'Was she on to something in connection with Polly Sinclair?' she asked. 'Or with Rachel Moston's murder? Do you know?'

'I thought you might.'

She ignored his clumsy innuendo. 'You printed a story

about Pawel Zawodny,' she said. 'It contained information we hadn't released. How did you obtain it?'

He noticed Hilary shift nervously on her chair. And did he after all detect a flicker of apprehension in the Ice Maiden's eyes? 'Remind me,' he urged.

'You knew he had a cabin cruiser and that we were looking at it. You knew we had a vodka bottle in evidence.'

He nodded, watching her carefully. 'Roxanne tipped me off that the police were asking questions about a boat and about a vodka bottle.' He'd already admitted that to Keith, so he wasn't giving her anything new.

'A vodka bottle? No more than that? Please think, it's important.'

He nodded, trying not to recall the photo he'd taken of the wine bottle between Roxanne's thighs. 'I put the rest together myself.' He hesitated, then decided to let this be his good deed for the day – for the bloody decade, let's face it. 'The *Courier*'s research department found out the brand for me, and that it was recovered from the scene.'

'Your research department?'

Ivo shrugged. 'Some necromancer in the basement with a scrying mirror, for all I know. I don't ask, and they don't tell.'

'But you were told the bottle came from the scene, not the body?'

'That's all I had. Until last night.'

She leaned forward. 'Roxanne said *we* were asking questions. Did she say who we'd been talking to?'

He shook his head. DS Fisher's eagerness surely confirmed it couldn't have been her who'd fed Roxanne those details: that ambitious little minx must have sniffed out some other clandestine informant. And not let on to him. But the Ice Maiden's lustrous grey eyes weren't getting any more out of him; whatever ideas Ivo might have concerning the identity of Roxanne's informant he'd keep to himself, thank you very much.

'We never mentioned those things to anyone,' she told him. 'Only a handful of people knew about the vodka bottle, including, of course, Rachel Moston's killer. Which is why it's so important that we find out who told Roxanne. And why the media respect the embargo.'

'Can't help you, I'm afraid.' He gave her his best candid look, inviting her to work harder, dig deeper. You could often learn far more from the questions people asked than from their answers.

'You're sure you didn't see Roxanne last night with anyone who might have been her source?'

He thought back: he'd seen Roxanne chatting with lots of people, but no one he recognised, no one who'd stood out as significant. He shrugged. 'I want that story every bit as much as you do.'

'Did you see her anywhere near Pawel Zawodny?'

'Definitely not. And if I had, I wouldn't have waited for an invitation to crash that particular party.'

'Mr Sweatman, I don't think you realise what you were meddling with.' She fixed those eyes on him again. 'Roxanne may have been killed because of what she knew.' Her voice faltered. 'It may have been you publishing your *research* that placed her in danger.'

Ivo's sharp mental picture of Roxanne flitting about the grass in her gypsyish skirt and denim jacket had the effect of snapping some small cog or flywheel inside him, sending his internal machinery into reverse and forcing his blood to flow backwards through the valves of his heart. He focused on this other lovely young woman who sat before him, her beauty different to Roxanne's but equally fresh and alive. 'I *was* fond her, you know,' he blurted out. Fuck! What was happening to him? 'Youth.' He turned to Hilary, trying to recover himself. 'Wasted on the young.'

'It's why we need to work together,' said the communications director. 'Not risk losing another young life.'

'I should do a piece about you,' he told DS Fisher impetuously. 'Roxanne's old buddy from student days working her butt off to track down her killer.'

'How did you know we were friends?' she asked sharply. As the obvious answer occurred to her, she seemed to deflate. 'Roxanne told you.'

Ivo nodded, leaning forward eagerly. 'A friend's personal appeal for help. That would stir a few hearts.'

Hilary turned to the younger woman, put a hand on her arm. 'It's a good idea,' she enthused. 'It would jog people's memories. Draw a good response.'

'Give the police a human face, too,' said Ivo winningly. 'Make up for lost ground.'

'Lost ground?' Ivo saw a flash of anger in Grace's eyes as she bit back whatever else she had evidently been going to say. Instead, she shook her head firmly. 'I'd be glad of your help, Mr Sweatman,' she replied. 'But let's keep it official.'

'OK,' he said. Suddenly he wanted to be out of here. It was all getting a bit much. DS Fisher was cool-headed and smart-thinking, yet not at all the Ice Maiden he'd imagined. Perhaps the impression of aloofness she gave came from being totally unconscious of her own loveliness. He had taken it for haughtiness, but she was far from that: she was warm and quick and he liked her. Her thug of a husband was not merely a thug but must also be a fool if he was stupid enough to have thrown away such a prize.

'Well,' he said, pushing himself to his feet, 'if we're finished, I've got work to do.' Seeing Hilary purse her lips, he laughed. 'Yup, another hard day's muckraking and scandal-mongering!' He turned to Grace; he must be going soft in the head, but he said it anyway. 'If you ever want my help, DS Fisher, it's yours.' He wasn't about to hand anything to anyone on a plate, but he'd be tickled pink if she ever came to him and asked.

THIRTY-SIX

Grace was relieved to accept Hilary's offer to escort Ivo Sweatman out of the building: she was angry and wanted to see the back of him. This man and his dubiously obtained story had treated her to an unwelcome interview with the chief con and nearly derailed the investigation; far worse, he'd inveigled Roxanne into unwitting danger and then stood over her lifeless body in order to steal an image shocking enough to sell a few extra hundred thousand newspapers. And yet, while Grace knew him by his deeds to be utterly loathsome, if she was honest, she'd also been unwillingly drawn to some kind of warts-and-all humanity in him.

She hoped that her reluctant whisper of liking was not merely because what he'd said had given her additional reason to hope she hadn't said a word to Roxanne about the vodka bottle: for if she'd put away too much tequila that night to keep her mouth shut, surely she'd have divulged everything, including the intimate part it had played in the posing of Rachel Moston's body? Yet Roxanne had clearly not even known what brand it was – Ivo's paper had somehow managed to blag that. CSIs weren't paid a great deal – perhaps not enough, anyway, to resist the temptation of an envelope stuffed with red-top cash – but only the crime scene manager and the photographer had been inside the tent and seen the body in situ. No one else at the scene knew that the bottle had been placed in the victim's vagina.

It was a relief. But a more intense relief was that Roxanne herself had been absolved. Only now could Grace fully admit the horrible fear that had been eating away at her: that her friend had sold her down the river in exchange for a few coveted shifts on a London daily. Ivo would never know it, but he'd finally freed her to think well of the dead.

All the same, that still left the burning question of who *had* told Roxanne about the bottle? How? When? Why? Grace considered Pawel Zawodny too clever and controlled to slip up like that. Unless he had deliberately chosen to feed Roxanne that morsel of information. But why? For what possible reason?

Grace tried to recall what it was Lance had said to her the morning Rachel Moston's body was found, about the bottle of Fire'n'Ice being a message for the police, a way for the killer to engage his pursuers in some game. Lance also reckoned that Roxanne's murder had been a kind of challenge. Was her killer's decision to reveal to a journalist a secret so far known only to himself and the police a move in some game he imagined he was playing?

If so, what was the game about? Control and domination? Or, as Lance had said, being the centre of attention? What was he trying to communicate? And at what point would he decide he'd won? Grace's brain was too tired from lack of sleep to do more than go around and around in circles, but it all kept coming back to one simple question: who was their opponent? Who had Roxanne been speaking to? Was it Pawel Zawodny?

Reaching the main MIT office, Grace asked Duncan if they had a transcript yet of the shorthand notebook they'd found in Roxanne's handbag.

He shook his head. 'She'd adapted her own style of short-hand. One of the PAs upstairs was able to make out the odd word, but most of it's indecipherable.'

'Shit!'

'We can't hang on to it much longer, either. The boss had a call from the *Mercury*'s lawyers demanding we return all unpublished journalistic material. We've no choice but to comply.'

'Yes, I know. Any names at least?'

'Some girls' names, a few initials. No PZ.'

'Maybe Gareth Sullivan will be able to translate it,' she said. 'What about her phone?'

Duncan brightened up. 'She received a call from the payphone at Colchester Town railway station at six-fifteen on Monday.'

Grace prayed that Duncan would assume she'd flushed not from guilt but with pleasure at such a promising lead.

'Why would anyone use a payphone except to hide their identity?' Duncan asked eagerly. 'Someone's down there now retrieving all available CCTV.'

'That was the day the *Courier* published its story about the bottle, wasn't it?' asked Grace. The fear gripping her vocal chords made her voice sound unnaturally shrill.

'Yes.'

'Where's the boss?' she asked, swallowing hard. 'Is he here?'

Duncan looked towards heaven. 'Upstairs. Big pow-wow. The university vice chancellor's not at all happy about a fatality right in their backyard and is out for blood. I'd give Keith a wide berth when he comes back down if I were you.'

'And Lance?'

'Over at Roxanne's flat.' Duncan gave her a kindly smile. 'Thought we'd spare you that.'

Grace wanted to run away, but she managed a smile. 'Thanks.'

She went to her own desk and hid her face in front of her computer screen, scrolling through meaningless emails. She would have to own up that she'd made that call. Even for such a narrow time frame, she couldn't possibly allow them to waste the man-hours it would take to trawl through the CCTV footage from the railway station and perhaps miss other opportunities to catch Roxanne's killer.

But a craven little voice whispered in her head: why rush to own up? No one would believe she hadn't leaked details of the investigation, and she'd never be able to prove her innocence. Ivo couldn't confirm where Roxanne had got her information, and Roxanne, the only person who could exonerate her, was dead. The chief constable had vowed to treat any unauthorised contact with the media as a serious disciplinary offence. Given the reputation that had travelled with Grace from Kent, she'd be out on her ear by the end of the day. For good this time.

Yet what if there was no CCTV of her making the call? Why not wait to find out?

But she knew she could never forgive herself if she allowed a false lead to divert attention from what was really important. It was no good: she would have to confess to Keith and take her chances.

Grace tried to control her panicky breathing. She longed to escape, if only to the toilets for a moment's privacy, but she didn't trust her legs to carry her. Was her career about to end? She had a sense of a net tightening around her. She had no friends. No spare money. She'd signed a short lease on her horrible flat. With no job, no prospects, nowhere to go, what on earth was she going to do with herself?

Keith came through the door looking grimmer than she'd ever seen him and shut the door of his own office behind him. Grace got to her feet: she knew that if she delayed for a second she'd lose her nerve. When Duncan saw where she was heading, he frowned and shook his head but, ignoring him, she tapped on the door and went straight in.

'Not now!' Keith spoke without looking up from his desk where he was gathering papers into one big untidy bunch.

'Sir, I need to tell you something.'

'Not me. They're sending in a team from the Murder Review Group.'

'What? Why do we need an external review? Why so soon?'

ISABELLE GREY | 289

'It's pass-the-parcel upstairs. Everyone shifting the blame.' He sighed heavily. 'Sorry. What did you want to tell me?'

Grace hesitated. 'It's going to cause more trouble.'

Keith looked at her keenly, and must have seen how shaken she was. 'Do I need to know?'

'I think you do. It affects an operational decision.'

He nodded. 'Well, they'll be glad of a final nail in my coffin. Might as well get it over with. Go on.'

Grace had no idea what to say. How could an innocuous phone call put two careers at risk when the only priority, surely, was that they were in the middle of a major inquiry? 'Could we have done anything differently?' she asked.

Keith sighed heavily and leaned back in his chair, his hands resting on the arms. 'Not made the university look bad when it might negatively affect student applications for next year. Not embarrassed the chief constable when she's a close friend of the vice-chancellor. Not allowed the *Courier* to make us look like idiots. All I want is to find Polly Sinclair and to put a killer behind bars before anyone else gets hurt. What about you?'

Keith's stare held more than mere rhetoric, and Grace hoped that she was interpreting it correctly. 'A call was made to Roxanne Carson's mobile from a payphone at Colchester Town station,' she said carefully, holding his gaze. She paused, waiting for his affirmative nod before continuing. 'I'm suggesting we don't need to spend too much time on it, sir.'

'You know that for certain?'

'One hundred per cent, sir. We were friends, if you remember.' Grace could see him take on board what she meant and then struggle with his fury. He had every right to be angry: she'd disobeyed a direct order and now the fall-out would be serious.

He thought through his options and then let his chair bounce forward again. 'How do we convince the incoming review team of that?'

'That's the trouble.'

'Anything else that I'll end up being sorry I didn't know?'

'Not in terms of the investigation.'

He nodded. 'Right now I need to buy time.'

'I understand. And I'm sorry, sir. I'm ready to take the consequences.'

'Yes. And you probably will. But I'm not handing Irene Brown an opportunity to sack both of us until I absolutely have to.'

'OK.'

'Though if push comes to shove, DS Fisher, then you haven't told me anything about this phone call, right? This conversation never took place.'

'Understood, sir. And thank you.'

'Get out.'

Grace went, almost colliding with Lance as he hurried into the main office. 'There's a team from the Murder Review Group downstairs.' He leaned in to speak confidentially. 'Any idea what's going on?'

'External oversight, courtesy of the chief con.'

'Nice of her to have such confidence in us.' Lance nodded towards the SIO's office. 'How's he taking it?'

'You know.' She shrugged, then looked at him anxiously. 'We are going to close this case, aren't we?'

He smiled. 'You bet.'

She let him propel her back to her desk, glad of the touch of his hand on her shoulder.

THIRTY-SEVEN

Nick Warleigh, a slight, taut man with a shaved head and smooth dark skin, was the head of the Serious Crime Division unit assigned to the surveillance of Pawel Zawodny. Grace had invited him to grab a coffee with her and Lance in the busy cafe round the corner from the police station, and now he greeted them with an understandable defensiveness: his team had, after all, lost sight of a suspect for a full twenty-six minutes during which Roxanne had been murdered. Warleigh must also have heard on the grapevine that Grace had been a friend of the victim, for his next words were to offer his condolences.

'Thank you,' she replied, touched by his consideration. 'We wanted a chance to get some direct feedback on your observation of Zawodny.' She didn't add that she'd worked occasionally with a covert operations specialist in Kent whose gut instinct about a suspect's pattern and style of behaviour had proved even more invaluable than his hi-tech vans, cameras and listening devices. 'What do you make of him?'

'We've hardly been on him forty-eight hours,' Warleigh pointed out. 'And most of that he's either been working on the house he's renovating or at home in his flat. One trip to the supermarket for newspapers and food, one stop at the florist en route to the campus vigil last night. Calls have been work-related or we think to his mother. Recordings have gone to a Polish translator.'

'First impressions?' she prompted.

'Well, he obviously knows now that we're there. But my guess is that he's been aware of us right from the off.'

'Whatever gives you that idea?' Lance asked sarcastically.

'Not because he gave us the slip, if that's what you mean.'

'We were the ones who released him from custody,' Grace reminded them both, wishing that for once Lance wouldn't come out of his corner fighting. 'Not that we had much choice about it.'

'Yeah, I'd never have known that if yesterday's *Courier* hadn't reminded me.' Warleigh gave her a wry smile and she returned it: now that both sides had scored a point, maybe they could get on with business.

Warleigh spooned aside the froth on his cappuccino, thinking for a moment before continuing. 'Zawodny's been meticulous,' he said. 'Drives bang on the speed limit. Stops for orange lights. Even parks precisely within the bay markings outside his flat.'

'So he's organised and law-abiding?' said Grace. 'He likes routine?'

Warleigh shook his head. 'Feels like it's too much. Over the top.'

Lance leaned forward over the little round table. 'A performance?'

'As I say, we've only been on him forty-eight hours. Give me a little longer, and I might have an opinion on whether his patterns are natural or contrived.' Warleigh sipped his coffee. 'He could just be a bit OCD.'

'But you don't think he is?' urged Lance.

'He seems hyper-vigilant. And he has an unusually light data footprint, too. Pays cash for everything, even petrol. Has a smartphone, but no computer or wi-fi.'

'See? He has something to hide,' declared Lance, looking to Grace for endorsement.

'He could just be keeping his costs down. Or he's worried about being caught not paying his tax.' She was as pleased as Lance that Zawodny's behaviour had provoked suspicion in such an experienced surveillance officer, but she wanted to prevent Lance railroading Warleigh into seeing only what they wanted him to see. That kind of tunnel vision tended to lead to bad consequences.

'It's probably best we don't share our theories yet,' she told Warleigh, hoping that Lance might also take the hint. 'Not until they're more than theories.'

'Fair enough,' Warleigh said, finishing his coffee. He pushed his chair back and looked at the door. 'If you don't mind, I need to get back to work.'

'Please, go,' she told him. 'We appreciate you making the time.' She saw him reach into his pocket. 'No worries, we'll get this.'

'Thanks.'

Lance shuffled his chair out of the cramped corner into which he'd been forced so the three of them could fit around the table. 'You getting cold feet about Zawodny being our man?' he asked crossly.

'Not at all. He *is* organised and meticulous and probably keeps an eye on costs, but then his ambition when he came here was to do well, make some money, go back to Poland and watch his Catholic mother shed tears of pride. So you can imagine his reaction when he saw what the *Courier* had written about him. My guess is he could well have felt pretty murderous.'

'So we let him go on Monday,' said Lance. 'He went to the railway station to make an untraceable call to Roxanne and arranged to meet up with her at the campus vigil.'

Grace winced: there was no way she could keep her part in this buried for much longer.

'He was angry and resentful. That's why nothing soft was placed under her head.'

'We're pretty certain the bottle of wine was bought at the campus shop, by the way,' said Lance. 'Did Duncan tell you?'

'No. Any prints?'

'Wiped clean. We know he never went there, so it may have been rubbish that he picked up.'

'Rubbish,' Grace echoed, a sob of horror for her friend rising in her throat.

'Sorry.' Lance touched her arm. 'But every bit of meaning shows he's talking to us. He wants a conversation, even if it's to punish us, to demonstrate his contempt.'

She nodded miserably, aware of his friendly scrutiny. 'Did you look at the Facebook page the *Mercury* set up for Roxanne?' she asked.

'No. Why?'

She shook her head, wishing now that she hadn't brought it up, but words like 'rubbish' and 'contempt' were painful to hear.

'Go on,' he said.

'I know every website gets them,' she said, 'but there are a few horrible comments. Stuff like: "She got what she deserved." "Strangling too good for her." And one or two pretty explicit suggestions about what else should have been done to her body.'

'Have you told the SIO?'

She shook her head again. 'No. What's wrong with people?'

'Tell Keith,' he said, his urgency betraying his excitement. 'Could be that some of them at least were left by our guy.'

'You think Zawodny would write that kind of stuff?'

'Abuse is about power. He's taunting us, daring us to stop him, proving how far he can go, how much he can get away with.'

It struck Grace that if Lance was right then the killer would probably be pleased with the effects of his nasty game: he'd certainly upset her and got Lance all riled up. But she kept that thought to herself.

'So where does Polly Sinclair fit in?' she asked instead. 'If the conversation's so important to the killer, why wasn't she displayed? Why doesn't he produce her body? Why the silence?'

Lance shrugged. 'Something went wrong, or he got spooked or realised he'd left evidence on the body he couldn't get rid of, so he dumped her at sea. Then, when maybe it began to piss him off that no one would know what he'd done, he went after Rachel so we'd get the message.'

'But he was sorry about Rachel,' Grace pointed out. 'He put her jacket under her head.'

'Wants us to think he's a nice guy really. It's these ungrateful women who take advantage, don't show proper respect, and need to be taught a lesson. They're to blame. They make him do it.'

'We still need something to tie him directly to Roxanne.'

'We'll get him on the CCTV from the railway station,' Lance said confidently.

'And if we don't?' she asked, feeling sick and shivery.

'Then we do it the old-fashioned way,' he said. 'We've got hundreds of statements to plough through. The switchboard has been overloaded with calls since the *Courier* posted its reward. Someone will have noticed something, even if it takes us weeks to find it.'

'I feel like we're drowning, Lance.'

'You need a good night's sleep.'

'Yes.' She smiled at him. 'Thanks for last night, by the way. Don't know what I would have done without you.'

'No problem.' He put a ten-pound note on the table, waving aside her objection. 'I'm off home. See you tomorrow.'

'Sure. Bye.'

Grace was in no hurry to return to her poky, sterile flat, so signalled to the waitress and asked for a glass of water and a toasted panini. Better stay off the coffee or she'd be too wired to sleep, but if she ate here, she wouldn't have to bother about what wasn't in her fridge, plus she could put off the evil hour when she'd have to go back to the flat. Unthinkingly, she reached for the newspaper discarded by a departing customer at a nearby table, only to drop it again as if the touch of newsprint on her fingers were a deadly poison.

Leaving the cafe half an hour later, Grace decided to loop through Castle Park before it closed for the night. It was a melting June evening and the wide lawns, cafe and play area were still busy. Nevertheless, as she skirted the impregnable Norman ramparts, she had a fleeting sensation that someone was dogging her footsteps, weaving from path to path between the flower beds and the steep earthworks. She knew where the feeling originated: though she told herself she was glad that Pawel Zawodny was under close observation by Warleigh's team, the truth was that Trev's text this morning, followed by two missed call alerts from him during the day, had spooked her. She checked her phone again now as she walked, just to make sure there'd been no further calls, and hoped she wouldn't find him waiting for her outside her flat again.

Trev, no doubt, would insist he was merely concerned about her and trying to be supportive, but that's not how his intrusions made her feel. She felt threatened, vulnerable, scared. She hadn't heard from him at all over the past couple of months, so what had stirred him into action now? Was it that she was forcing through the sale of the house? Or that she had a job and was back on her feet, was right at the heart of a major murder inquiry while he had to work in a shop? She guessed he felt aggrieved and, if he couldn't control and dominate her in any other way, intended at least to make it impossible for her to remain oblivious to his presence in her life. He couldn't possibly kid himself that she felt comforted by a text promising her that she was *not alone*, must know his unwanted attention could only revive visceral memories of helplessness and pain. But if she called him on it, he'd merely say he was trying to be supportive and that she was being neurotic, suspicious and ungrateful.

She shook herself and, spotting a young couple ahead of her rise from a bench, nipped over to sit down before anyone else could claim it. She had a choice: she could either let a few unanswered calls fuel imaginary fears or she could treat them seriously and consider going down official routes to protect herself. She didn't want to be afraid, but past experience had proved what Trev was capable of. She must send an email tonight to her solicitor asking again that all contact go through him and that the house be sold as quickly as possible.

Meanwhile, Grace told herself, it was more important to think about what had happened to Roxanne. Although it hurt, like deliberately touching an inflamed tooth with the tip of her tongue, she forced herself to think clearly and professionally. At least Roxanne hadn't been beaten or raped. Dr Tripathi thought it likely she'd been taken by surprise as a ligature was thrown around her neck from behind and then tightened too rapidly to give her any chance of escape. She was petite, shorter and lighter than the strong, muscular builder. But what on earth had she been doing alone with him amongst the trees?

Grace needed to put herself inside Roxanne's head. Had her friend's ambition led to her death? Rachel Moston's murder and the mystery surrounding Polly Sinclair's disappearance were the biggest stories to hit Colchester in years, and in Roxanne's hunt for a fresh angle, she had been facing massive competition. The media had latched on to the girls' landlord before his arrest, so it wasn't impossible that she had approached and even spoken to Zawodny before the vigil. But Roxanne also knew about Zawodny's boat; she had been the source of the *Courier*'s story about the police searching it. She knew that a bottle had been retrieved as evidence from the murder scene. If that hadn't come via a leak from within the investigation, then she must have realised that only the killer could possess this particular piece of information. But had she heard it from Pawel? And if so, even in pursuit of a career-changing scoop, would she honestly have believed she could tough it out alone with Rachel's killer? However badly Roxanne wanted to schmooze the national dailies and get a foot in the door in London, surely she'd never have been stupid enough to place herself in such danger?

Grace looked out across the grass. Some young men in

shorts and bare feet were throwing a Frisbee to one another; a group of tired mothers were fastening fractious children into buggies ready for the walk home; and an elderly couple holding hands on the bench opposite caught her eye and smiled. It was hard to believe that death might be waiting under the shadowy trees that cloaked the picturesque castle walls, yet it was true. Grace shivered. Maybe Roxanne had convinced herself it couldn't happen, that she was invincible. It's probably how Roxanne *would* think. It's how Grace had once thought. Before Trev broke three of her ribs and fractured her cheekbone.

She was suddenly weary. Besides, it was no good: some piece of the puzzle was always missing. She'd never solve it by thought alone.

Yet the moment Grace rose and set off across the grass, avoiding the Frisbee players, she began to spy a fresh possibility. According to Ivo Sweatman, Roxanne's source had claimed it was the *police* who'd been asking about the boat and the bottle. What if it hadn't been Zawodny that Roxanne had expected to meet? What if Roxanne had gone to talk not to a suspect at all but merely to someone she believed had access to inside information? Expecting to talk to someone who posed no threat, she had instead encountered her killer.

THIRTY-EIGHT

Grace looked up curiously as the door to Keith's office finally opened on Thursday morning. When the Murder Review Group team had arrived late yesterday afternoon, they had been whisked off upstairs, and they were already closeted with Keith when she'd got here first thing this morning. She was eager to meet them. It would be good to set out the facts and ideas she'd connected up last night about who Roxanne might have been talking to, and to see if the new team would reach similar conclusions. But as the first figure exited behind the SIO, her heart jolted into her throat: Colin Pitman, her old DCI from Maidstone.

Over the four years she'd worked with Colin, she had considered him a great boss, funny and astute, who wielded his authority with a light hand. Once upon a time he'd gone out of his way to make her feel a vital member of his team and supported her promotion to DI. But watching him now beside Keith Stalgood, she knew she'd take Keith's stern expression over Colin's easy smile any day. She'd learned the hard way that Colin's constant search for consensus had been at best pragmatic and at worst a gutless need to be popular – she'd seen it in his face when she'd handed him her resignation. She watched him now, trying so hard not to meet her eye, just as he had that freezing February day outside Maidstone Magistrates' Court when Trev was convicted. She felt a weight settle round her heart. Last night she'd emailed her solicitor and had been relieved to receive no more calls or texts from Trev. She'd made an effort, as she settled to sleep, to rinse the past out of her mind. And here it was, walking in the door and expecting her to smile politely at it.

Keith introduced the three senior officers as John Kenny, Lena Millington and Colin Pitman. Grace had heard that Colin had been made up to superintendent, and now wondered how much his relief at her departure had been due to getting rid of a problem that might jeopardise his promotion. If so, he owed her one! Meanwhile she found comfort in the idea that he might be dreading their imminent encounter more than she was, and when he could no longer avoid acknowledging her, watched him flush with what she hoped was shame.

Keith explained that the review team had been given an office upstairs, where they'd be evaluating the evidence, strategy and direction of the investigation and making recommendations for how to progress it. The team were authorised to ask questions and check facts as and when necessary. There was no denying the sour resentment that washed around the office: it was not just highly unusual for the chief constable to have called for an external review so early in an inquiry, it was humiliating. Nevertheless Keith now set a positive tone, insisting it was vital to ensure nothing had been overlooked, especially in the search for Polly Sinclair, and urged them all to welcome the team and make good use of fresh oversight.

Keith moved quickly on to an efficient round-up of reports on the various lines of inquiry – DNA, toxicology and other results from the post-mortem wouldn't be in for a while yet – and was keen to tell them that, thanks to Superintendent Kenny's intervention, all the data gathered about who was where and when at the campus vigil was now being fed into a simulation programme that would allow them to track any given individual in real time. They had already constructed skeleton outlines for the routes followed by the victim and other persons of interest, including Pawel Zawodny, which they hoped would prove fruitful.

Lance reported that so far today Zawodny was sticking to the same routine as the previous two mornings, and shared Warleigh's sense that Zawodny was on his best behaviour because he knew he was being watched, stressing that at this stage that was only a hunch. Duncan hoped today to get the CCTV footage – which had been held up by the usual bureaucratic nonsense – from Colchester Town railway station. And Grace confirmed that she had sent a preliminary list of questions over to Gareth Sullivan at the *Mercury*, but he'd come back to her saying that he, too, was having difficulty deciphering Roxanne's personalised short-hand squiggles; she promised to chase him up by lunchtime if she hadn't heard from him again by then.

After a word with the review team, Keith returned to his office, closing the door. Lance turned his back on the intruders so that he could grimace at Grace without being observed. She leaned closer, angling her head towards where Colin stood with his colleagues talking to Joan on the far side of the room.

'He was my guv'nor in Kent.'

'No way!' Lance swivelled to take a better look. Her former DCI was an attractive man: fit, dark-haired and bright-eyed, always dressed in a spotless white shirt; she'd probably even quite fancied him when she first joined his team. She'd certainly been aware early on that he cheated on his long-suffering wife. Now, although Colin didn't acknowledge their inspection, Grace saw his neck stiffen. It almost made her want to laugh; for a second she felt free, like a kid no longer afraid of a bully because she was safe with the cool gang at the back of the classroom.

'He's actually not stupid,' she said. 'Maybe Keith's right and fresh eyes on the case can't hurt.'

'We're not stupid, either,' Lance retorted.

'True,' she said, pulling her chair closer. 'I need to speak to Keith, but d'you mind if I run something by you first? Something that occurred to me last night?'

'Go ahead.'

'Remember Danny Tooley, the kid in the bookshop on campus?'

'The one we saw Roxanne talking to?'

'Exactly,' she answered, matching his matter-of-fact tone, despite her flare of grief at the recent memory of Roxanne flitting from bookshop to cafe. 'We know Roxanne was keeping tabs on him. Schmoozing him.'

'And we spoke to him at the vigil, right?'

'Yes. What if he knew who Roxanne was planning to meet?'

'Is his statement not amongst the rest?'

Grace shook her head. 'I checked. He never made one.'

'Then we should chase it up,' agreed Lance.

Grace nodded uncomfortably and looked at her watch. 'I'm going to have to shoot off in a second. Hilary wants me at the media conference. The chief con's coming over for this one, and they're expecting a big turnout. But there's one other thing.' She lowered her head, speaking more quietly. 'I only remembered last night. When I went to speak to Danny about Polly wanting a lift home, I asked if he knew Pawel Zawodny, if he'd ever seen him with Polly in Colchester.' She made herself meet Lance's curious gaze. 'Danny lives in Wivenhoe, so I also mentioned that Zawodny has a boat on the river. I hoped it might jog his memory.'

'Shit!'

'I know. At the time I spoke to Danny, it seemed more important to try and place Zawodny with Polly than to worry about something Danny might have known anyway. But it means he could have told Roxanne we were asking about the boat. And it weakens the argument for it being Zawodny himself who told her.'

'Still doesn't explain the bottle.'

'No,' she agreed. 'And it's possible Roxanne got that

from someone else. But if Danny did tell her about the boat, then we need to find out what other information he gave her.'

Lance nodded. 'And where he was getting it from.'

Just as Grace twisted in her seat to see whether the SIO was still in his office, he came back out, accompanied this time by Duncan.

'Listen up.' Keith had everyone's attention. 'Some violently offensive comments have been left on the *Find Polly Sinclair* Facebook page and on the memorials set up for Rachel Moston and Roxanne Carson. We've now established that the most unpleasant messages originated from Matt Beeston's IP address.'

As Keith waited for the ripple of hushed comment to subside, Lance looked at Grace in astonishment: Matt's was the last name they'd expected to hear.

'Two particularly vicious new Twitter accounts have also been traced back to him,' added Duncan. 'He's used them to slag off the women who made allegations of rape or sexual assault against him.'

'What a sweetheart!' muttered someone at the back of the room.

'The chief constable rightly feels that none of the young women or their families should have to tolerate such distressing and distasteful abuse,' Keith continued, 'and that we should make it a priority to be seen to take decisive action as part of our ongoing inquiry.'

Strictly speaking, such offences did not fall under MIT's remit, and there was an undercurrent of grumbling that, with resources already at breaking point, they were being dictated to from above for the sake of PR.

'Matt Beeston had no particular connection with Roxanne Carson, did he?' asked Lance. 'No reason to troll her that we know of?'

'She wrote a piece condemning the university authorities for failing to discipline him sooner,' Keith reminded them. 'That kind of publicity is likely to put paid to him ever finding another academic job.'

'The worst of the Twitter abuse is about Roxanne,' said Duncan.

'But she was hardly the only reporter to lay into him,' said Grace. 'Some of the other newspapers were far worse. Why target her?'

Lance turned to her, a note of apology in his voice. 'Because she was a woman?'

Grace felt sick. 'Then surely this should put him back in the frame, boss?' she asked, knowing full well how her question implied they'd made a mistake letting Matt go the first time. 'Venting such an un-self-censored hatred of women when he's already in a deep enough hole strikes me as pathological.'

'He remains under investigation,' said Keith. 'The case papers for the rape allegations are with the CPS lawyers.'

'What about the link between online abuse and domestic violence?' she pressed. 'This kind of harassment with constant texts and threatening messages is known to precede violent attacks.'

Grace noticed Colin nod sagely and fold his arms.

Although his expression remained neutral, it was a familiar gesture that she knew signified opposition. It only served to make her persevere. 'There's a pattern of behaviour here that we should look at again.'

Keith thought it over before he nodded. 'Find out first if Matt was seen at the campus vigil,' he ordered. 'Let's not assume anything. But if he *was* there, bring him in immediately.'

Grace turned to Lance, who raised his eyebrows. He leaned over. 'What about Danny Tooley?' he mouthed.

She didn't need reminding: the investigation was starting to go around in ever-decreasing circles, and they knew it.

THIRTY-NINE

Ivo wasn't himself, and he didn't like it one bit. It had got so bad last night that he'd had to get out of bed and empty all the alcoholic drinks in the hotel minibar down the toilet. Though that had raised the spectre of another far more dreadful night when he'd done the same thing, only to regret his action, take the scuffed plastic toothbrush mug from the mean little shelf above the hotel basin and scoop as much as he could of the diluted liquid back up. Mercifully the flashback had ended at the point when he'd lifted the mug, smelling of stale toothpaste, to his lips. As he'd done so, he'd known for sure that, over the long preceding hours of steady drinking, there was no way he'd have bothered to flush. He'd never been able to stomach the smell of toothpaste since.

Last night he'd flushed the toilet twice just to be on the safe side. He'd come a long way since then, he knew he had. He was supposed to look at the glass half full, not half empty – a handy metaphor for an alcoholic if ever there was one. But sometimes the shame of those days – who was he kidding? Those *years* – caught up with him and sent him

reeling. The quacks had told him he must have the consti-
tution of an ox, or he'd be long since dead from sclerosis
of the liver. On the other hand, the absence of hangovers
meant that it had taken him a whole lot longer than
everyone else to accept he had a problem. All those light-
weights who'd sloped off home when his own personal
party was just getting started, those wimps moaning and
crawling around the next morning in the office when he'd
been fresh as a daisy – they'd had the luck to learn their
limitations. He never had any limits. None at all.

Only one thread of life had remained throughout it all
– work. Words, headlines, type, reels of newsprint, rolling
presses; the ceaseless cycle of production had given him a
pulse, kept his heart beating, stopped him ever quite
drinking himself to death.

When he'd first started, the industry was still unionised,
and he'd had to do his indentures on a local paper up in
Yorkshire where they used hot metal to print the paper. If
some upstart reporter upset the temperamental and highly
paid nabobs of the compositing room, they'd discover their
story covered the next day in a rash of especially embar-
rassing typos. By the time Ivo collected his union card, he'd
progressed from flower shows and Women's Institute meetings to the coroners' and magistrates' courts. And, when
he made it south to Fleet Street, his first encounter with
the rumbling, heavily laden lorries setting off into the cold,
dark night and leaving behind the sharp scent of ink and
the aroma of warm paper had been the most romantic of
his life.

He'd been sent once by his then editor to see some swanky hypnotist in Harley Street who 'addressed addiction issues' (so that if his liver packed up he couldn't later sue his employers for failing to address his 'problem') and the guy had asked him to go in his imagination to a place where he'd feel totally relaxed and content. Immediately he was standing in the yawning mouth of a delivery bay at one in the morning as the last load of newspapers went out, and some gaffer wearing an old coat and fingerless mittens, no doubt knitted by his old lady back in Southend, cut the string on a damaged bale to hand young Ivo a copy of next day's news. He thought then he'd been inducted into the most glamorous and seductive club in the world. And he had. Not even a Maxwell or a Murdoch had since stained the purity of his love.

And now here he was, on a Thursday morning, sitting on a red plush and fake gilt ballroom chair, crammed in beside the crack troops of the world's media, waiting for Chief Constable Irene Brown, no less, to take to the stage. Now there was a second body it was standing room only, and he'd arrived well over half an hour ago to make sure he bagged a place near the front. A seat in the middle of the front row had been reserved for the editor of the *Mercury*. Their headline this morning had been *KILLED FOR DOING HER JOB*, and no doubt Sullivan was now making a killing out of syndication rights. Ivo himself, having scooped everyone yesterday with his own first-hand report of discovering the body, had been under some considerable pressure to maintain momentum. In the end, while everyone else was kindly setting the scene for him by extolling the virtues of the cream of the nation's young womanhood, praising the three girls' youth, beauty and accomplishments, and demanding greater protection for all students in the face of still-nameless danger, Ivo had found a way to set the *Courier* up as their champion.

Nothing the readers liked better when facing a slaughter of the innocents than a healthy dose of outrage. Blaming a university for poor security, as the *Mercury* had done, was by now a bit limp, so Ivo had been thrilled to come across some hideously misogynistic messages and tweets amongst the tributes to 'our' Polly, 'tragic' Rachel and 'brave' Roxanne. Talk about disrespecting the dead! His editor had lapped it up, and it made the perfect smokescreen for the absence of any actual news.

But now he'd have to find a story to top that, and unless the police were about to set a new agenda, finding a fresh angle was going to be a struggle. These press conferences were fast turning into a variety show as compère Hilary Burnett attempted to ring the changes with the same few tired acts, and Ivo wondered what juggling, dancing dogs she'd roll out for them today.

As the communications director led the way punctually onto the stage, Ivo was pleased at least to see that DS Fisher was back in the line-up; she'd been absent yesterday, no doubt out of respect to her friend. He'd thought about her quite a bit since their meeting yesterday morning. If truth be told, she was probably responsible for the desperation that had had him pouring good money down the khazi in the wee small hours – there was no way he'd be able to wing that tab onto expenses. If he tried it, they'd probably send him back to the hypnotist, and he'd rather slit his wrists. Still, never mind: he had a blank sheet of paper called a front page to fill and nothing as yet to put on it. The same went for every bum on every seat in here. With two murder victims, a young woman now missing for twelve days, and at least two known suspects walking around free, Hilary had better bloody well throw a decent bone to this hungry pack of wolves before she had a massacre on her hands.

FORTY

Grace was exhausted. She had come under increasing pressure from Hilary to be at today's media conference before her absence itself became a story. And she'd had to spend twenty minutes with Hilary and the chief con beforehand, rehearsing how best to answer the inevitable questions from the *Courier*'s chief crime reporter about her friendship with the murder victim. In the event, most of the questions had come not from Ivo Sweatman but from the *Mercury*'s acting news editor, a sign that the local paper was eager to retain ownership of the personal angle for as long as it could. But the *Mercury* opened the door to the rest of the world, and although Irene Brown fielded many of the questions, Grace had been bombarded by reporters from TV stations she'd never even heard of. At the end, once the chief con had congratulated her and been escorted away, Hilary had insisted Grace remain behind to record individual segments to camera so that every news programme had their own unique package. As a result, Hilary was ecstatic, but Grace just wanted to get back to the office and find out what was happening with Matt Beeston.

As Hilary finally allowed Grace to escape, Colin Pitman materialised beside them outside the conference room. 'So you knew Roxanne Carson?' he asked.

'Yes,' Grace replied wearily. A display of sympathy and concern from Colin was the last thing she needed right now.

'She acquitted herself well, didn't she?' Hilary appealed happily to Colin. 'It's not easy, managing to sound so authentic in front of such a mass of people and cameras, but you're a natural,' she told Grace. 'The chief constable will be delighted with all the positive coverage.'

'Brilliant,' Colin said, with an ironic glance at Grace that she was almost too tired to resist. It had been easy once to like this man. And it was pointless to waste energy fending off every meaningless encounter.

'Well done,' said Hilary, squeezing her arm affectionately. 'And thank you.'

As Hilary tapped off along the corridor on her high heels, Grace sighed in relief, letting her shoulders drop. 'That was all a bit much,' she admitted.

'Hilary's right, though. You did do well.' Colin came an inch closer. 'I'm so glad the move here was the right decision. I knew it would be.'

Grace bit back the angry words; what was the point?

'You'll make it back up to DI in no time. And I'd be happy to put in a good word for you with Superintendent Stalgood, if you'd like.'

Colin assumed her assent, so she didn't bother answering and merely stared at him. He, however, took her incredulity for pain, and shook his head in sorrow. 'I wish I'd seen what was coming with Trev. We all do. I blame myself, I really do.'

She almost laughed in his face. So far as she knew, Jeff, Margie and no doubt Colin, too, were still best pals with Trev.

'Thanks.' She managed to keep a straight face: maybe her twenty minutes of media training was paying off. But Colin continued to hold her gaze.

'I know what you went through,' he said, clearly striving to sound wise. 'But look, it's over now. Fresh start. I couldn't have been more sorry to let you go, except I knew it was the best thing for you.'

She realised that he'd convinced himself to believe this tosh. She'd seen such delusion many times when interviewing suspects, or with the parents or partners of perpetrators who'd committed monstrous acts. People had an uncanny ability in the face of unbearable truth to weave their own narrative and stick to it through thick and thin, she thought. She saw now how Colin, since her departure, had told himself this story to escape his own cowardice, and could now without a glimmer of irony pat himself on the back for his foresight and compassion. It was impossible to imagine anything she could say that would pierce the cloak of fiction he'd wrapped around himself. So she let it go.

Falling into step together, they made their way slowly

upstairs. When they reached the MIT office, Colin held open the door, letting her go first, an instinctive courtesy that she used to think was quite sweet and now would have preferred to flatly reject.

They sensed the electricity in the room immediately. Duncan, nearest the door, swung around in his chair. 'Matt Beeston was on campus on Tuesday night! A couple of his former students who were at the vigil reported seeing him. We're checking back with them now.'

Keith came out of his office. 'Lance. Grace. Go pick him up.'

It did not take them long to reach Matt's town-centre flat. When he opened the door to them, he looked even worse than the last time Grace had seen him. He'd cut his hair short and dyed it blonde, a cheap yellowish shade that didn't suit his skin and certainly didn't enhance either his stubble or the dark rings under his eyes.

'Bit of a disguise,' he mumbled when they failed to hide their reactions to his altered appearance. 'So I can buy some milk without being papped. Probably a mistake, in retrospect.'

His flat seemed orderly enough – his cleaner must still be doing her stuff – but there was a pile of pizza boxes on the floor that wouldn't fit in the over-crammed kitchen bin and Grace caught a distinct aroma of stale takeaway curry.

'What is it you want?' he asked.

'We are arresting you on suspicion of sending by means of a public electronic communications network a message or other matter that is grossly offensive or of an indecent, obscene or menacing character,' Lance told him. 'You do not have to say anything, but it may harm your defence –'

'Yeah, I know,' Matt interrupted.

'– if you do not mention when questioned something which you later rely on in court. Anything you do say may be given in evidence.'

'OK. So what happens now?'

'We need to take every electronic device you have here.'

Matt pointed to his laptop. 'Help yourself.'

He sat listlessly in the back of the car on the short journey to the police station, staring silently out of the window. His passivity continued as he was booked in and taken to an interview room. When asked, he waived his right to a lawyer, saying that it would only mean a bigger bill for his parents to pay. 'I'm not going to argue with you,' he said, as soon as they had finished the formal preliminaries. Even when they reminded him that he was still under caution for suspected murder and suspected rape, he just shrugged. 'You do what you gotta do.'

'This isn't a game, Dr Beeston,' Grace reminded him sharply. His attitude was more than unhelpful: she'd read of cases where such fatalism had led to false confessions.

'I'm not stupid,' he retaliated. 'I've been waiting for the knock on the door. I realised after it was too late that you'd track everything back to me eventually.'

She was itching to say a sarcastic 'Poor you' but stopped herself in time. However provoking his air of victimhood, she must curb her desire to give him a good hard slap. He was like a toddler pushing his limit to get attention, however negative the consequences.

Grace's temper wasn't improved by Lance reading aloud the stream of violent abuse and threats of sexual mutilation that Matt had spewed out into cyberspace, though she was glad to see that even Matt seemed cowed by the sheer nastiness of what he'd written.

'Did you send these electronic messages?' asked Lance.

'Yes.'

'And would you agree that they are grossly offensive, given that all of them relate to young women who are either dead or missing?'

'If that's what you need me to say.'

'Yes or no?'

'Yes.'

'So why did you do it?'

'It seemed like a good idea at the time. I was rat-arsed. And very pissed off.'

'What were you angry about?'

'It seemed like everything was their fault.'

'Whose fault? How?'

'Oh, for fuck's sake!'

'For the tape,' Lance replied.

Matt shook his head in misery. 'Why don't you go out and arrest the cretins who sent me their turds, or the middle-aged ladies who wrote on Basildon Bond notepaper with second-class stamps to tell me they ought to bring back hanging? They're the ones who gave me the idea in the first place.'

Lance ignored Matt's self-pity. 'Did you go to the candlelit vigil on campus on Tuesday evening?'

Matt voice rose in indignation. 'Yeah. So what? I didn't murder anyone!'

'But you are suspended from your job at the university.'

'So? Doesn't give them the right to tell me where I can and can't go.'

'Everyone at the vigil wanted to pay their respects to Polly and Rachel.' Grace took over, speaking softly, testing to see if his anger would still encompass the real victims in the case. 'You knew both Polly and Rachel, knew them better than the majority of people there. Is that why you went?'

'No.' He stared at her with a mixture of contempt and distress.

'So why were you there?'

He looked away again, his jaw working as if he were grinding his teeth. 'They ruined my life. If nothing had happened to them, if they hadn't got themselves killed, I'd still have job, a future.' He muttered another word under his breath, but Grace couldn't catch it. She looked at Lance, but he shook his head.

'What did you say?' she asked.

Matt raised his head and looked at her full in the face. 'All those fucking bitches,' he said again, loudly and clearly.

FORTY-ONE

'Being a total arsehole doesn't automatically make him a killer,' said Lance, as he and Grace made their way back upstairs after the interview. 'I'm still not convinced he's together enough to be our guy. Our guy is smart.'

'True.' Grace shared some of Lance's doubts, yet all the same she'd been deeply shocked by Matt's undisguised hatred of blameless young women. Had his anger and resentment erupted only in response to recent events, or had a capacity for lethal violence always been there, lying deep, expressed in the sexual exploitation and humiliation of his students? Matt might not be very shrewd or cunning, but he was well educated and intelligent. Surely his response to not getting his own way couldn't simply be rooted in some warped sense of privilege and entitlement? But then it was his position that had protected him: either not a single one of his academic colleagues had picked up strongly enough on his misogyny to demonstrate any practical concern for his female students or they had simply and expediently chosen to look the other way.

Grace knew which answer she favoured.

'You OK?' asked Lance. 'You're shivering.'

She stopped on the stairs, unable to catch her breath enough to continue.

'Grace? What's the matter?' Lance took hold of her shoulders and guided her gently downwards. 'Here, sit on the step. Can I get you anything?'

She shook her head, unable to speak, her heart pounding against her ribcage.

Lance sat down beside her. 'It's OK. Keep breathing. It'll be OK.'

Slowly his warmth began to seep into her, and the darkness receded enough for her to take a breath. 'Sorry.'

'Don't be. He really got to you, didn't he?'

She concentrated on breathing through her mouth, waiting for her heartbeat to return to normal. 'Having my old DCI here doesn't exactly help.'

'Is this about what happened in Maidstone?'

Grace nodded reluctantly.

'Want to tell me about it?'

She waited until she could keep her voice steady. 'They turned on me, all of them, even my husband. I think Trev believes it when he says he did it for them. No one spoke up for me. Colin never said a word. Not a word. I was completely on my own.'

Lance rubbed her shoulder gently. 'You're here now.'

'Matt's students. Someone should have listened to them.'

'I know.'

They sat in silence for a few moments. 'Can I ask you something?' she said.

'Sure.'

'I told you about the officer in Kent, Lee Roberts, who got busted.'

'Yes.'

'He was a liability. Dangerous. A very, very short fuse. And no one was prepared to do anything about it. It was me who called in the tip-off about his dealer. If I'm honest, I suppose I did kind of hope Lee would get taken down, too, but I never gave his name. I wouldn't have done that.'

'OK.'

Grace wasn't sure from Lance's tone what he was thinking. 'What would you have done?' she asked.

'Would I have made the call?'

'What would you have done to me if you knew I had? If Lee was your fellow officer?'

'And I'd known what state he was in?'

'Yes. Do you think I had it coming? What they did to me?'

Lance shrugged. 'Lee pops pills and then gets busted, that's his problem.'

'You wouldn't have sent me to Coventry? Put dog shit in my desk drawer?'

'Jesus, is that what they did?'

Grace nodded, not trusting herself to speak.

'Bastards. And that creep Colin Pitman was your DCI?'

'Yes. He refused to take any official action. Said it wouldn't be in my best interests.'

Lance shook his head in disbelief. 'I don't know if I'd

have made the call. But I would never have treated you like that. Never.'

Grace sighed. 'Thanks.'

Lance put an arm around her shoulder, tugging her closer. A couple of community support officers came up the stairs towards them, awkward in their bulky vests, belts and hooked-on radios. Grace and Lance remained where they were, making the two young women pick their way around them. They turned, curious, and glanced back at them.

'Kiss and make up,' Lance called after them. 'It's just the best, isn't it?'

Grace meant to laugh but it came out as half sob, half hiccup, making Lance laugh as well. The two support officers snatched a second look, and Grace turned to smile at their discomposure. 'Ignore him,' she told them, digging Lance in the ribs with her elbow. She stood up, dusting off the seat of her skirt, then kissed Lance lightly on the top of his head. 'I mean it. Thanks.'

'Any time.'

Keith was waiting for them impatiently. They weren't sure how much of their interview with Matt he would have observed as Hilary had been eager for Keith personally to inform the victims' families that the Internet troll had been arrested, and also then to field their difficult questions about why Matt Beeston had not been kept in custody since his initial arrest. But Grace discovered, as soon as he'd closed his door behind them, that he had something else to tell them.

'Gareth Sullivan just got back to me about Roxanne Carson's notebooks. They're having almost as much trouble as us trying to decipher her shorthand –'

'Can't we send them to a code-breaker?' Lance interrupted. 'GCHQ or something?'

'I tried suggesting that,' Keith replied tersely. 'He told me to get a court order.'

'So could he decipher anything at all?' asked Grace, still jittery over whether her friend's notes would reveal her phone call and their clandestine meeting at the coaching inn.

'Sullivan was pretty sparing with the detail, but because Matt Beeston is under arrest, he was good enough to share with me that Roxanne was aware that Polly Sinclair took Matt Beeston home with her the night before she disappeared. Something that was never actually spelled out to the media.'

'So does Sullivan know who told her?' Lance asked eagerly.

'He knows,' said Keith disgustedly. 'But, in the name of journalistic ethics, he wants to seek permission from the person concerned before he gives us a name.'

'Zawodny saw Polly in bed with *someone*,' said Lance robustly. 'And Matt's arrest has been more than public knowledge. He could've put two and two together and told Roxanne.'

'Why?' asked Keith.

'Take the heat off himself,' Lance replied.

'It could also have been Polly's housemate,' suggested Grace.

'If Roxanne had been tipped off and arranged to meet Matt at the vigil,' said Keith, 'then how did she make contact? When did they speak?'

'Easy enough to make an anonymous call,' said Lance. 'From the train station, for example.'

Grace avoided Keith's eye and swallowed hard before speaking. 'There's someone else who could have told Roxanne about Matt and Polly.' She turned to Lance, enlisting his support. 'Danny Tooley.'

'Of course,' said Keith. 'I remember you said that Polly asked Danny for a lift home when she was with Matt in Colchester.'

'Yes,' said Grace. 'Danny told us he refused because he knew Matt had a bad reputation amongst the female students.'

'And we know Roxanne was keeping tabs on Danny,' added Lance.

Grace shot him a grateful look, then took a deep breath. 'I think Danny told her about Zawodny's boat, too. It's my fault. I asked him about it, if he'd ever seen Polly with Zawodny in Wivenhoe.'

'Why the hell haven't you told me this before?'

'I was about to. But things got busy. I'm sorry, sir. It's not an excuse.'

'No, it's not.' Keith frowned in irritation. 'Should we be looking at him as a suspect? Was he was in town the night Polly disappeared?'

'We don't know,' said Lance. 'But he doesn't drive. Where would he have taken her?'

'What about Rachel Moston?' asked Keith. 'Did he know her? Would he have any reason to kill her?'

Lance looked to Grace to answer. 'He knew who she was. But we're not aware of any connection. I don't think he's a suspect. It's more whether he was telling Roxanne more than he ever told us.'

'You think?' asked Keith with heavy sarcasm.

'In which case he might also have known who Roxanne was planning to meet up with at the vigil,' said Lance, giving Grace a look of encouragement.

'We should bring him in,' she said. 'Take a statement under caution.'

'Get on with it, then,' said Keith. 'And I'm sick of pandering to Gareth Sullivan's journalistic ethics. Tell Duncan to organise a court order to seize all Roxanne's notebooks.'

FORTY-TWO

Danny was reluctant to leave the bookshop, explaining discreetly that there were supposed to be at least two people on the floor at all times. Lance responded cheerfully that a word with his manager or, failing that, a call to his head office, would clear the way, leaving Danny little choice but to accompany them.

He was quiet in the back of the car, despite Grace's attempts to chat and resume their earlier rapport, and baulked at the brick facade of police headquarters, shrinking into himself and waiting to be led through the lobby and on into the secure areas of the building. As Lance set up the tape in one of the more pleasant interview rooms, Grace watched Danny take a careful look around at his surroundings. Finding himself under observation, he gave her a wary smile.

'So, Danny,' she began, 'you know that Roxanne Carson has been murdered?'

He nodded.

'Almost certainly by the same person who murdered

Rachel Moston. We're looking at the possibility that Roxanne was killed because she was a journalist, because she knew something as a result of her work that the killer felt threatened by.'

Danny looked alarmed, but nodded to show he understood.

'Roxanne herself might not necessarily have realised the significance of what she'd heard or been told,' Grace continued, 'and therefore we need to piece together precisely what she knew and who she'd been talking to. You're aware that we already know that she'd spoken to you.'

'You think I killed her?' he blurted out.

Grace was about to reassure him, but Lance got in first. 'Did you?' he asked.

'Maybe you're going to say I did.'

'Is there a reason we should say that?' Lance pursued.

'I talked to her quite a lot,' said Danny. 'She'd text me if she had questions, about stuff on campus and things.'

'It would be really helpful if you could tell us absolutely everything that you told Roxanne,' Grace said in her most soothing voice: making Danny panic wasn't going to assist his accurate recollection. 'And everything that she asked you.'

'OK,' he told Grace, flicking a worried look at Lance, who, perhaps realising he'd gone in too hard, smiled encouragingly and sat back, leaving the stage to Grace.

'I don't like these places,' Danny said unexpectedly. 'They remind me of when I was a kid, when my mum was ill.'

'You're here as a witness,' said Grace. 'We're grateful for your help.'

He nodded and settled himself in his chair, reminding Grace of how a fretful dog might tread out his bed.

'What kind of questions did Roxanne ask you?'

'She wanted background. What the students are like, whether they do much partying, who they go out with, that kind of thing.'

'And did you see her or speak to her at the vigil on Tuesday night?'

Danny nodded. 'Early on, before you and I spoke.'

'What did she say?'

'She was busy, said she needed to keep moving.'

'Did you see who she talked to?'

'Some of Polly's friends, and I think some friends of the other one.'

'Friends of Rachel Moston?'

Danny shrugged. 'I hardly knew her.'

'OK. Did Roxanne ever ask you specific questions, then or earlier? About what she thought we – the police – were doing or wanting to know about?'

'I told her you'd asked about the Polish guy, their landlord. That he had a boat. She was interested in that. Wanted to know what else you'd said.'

'And what did you tell her?'

'I didn't know anything else.'

'You saw the newspaper article, speculating that a vodka bottle played a part in Rachel Moston's murder?'

'Yes.'

'Can you remember if Roxanne asked you about a bottle, either before or after that article?'

Danny hung his head. When he raised it again, his eyes were wet. 'I'd been telling her about Polly. About how upset she was, how Dr Beeston hadn't been very nice to her. I feel really bad about that now. Polly trusted me.'

Grace fought the urge to lean forward, tried her best not to betray her eagerness. 'What did Polly mean when she said he hadn't been very nice?'

Danny met her gaze with a fierceness she hadn't seen before. 'It wasn't her. She wasn't like that. He got her really drunk. It was his fault.'

'What was his fault?'

'That she did those things. It wasn't her.'

'What things, Danny? I know you cared about Polly and don't want to say anything bad about her. But we need to know exactly what she said.'

'It was something about a bottle. I didn't really understand what she meant.'

'What were her precise words? Can you remember?'

'She wasn't like the others! She wouldn't have done that sort of thing!'

Not wanting to push Danny too hard when it was clear how upset he was at betraying the girl of his dreams, Grace decided she could always come back to this later. 'And you told Roxanne?' she asked instead.

'I shouldn't have said anything,' he cried. 'Polly trusted me!'

'But you said enough for Roxanne to go away thinking that Dr Beeston had done something to Polly with a bottle? Something sexual perhaps?'

Danny shrugged, the fierceness fading away. 'I didn't say that. Roxanne did. He got Polly drunk. She didn't know what she was doing. She was sweet and lovely and kind.'

'And can you remember *when* you told Roxanne what Polly had said? Was it before or after the newspaper article last Monday?' she asked. 'Please think hard, Danny. It's important.'

'Before.'

Grace looked at Lance. His eyes were dancing with excitement but, taking up the reins, he changed the tone, making his voice light and chatty.

'And did Roxanne say if she was going to speak to Matt, to get a response from him? Or maybe had already?'

'I don't remember. I don't think it came up.'

Danny looked exhausted.

'OK, thanks. I think we've pretty much covered the ground now, Danny. We really appreciate you helping us like this. I know you need to get back to work, so we'll organise a car for you in a moment.' Lance flicked through his notebook as if double-checking that he hadn't forgotten any unimportant details. 'Oh yes, the landlord, Pawel Zawodny. He came to the vigil.'

'I don't know him,' said Danny.

'You might have noticed him. He brought a massive bouquet of flowers, caused quite a stir.'

Danny shook his head, clearly not interested in the subject.

'Roxanne didn't mention wanting to talk to Pawel

Zawodny?' Lance pressed. 'Even though he'd recently been in custody?'

'Not that I remember.'

'Not to worry.' Lance wound things up and switched off the tape.

'So you think Roxanne knew who killed Rachel?' Danny asked, as they all got to their feet.

'It's possible,' said Grace.

'Is it Dr Beeston?'

'We're working on it.'

'When will you know?'

Grace caught something in Danny's eyes, just a flash and then it was gone, but enough to convince her that he was still holding something back. A crazy idea jumped into her mind, but she wanted to voice it, just to see if she was right, if she could catch him unawares.

'If you know where Polly is, you would tell us, wouldn't you, Danny?'

He gave an awkward laugh. 'Me? Why would I know?'

'Because she came to you. She trusted you.'

Lance jerked his head up in surprise, but then nodded. 'Was Polly afraid of Dr Beeston?' he asked eagerly. 'Is she hiding from him? Because if she is, you can assure her that it's safe to come out now.'

For a moment Grace almost thought Danny was going to crumble and tell them whatever secret he was keeping, but then his eyes filled with tears. 'I only want her to be cared for,' he said.

'We all do,' Grace assured him. 'Especially her family.'

'But if you know where she is, Danny, you can tell her she doesn't have to hide away any longer,' said Lance. 'I promise we'd make absolutely sure she'll be safe.'

Danny kept his head down and walked to the door without answering.

'Even if she could just let her parents know she's alive.' Lance spoke to the back of Danny's head, which hunched more deeply into his shoulders.

He turned back to face them, brushing his eyes with the back of his hand. 'I can't help them. I'm sorry. But I don't think she'd ever deliberately do anything to hurt them. She's not like that.'

They left Danny in the lobby to wait for a car to take him back to the bookshop. As soon as they'd returned through the inner door to the station, Lance turned to her. 'Do you think he knows where she is?'

Grace shook her head. 'For a moment there I did. But do you remember how upset he was when we saw him at the vigil? He was crying. Why would he weep like that for her if he knew, or even had good reason to hope, that she was safe?'

'Yeah, I guess so,' Lance conceded.

All the same, as they made their way upstairs, something about that flash in Danny's eyes stuck at the back of Grace's mind like a forgotten word or name on the tip of her tongue that would only come back once it was too late to matter.

FORTY-THREE

'How did you get on?' Duncan asked as Grace and Lance appeared in the doorway to the MIT office.

Lance looked to Grace to respond, but she indicated for him to go ahead. 'Polly Sinclair confided something to Danny about Matt Beeston and a bottle.'

'And he told Roxanne?'

'Who told Ivo Sweatman, whose private investigators blagged the rest, about a vodka bottle being retrieved from the scene of Rachel Moston's murder.'

'Result!' said Duncan, as Keith emerged from his office and made them repeat it all again.

'OK,' said Keith with a nod of satisfaction. 'Let's run through what we've got on Matt Beeston.'

'We can place him in the Blue Bar on the nights Polly Sinclair went missing and Rachel Moston was killed,' Duncan began. 'He lives within walking distance. We have him on CCTV on the route between the Blue Bar and his flat at one a.m. on the night of Rachel's murder, which would have given him sufficient time after the last sighting of the victim to have carried out the crime and be heading home. He was also on campus when Roxanne Carson was murdered.'

'Hilary's set up a Facebook page for people to post where they were and who they saw at the vigil,' said Joan. 'And our nifty simulation programme lets us use that information to track individuals across a given timeline. Not much so far on this suspect, but we have got him heading down towards the lake.'

Keith nodded in approval as Grace took up the reins. 'Matt Beeston had sex with Polly and taught Rachel. As yet we don't know if he was in direct contact with Roxanne, but she had information harmful to him, and he's made his resentment against her and the other victims abundantly clear in his grossly abusive and violent messages.'

'There's also the post-mortem display of the bodies,' said Lance. 'Roxanne's knickers were stuffed into her mouth, which suggests a desire to symbolically shut her up. Plus, at the time of her death, only the killer would have known where to place a bottle.'

'And now we have hearsay evidence that Matt may have used a bottle as a sex toy with Polly,' added Grace.

'He has a known history of sexual predation against women he teaches and of using alcohol to disempower them,' said Lance.

'We must go back to the students who've given statements and press them further on the precise details of his sexual assaults,' said Keith. 'See if one of them mentions a bottle.'

Keith looked at Grace as he spoke, and she knew that this job would inevitably fall to her. She nodded reluctantly, reflecting that by the time this was over, Matt's victims would have paid a heavy price for falling for his charm and the offer of just one more drink.

Duncan pointed to the photograph on the board of the wine bottle retrieved from Roxanne's body. 'We've put out an appeal for anyone who bought this brand of white wine,' he said. 'It was on sale at the campus shop, so we've asked the university to email every student. We want to know who discarded an empty bottle and, if possible, where and when, which might also help us plot the killer's movements leading up to time of the murder.'

'Good,' said Keith curtly. 'It's enough to keep up the pressure on Matt in the next interview.'

'So where is Polly Sinclair?' No one had noticed Colin Pitman slip into the room. He stood beside the door, watching and listening. 'Matt Beeston doesn't drive,' he said. 'If she's dead, how come no one's found her body?'

An hour later Colin caught up with Grace as she set off to walk home through the car park that spread around one side of the police station. No one was using the front entrance any more, not if they could help it, for fear of being besieged by cameramen and journalists sticking microphones in their faces.

'You were pretty quiet back there,' Colin said. 'Anything you want you share? Off the record?'

Earlier, in the MIT office, he had stressed that while it was feasible for Matt Beeston to have murdered Rachel and walked home afterwards, and killed Roxanne before slipping unnoticed into the crowd at the vigil, they had never satisfactorily explained how Matt could have transported Polly Sinclair away from the town centre. By the time she disappeared the last train had gone, and exhaustive enquiries left them confident that neither Polly nor Matt had taken either a cab or a night bus. 'If Matt Beeston is responsible for her fate,' Colin had said, 'then where is she?'

With an air of quiet triumph, he had then left it to his colleagues to announce not only that an additional budget had been provided for a renewed search for Polly, but also that it had already been announced to the media. There was to be a full sweep of every building in a radius around the Blue Bar, taking into account any points at which victim and perpetrator could no longer have evaded capture on CCTV.

But if Superintendent Millington had expected an enthusiastic response, she had been disappointed: a suppressed groan had rippled around the room; Duncan had stared at the floor while Keith remained expressionless. Extra resources were of course welcome: it was nearly two weeks since Polly had vanished and they were no nearer finding her now than when Phil and Beverley Sinclair had first reported her missing. But everyone knew this new search strategy was a logistical nightmare that would require them to track down innumerable key-holders of commercial premises, some of them unoccupied, and secure their attendance. Dozens of specially trained officers and dog-handlers would not only search but also have to ensure that they didn't trample all over any evidence that was found. With no new lead to suggest that Polly's body might be hidden in Colchester town centre, it was little more than an expensive and distracting PR stunt. Grace was not the only one willing to bet that the chief con would find time to be on hand tomorrow to make a statement against the impressive backdrop of TV news footage of the sweeping new search.

'Detective Superintendent Stalgood is pretty much on top of things,' Grace told Colin now.

'Any part of the investigation you think we ought to be looking at in particular?'

Grace shook her head and tried to keep walking. She had listened to the muttered grumbling that went on once Colin, Lena and John Kenny had departed. Although it was true that whoever killed Rachel and Roxanne had managed to get in and out without being seen or leaving forensic traces, she couldn't believe the review team seriously supposed that whoever had taken Polly had access to somewhere in the centre of Colchester where she had either consented to go or been dragged or carried, where the initial search team had failed to gain entry and where, after several hot June days, the cadaver dogs they had already employed hadn't picked up any scent.

Colin turned to look back at the modern, fortress-like brick building, forcing Grace out of politeness to hover beside him. 'We all know how vital it is not to get sidetracked by a single mindset,' he said. 'If there's any chance that our focus so far is wrong – out-of-the-ball-park wrong – then I'd like to hear your thoughts.'

'What's your thinking?' she countered. While she had to admit that there'd been a time when she would have welcomed such a private approach from her boss as a sign of how much he valued her opinion, now she saw it for what it was – a petty manoeuvre to divide and conquer.

Colin smiled. 'We can hang onto Matt Beeston until tomorrow. Then we need to apply for an extension. I'm not sure we've got enough on him to wrap all this up.'

'He's been charged under the Communications Act. He's admitted those offences.'

Colin shook his head. 'Doesn't prove murder. All we've got is circumstantial, especially when it comes to tying him in to Polly Sinclair's disappearance.'

He was right: Grace knew it was at the back of everyone's minds that if, right from the start, they'd got it all wrong about linking Polly's disappearance to Rachel's murder, then they'd missed opportunities both to prevent Roxanne's death and possibly to save Polly from God knows what fate. '*On* the record,' she said, giving him a straight look, 'all we've got so far to keep us focused on those suspects connected to both Polly and Rachel is victimology.'

Colin nodded, pleased by her answer. 'The review team's looking at the possibility that Polly's disappearance isn't connected to the murders, that we should be looking for two separate perpetrators.'

He turned back again to face the direction in which Grace had been walking. 'The big question is this,' he began. 'Are we tempted to split Polly's disappearance off as a separate investigation merely to rid ourselves of inconvenient

pieces of jigsaw that won't fit into the murder enquiries?'
He gave a rueful smile. 'On the other hand, there's zilch to
point us in any other direction.'

'I know,' Grace admitted. She was already regretting her
rash impulse to speak, but it would be wrong to allow an
old grudge to impede an active investigation. Colin might
be a snide political operator out for his own advancement
but, as an SIO, he'd had some notable successes. 'If the new
search draws a blank,' she began carefully, 'then there are
other scenarios.'

'Spell it out,' he said, smiling at his reference to their old
joke.

'One, that Pawel Zawodny killed Polly and disposed of
her body at sea.'

'And Matt Beeston murdered Rachel and Roxanne?'

'Yes,' she said. 'It could just be coincidence that each
happens also to be connected to the other's victim.'

Colin nodded in satisfaction, making Grace wonder if
this was precisely what he'd hoped she'd say. 'That would
work,' he agreed cheerfully. 'And the other?'

'That Polly is still alive. I'm not saying that I think she
is, but we should keep an open mind.'

'Quite right. Thanks, Grace. Have a good evening.'

Abruptly dismissed, Grace was nevertheless relieved to
make her escape, crossing the main road that bordered the
police station and heading downhill towards her flat. She
felt itchy and uncomfortable. It wasn't the warm evening
trapping the rush-hour traffic fumes between the buildings;
it was a nasty sense that Colin had been subtly inviting her

to be disloyal to Keith and the rest of his team. Had she been? She didn't think so, but then neither had she considered it wrong to report Lee Roberts's increasingly volatile behaviour to her trusted DCI. And, she reflected sourly, look how well that had worked out.

Why did Colin Pitman of all people have to be part of the review team? It wasn't fair! She felt the past smearing itself over her again and suddenly realised with surprise just how angry she was that it could happen. Her phone signalled a message alert, and she looked at the screen. Trev! Without even reading the message, she tapped out her own message and pressed send, hoping that *Fuck off!* would be clearly enough understood.

FORTY-FOUR

Ivo was surprised when Trevor Haynes rang back and agreed to speak to him after all. The disgraced copper insisted Ivo come to the bike shop where he worked, as it kept late opening hours. The place was like a small cave crammed with brightly coloured helmets, jerseys and reflective strips childishly at odds with the precision engineering of the frames, wheels and gears that gleamed from great spiked hooks on the walls. Some wag – the Young Ferret, no doubt – had once suggested that Ivo take up cycling, probably when it was discovered that Ivo had never reapplied for his licence after his driving ban expired. But the joke just went to prove that the lad hadn't yet found his way through those arcane intricacies of the expense account in which any number of eye-watering cab fares could be lost like invisible galaxies in outer space. Besides, Ivo had never understood the attraction of physical competition – apart perhaps from a spot of vainglorious arm-wrestling on a beer-washed pub table – and the only bit of specialist kit he'd ever coveted had been a trigger-lever corkscrew. Now, hearing how much all this cycling stuff cost, let alone the special shoes and Lycra outfits that would frankly look more at home in a Streatham brothel, Ivo was doubly glad he hadn't bothered.

But he was prepared to let Trev wax as lyrical as he liked about his sporting kit: after all, the man wasn't stupid – indeed, he looked wily and shrewd, like a good beat copper should – and Ivo wanted him to relax his guard before going in under it to stick him with the killer question. He'd already prepared the ground when they'd spoken on the phone, offering the merest of hints that the Colchester murder inquiry was being hampered by internal strife and that Ivo had picked up the teeniest, tiniest rumour that DS Fisher was regarded as a bit flaky, perhaps even a loose cannon.

Now Ivo stared into Trev's blue eyes. The man was attractive, even charming; lithe, tanned and obscenely healthy-looking, with one of those boyish, lop-sided grins the ladies seemed to go for. But Ivo had seen enough of DS Fisher to hope she'd fall for more than a mischievous smile, so there must be a bit more heft to this guy than the brutality required to inflict the injuries Ivo had read about in the copy of the police surgeon's report the Young Ferret had provided.

Ivo gave himself a shake: dislike always showed itself, and he needed Trev to trust him. Ivo might never have been physically violent himself, no matter how pissed, but, he reminded himself sternly, for a drunk who'd screwed up the lives of everyone around him to look down on a man who kicked the daylights out of a woman was like the prison inmate who robbed old ladies thinking it was OK to shank the nonce. So get a grip, he warned himself, and play nice.

Half an hour later Ivo was glad to get out of there, having finessed his well-practised manoeuvre of fussing over notebook, pen and pockets so he didn't have to shake the bastard's hand. In his taxi back to the train station his blood boiled. Trev had answered the killer question all right. Hadn't even needed much encouragement. Had been only too glad to supply the perfect quote: *Trouble with Grace is, she just won't listen to reason.* Put that next to the photo that Ivo had managed to wheedle out of the local rag of Trev leaving the magistrates' court – they'd Photoshop it into grainy black and white to make him look like some syphilitic Public Enemy Number One – and the cycling champion would rue the day. At least, Ivo bloody hoped he would.

He didn't understand why the Ice Maiden's history had aroused his indignation so strongly, but he'd learned not to question his instinct for a good story. And somehow, for him, she *had* become the story, the beating heart of this investigation.

As the train pulled out of Maidstone, Ivo opened an email sent earlier by some minion in the office who should have known better than to treat such an overture so cavalierly. *Danny Tooley rang the office, asking to speak to you*, it read. *Refused to say what it was about except to tell you he was a friend of Roxanne Carson.* The name meant nothing to Ivo, but he punched in the number left for him to call, and was answered almost immediately by a low, wary voice. The moment Danny Tooley informed Ivo that he worked in the bookshop on campus, Ivo knew he'd hit pay-dirt: this was the kid Roxanne had been schmoozing!

By midnight Ivo had Danny safely ensconced in one of two adjoining rooms in a budget hotel on the edge of Colchester. It was all a bit cloak and dagger, but it never did any harm to romance the punter a bit, make them feel important and then encourage them to live up to the hype by spilling their guts right onto the front page. He'd get him settled in first, order some food, watch a bit of TV, get chummy, and then they could start talking. Ivo had no idea what he was likely to get, nor quite what to make of him. Danny said he was twenty-three, but came across as much younger. He wore cheap clothes and looked like he'd never had a square meal in his life, yet didn't appear the least interested in money, not even the *Courier*'s hefty reward. Ivo had called his editor from the train to get him to sign off on a decent scale of discretionary payments for anything less than a full confession – should Danny unexpectedly cough to the murders, then the sky's the limit: once he was convicted, their lawyers would make damn sure they'd never have to pay out anyway – but Danny was eager to tell his story without any upfront cash offer.

So what did he want? Fame? Glamour? To be seen as the hero of the hour? Despite the young man's self-effacing manner, Ivo reckoned he was sharp-minded and capable. No wonder Roxanne had held out on him and been so keen to keep her source under wraps. And now Danny would tell him whatever it was he'd told Roxanne.

Ivo still found it difficult to bring the eager young reporter to mind without his thoughts being flooded by the razor-sharp image of her body as the flash on his phone camera had gone off. He moved to stand beside the window so he could stare down into the darkness of the hotel car park without Danny noticing that he was spooked, but all he could see reflected in the double-glazing was his own fingers lifting Roxanne's skirt, exposing her, exposing what had been done to her. He prayed to whatever god might exist that it hadn't been him who'd pushed Roxanne into danger, which is what the Ice Maiden had insinuated. Sure, he'd dangled a carrot or two, egged her on, got her nostrils flaring for a good story, but she'd have been up for it with or without him. He had to keep telling himself that.

But, as it turned out, it wasn't Roxanne that Danny was so eager to talk about. It was Polly Sinclair.

FORTY-FIVE

Friday did not begin well. Everyone was tired after nearly two weeks of late nights and snatched meals, too much coffee and adrenaline, and they certainly didn't need the morning papers to tell them that the investigation was no further forward. Although the majority of the tabloids had run with the upbeat story from yesterday's press conference of Detective Sergeant Grace Fisher's long-standing friendship with the second murder victim, the *Courier* had once again bucked the trend. *CLUELESS!* screamed the huge black type above two photographs, one of *Our Polly*, laughing, blonde-haired, and now missing for almost a fortnight, the other a snatched image of a harried-looking Keith taken, so the caption explained, as he'd left the inquiry into the botched Chalmers case two years earlier. In the column below, the *Courier*'s crime correspondent demanded to know for how much longer this murder spree could continue under the very noses of the police, who were still no nearer either to finding Polly or to charging a twisted serial killer with two murders. *Essex police have repeatedly questioned the same two suspects,* Ivo had written, *but do they actually have a clue about the true identity of the elusive monster preying on the once-peaceful streets of Colchester?*

The *Courier*'s destructive slant left the team demoralised and acutely aware that Keith was pretty much helpless in the face of the review team's determination to cement their *de facto* command of the investigation. So everyone was relieved when Keith emerged from his office to announce that the Met's Sapphire unit were talking to a woman who claimed she'd been sexually assaulted on their plot by Matt Beeston. Not only would Sapphire like to interview him, but they'd also be happy to pursue all the rape allegations against him. It was an answer to a prayer: this would give them the time they needed to press on with the murder enquiries knowing that their main suspect would be safely under lock and key in London.

It was while Grace was making arrangements for the Met to take Matt off their hands that she answered a call from Jessica, letting them know that she was about to leave Colchester for the long summer vacation. It was mid-afternoon by the time Grace and Lance were free to hurry over to the little house in Station Road, where they found Jessica packing up her belongings.

'It's horrible,' she told them, crossing her arms tightly across her chest. 'Packing up all my stuff, yet leaving Polly's. I feel like I'm abandoning her, like I don't care or something, but I can't stay here any longer on my own.'

'No, of course not,' said Grace. 'Are her parents coming to collect her things?'

'No. They're worried in case she comes back, finds all her stuff cleared out and goes away again.'

Grace nodded. 'Of course. It's tough for them.' And not made any easier, she thought bitterly, by the morning headlines.

'But Pawel told them it's fine for them to leave everything here,' said Jessica. 'Offered to let me stay on for free, too, if I want. He's being pretty decent about it all.'

'That's good,' Grace answered. She risked a cautious glance at Lance, but Jessica spotted it and raised her chin obstinately.

'He said he hasn't been able to let the house for next term anyway,' she said. 'The university Accommodation Office has taken him off their lists, and no one's going to rent from a murder suspect.'

'Sounds like you're still quite friendly?'

'Not friendly, but it's hard to believe Pawel would hurt anyone.'

'You should still be careful,' Lance warned.

Jessica's head drooped and she was silent for a moment. When she spoke, they could hardly catch her words. 'She's not coming back, is she?'

Grace told the truth. 'Two weeks is a very long time to have absolutely no sign of her.' She waited until Jessica took a deep breath and went back to packing up her mugs and dishes. 'I'm afraid we need to ask you some more questions about Polly. About things she might have said to you.'

Jessica stopped what she was doing and placed a half-wrapped cereal bowl into the cardboard box at her feet. 'Then do you mind if we get out of here?' she asked. 'This place just gets a bit too much.'

Lance and Grace agreed, and followed her across a playing field on the far side of the railway line to a footpath that led into Wivenhoe Woods. From a distance, the shade under the trees had looked inviting yet, once under the leafy canopy, the air quickly become close, and Grace caught an occasional fetid scent of mouldering vegetation. The dry mud pathways were well worn but the brambles and deliberately placed brushwood made the tangled heart of the ancient woodland that stretched away beyond the tree trunks appear impenetrable.

Grace was content to let Jessica walk in silence until the unhappy hunch of the young woman's shoulders began to ease. 'So what was it you wanted to ask me?' Jessica said at last.

'I know you've told us before, but we'd like you to go over everything that Polly said to you about the night she spent with Matt Beeston,' said Grace. 'Really everything.'

'She didn't say much.'

'But you told us earlier that she regretted bringing him home.'

They came into a clearing, and Jessica stopped in front of a large board with captioned illustrations of local fauna and flora. 'She said she'd been really drunk. Like more than she should've been.'

'Did she think her drinks had been spiked?' asked Lance.

'Not really. Maybe a double when she asked for a single.

She thought it was more the release of tension because the exams were finally over.'

'Sure,' Lance said reassuringly.

As Grace slapped away hovering midges, feeling the stillness of the late afternoon air prickly and oppressive, Jessica reached out and stroked the bright scarlet markings on the image of a great spotted woodpecker on the board. 'I think it was just one of those awful shags you have when you've drunk a bit more than you should,' she said, cringing with embarrassment. 'You know?'

'Can you remember exactly what she said?' Grace asked gently.

Jessica stared away into the trees. 'She couldn't get him to go the next morning. Had a really bad hangover and was too ill to argue. Said she had to put out again before he'd leave. That's when Pawel caught them at it. She was pretty stressed.'

'You think it was rape?'

Jessica shrugged miserably and began to walk again, striking off into a smaller side path to avoid a group of noisy kids on mountain bikes.

'What kind of sex was it?' Grace asked, checking over her shoulder that no one was close enough to overhear. 'I'm sorry to ask, but it's important.'

'Like what was done to that journalist, you mean?'

'Not necessarily.' Grace feared putting words in Jessica's mouth, but the young woman shook her head.

'I don't think so. Polly was fed up with herself. She shouldn't have let it happen with Matt, but I don't think she was scared or particularly shocked or anything. He's such a loser.'

Grace nodded. 'The two of you were close, right? She'd have told you if there had been more to it?'

'I don't see why not.'

'Is there anyone else she might have confided in? Anyone she'd trust with her deepest, darkest secrets?'

'Maybe some friend from home? I don't know. We got on pretty well. We were going to share a house again next year.' Jessica plucked at a strand of hair, as if examining it for split ends. 'Right now I'm not even sure I want to come back next year.'

'People often feel like that,' said Lance comfortingly. 'Wait and see. Once things are resolved you may feel differently.'

Grace thought hard: had Polly really chosen to tell Danny but not her housemate such crude details about her sexual encounter with Matt Beeston? It seemed extraordinary. Was he a fantasist? Or had there been something between them, something Danny still wasn't coming clean about? And what about the notion that both she and Lance had picked up, that Danny knew where Polly was? She had to find out. Frowning, she turned to Jessica again. 'Do you know who Danny Tooley is?'

'Yes.' Jessica pointed through the trees to where it was possible to make out a line of low rooftops. 'He lives over there. Gives us a lift sometimes.'

Grace froze with fear: what had she missed? 'He gives you a lift?'

'Yes. He works in the campus bookshop.'

'Is it a regular thing, getting a lift with him?'

'No. Just once or twice when one of us missed the bus. And home from town late once when we happened to bump into him.'

'What sort of car does he drive?'

Jessica thought for a moment. 'A BMW. One of those old square ones, – dark red, I think.'

'Thanks.' Grace's fear lessened a little as it struck her that of course Danny was bound to lie to a police officer about driving without a licence or insurance. But the urge to dash off and begin checking out this unexpected new information was overwhelming. Lance caught her eye, clearly in the grip of exactly the same impulse. 'Shall we turn back?' Grace started to walk a little more briskly. 'What did Polly make of Danny?' she asked.

'Thinks he's sweet,' Jessica answered without too much reflection. 'Says he makes her laugh. Don't see it myself, but I guess it doesn't hurt that he's, like, totally nuts about her. I'd find it annoying more than funny.'

'In what way?'

'Oh, you know, if he sees us in town, he'll always come and say hello. Stands around making lame jokes. Sometimes he can be a bit hard to shake off.'

As they emerged from the woodland path back onto the open expanse of grass, Grace was glad to breathe in the freshness of a light breeze from the distant water. Jessica was happy to part company at the edge of the playing field, promising them both that she'd stay safe and get in touch if she had any anxieties about her landlord. As soon as she'd gone, Grace turned to Lance.

'I checked!' she said. 'Unless he uses a different name, he's not on the DVLA database. Never even applied for a provisional licence.'

'You think he's spirited her away somewhere?' Lance asked. 'Her knight in shining armour?'

'We need to find the car he's driving. And then have a word.'

'He obviously uses it to get to work,' said Lance. 'Let's go check.'

But there were no BMWs amongst the few staff cars parked beside a row of industrial-sized wheelie bins in the service area behind the campus buildings, and when they went into the bookshop in search of Danny, the manager told them that he'd called in sick this morning and had said he wasn't sure when he'd be well enough to return to work.

Grace was tempted to put her foot down and speed back to Wivenhoe as fast as she could. As the yellowing summer fields whisked past the windows, she kept telling herself that her alarm was only because she'd messed up and not asked the right questions early enough, not because she feared that Danny might have reason to know where Polly was.

She turned into Rosemead Avenue and drew up outside number twenty-seven, a modest little house, neatly kept but with a run-down, dilapidated look to it. Lance went to ring the doorbell. When there was no answer, he peered in through the front window, then shook his head: nothing.

'If he's ill, he may not come down,' Grace pointed out, joining Lance at the window. Inside she could make out a wooden bookshelf against the back wall, well stocked with paperbacks, a shabby old couch and a worn patch of carpet. Grace thought about Danny's brother away in the army, about an isolated young man, unable to continue his education because his mother was ill, who had chosen to work in a place where he'd never belong. Who knew what frustrations or odd desires he might harbour?

She led the way around the side of the house to a featureless little garden laid entirely to lawn. The grass had been cut, although not recently, and was covered in clover, daisies and dandelions. She looked up at the back windows. There was no sign of life. Through the kitchen window they could see everything kept neat and tidy on the beige countertops. On the windowsill, facing inwards, was a little shepherdess made out of lacquered seashells.

They rang the front doorbell a couple more times, but either Danny didn't want to leave his bed or he wasn't there. Grace cursed herself. However understandable Danny's lie about driving without a licence, he had misled the police in a murder investigation. The big question now was how much else he'd lied to them about.

FORTY-SIX

There was an unexpected mood of elation when Grace and Lance got back to the MIT office, and they hurried over to Duncan to find out what was going on.

'We just got the transcripts of Roxanne Carson's reporter's notebooks back,' Duncan told them. 'The boffins have untangled her shorthand.'

'That was quick,' said Lance while Grace hoped they'd interpret her gasp as anticipation of a breakthrough rather than apprehension at what her friend's notes might reveal.

'What's more, they confirm that Matt Beeston had motive for killing her!' said Duncan excitedly. 'Danny Tooley had told her that Matt and Polly went home together. So, according to her notes, she ambushed Matt's takeaway delivery, got up to his flat and asked him about the night he and Polly had sex!'

Grace leaned against the nearest desk. 'When was that?'

'Lunchtime Tuesday. The day of the vigil,' said Duncan. 'It'd be crazy not to assume that Roxanne wouldn't also have asked him about the bottle. That would be more than enough to get him rattled.'

'Is that not in Roxanne's notes?' queried Grace, frowning.

'I haven't seen the transcripts,' said Duncan. 'So I don't know how detailed they are. But it makes your point, Lance, about why the killer stuffed her knickers in her mouth. Matt would have good reason to want to shut her up.'

'What about Zawodny?' asked Lance. 'Does she mention him? Did she speak to him?'

Duncan shook his head. 'Nothing in what we have here.'

Disappointed, Lance shook his head in irritation.

'Matt's still in London?' asked Grace.

'Yes,' said Duncan. 'We'll get him back as soon as Sapphire have finished with him.'

'Are they charging him?' asked Lance.

'With the rape? Hope so.'

'Bastard!' Grace couldn't stop the wave of anger she felt towards the spoiled, selfish young man who may have robbed her friend of life. Lance and Duncan both did an embarrassed little shuffle by way of apology that, in their eagerness, they'd forgotten her private distress.

'What does Keith think?' asked Lance.

Duncan nodded towards the SIO's office, where the blinds were down. 'He's in with the superheroes,' he said with a snort of contempt. 'Don't reckon he's enjoying himself much, either.'

Duncan turned away, and as Grace and Lance returned to their own desks, she spoke softly, not to be overheard.

'You do realise that this all depends on whether Danny was telling the truth?'

'How else would he know about the bottle?'

'The first time he mentioned it to us was after Roxanne died. He could have read it in the paper like everyone else.'

Lance shook his head, unconvinced.

'Why did Polly tell Danny about it but not Jessica?' Grace pressed. 'If Polly was prepared to tell anyone, she'd have told her best girl friend.'

'Why would he lie to us?'

Grace shrugged. 'To big himself up? Keep himself in the loop because it's exciting? Or maybe it's all to do with some sad little fantasy about how close he and Polly really were.'

'In his dreams,' said Lance.

'Exactly!' said Grace. 'It makes no sense that Polly would talk to him like that. He's too inexperienced, too dreamy-eyed and romantic about her.'

'Maybe that's what she liked about him?' said Lance. 'Still, we need to speak to him. Make him see that he might actually have to swear under oath in court exactly what he told Roxanne, and when. That might shake him down.'

'I'll send someone over there to turf him out of bed,' said Grace. 'Then we can find out what's going on.'

The blinds covering the SIO's glass partition opened, and Colin led the team out into the main office. It was the end of a long day, yet he looked fresh and invigorated, his white shirt pristine. Keith exited behind the others, looking drawn and angry, his hands thrust deep into his trouser pockets and his lips pulled tight together as if he didn't trust himself to speak.

'We have jointly decided to refocus the investigation,' began Colin, looking right around to room to make sure that he had captured everyone's attention. 'We want to explore the possibility that the disappearance of Polly Sinclair is unrelated to the murders of Rachel Moston and Roxanne Carson.' He paused as people exchanged glances and either nodded in agreement or raised sceptical eyebrows at one another. 'Now that we have the contents of Roxanne Carson's reporter's notebooks, we are moving closer towards the possibility of charging Matt Beeston with both murders.' That did win a murmur of approval, and Colin allowed himself a small nod of acknowledgement, as if this imminent victory was due to his leadership. 'We therefore want to look afresh at Polly's disappearance,' he concluded.

Everyone knew that the specialist search teams had spent the day combing the centre of Colchester and found nothing, but Lena Millington, who now took up the baton, seemed to regard this as useful new intelligence. 'It firms up the likelihood that Polly did somehow leave Colchester that night,' she said. 'We know she didn't take public transport, nor a taxi, so we can assume she travelled in someone's car, either willingly or not.'

'She was never picked up on CCTV as a passenger,' said Duncan. 'We've been over everything twice.'

Superintendent Millington nodded. 'Which suggests she was abducted.' Stationed behind her, Keith gave a tiny shake of his head and folded his arms grimly. Grace understood why: absence of proof was not itself proof of anything. 'We want to look again at Pawel Zawodny,' Lena Millington concluded. Colin and John Kenny, who flanked her, both nodded in agreement.

Beside Grace, Lance made his own small clenched-fist gesture of triumph. 'Told you!' he whispered to her.

But Keith took a step forward. 'We're covering old ground,' he said impatiently. 'There's no new evidence.'

'It's a fresh perspective,' Colin said firmly but pleasantly. 'The chief constable brought us in to provide strategic oversight.'

'If that's what you call rearranging the same pieces into a different pattern! Using one theory to plug the holes in the other, and vice versa.'

'Keith, we've discussed this.' Colin might be smiling, thought Grace, but behind the charm there was an unmistakable note of warning.

'And I told you I disagreed,' said Keith. 'What if both theories are wrong? Do you want to be the one to tell the parents?'

'There is a pretty good case for looking again at Zawodny, boss,' said Lance as mildly as he could. 'Polly may well have accepted a lift home from her landlord, a man she knew and trusted.'

'Even though she'd caught him spying on her that very morning?' demanded Keith.

'He admits disposing of something large enough to be a body at sea,' Lance persisted. 'He admits having sex with another tenant in lieu of rent. And he has contempt for women who go to bars and get drunk. It may not have been premeditated. He could have tried it on with Polly and ended up killing her.'

'You show me solid evidence that he or his truck were in town that night, and I'll buy it,' said Keith.

Lance fell silent, unable to argue with Keith on this point. And Grace realised that her instinct, too, still baulked at the idea of Pawel Zawodny as a cold-blooded killer. True, the builder held old-fashioned views on how women should behave, and had become angry when Grace had challenged him in interview, but that could have been merely the natural anger of a hard-working man insulted by abhorrent and unjust accusations. Yet if Lance was right, and Pawel *had* made a pass at Polly and, when she objected, it had got out of hand, then it was striking that he had never once protested his innocence: was that from pride or guilt? If Polly's disappearance was unconnected to the murders, then Colin was right to insist that Pawel did, at the very least, belong in the frame. She was going back around in circles again!

'We still have Zawodny under surveillance,' said Colin in an encouraging tone, reminding Grace of a good-looking football manager, always ready to defend his team in public however he might blast them in private. 'Meanwhile, our recommendation is that we seek advice from the CPS on whether we have enough to bring separate charges against him and against Matt Beeston.'

'And if we're wrong,' said Keith, 'the media will flay us alive. Might as well shut up shop.'

'We've just been speaking to Polly Sinclair's housemate, Jessica,' began Lance as diplomatically as he could. 'Polly said nothing to her about Matt using a bottle as a sex toy.'

'There could be any number of reasons for that,' said Lena Millington tartly.

'We could ask Zawodny if he noticed anything when he spied on them,' suggested John Kenny. 'After all, didn't he say he went upstairs because he thought the girl was in trouble?'

'Do we ask him before or after we charge him with Polly's murder?' asked Keith sarcastically.

'What did Roxanne write in her notebook?' asked Grace. 'What were her actual words about what Danny Tooley told her?'

'There's nothing written down about a bottle,' said Colin. 'Just that she tried to get as much as she could from him about Matt going home with Polly.'

'So we've only got Danny's word for it,' said Grace.

'Which may be why he's avoiding us,' suggested Lance.

'What do you mean?' asked Colin.

'He's not at work. Called in sick. And he's not answering the door at home,' said Lance. 'Could be that he's understandably reluctant to admit that he's been telling us porkies.'

'I checked back with the two students I spoke to who'd accused Matt of rape,' said Grace. 'Neither described being assaulted with a bottle or any other object.'

'Maybe the victim Sapphire are talking to will add to the picture,' said Colin with a confidence Grace couldn't believe he really felt. 'Find Danny Tooley and bring him back in. Be ready to throw the book at him if he's misled us.'

'We now also know that he has use of a car,' said Grace. 'Even though he doesn't hold a licence. An older model dark red BMW.'

'Registration number?'

'Don't know, sir. There's no car registered to Danny's address and there was no dark red BMW near his house, nor in the parking area where he works.'

'So whose car is it?' Colin demanded, finding a welcome outlet for his impatience.

'He mentioned a brother,' answered Grace. 'In the paras, serving abroad. Danny could be borrowing a car belonging to him and driving it illegally.'

'The army can be slow to respond,' said Keith, 'but it shouldn't be too difficult to find that out.'

Grace gave him a grateful smile, then turned to face Colin again. 'Sir, I'm aware that, without Danny Tooley's testimony, the case against Matt remains circumstantial, but –'

'You have serious doubts about Tooley's reliability?'

'Yes, sir.' Grace saw Colin's cheeks redden in frustration, but she continued anyway. 'Until we find Danny and clarify matters, I think we should treat his statement with caution.'

'I am aware that it is in any case only hearsay evidence.' Colin strove to make his tone pleasant, but Grace could see how angry he was. It only served to make her more determined.

'But don't you see? Danny has a car.' She spoke impetuously, barely conscious of what she was about to say. 'He could have given Polly a lift home the night she went missing. He's not been picked up on any CCTV driving out of Colchester only because we've never been looking for him. *He* could have killed her.'

To her surprise, Colin didn't contest her assertion. Instead he looked calmly first at John Kenny and then at Lena Millington, who both appeared to give their assent to something previously discussed. Then he turned back to face Grace. 'Roxanne Carson's notebooks threw up another issue that we need to discuss. Perhaps best done in private, if you don't mind, DS Fisher?'

Colin pushed open the door to Keith's office and waited, a triumphant gleam in his eyes. Grace knew immediately what this was about. She had no choice but to walk past him, sickeningly aware as she did so that the curious eyes of everyone in the room were upon her.

FORTY-SEVEN

Half an hour later Grace walked down North Hill feeling as if she was hurtling down a precipitous slope. Was it over? Had her call to Roxanne from Colchester Town railway station and their subsequent drink at the old coaching inn – both of which she had just admitted to the three superintendents – ended her career? She was certain that if it had been up to Lena Millington and John Kenny she'd already be suspended. And she had no illusions that Colin's delay had been prompted by kindness or even to make amends for the past; she knew him well enough now to be convinced that he'd been hedging his bets, sliding away from accepting responsibility by suggesting that, given Grace's recent media exposure, they wait to inform both the communications director and the chief constable.

But Grace knew it was only a reprieve. Given this morning's hostile coverage in the *Courier*, the chief con might prefer to seek a discreet route by which to institute disciplinary proceedings, but the result would be the same: Grace would be out on her ear. Where would she go? What could else she do? She began to panic: no income, no friends, nowhere where she belonged, saddled with the lease on a flat she hated while still paying the mortgage on the house in Maidstone. She must call her solicitor first thing on Monday, push to get the divorce settlement finalised and the Maidstone house on the market. There wouldn't be much left once it was sold, but it would be something.

She stopped at a crossroad, waiting for the traffic signal. It was rush hour, and even though the good weather was supposed to break soon there was a long queue of cars thanks to people heading off to weekend escapes. She looked at the tired drivers with elbows stuck out of rolled-down windows, fingers drumming on shiny paintwork, waiting for the red lights to change. When she'd been offered this job, she, too, had fondly imagined exploring a new area – Dedham Vale, Southwold, the Broads or the sweeping sands of Holkham beach – but now she had nothing.

Her phone buzzed and she felt a sour taste in her mouth as she looked at the screen, hoping it wouldn't be Trev – again. But it was Hilary, who had just heard the news; shocked yet genuinely sympathetic, Hilary offered to meet for a coffee the following morning to discuss the best way to handle the inevitable interview with Irene Brown. Grace was grateful once more for her kindness, and gladly agreed.

The lights had changed again while Grace was on the phone, and she had to wait once more for the green man to appear. On the opposite corner, outlined against the evening sun, she spotted an all-too-familiar silhouette and laughed: a bad day was turning into farce. Trev waited for her to come across to him.

'Grace! I didn't expect you so early. I know you don't want to see me, but I have to talk to you and you won't take my calls.'

'Now is really not a good time.'

'Please, love. It's important. I've done something really daft. And you need to know. I had to come and warn you.'

'What?' she asked in alarm.

'I was angry,' he said with a rueful shrug. 'You sent that text, telling me to fuck off, and then there was this journalist banging on my door. So I let him in.'

'Oh Jesus, Trev!'

'I know, I know. It was stupid. But you kept rejecting my calls.'

'So it's my fault?'

Trev didn't answer. Grace set off at a march, intending in her blind fury just to escape him, reach her flat and barricade herself inside. He followed at a distance, trying not to crowd her. By the time she reached the entrance to her building it had sunk in that he was right: whatever he had done, she did need to know.

'Who was it?' she asked, though she could already guess the answer. 'Which paper?'

'Some guy from the *Courier*. Ivo Sweatman.'

'What did you tell him?'

'He already knew quite a lot. All I really did was confirm it, you know? They're clever, these guys. Make out like they're just asking questions, that you're not really telling them anything they don't already have, but they sure know how to press the right buttons.'

Grace was afraid she was going to throw up. She leaned a hand against the rough brick wall beside her and bent over, breathing slowly through her mouth.

'I'm sorry, love, I am,' said Trev, 'but he wound me up. You wound me up.'

'And you just can't help yourself, can you?' she shot at him, her eyes blazing. She had never hated him more than she did at this moment. This was worse even than the night she'd spent nursing broken ribs in a freezing cold hotel bed. Then she'd struggled to find explanations, to understand, desperate to find some way to forgive and conserve all the love that she'd poured into their relationship. Now her hatred was like a fire, burning up the past – their first night together, the moment he proposed, their honeymoon, everything – in one mighty conflagration. It felt good: empty and terrifying and soulless, but good.

'Fuck off, and don't ever, ever come near me again,' she said. Her hand was steady as she got the key in the lock, opened the street door and slammed it in his face.

Once inside her flat, she felt like an automaton. She was able to kick off her shoes, fill the kettle, drop a tea bag in a cup. She imagined that soldiers about to go into action must feel this way. Life might be about to be extinguished but the body went on functioning.

But as she carried her mug of tea over to the square window that looked across to a row of identical square windows, her hand began to tremble. What did Ivo Sweatman know? What *didn't* he know? The thought of what that man might do with the details of her past made her feel sick again. She wondered if she should call Hilary, but the idea of having to explain, to tell her story, was too much.

She made herself sip the hot tea, trying not to slop it on the anonymous beige twill carpet. How had Ivo Sweatman managed to latch onto Trev? How had he found out enough about her past to bother doing so? The answer was a body blow: Roxanne!

Grace was barely conscious of putting down her mug, sitting on the uncomfortable couch, placing her arms around her head and rocking with the pain of the betrayal. Why would Roxanne have passed on Grace's most intimate secrets to Ivo Sweatman? For advancement? Was that all Grace's friendship had been worth? A trade in return for the promise of some part-time shifts on a national newspaper?

Grace got up and went to rummage in the boxes lined up against the living-room wall that she had yet to unpack. In one of them was her running gear. She had to get out of here. Had to do something that would empty her mind and enable her to survive the next few hours at least. She would worry later about how she'd get through the night.

As she pulled on her crop pants, then laced up her trainers, she told herself that there was no point in nourishing her anger against Roxanne. OK, so she could add her to the list of people she'd been wrong to trust, but Roxanne was dead, and she was alive. It was irrelevant what Roxanne had or hadn't done; her life had been taken from her, and – forget Colin Pitman, Trev, Ivo Sweatman, the lot of them! – it was still Grace's job, officially or not, to track down her killer.

After two circuits of the cricket ground, she crossed the river and jogged up towards the castle. She was out of condition and, feeling a stitch in her side, was glad to drop onto an unoccupied bench that looked back down the gentle slope up which she had come. Grey clouds were gathering on the horizon, but for now the view was green and restful, and the people around her were out to enjoy their start to the weekend. She reminded herself that for most people in this unremarkable market town life went on as usual, that violation, death, suspicion and betrayal were rare aberrations. She tried to tell herself that it wouldn't be the end of the world if she could no longer be a detective but, however sensible, the thought was like facing some kind of ritual disembowelment. It would be the end of *her* world.

She recalled the idea she had voiced earlier, that Danny could have killed Polly. Did she really believe that? Could she back it up? It would be a calming distraction from her own problems to think this through, even if there was never going to be another chance for anyone to take her seriously.

If the question was why such a mild and unassuming young man would do something terrible to a young woman he liked so very much, then the answer was coursing through her own veins: hurt, rejection, disappointment, betrayal. Such emotions turned you inside out, made you into someone you barely recognised. Yet however absolutely she had hated Trev when he'd stood before her, however much she might have wished him in some way instantly struck down, if only to *know* the intensity of her reaction to what he'd done to her, she had not raised a hand to him. She had not wanted to actually kill him.

She remembered Lance's sense, after they'd interviewed Danny, that he knew where Polly was. She'd discounted it, recalling his grief at Polly's candlelit vigil. That had been real, she was convinced. But what if he did know where her body was?

Danny was isolated, sensitive, unable to finish his education, soft on a girl even after she'd been rude to him and paraded the fact that she was taking a university lecturer home to her bed. Had he suffered so much that his resentment became murderous? And had he resented Matt Beeston enough to get a kick out of implicating him, knowing that with Roxanne dead there was no one to call him a liar?

Grace felt the pieces click into place. If Danny was responsible for Polly's disappearance and feared Roxanne suspected him, then he had a motive to kill her – and shove her knickers in her mouth to shut her up. How had they missed it!

But what possible reason did Danny have to kill Rachel Moston, with whom he had no apparent connection? And yet whoever had strangled Roxanne had positioned the wine bottle in a way known only to Rachel's killer. Granted, such an ambitious high-flyer as Rachel would never have given a shop assistant the time of day, but would her attitude have pissed Danny off enough to make him want to kill her? And then violate her body?

Except, thought Grace, he was sorry afterwards.

Keith and the rest of the team always discounted the cushion under Rachel's head, but it spoke more powerfully to Grace than anything else. For her, it always came back to that. Where the others saw misogyny, sexual dominance, humiliation, power and control – all common reasons why men killed women – Grace saw only that folded red jacket.

Matt Beeston was too narcissistic for such a gesture: she simply couldn't see him bothering. Pawel Zawodny had a short fuse and might have been driven by his Catholic conscience to show remorse, yet she still couldn't quite see his anger as murderous. But she could so easily picture Danny neatly folding Rachel's jacket and lifting her head to place it softly underneath, imagine him pulling down the patterned skirt to hide what he had done to her with a half-empty bottle of vodka.

So where was Danny now? And, even when they found him, would Keith and the rest of the team be willing to trust her?

FORTY-EIGHT

Ivo got to the meeting early. He was hoping to see Keith, but he would have come anyway. He was shaky, no doubt about it, and he needed to acknowledge it here in the fellowship. Even after all this time, it still scared the hell out of him to stand up and speak about himself. But he had to say something, even if only to hear his own words spoken aloud. He had taken photographs of a dead girl, a young woman he knew and liked. He had been stone-cold sober and taken photographs of a dead girl when any normal human being would have been weeping or kneeling to pay their respects. And he couldn't even get away with saying it was his job. It was him. He wasn't normal. Wasn't sure he ever had been. Maybe that's why he did this job. It was no excuse to spout all that bullshit about the romance of Fleet Street; there was no romance in what he'd done. He must be fucking psychotic to do a thing like that.

A few regulars stood in a group chatting, and Ivo knew he'd be welcome to join them, but he went over to the window that looked onto a walled garden, laid to lawn and dotted with small trees. Gardens weren't his thing: he had no idea whether this was a nice garden or not, but it was green and empty of people. But as he stood there it seemed to darken and the trees to grow alarmingly in stature, their shadows like bony fingers creeping towards his throat: fuck, it was happening again! He kept seeing her, kept seeing the flashlight from his phone throwing into pin-point-sharp focus the neatly waxed line of her pubic hair and the glistening wine bottle. He wanted to throw up. Maybe he should just get out of here, find the nearest bar, drink himself to death and be done with it.

But that would be sheer self-indulgence. This wasn't about him. Roxanne was the victim here, Roxanne and the other two. This was about getting the twisted little fuck who'd done these things banged to rights. Ivo wanted to see a diabolically Photoshopped portrait of the bastard adorn the front page once the guilty verdict came in. Ivo owed Roxanne that much at least. Better than flowers on her grave any day.

But it helped to be amongst others who understood what it was like to live with this demon on their shoulder, whispering in their ear, promising how simple it was to make the relentless shame and anxiety vanish: one drink, only one! Pouff! Just like that! Gone. Go on, what's not to like? He hadn't had it this bad in a long time.

He turned around, looking to see if Keith had arrived. No sign of him yet, even though people were sitting down ready to start. Not that he expected Keith to give him a warm welcome, not after Ivo had called him clueless in

72-point bold type. But he wanted, given the chance, to offer him a heads-up on tomorrow's story which, let's face it, was going to be huge. His editor had already increased the print run on the back of it.

Danny Tooley was about to spend a second night holed up in his cheap hotel room on the ring road. Ivo had called for back-up, stipulating that a reporter who was young, female, pretty and preferably blonde come be Danny's minder. Sharon might succeed in getting Danny to open up on topics where all Ivo's best tactics had so far failed.

He took a chair at the edge of a row and made himself listen to what others were saying, trying not to dismiss their confessions as minor compared to his violation of the dead. That would be vanity, another snare. No slip-up or failure was small or insignificant to an addict; constant vigilance was required. When his moment came, he stood up, holding on to the back of the chair in front and feeling his palms clammy and slippery. 'My name is Ivo Sweatman and I'm an alcoholic,' he began, hearing the nervous rasp in his voice. 'I haven't had a drink in four years, but –' He paused to let the ripple of approving nods fall still again. 'But I'm still an addict. I'm a reporter, a journalist, and I'm addicted to the thrill of getting a story. Sometimes I go too far.'

Some small disturbance made him turn towards the door. He found Keith standing there and caught the unmistakable flash of contempt in his face. Ivo faced front again. 'Thank you for letting me share that,' he said, and sat down. His heart was pumping in his chest and he felt his face burn.

The person next to him patted his arm as someone else stood up and began to speak. He didn't hear what the woman was saying. It didn't matter. Tonight he was here for Roxanne.

The first part of the meeting passed in a kind of daze as Ivo's heart continued to thump and jolt against his ribcage. Finally he heard the familiar rattle of the coffee urn, and looked around just in time to catch sight of Keith making for the door.

He caught up with him on the paved frontage of the Friends' Meeting House. 'Hey, Keith, wait up a second. I need to talk to you.' Keith stopped and spun on his heel: Christ, the man looked like shit! Ivo almost wondered if he was drinking again, but the needle-like intensity of the fury in his eyes was too clear to be polluted by alcohol.

'I have nothing to say to you, Ivo!'

There was nothing for it: he'd have to go straight in with an attention-grabbing headline. 'Polly Sinclair is alive. She ran away. Danny Tooley helped her.'

'Danny Tooley?'

Ivo nodded. 'He's given us an exclusive.'

'How much are you paying him?'

'He's never so much as asked about the reward, or payment.'

'Do you believe him?'

'We're running it tomorrow.'

'Fuck.'

A young man came out of the Meeting House and tried not to stare curiously at them as he walked past. Keith looked around, then drew Ivo through a side gate into the garden, which Ivo now saw was part of an old graveyard. He could hear traffic from a nearby main road, the air was muggy and he could feel the first light misting of rain.

'What's he saying to you?' Keith demanded.

'He bumped into Polly in Colchester. She was drunk and on her own, so he offered her a lift home.'

'Whose car?'

'Belongs to his brother, Michael. He imagines Michael hasn't twigged that he uses it. It was the only detail he was bothered about us printing.'

'Go on.'

'In the car, Polly started crying. He knew what it was about because she'd already told him earlier in the day about her romp with the randy lecturer. She said she couldn't face telling anyone else what had happened but knew she wouldn't be able to hide from her parents how upset she was. She spent the night at Danny's house and first thing in the morning he drove her to Ipswich and dropped her at the train station. He gave her some cash and lent her a hoodie and some other clothes. She said she was going to a friend in London. She wouldn't say who, and swore Danny to secrecy.'

'So why is he breaking his promise now?'

'Because he's worried about her. Two weeks is a long time.'

'Where did he get the cash?'

'Said he already had it at home. His emergency stash.'

'What about her phone?'

'She chucked the SIM card out of the car window.'

'It's a fairy-tale!'

Ivo made no comment. So far as he was concerned, the story lay in Danny saying all this stuff, not whether or not it was true. Not knowing was half the fun. The human interest of IS he, isn't he? Did she, didn't she? That's what his readers loved. It was Keith's job to hunt down the killer. Ivo's quarry was a sizzling-hot story.

'Where is Danny now?'

'Safe. And staying that way until tomorrow's paper hits the streets.'

'Have you told Polly's parents?'

That particular phone call had not been Ivo's finest hour, but his editor had insisted on it. He relayed their response exactly as he planned it would appear in tomorrow's column heading. 'They're praying it's true.'

'Jesus, Ivo. Have you no pity?'

'I just report the facts. And the fact is, he's saying it.'

Keith blew out a scything breath through clenched teeth, threw up his hands and took a few agitated steps away across the dampening grass. Ivo watched him shake his head a few times and run a hand across his short, springy hair before turning back to face him again. 'Off the record, Ivo. Do you believe him?'

It must have been the fact that Keith was standing smack in the lengthening shadow of a tree that made Ivo weaken. After all, why waste the man's time? He shrugged and moved closer, speaking confidentially. 'The *Courier*'s crime desk spent all day checking out Polly's social media contacts. Zilch. We sent someone to talk to the ticket staff at

Ipswich station. Nada. Tried to blag a copy of their CCTV, but they weren't in the market.' Ivo dug in his trouser pocket and dangled a car key in front of the detective. 'His brother's car won't go anywhere 'til you say so.'

'We need Danny. Tonight.'

'My editor's not going to allow that. I'm sorry.' Ivo was surprised to discover that he meant it.

'What if he killed her?'

Alone in the hotel room with Danny, the thought had crossed Ivo's mind more than once. He had not felt a single twinge of fear or danger – though he was waiting to get Sharon's take on that – but, no question, he'd occasionally caught a whiff of being very expertly played. Over the years he'd met more than his fair share of incredibly convincing and plausible psychopaths – it took one to know one, probably – and he wasn't about to have a fit of the vapours if this diffident, helpful, naive-looking young man turned out to be anything but.

But it would be insane to spike a scoop of this magnitude just to make Superintendent Stalgood's life easier. 'I'm a reporter,' he said, raising his hands and swallowing down his distaste for himself. 'I just report on what I see and hear.' Besides, if it *did* turn out to be true, and the *Courier* could take the credit for rescuing a damsel in distress, he'd probably get a fucking OBE. Certainly a pay rise.

'And what if your report makes it impossible later to get a conviction in court because any half-way decent barrister claims the evidence against his client was tainted?'

'I'm just giving my readers what they want.'

'Don't hide behind that nonsense.' Keith leaned forward, right into Ivo's face. 'Listen to me. I really don't care what you do to me. You can lampoon me and bang on about the Chalmers fiasco 'til you're blue in the face. But Polly Sinclair has a family. As does Rachel Moston. And Roxanne Carson. Meanwhile there's a killer out there, I've got an external review team up my arse, and come Monday morning I'm likely to lose a perfectly good officer for no good reason. So tell me where Danny is!'

'Which officer?'

'What?'

'Which officer are you likely to lose?'

Keith sighed. 'DS Fisher. She'd been talking to Roxanne. It's a disciplinary offence.'

'Giving Roxanne information?'

'No. Just talking. They were old friends.'

'Colin Pitman's on the review team, isn't he?'

'So?'

Ivo considered telling Keith all that he'd learned in Maidstone, but then thought better of it. Knowledge was power. He could put what he knew about Colin Pitman to better use elsewhere. 'You can have Danny first thing tomorrow morning,' he said. 'I'll call you and tell you where he is.'

'I don't think so,' said Keith. He walked away without another word. Ivo shrugged. He guessed it wouldn't take the police long to track down the hotel and snatch Danny away, but right now he didn't care. He had another story to write. There was still time for the news desk to shift things around for the early edition.

FORTY-NINE

After Hilary's call alerting her to the *Courier*'s story about Danny, Grace wasn't able to resist running out to the newsagent to pick up a copy. The headline *IS POLLY STILL ALIVE?* was shocking enough, but Grace couldn't wait to turn to the inside page where sure enough there was a blurred over-the-shoulder shot of Trev beside an admittedly rather nice picture of her taken at one of this week's press conferences.

Brave officer's torment at hands of police thug husband ran the strapline. Her mouth dry, she read on: *DS Grace Fisher, the detective at the heart of the Colchester murder inquiry who has sworn to bring the killer of best friend plucky local reporter Roxanne Carson to justice, was driven out of her job as a detective inspector in Kent by uncaring boss Detective Superintendent Colin Pitman, who is now part of the three-man review team scrutinising the Essex investigation.*

She just won't listen! ran a smaller heading below. *Disgraced ex-police constable Trevor Haynes claimed that his former wife's 'problem' was that she wouldn't stay in line and cover up for a*

violent, drug-abusing colleague. Both Lee Roberts and Trevor Haynes
were convicted earlier this year on separate charges of . . .

Grace skipped the few sentences that graphically described the injuries she'd sustained from Trev's beating and jumped to the last paragraph, which lambasted her spineless former boss Colin Pitman for presiding over a bullying police culture that encouraged wrongdoing by a handful of bad apples.

Part of her wanted to both laugh and cry with relief that someone had, for the first time, stuck up for her against the bullies, but a larger part cowered away from the bruising truth that this article would merely reopen old wounds and leave her vulnerable to yet more sideways looks and sneering comments. Colin, too, would never forgive her, even though this time it had been his mate Trev who had stepped out of line.

Grace's sister rang just as she finished reading. She had never told Alison the full horror of Trev's assault – either too proud or too afraid that even Alison would, deep down, believe Grace had brought it upon herself – and Alison was calling to tell Grace how hurt and offended she was at having to learn such details now from a national newspaper. Grace appeased her as best she could and promised to visit at the first opportunity. She didn't tell her sister that by the end of the weekend she might again be out of a job.

When the next call flashed up, Grace was tempted to reject it, but was soon glad she hadn't: it was Lance, wanting to check she was all right and offer any help or support she wanted – any time. She thanked him warmly, and explained that Hilary Burnett was on her way over. As soon as the chief con had been made aware of Ivo Sweatman's interview with Trev, she'd insisted on seeing Grace immediately, even on a Saturday, to deal with the outstanding disciplinary matter. Hilary had offered to accompany her to Chelmsford and Grace had gratefully accepted.

Not long afterwards, in the passenger seat of Hilary's Audi, Grace watched the windscreen wipers steadily clear away the morning drizzle and was relieved that the communications director didn't expect her to chat. She wished now that she'd read Ivo's interview with Danny more carefully so that she could decipher the detail. She didn't believe a word of it. Despite hundreds of unconfirmed sightings of Polly up and down the country, there had been absolutely no activity on her phone, bank account, credit cards, email or social media. It remained a possibility that she had committed suicide, but there was no body and no note. The sad truth was that the police could offer her parents no real hope that she was alive.

Whatever Danny's warped reasons for spinning such a tale – and she'd think about that later – it was cruel of Ivo to have run the story. The torment that Phil and Beverley Sinclair must be going through was unthinkable. Reflecting on her own conversation with her sister, she could barely imagine the phone calls from friends and family that they would now have to deal with. Grace couldn't conceive how any civilised country could allow such irresponsibility, yet millions of people would buy today's *Courier* and genuinely believe it was because they cared about the fate of 'Our Polly'.

They arrived at Essex Police HQ. Hilary had an electronic pass for the car park and took a visitors' spot near the entrance. She switched off the engine and turned to Grace. 'Ready?'

'Not really.'

Hilary scrutinised her. 'Got some lipstick? Go in fighting.'

Grace laughed and rummaged in her bag. As she used the visor mirror to apply some dusky pink to her lips, Hilary patted her leg. 'I know it's horrid to have your dirty linen spread out in public, but Ivo Sweatman has actually done you a real favour,' she said.

Grace concentrated on keeping her hand steady and did not reply.

'The chief constable's priority will be damage limitation. And this timely reminder to the public that you're our very own plucky heroine will have put a very different spin on things.'

Grace nodded reluctantly as she capped her lipstick and stowed it away. She simply dare not allow herself to hope that her career could be saved: better to face the worst and get it over with.

'Will you let me do the talking?' asked Hilary. 'Trust me, I know how to press the right buttons. I'll have you walking out of here with a commendation!'

Grace couldn't help laughing again. She knew this last boast was a joke, but began to realise that perhaps she'd been unfair to Hilary: she was just as skilled in her way at reading, managing and defusing people as any Tier 3 police interviewer.

They were shown straight into Irene Brown's spacious corner office. Hilary glanced at a thermos jug and cups and saucers already laid out on the coffee table between two brown leather sofas and raised an eyebrow at Grace: this was a favourable sign. The chief constable, relaxed in a uniform dress shirt rather than the full regalia of a buttoned-up jacket, came out from behind her desk to greet them.

'Hilary, DS Fisher, please.' The chief con sat in the middle of one sofa, gesturing to them to sit beside one another facing her. 'Coffee?'

Grace was about to refuse, not sure she could cope with managing a cup and saucer without spillage, but a nudge from Hilary made her accept.

'I was very disappointed to receive Superintendent Pitman's call yesterday,' Irene Brown began without preamble, 'suggesting that you have had further unauthorised contact with the media, in direct contradiction of my express orders the last time we met. I'd like to hear what you have to say.'

'It is true, ma'am, that I met a second time with Roxanne Carson.'

'Without informing your SIO?'

'It had nothing to do with any operational matters, ma'am. Our meeting was of a purely personal nature.'

'Because Roxanne Carson was an old friend?'

'Yes, ma'am.' Grace felt a leap of hope: if the chief con was feeding her own witness and showing a readiness to describe Roxanne as a 'friend' rather than a journalist, then maybe Hilary's prediction was right and she was being handed a lifeline. But then the bitter taste of betrayal flooded the back of her throat: *was* Roxanne a friend? How much of what Grace had so gratefully confided in her that drunken night at the Blue Bar had she passed on to Ivo Sweatman?

'DS Fisher was one of the first officers at the scene when Roxanne Carson's body was found, ma'am,' said Hilary gently. 'She was understandably reluctant to talk to the media about their friendship so soon after such a distressing experience, but was professional enough to be persuaded of the benefit to the investigation. You yourself have seen first-hand the value of her contribution.'

Irene Brown gracefully accepted Hilary's deft reminder that she had specifically asked to be seated beside Grace when facing the TV news cameras at the media conference. 'The human face of modern police work,' she acknowledged. 'Not that I intend to be held to ransom by the media,' she added pointedly. 'However, I have also received an email from Superintendent Stalgood.' She turned to Grace. 'He wished to make me aware that your actions, although regrettable, had not in his opinion impacted negatively on the investigation. He feels that, going forward, the needs of the inquiry should override any draconian disciplinary procedure.'

'I can only apologise, ma'am, for a regrettable lapse of judgement and for wasting everyone's time.'

'I will leave it to Superintendent Stalgood to impose an

appropriate redress.' The chief constable rose to her feet, smoothing down her immaculately fitted black uniform skirt. Grace put down her untouched cup of coffee and stood up.

'I won't take up more of your time, Hilary,' the chief con continued. 'I imagine you're needed back in Colchester to deal with this latest story about Polly Sinclair.'

'It's going to be extremely difficult,' agreed Hilary, following Irene Brown to the door of her office. 'I'm sure that the parents would really appreciate it if you could send them a personal message.'

'Absolutely. Draft something for me to approve. And let me know if you want me to add weight to today's media conference.'

'Thank you, yes. I think your presence would definitely set the right tone.'

'Then I'll see you later.' With a brief nod of farewell to Grace, Irene Brown shut the door on them. Grace could hardly believe it. She was safe. Her job was safe. She felt like dancing down the corridor. Cue lights! Cue music! She could go back to work!

'Told you,' said Hilary gleefully, as soon as they'd reached the privacy of the lift. 'Last thing on earth she wanted was to have to take any action against you. Can you imagine the media backlash if she had?'

'Thank you so much, Hilary.'

'I just offered her what she was looking for: a way out.'

'No,' said Grace, hugging her, 'you were wonderful. Played a real blinder in there!'

Hilary went pink and turned to the mirrored wall of the lift to primp her perfect hair. 'I don't know why Superintendent Pitman felt he had to refer it to her at all,' she said. 'Though maybe it's just as well he did.'

Grace's heart sank. Colin had referred it because he hoped she'd be sacked. He wasn't going to be the least little bit pleased to see her walk back into the MIT office, especially not after the hatchet job Ivo Sweatman had done on him in this morning's paper. He wouldn't even be able to avoid it: a copy of the *Courier* would be on every desk because of the interview with Danny Tooley. Colin was just going to have to suck it up.

FIFTY

Grace phoned Lance from the car and was thrilled by his genuine pleasure and relief at her news. He was at work and, hearing an unusual amount of noise in the background, she asked what was going on.

'Colin's just announced that Sapphire have charged Matt Beeston with rape.'

'That's good.' Grace relayed the information to Hilary, who let out a sigh of relief that she would have at least some positive news to present to the media.

'Once Matt's been before the magistrates, they'll send him back to us,' Lance continued. 'Colin's looking to bring murder charges by Tuesday at the latest.' Grace began to object, but Lance cut her short. 'Don't rain on his parade,' he warned, lowering his voice. 'Right now he needs every bit of reflected glory he can lay his hands on.'

'Maybe I should take the day off? Come in on Monday?'

'I think that would be wise. I'll keep you posted if there are any developments.'

'Thanks, Lance. Hang on, what about Danny?'

'He's downstairs. We're waiting on a shrink to say he's fit to be interviewed. But he's a time-waster. Twisted wannabe. We know that.'

Grace decided now was not the time to argue. 'OK, thanks.'

'Take care of yourself.'

Hilary dropped Grace at her flat and sped off to prepare for the daily press conference, which promised to be the liveliest yet. Grace slipped out of the formal grey suit and pale blue blouse she'd worn for her meeting with the chief con and pulled on her most comfortable jeans, a yellow vest and a peach-coloured short-sleeved T-shirt. The rain had cleared, the sun was back out and she wanted to celebrate her reprieve, so bright colours seemed like the right idea. She tied back her hair and dug out a pair of bug-eye sunglasses, hoping they'd be enough to stop anyone recognising her. She didn't want the fragile balloon of her positive mood burst by anyone connecting her with the 'brave officer' stupid enough to have let her 'thug husband' beat her up.

As she locked the door to her flat and made her way downstairs, she thought about Danny, waiting in the bowels of the police station. She didn't need a psychiatrist to tell her that he was more than a time-waster. It was not unusual for a perpetrator to hang around an investigation, courting great risk but apparently unable to leave it alone. Some try to be helpful, offering tea and biscuits to officers guarding the perimeter of a crime scene. Some turn up at their victims' funerals. And quite a few over the years had volunteered to talk to the press.

Grace considered what lay behind Danny talking to the *Courier*. She doubted that he craved celebrity or notoriety, nor that he resented another suspect taking credit for his crimes, though she knew that both were motives that had driven other infamous killers to seek publicity. It could be an attempt to mislead the police and muddy the waters of the investigation, or in hope that Ivo Sweatman would, in return, give him the inside track on what the police already had on him. But she believed Danny's purpose lay deeper: maybe, driven by guilt, it was his wishful thinking that the girl of his dreams *was* still alive that had created this fantasy of rescuing her. Saying it aloud and then seeing it in print might make it seem real.

She had intended to walk to Castle Park but now changed direction. So far none of the evidence she had gathered against Danny was any stronger than that against either Matt Beeston or Pawel Zawodny. She needed more than cod psychology if she was to stand any chance of persuading the team to listen to her. Back to basics: Danny had said that on the night Polly had asked him for a lift back to Wivenhoe he'd been drinking with some of his brother's army friends. It shouldn't be too difficult to work out which of the pubs near the garrison the paras had claimed as their own.

It was clear that the Armoury was a venue where local girls on the pull could chat up squaddies to their hearts' content. Even on a Saturday lunchtime the tight group of tanned, exceptionally fit young men at the bar was already surrounded by a flock of admiring and scantily dressed young women. It was easy to see how the soldiers' training and experience gave them a glamour reflected irresistibly back at them in the girls' shining eyes. Grace couldn't imagine Danny lasting two minutes in such company.

The landlord, who looked like a former drill sergeant, shook his head and directed Grace to the Dog and Whistle. 'Ask for Mandy,' he told her. 'It's the army wives who keep tabs on everything around here. Mandy's the mother hen and if she can't tell you what you want to know, no one can. And catch the bastard,' he called after her, waving an arm to encompass the excited girls around the bar. 'They're sitting ducks, this lot. No point telling them to go easy because they don't bloody listen.'

As Grace made her way to the Dog and Whistle, it occurred to her to wonder if the existence of a brother, too, might simply be another lie, an imaginary friend Danny had conjured up out of his need to belong. The pub, half empty and low on charm, was a featureless Sixties building with big windows along one wall through which the midday sun remorselessly illuminated every mark and stain on the red-patterned carpet. Grace ordered a water with lime juice from the barman, who, after a quiet word, pointed out a whippet-thin woman nursing a half of lager and chatting sedately to a couple of other women. 'Mother hen' was not the description Grace would have chosen. Mandy was probably about the same age as Grace but had a smoker's prematurely aged skin and the sinewy arms of someone used to hard manual work. Grace introduced herself, showed her warrant and apologised for disturbing her.

Mandy gave her an undisguised up-and-down look. 'It's OK,' she said, picking up a packet of Silk Cut and a disposable lighter. 'Mind if we chat outside?'

Grace followed her out to a small fenced-off area of damp concrete with a picnic table and a rubbish bin. Mandy lit a cigarette and perched up on the table, resting her feet on the grey wooden seat. She wore a gold ankle chain and her toenails were painted a frosted emerald green.

'What d'you want?' she asked.

'I need to speak to a para serving at Camp Bastion, name of Tooley,' said Grace. 'He's absolutely not in any trouble, but I need to check something with him.'

Mandy nodded, considering her response. 'Michael Tooley?'

Grace gave a slight nod, hoping this wasn't just coincidence. 'We think someone's been using his car without his permission.'

Mandy raised an eyebrow. 'His pimped-up Beemer? He won't be happy about that.'

'I'd rather not hang about waiting for official wheels to turn,' said Grace, hoping her excuses didn't sound too dodgy.

'It's important?' asked Mandy, turning her head to blow smoke out sideways, away from Grace.

'Yes.'

Mandy eyed her shrewdly. 'It'll be about young Danny, then?'

'Possibly. You know him?'

Mandy nodded. 'There's no harm in him, but he can be a pain in the arse.'

'What do you mean?'

'So it is about him, then?'

Grace smiled and sat up on the table beside her. 'Does he hang out much with his brother's mates?'

'Hangs on sometimes.'

'Might he have spent an evening drinking with them?'

Mandy's laugh turned into a cough, and she never replied. Grace sipped her cold drink, realising she was glad of the refreshment, and waited comfortably for Mandy to decide how much she wanted to say.

'Michael joined up to get away from home,' Mandy said after a few drags on her cigarette. 'Although I'm pretty sure his mum died three or four years back. Whatever, Danny's not a kid any more. He needs to get a life of his own. Michael's older and they had different dads, so there's only so much Michael feels he has to do for him. And I very much doubt that includes letting him chief his car.'

'I need to speak to Michael,' said Grace. 'Skype him if possible.'

Mandy shrugged. 'He'll only get so much Internet access a week. And that's only when he's on base.'

Grace fished in her bag for a card. 'I understand. But is there any way you could get word to him, ask him to get in touch with me?'

Mandy dropped the remains of her cigarette on the ground so she could take the card and tuck it away. She slipped off the table, sliding her flip-flop over the cigarette to extinguish it. 'Leave it with me,' she said, picking up the butt and then looking directly into Grace's eyes. 'Danny's not a bad lad, not at all. But his mum –' She pursed her lips in distaste as she walked over to the rubbish bin. 'Poor kid never stood a chance.'

As Grace hurried back to her flat, she thought about what Danny had said about his mother being ill. Her first impression of him had been that he was poor and undernourished. He'd said in the police interview room that 'these places' reminded him of when he was a kid, and that he'd had to leave school to look after his mum. She'd naively assumed that 'these places' meant a hospital, that his mother had been disabled or chronically ill. But what if she'd missed the most vital clue of all? Polly and Rachel had both been drunk. Rachel had been violated with a bottle of vodka, Roxanne with a discarded wine bottle. She'd always believed that booze was in some way an important thread in this case. What if Danny's mother had been an alcoholic?

Instead of going up to her flat, Grace got in her car. Danny was at the police station so it would be safe to take another look at where he lived. She wanted to focus her thoughts, and she hoped maybe there'd be something about that carefully tended, worn-out little house that would speak to her.

The main car park in Wivenhoe was full, so she left her car on a side road and took the path through the woods that she and Lance had followed with Jessica the day before. Even though the night's rain had fed the parched undergrowth, Grace found the trapped air beneath the trees claustrophobic and was glad when the path emerged into a small clearing where three cars were parked. She had not noticed it before when she'd cruised around the block with Lance, but she found that it opened directly onto Rosemead Avenue. Close by was a little row of garages from where she could see Danny's house. She asked herself what kind of life he lived there, what kind of childhood he'd had. A boy who loved reading yet had given up his education to care for his mum was someone who might plump up a pillow and slip it comfortingly under a woman's head. But Grace had seen too many chaotic families with kids both scared of and protective of erratic, neglectful, addicted parents to think that could be the whole story. If Danny had grown up forced to take responsibility for a parent lost to substance abuse, might he also be capable of punishing a woman for being drunk by pushing a vodka bottle into her vagina?

FIFTY-ONE

When the Child Intervention Team offices opened on Monday morning, Grace was already waiting outside. Over the rest of the weekend, with Lance's help, she had run what checks she could on Danny's mother. Retrieving her name from an old electoral roll, they'd learned that Marie Tooley had been arrested three times for being drunk and disorderly. Cursing herself for not having made this vital connection earlier, Grace had done her best to glean what information she could from the Child Protection weekend skeleton staff, and was trying hard not to let the hours she'd spent on hold or being told she needed to speak to someone who was on indefinite leave colour her attitude when she finally came face to face with an individual.

Charmaine Worrell's cramped office had all but vanished beneath a warehouse of dusty brown folders, each one of which Grace presumed must represent a family in crisis. It had been no different in Kent, where the same handful of families was known not only to the social workers but also to teachers, police, duty solicitors, magistrates and prison officers. In many ways Danny had done pretty well just to hold down his job in the bookshop and keep the grass cut in his back garden.

Charmaine had bright, intelligent brown eyes, and Grace imagined she ran a tight ship, despite the overload. Grace wasn't too surprised when she didn't need to open a file to respond to the name Danny Tooley. 'His mother was a chronic alcoholic,' she told Grace. 'By the time Danny was thirteen he was bathing her, cleaning up her vomit, keeping the house decent and somehow managing to buy her booze for her while she stayed in bed for weeks in a drunken stupor.'

'Why did no one do anything to help him?' asked Grace, appalled.

'He loved her,' Charmaine answered with a shrug. 'We removed Danny from her twice and each time he ran home, so in the end we more or less gave up.'

'What about his brother, Michael?'

Charmaine shook her head, her eyes straying to the lights blinking on the multi-line handset on her desk.

'He's older. Had a different father,' prompted Grace.

'Sorry, no memory of a brother. Maybe he never came to our notice. It'll be in the file.' She looked around her office. 'Somewhere.'

'Anything else you can tell me about the family? About Marie?'

Charmaine sighed. 'Only that she loved her booze an awful lot more than she loved her son. There were times when she treated him like dirt, or simply ignored his existence. Every once in a while she'd get sober and try to make it all up to him, but it never lasted more than a few weeks. Only Danny knows which was worse.'

Grace got to her feet. 'Thank you. You've actually been a great help, and I appreciate you making time to see me.'

Charmaine also rose courteously, smoothing her suit skirt over her wide hips with neat hands with freshly painted red nails.

'No doubt we'll be in line to share the blame, if it turns out there's been another avoidable tragedy,' she observed with discernable irony.

'I hope not,' said Grace, smiling.

Charmaine shrugged, one hand already hovering over her flashing phone.

As Grace made her way out through the narrow reception area, she came face to face with Ivo Sweatman, who sat in one of a row of beechwood chairs upholstered in a variety of soothing colours. Recognising her, he smiled as if he were pleased to see her. 'DS Fisher!'

Grace struggled to make a sound that wasn't an outraged groan. 'I don't want to speak to you.'

'You're here about Danny Tooley?'

Speechless, she pushed through the door beside him and headed down the stairs but soon heard his heavy footsteps behind her.

'Wait, please. I've spent time with Danny. I can help you. Let me help you.'

Grace was too angry and confused to listen. She banged on the green knob that was supposed to open the outer door but nothing happened. Ivo caught up with her.

'You have to keep pressing it,' he said.

She dropped her hand and stood aside. He pushed his palm against the button and the door swung open. He followed her outside onto the pavement. Realising that he wasn't about to give up, she turned on him. 'Who the hell do you think you are?' she demanded. 'What gives you the right to go grubbing about in my life? Just so you can sell newspapers!'

'I did it for you,' he said simply. 'I heard your job was on the line.'

She stared at him, not comprehending.

'It worked, didn't it?' Ivo grinned. 'I thought it was a nice piece. It was your idiot husband I skewered. And I bet you enjoyed watching your old boss Colin Pitman squirm.'

'I want you to leave me alone,' she said. 'Whatever happened to me, it's none of your business.'

She walked off, but he followed her again.

'What did you find out about Danny-boy, then? Did they tell you in there that his mum's favourite tipple was vodka?'

'What?' In spite of herself, Grace spun around to face him. Ivo nodded slowly, not taking his eyes off hers.

'Look, I'm sorry, OK?' he said to her. 'No one likes their dirty linen, and all that. But I was right, wasn't I? I bet the chief constable lapped it up.'

'How did you find out about Trev and me?' she asked. Her throat felt tight and she was suddenly afraid that she was going to cry. But she had to know the truth. 'Did Roxanne tell you?'

Ivo looked surprised more than surprised, wounded.

'Only that you knew each other at university, that you'd been with the Kent force. The rest wasn't exactly hard.' He must have seen her doubt, for he raised a hand. 'Scout's honour. Roxanne never breathed a word of it. Anyway, give me some credit. Finding stuff out is what I get paid to do.'

'She never told you about me and Trev?'

'Not a word. And I tried, believe me.'

Grace nodded, relief washing over her. She took a deep breath and blew it out again slowly.

'That's better,' he said. 'Now, tell me you weren't in there asking about Danny Tooley?'

As Ivo looked at her quizzically, she thought that he must have been a good-looking man when he was younger. His eyes shone with intelligence and, despite the broken veins in his cheeks, the sagging chin and the bald patch, he wielded his charm as if, once upon a time, he'd been used to women falling at his feet.

'So how far have you got?' he asked.

'I shouldn't even be talking to you!' She set off again along the pavement, but he fell in beside her, tucking a hand lightly under her elbow. It was an old-fashioned gesture that reminded Grace of her father, and she didn't shake him off.

'I realised something this week that I'd never thought about before,' he told her. 'I don't generally give a shit about who did the crime. I don't come at it from that angle. That's your job. But this one got personal. She was a sweet kid, your friend, and I owe it to her.'

Grace asked herself if he was spinning her a line, feeding

her the irresistible bait that would persuade her to drop her defences. If so, she wasn't rising to it.

'Truth is, I'd been coasting on this story,' he went on, ignoring her silence. 'Roxanne did all the work and I took all the credit.'

She nodded to show that she was, after all, listening.

'I think Danny Tooley killed her.' Ivo said it so quietly that at first Grace thought she'd misheard. 'I reckon you think the same,' he told her. 'Why else would you be talking to Child Protection first thing on a Monday morning?'

Grace stopped and drew back against a shop window to let other pedestrians go past. 'OK,' she said. 'Why don't you start?'

'As the actress said to the bishop.' Ivo dug in a pocket and pulled out his phone. He tapped and swiped and then handed it to her. On the little screen was a faded colour image of a small boy sitting cross-legged beside a thin, dark-haired woman in white leggings and an oversize pale-blue sweatshirt who sat hugging her knees on the floor of some kind of small outdoor wooden structure, like a toy fort in a children's playground.

'Is this Danny?' she asked.

Ivo nodded. 'With his mum. Fifteen years ago. Probably his only picture of her. It means a lot to him.'

Grace looked at it again. Danny and Marie each held a packet of crisps, and Danny was smiling with pure happiness. Marie, too, smiled for the camera, but not enough to hide the strain in her eyes. 'Did Danny really tell you she drank vodka?' she asked.

'No,' said Ivo with a wink. 'I made that up. But I hit the bullseye, didn't I?'

'Yes,' said Grace, intrigued that someone else had come to the same conclusions. 'Polly and Rachel were both drunk. I think that's what this is all about.'

'I know more than a little about what it's like to live with an alcoholic,' he told her. 'Two wives and a daughter all really believed they could help me beat this thing.' He shook his head. 'Doesn't happen like that. You'd be amazed how many times you have to let someone down before you finally convince them you're not worth it.'

'Are you still drinking?' asked Grace.

'No. But I had a long chat with Danny-boy. His mum obviously did her best, gave that vodka bottle some real welly and still couldn't get him to wipe his hands of her. Unlike his older brother. He saw sense and scarpered as soon as he could.'

'So when Danny wanted to take care of Polly, but she got drunk and slagged him off, he –'

'He lost it.'

It gave Grace confidence to hear someone else so perfectly in tune with her own thoughts, but there was no way she was about to get into an involved discussion with the chief crime correspondent of the *Courier* about a suspect in an ongoing murder inquiry. 'I need to get back to work,' she told him.

'I don't blame you for not trusting me. But I meant what I said before. If you ever need my help, it's yours.'

'Will you send me that photo?' She nodded towards the phone still in his hand.

'Sure. But don't forget, young Danny-boy isn't who he wants you to think he is.'

As Grace handed Ivo one of her cards, she reflected that he probably already knew her shoe size, never mind her email address. But nevertheless she felt awkward and embarrassed, as if something intimate had just passed between them, although to anyone passing by they were merely two people who'd apparently stopped on the pavement for a chat on their way to the office.

Ivo left her to head back the way they'd come. As she set off towards the police station, she remembered – almost with a stab of joy – what he'd said about Roxanne. Her friend had never betrayed her! It had all been her own paranoia and stupidity, which left her with the terrible realisation that if she had only listened and trusted and shared when they'd met that evening in the coaching inn, instead of making ridiculous accusations, Roxanne might still be alive.

FIFTY-TWO

Grace tried not to look surreptitious as she slipped into the MIT office as unobtrusively as she could. She made it to her desk without meeting anyone's eye; pity, contempt, embarrassment, she didn't want to know what anyone thought of the *Courier*'s revelations about her marriage. Lance seemed to sense her purpose, for he gave her merely an ordinary casual Monday morning greeting. 'OK?'

Grace smiled her thanks. 'Yes. Where are we up to?'

'Matt Beeston should be up before the magistrates in London on rape charges as we speak. Then the plan is that he'll be brought back to us. Keith's talking to the CPS lawyers to see if we've got enough to charge him with murder.'

Grace nodded.

'And the surveillance team have reported that Pawel Zawodny is taking steps to put all four of his houses on the market,' said Lance.

'Well, if he can't rent them,' said Grace. 'He told us it was always his intention to sell up and go home to Poland eventually.'

'Or off to some country with no extradition treaty,' said Lance darkly.

'You still think he killed Polly?'

Lance nodded. 'Sure of it. We'd have found her otherwise.'

Lance's certainty gave her pause. Where was Polly? If she was right, and Danny *had* killed her, what had he done with her body? That inkling of doubt raised another: why would Danny have wanted to kill Rachel Moston, a young woman he barely knew?

'Who interviewed Danny?' she asked, ignoring Lance's look of surprise at her sudden jump from Zawodny to Danny Tooley.

'Me and Duncan. He stuck to the same story he told Ivo Sweatman. Nothing would budge him.'

'And you don't believe him?'

Lance laughed. 'Keith was all for arresting him for wasting police time! This story about saving Polly, it's all in his head.'

'But you checked it out, what he said?'

'Of course.' Lance sounded a little irritated. 'Polly doesn't show up on the CCTV from Ipswich railway station where Danny said he dropped her off, and all the reported sightings coming in are still random, from all over the country. None of them so far stack up. All her cash, credit card, mobile network and social media links remain inactive. Dead.'

'What about Michael Tooley's BMW?'

Lance held up his hands. 'Yeah, OK, we picked it up on

CCTV in Colchester the night Polly went missing, but Danny says he was out drinking with his brother's friends. We're checking, obviously.'

'When will you know?'

'The army will get back to us in their own sweet time.'

'I'm hoping I might get to speak to Michael Tooley,' Grace told him. 'One of the army wives promised to get word to him, though he hasn't managed to make contact yet.'

'Why do you need to speak to him? We've got the car.'

Grace could see that Lance was losing patience with her. She looked around the room. The MIT office had a good buzz to it today in busy expectation of getting some positive results and successfully ending this first phase of the investigation. Even after the two suspects were charged, there'd still be plenty of work to do, but the fear – of failure, ridicule, another tragedy waiting to happen – would be gone. She understood why none of them would want her to tell them that they were wrong and should start over again.

'Danny's mother was an alcoholic,' she said. 'Twice they tried to take him into care, but he ran away, ran back to her. He missed out on his education so he could take care of her. His alcoholic mother was all he had. Polly and Rachel were both drunk. The bottles were about alcohol.' As Grace made each point, her own earlier doubts evaporated.

'Matt got women plastered so he could have sex with them,' argued Lance. 'Told himself that, if he was too rat-arsed to be responsible for what he was doing, it wasn't rape.'

'And Polly?'

'Matt didn't kill Polly. Pawel did. Look, Grace, I spent a good couple of hours running through Danny's story with him. He's a fantasist. Do you honestly think a sweet kid like Polly Sinclair is holed up somewhere, waiting for the heat to die down, knowing the hell her family must be going through? For two whole weeks?'

'No. I think she's dead.'

'But these were confident, aggressive crimes, probably very well organised, with split-second timing. Not Danny's style. He wouldn't hurt a fly.' Lance paused, clearly concerned that she'd take his opposition the wrong way. 'Not unless you're thinking of Anthony Perkins in *Psycho*, anyway!'

Grace tried to smile. 'Well, he's not a psychopath, but he has been damaged. I think badly damaged.'

'So Danny was in care, had an addict for a mother, so what? He wouldn't have got near Rachel Moston that night. She'd have eaten him for dinner.'

'That I agree with,' said Grace. 'And if he didn't kill Rachel, then he'd have no reason to kill Roxanne. Yet I still think the vodka bottle, the wine bottle, the jacket under Rachel's head –' She frowned and let out a sigh of frustration. 'Look, Lance, would you come with me to talk to Danny?'

Lance shook his head. 'They're bringing Zawodny in. Sorry, but I want to be here, be first in line to interview him.'

'Fair enough. But, please, don't forget Danny's crush on Polly was weird enough for him to come up with this whole rescue fantasy, this powerful wish for her still to be alive.' Grace almost added that Ivo was suspicious of Danny, too, but caught herself in time: seriously bad idea to admit she'd been passing the time of day with Ivo Sweatman! 'I think we'd be crazy not to take at least one more look at him,' she said instead.

It was Lance's turn to glance quickly around the office. 'First off, I really do think that Zawodny is our man. He killed Polly. He may not have meant to but, if you ask me, thanks to him she's feeding the fishes. And Matt Beeston's a nasty piece of work, more than capable of the other two killings. And second' – Lance lowered his voice – 'you'll be doing yourself no favours right now if you stick your neck out. No one else is going to run with you on this. You're new here. You have a history. You *were* talking to a journalist, even if the chief con decided to let it go. Don't get me wrong, I'm delighted she did!' he added hurriedly. 'I really am. But you must realise that you've seriously pissed off Colin Pitman. And I very much doubt he's a good enemy to have.'

'*I've* pissed him off?' demanded Grace. A dream she'd had last night came rushing back. It was one she'd had several times since Trev's mates had taken him away in a police van, a nightmare in which there was something stuck to her that she couldn't get rid of, no matter what she did, how hard she tried. She was beginning to realise that it was not about rejection or punishment, but shame at her own stupidity for ever imagining it would be all right, ever supposing that she deserved to have her life work out OK.

And now, did she honestly believe that the rest of the team were getting it wrong and she was the only one to see clearly? Or was she, as Trev, Colin and the others had repeatedly told her, obsessed with her own bloody-minded ego? Still out to prove that she was right?

She realised that Lance had a hand on her arm. 'Sorry,' he said. 'I didn't mean that. But' – he moved even closer and lowered his voice even further – 'there's been a rumour this morning that Colin could be disciplined over his failure to investigate that assault on the prisoner in the van back in Kent. Your ex-husband confirmed to Ivo Sweatman that Superintendent Pitman *was* aware of it and failed to investigate. So he'll be out to discredit you any way he can. Seriously, you really do have to watch your back.'

'OK, thanks.' Grace's heart did a little leap in hope that, however vindictive Colin might prove to be, the whole sorry mess might finally start to unravel. Meanwhile, she had to decide whether she really wanted to stand out against every one of her new colleagues.

Lance must have seen her uncertainty, for he patted her arm. 'Get some evidence,' he told her. 'Look, Grace, you and I disagree; that's fine. Who knows, maybe I'm wrong. But you need evidence.'

'Can you cover for me if I disappear for an hour or two?'

'Go!'

On her way out through the car park, Grace saw Pawel Zawodny getting out of a police car, escorted by two officers. His clothes and hair were dusty, as if they'd pulled him off a job and not given him a chance to change or even wash, but he stood up straight, his expression calm. She was too close to pretend she hadn't seen him, so she greeted him politely as she walked past.

'One day maybe I'll understand why a woman like you would want to do such a dirty job,' he said, looking at her sadly.

One of the officers caught Grace's eye and gave a tiny shake of the head. In any case, she knew better than to engage with such a remark and kept walking. Yet she felt a pang of guilt. It seemed to her that in two short weeks Pawel had been robbed of that golden edge of self-assurance with which he'd looked her up and down on her first morning with the Essex force, as though their suspicions and accusations had stolen something vital from him. But she beat down her feeling of regret. She owed him nothing. He was a suspect in a murder inquiry. And she had a job to do.

FIFTY-THREE

In pride of place on the tiled mantelpiece that surrounded a flame-effect electric fire was a framed 6x4" colour print of the photograph Ivo had shown Grace earlier this morning of Marie Tooley with her son. Danny placed an old-fashioned wooden tray down on the smoked-glass coffee table, then sat beside her on the couch. He wore the same kind of grey trousers and white shirt that he wore to work. He poured tea from a brown pot covered with a knitted tea cosy made to look like a country cottage, with flowers round the door and a red chimney as a bobble on top; the milk jug had roses on it, and he apologised for having no sugar. As Grace accepted a cup and saucer, she wondered where his good manners had come from, if perhaps there had once been grandparents on the scene.

She leaned back against the lumpy cushions of the dark-brown needlecord couch. 'So is this where you sat with Polly?' she asked.

'Yes,' he answered warily.

'What did you talk about?'

'Not much. Books. It was late and she was tired.'

'So had you arranged to meet that Friday evening or did you just bump into her in town? Or, given how upset she'd been, when she came into the bookshop to apologise to you that afternoon, maybe you were keeping an eye on her? Making sure she was safe?'

'She knew I'd always look out for her.'

'And you gave her a lift home?'

'Yes.'

'That was kind. But you brought her here rather than back to her place?'

'I've told all this to the other policemen.'

'I know, Danny, and I'm really grateful to you for going over it again.' Grace sipped her tea, looking around the threadbare lounge. 'Tell me, did Polly ever invite you to her house? It can't be far from here.'

'No, it's not.'

'So did you ever go there?'

'I liked it when she came here.'

'So when did she tell you that she wanted to disappear for a while?'

'She'd seen Dr Beeston again in the bar that night, and that upset her.'

'So did she first mention it in the car, or when you were sitting here with her?'

'It must've been in the car. She didn't want to go back to her house.'

'She'd been drinking quite heavily, hadn't she? You didn't

think maybe this plan to disappear was just the booze talking?'

Danny put his cup and saucer neatly back on the tea tray. 'I made her some tea, told her we could talk about it all calmly in the morning, but her mind was made up.'

'Where did she sleep?'

'Upstairs. Your tea's going cold.' He stood up, fidgety and nervous. 'Shall I get you some hot water?'

'No, I'm fine, thanks.' Grace sat quite still, waiting to see how Danny would deal with his agitation.

'I don't use the front bedroom, so I gave her my bed. I can show you, if you like.'

'OK, thanks.'

'I slept down here on the couch.'

Grace smiled. 'Like a proper gentleman.' She got to her feet, pushing herself up awkwardly from the saggy foam cushions.

She followed him up the narrow staircase and into the little back bedroom. It was furnished as if for a child, with a single bed and matching single white melamine wardrobe and chest of drawers. There were more books and a couple of framed black-and-white photos on the walls that she recognised from Ikea; one of Audrey Hepburn in *Breakfast at Tiffany's* and the other of Brooklyn Bridge. The sheets and duvet cover, too, though faded from frequent laundering, were cheerful Scandinavian patterns: she wondered if someone had taken Danny shopping or whether these were the spoils of a solitary trip in his brother's illicitly borrowed car. But any sense of pity she had for him was swiftly overlaid by the acute awareness that Polly may have died here. Grace simply couldn't imagine the young woman electing to sleep here, given that her own bed in Station Road was barely five minutes' walk away. Unless she'd not been sober enough to get there. Or dead. The thought made the hairs on the back of Grace's neck stand up.

'So did you, like, lend her a toothbrush and stuff?' she asked as cheerfully as she could, and watched Danny struggle to maintain the rosy fiction he'd offered Ivo of how he'd lent Polly some of his clothes and made sure she had everything she needed for her desperate adventure. The more questions Grace asked, the more she felt as if she were taunting him with his own lies; she could see that here in the reality of these rooms it became harder and harder for Danny to believe in the fairy-tale he'd spun himself of how he'd rescued his damsel in distress. Somehow, late that night, his fantasy had come to an abrupt end, and now he couldn't bear to admit to himself what he'd done to the girl he loved.

He was reluctant to let her look in the front bedroom, but she insisted politely until he had to open the door. She didn't go in: if this house *was* a crime scene, then the less she contaminated it the better. Even if there were no blood-stains, nor even the signs of a struggle because Polly had been strangled or smothered, there might still be other evidence here that would enable them to interrogate whatever account Danny gave of Polly's presence.

The bedroom had been completely stripped, right back to the floorboards; only the pale, sprigged wallpaper remained, with unfaded shadows where furniture or pictures had once been, along with old spattered stains that had been inadequately wiped off. Grace wondered with distaste if they were the ghostly marks of Marie Tooley's vomit.

'Was this your mother's room?' she asked.

'It's where she died,' he said.

'I'm sorry. You said she was ill and you took care of her. What was wrong with her?'

His reply was reluctant. 'She had problems. She was depressed.'

Danny immediately turned away and went downstairs. Grace took a last look around and then followed him back down to the dingy front room. Through the window, keeping to the public highway at the end of the driveway, she could see the little knot of photographers who'd been there when she arrived. They'd snapped her, just in case, but hadn't been unduly interested. She sat down again on the uncomfortable couch.

'Danny, we have CCTV images of Polly in Colchester on the night you brought her back here. She was so drunk that she could hardly stand up.'

'It was the night air. It went to her head.'

'What do you think about young women who get as drunk as that, like Polly was that night?'

'They can't help it.'

'Why's that?'

'It's not their fault. It's not what they're really like. Polly just needed someone to take care of her.'

'Just as well you were there for her, then. Tell me, do you drink?'

'No, never.'

Grace pointed to the photograph on the mantelpiece. 'Is that your mum?'

Although Danny nodded and smiled, Grace saw his body tense up.

'Before she got ill,' he said.

'How old are you there? Six, seven?'

'Yes. She was a good mother. She loved me.'

'I'm sure she did. What were you doing? Looks like you were having a picnic or something.'

'She liked picnics. When she was well, we used to do all sorts of nice things together.'

Danny put his hands around his knees and hugged them to him. As he began to reminisce, Grace could see that he had all but forgotten she was there. The longer he talked about cherished treats and remembered outings, the more she thought about the catalogue of neglect, chaos and degradation that must have been Danny's actual childhood.

As he showed her out twenty minutes later, standing back in the shadow of the door so the photographers couldn't catch a decent shot of him, she thanked him for the tea and was rewarded with his familiar sweet smile.

She could easily have walked down to the quay, but decided to move her car so she wouldn't have to face the cameras again when she returned for it. The car park wasn't too crowded on a Monday, and she made her way down to the water and sat on a bench looking out across the jingling masts of the boats to the mudflats on the far side of the river. What she'd learned was hardly going to satisfy Lance: it wasn't evidence. Yet she was more certain than ever, from Danny's body language, his evasions, his hopeless loyalty to his mother, that he had murdered Polly Sinclair.

Whether or not Polly had been too out of it to know where he was taking her or what she was agreeing to, his princess had assented to come home with him. Had he believed this was the start of the love affair he'd dreamed about? If so, then if Polly had probably been sober enough to reject him: for Danny, the shame of her rejection must have been unbearable.

What was it that Ivo Sweatman had said to her? *You'd be amazed how many times you have to let someone down before you finally convince them you're not worth it.* But did it work like that? What about the person whose faith and hope is endlessly thrown back in their face? How worthless do their efforts feel? How angry does that make them?

Grace was more convinced than ever that she couldn't follow Lance's well-meant advice to watch her back: Danny was too damaged, too vulnerable, too lethal. She couldn't just pipe down and let it go. But Colin and the review team were in charge now, and they were all gung-ho about charging Matt Beeston and possibly Pawel Zawodny, too; they weren't about to listen to her. Besides, she already knew exactly what her old DCI would say: Clear the ground beneath your feet. Go for the obvious before the fantastic. Bring me evidence, not mumbo-jumbo. She might hate Colin Pitman's guts but sometimes he was right.

There was only one way to prove this to herself. Grace had noticed a payphone near the entrance to the car park and made straight for it. Ivo Sweatman picked up after a couple of rings.

FIFTY-FOUR

Ivo couldn't even remember the last time he'd been up and dressed at this ungodly hour, let alone out of doors. And come to think of it, whenever the last time had been, he was more likely making his unsteady way home rather than standing around in the morning chill at the edge of a playing field, listening to the birds chirruping away like they were tuning up for school orchestra practice. He felt like Little Lord Fauntleroy or Fotherington-Thomas or some other childish sap who could actually tell the difference between one little brown bird and another. Fair enough, the Ice Maiden had asked him if he'd mind looking a fool if she turned out to be wrong, but when he'd told her he'd be honoured, he hadn't reckoned on a bloody nature ramble at first light on a Tuesday morning.

She'd told him to take another look at the photograph of Danny-boy's mother, and then to start in Wivenhoe Woods, especially any really overgrown areas close to the little car park at the end of Rosemead Avenue. He hadn't parked there for fear, at this unseemly hour, of attracting unwanted attention, which was the same reason he'd said he'd meet the dog-handler here on the playing field that bordered the woods. There was a middle-aged guy heading across the grass towards him now with a black-and-white dog on a lead, a kind of spaniel, Ivo guessed, though it looked too soft and playful to be capable of the kind of serious work he wanted done. And for which the Young Ferret had obligingly organised a handsome payment upfront.

Ivo hoped for her sake that the Ice Maiden wasn't clutching at straws. Danny-boy could have dumped Polly's body absolutely anywhere around here – in the creek, a gravel pit, beside a railway line where no one ever went – and he'd warned her that Whatshername from Sky News had already had her bonkathon ex-SAS tracker out here and found nothing. But the Ice Maiden hadn't cared. *She'll be somewhere safe, somewhere special, her head on something soft. That's how she'll be found.* That's what she'd said, and so here he was, prepared on her say-so alone to give it his best, even if that did mean risking every single brownie point he'd chalked up with his editor this past week.

He was wrong for starters about the soft-looking dog, for the guy came right up to him and greeted him by name, introducing himself as Martin and the spaniel as Lucy. Although Martin had explained it all to him on the phone, Ivo still couldn't for the life of him see how the cadaver dog wasn't going to get totally confused by all the different whiffs and odours that even Ivo's jaded nose could pick up as they drew closer to the trees, and Lucy herself seemed to be in such an ecstasy of busy excitement that Ivo figured it would take her all day to make her way through just the first few yards of vegetation.

Ivo showed Martin the photo on his phone: the background behind the amateurish wooden structure was out of focus, just fuzzy green outdoors, of no help at all. 'We're looking for something like an old den, that kind of thing,' he said. 'It'll be at least fifteen years old now, so there may only be a few bits of wood left, if there's anything at all. And it's likely to be well off any of the regular paths.'

'If there's something here, we'll find it,' Martin said calmly, and set off along the nearest track holding the eager Lucy on a short leash, leaving Ivo to resign himself to a long, footsore morning chasing around in ever-decreasing circles.

'And if you find anything, for God's sake don't touch it,' Ivo remembered to call after him. *Ring Keith, call 999, anything, but don't go near it* were the Ice Maiden's orders, not that he needed them: after Roxanne, the last thing on earth he wanted was the image of another dead girl in his head.

'I have done this before,' Martin called back over his shoulder, unperturbed.

And whatever you do, don't call me. You have to keep me right out of it. He'd heed that instruction, too, but found he couldn't summon up much relish for grabbing any glory that lay in finding the rotting corpse of 'Our Polly'. He'd gathered that DS Fisher was way out on the edge of a cliff here, backing her hunch about Danny-boy. He was convinced she was right, but feared that that poisonous little fart of a boss of hers, Colin Pitman, would probably be more keen right now on getting rid of her than convicting the right suspect. Ivo felt a stab of guilt that his headlines had helped to undermine Keith Stalgood's position, but hey, all's fair in love and war.

Lucy pulled her handler unhesitatingly along paths that all led in the same direction, and the dog was now clearly determined to continue in a straight line into less frequented undergrowth. Ivo and Martin had to fight their way through vicious brambles and thick, spiky bushes. By the time they came across a broken-down ladder which, though well hidden, was, as Martin pointed out, lying on top of this year's new growth, even Ivo could smell it. Fuck, it was horrible! But, peer as he might through the dense tangle that surrounded them, he couldn't see anything that resembled a den or a kids' stockade. Lucy sat back on her haunches facing the spreading base of a rugged oak tree, her nose pointing up at the trunk. As Ivo watched the dog sit there, so still, yet taut with quivering anticipation, his brain clicked into gear: a ladder! He looked up, and there above him, maybe fifteen or twenty feet up and laid across two thick branches, was the platform of what must once have been a fairly substantial tree house. Between the rotting planks Ivo could make out a bundled shape tightly wrapped in black plastic.

'Let's get out of here,' he said, blundering back the way they'd come, praying that he wouldn't throw up. Martin followed, making a big fuss of his dog, rewarding her for a job well done.

'Two weeks ago, you say she went missing?' he asked Ivo.

Ivo nodded, not trusting himself to open his mouth.

'Whoever left it there must've trussed it up tight or you wouldn't have needed the dog to find her. Not in this weather. Mind you, it's been protected from the worst of the rats and the carrion birds.'

Ivo wasn't listening. He was trying to keep his hand steady enough to find the right number on his phone. It was only when he heard Keith's sleepy voice that he realised he'd woken him up, that it was still only half-past five in the morning.

FIFTY-FIVE

Grace had been woken at two by the Skype ringtone on her laptop, which she'd left on the floor by her bed. The connection to southern Afghanistan had been patchy, but, as the sun was rising in Helmand, and before the 40-degree temperatures kicked in, she'd been able to have an illuminating conversation with Michael Tooley, a matter-of-fact professional soldier in khaki singlet and shorts sitting in what looked like a swelteringly hot metal shipping container. She felt like she'd only just fallen asleep again when her mobile rang sometime after six. It was Keith, calling from Wivenhoe Woods where he was waiting to meet the forensic pathologist and the crime scene manager. The second he'd heard that Ivo Sweatman, aided and abetted by a trained cadaver dog, had discovered what, according to the dog-handler, could only be human remains in the collapsing remnants of a kids' tree house, he'd driven there with blues and twos all the way from Upminster. Grace did her best to sound astonished.

By the time she was climbing the stairs to the MIT office

shortly before seven, all hell had broken loose. She met Hilary coming down. 'I've just been told a third suspect has been arrested,' she said, 'and there's not a single officer available for the morning press conference. What on earth am I supposed to tell the media this time!'

Hilary clattered off and Grace went into the office. Lance materialised at her side as if he'd been waiting for her. 'You have anything to do with this?' he asked with a sly grin, his eyes shining with excitement.

'Me? No!'

'Yeah, right. But don't worry, my lips are sealed. They're bringing Danny in now.'

'Good.'

'I told the superheroes it has to be you who leads the interview, that you're the only one who's had a real handle on this right from the start.'

Grace was surprised, and touched. 'Thank you.'

'Come on! It's your collar, regardless of whatever funny handshakes you've been having with Ivo Sweatman.'

Confirming Lance's words, Superintendent Millington immediately called Grace into her office, and she, Grace, Lance and Duncan spent the next hour planning the interview strategy. Before they were finished, Keith called from the mortuary to report that Dr Tripathi had now cut through enough of the tightly bound layers of black refuse sacks and gaffer tape to confirm that they contained human remains. It would take some time to fully uncover the body, which had been wrapped with great care in a clean bedsheet and then swaddled with an eiderdown, but the pale blue dress the corpse was wearing would appear to confirm unofficially that they had found Polly Sinclair. Formal identification and preliminary post-mortem results would follow later in the day, and they'd keep the interview team updated.

When Grace and Duncan entered the interview room an hour later, Danny was already sitting at the table beside one of the duty solicitors, who nodded familiarly to Duncan. Danny picked nervously at the loose cuffs of his plain white work shirt and listened numbly as Duncan went through the formal preliminaries. The dark hairs showing on Danny's arms above his bony wrists looked as if they had sprouted there overnight, making his pale skin seem naked and exposed, that of a child in an adult body.

It had been agreed, after some discussion, that Grace would begin by showing Danny the print-out of the photograph that he had framed on his mantelpiece. 'You know what this is, don't you, Danny?' she asked, identifying it for the tape as a numbered exhibit.

'How did you get that?'

'You let the journalist from the *Courier* take a photo of it. And we talked about it yesterday, didn't we?

'Yes.'

'Where was it taken, do you remember?'

'I was only little.'

'Was it in Wivenhoe Woods?'

'I don't remember.'

'Think hard, Danny. When's the last time you visited this place?'

'Not for years. I don't know where it is.'

'So it would surprise you, then, if we told you that we're pretty certain we've found it?'

Danny stared at her in obvious panic. Grace had tried earlier to explain to Lena Millington that Danny was immature, naive, a fantasist, but also ruthless, cunning and manipulative, not in pursuit of power over other people but in defence of his own self-delusions. He was panicking now from fear not that he'd been caught but that his precious house of cards would come tumbling down and leave him facing nothing but emotional and psychological ruin.

'I spoke to your brother, Michael, earlier this morning.'

'You can't have done! He's in Helmand.'

'He is, yes. But we had a video call. He told me about your mother's illness.'

'She was depressed. He never understood depression.'

'Your mother may have been depressed, but she was also an alcoholic, Danny.'

Danny smoothed his fingers over the photograph of Marie Tooley. 'This is my mother. Look at her. She's fine. She's lovely.'

'Yes,' agreed Grace. 'On a good day. A rare good day, from what Michael told me.'

'She was a lovely mother.'

'But there were also months at a time when she failed to get out of bed, soiled herself, vomited and refused to clean it up. And rewarded your devoted care with vile abuse.'

'She was ill. I looked after her.'

'You did, Danny. I know. Michael could never understand why you stayed. Why you didn't get out like he did. I spoke to the social workers who also tried to help you. They said you missed so much school on her account that it was a miracle you got any education at all.'

'She couldn't help it. She tried. When she was well, she promised it wouldn't happen again. She never meant to be like that. She was ill. It's not who she really was.'

'Like Polly?'

Danny's head shot up and he stared at her, his mouth hanging open in shock.

'Polly was really rude to you that night in Colchester when she asked for a lift. Even Dr Beeston was surprised that she had such a mouth on her.'

'She didn't mean it! She came specially to apologise the next day!'

'And when she got drunk again the next night, and was staggering around alone in the centre of Colchester at one in the morning, what did you think?'

'I took care of her.'

'But then she turned out to be just as ungrateful as your mother, didn't she, Danny? Polly didn't love you any more than your mother did.'

Danny placed both hands on the table, shoved his chair back and got to his feet. For a moment Grace thought he was going to attack her, and she tried hard to remain impassive, glad of Duncan beside her. But Danny turned to his solicitor. 'She can't do this. She can't talk like this. Make her stop.'

The solicitor soothed him and got him to sit down again, explaining that, though he was free not to answer, the police could ask him anything they liked.

'What did your mother like to drink?' said Grace. 'Did she like vodka?'

'Tea. She liked to drink tea.'

'Not according to your brother, Michael. If she got to choose, then she liked vodka, but most of the time she'd take whatever was cheap, whatever was on special offer. She made Michael give you an ID card so you could pretend to be eighteen and go out to buy her booze for her. You always had to buy whatever was on special offer, or she'd yell and curse at you when you got back.'

Danny folded his arms, sitting straight in his chair, chin down, legs pressed together, not looking at anyone.

'But it was the booze that stopped her loving you, wasn't it, Danny? Stopped her being the lovely mother who took you on picnics and ate crisps with you in a tree house in the woods.'

Danny went on pretending not to hear.

'Fire'n'Ice was on special offer the week that Rachel Moston was killed.' Grace tried to keep the excitement out of her voice. She still had some lingering doubt about whether Danny was really capable of luring a confident young woman like Rachel onto a demolition site in the middle of the night. She was desperate to get to the truth, to know finally what had happened that summer night when all the students were out celebrating the end of their exams.

She opened a folder she had placed earlier on the table.

'You'd have recognised Rachel from the bookshop, is that right?'

Danny nodded imperceptibly.

'For the tape, please.'

'Yes.'

'But she was never nice to you like Polly.'

'She had no idea who I was.'

'So it was OK to be angry with her. You were upset and distressed about what happened that night when, as you told us, you had given Polly a lift home. Unbearably distressed, perhaps. Rachel was strangled five days after Polly went missing. Whoever did that left a very definite message in the way he posed her body.' Grace dealt out three crime scene photos. 'What do you think this meant?' she asked. She placed her fingertip on the paper, pressing down firmly on the glistening bottle of Fire 'n' Ice between the pale thighs.

After a single glance, the solicitor looked away, his face contracting in disgust. Grace watched Danny carefully. Whatever he felt, it was not surprise: he knew exactly what to expect.

'I think whoever did this wanted to explain something, to explain his feelings,' said Grace. 'Rachel had been out celebrating. She'd completed her degree and would be leaving uni for a good job. She'd been out with her friends and had drunk one too many on a warm, balmy night. That's when you saw her leaving the Blue Bar, right?'

Danny stared at Grace, his mouth set with a belligerence she'd never seen in him before.

'So, what? You offered her a lift? Told her you also lived in Wivenhoe and that your car was parked nearby? Is that how you got her to walk with you?'

'She'd been sick,' he said abruptly. 'The cabs refused to take her in case she threw up again.'

'So you were looking after her?'

'I said I'd get her home.'

'But you didn't.'

He shook his head.

'For the tape.'

'No.'

'Where did the vodka bottle come from?'

'It was on a wall. Someone had left it there. She said it was a shame to let it go to waste and started drinking from it. She'd just been sick! It was disgusting.'

'So she deserved this?' Grace pointed to the crime scene images. 'She ought to be ashamed for being so drunk. For not being nice to you when you were trying to look after her. For not being Polly.'

'I'd never hurt Polly like that!'

'No. Not like this. You wrapped her up in an eiderdown. Put a frilly pillowcase under her head. Its pair was retrieved from your airing cupboard an hour ago.'

Danny stared at her as if she was speaking a foreign language.

'But afterwards, after you'd done this to her, you took Rachel's red jacket and folded it up, didn't you?'

This time Danny nodded. 'The bricks were filthy, sharp. The dirt was getting in her hair. I didn't know what else to do.' He raised his head with a look of pride. 'I'm good at looking after people.'

Now Grace was coming to the part that was hardest for her. She swallowed back the grief and squared her shoulders. 'And Roxanne Carson?' she asked, hoping her voice wouldn't tremble. 'You didn't take such good care of her.'

'She was going to write stuff about Polly.'

'And about you.'

'I didn't care about that. But she was going to put things in the paper that weren't true. All she wanted to talk about was Polly being drunk and having sex with Dr Beeston. She wouldn't stop asking questions.'

'And you wanted to stop her from printing that kind of stuff?'

'She didn't understand!' cried Danny. 'None of that stuff was Polly's fault. I loved her!'

'But Polly's dead, Danny. How did that happen, if you loved her?'

'I don't know.'

'I think that you hoped Polly would love you back. Especially after she came to the shop to apologise to you. That proved she liked you.'

Danny nodded.

'Maybe you even imagined that meeting up with her in Colchester, taking her home, was like a date. That maybe she felt the same way you did.'

He stared at her with anxious, poignant hope, as if somehow the past could be rewritten.

'But once she'd had a drink, she changed,' said Grace. 'She didn't like you so much after all.'

'No, we're friends.'

'It's the hope that's so cruel, isn't it? When you hope for something, hope for love, and it doesn't happen, you feel let down, stupid, ashamed, like it's your fault for wanting it.' Deep in her mind Grace heard the click of a kettle switching off: she knew in her very bones the shame of that moment when you realise that you are not loved as you stupidly believed yourself to be. That moment of shame could change a person forever. 'Polly turned you down, didn't she?' she asked. 'Destroyed your hope.' Grace had spent only one night alone in a budget hotel bed that never got warm. Danny's childhood had been unimaginably worse and gone on for far longer than that. 'Made you feel like you weren't worth bothering with.'

'She wasn't like that!'

'That must have been unbearable.'

'No. It didn't happen.'

'Which is why you wanted to show that you were looking after her, to leave her pure and safe in your special place, the place where you enjoyed lovely picnics with your mum.'

Danny stared at her.

'We'll be able to match the perforations of the bin bags you wrapped her up in to the remainder of the roll under your sink. We'll be able to work out exactly what happened that night. Danny?'

'What?'

'Have I understood? For the tape, please.'

But Danny smiled and shook his head, and then stretched out a finger and gently stroked the image of his smiling mother. 'Polly went away,' he said, still smiling. 'She wanted to go somewhere safe, where bad things wouldn't happen, and I helped her.'

FIFTY-SIX

As Grace turned into Alma Street, she could see Pawel Zawodny already waiting outside the house. He smiled as she drew near, his coat collar pulled up against the early autumn chill from the river.

'Thanks for coming yourself to meet me,' she said.

'My pleasure. I think I owe you something for my being free to come here and not in a cell.'

'Hardly!'

He had the key ready in his hand. 'You want to see inside?'

'Please.'

He opened the front door. The single downstairs space seemed much bigger now that it was unfurnished, with only the built-in shelves and slatted blinds remaining from when Caitlin and Amber had lived here with Rachel Moston. The wood-effect floor and all the surfaces were spotless, and the low September sunlight streamed in through the glass of the conservatory extension. She was happy that it was all so different to the Edwardian terrace she had shared with Trev. Her old home in Maidstone was now sold, her divorce would soon be final and she could at last abandon her featureless rented flat. This house would be a new beginning.

'It's just as lovely as I remember,' she told him.

'You don't feel it's unlucky? Or haunted?'

'No. Do you?'

Pawel pulled a face. 'Unlucky for me, maybe. But not so much as for those poor girls.'

'But you're still selling up?'

He nodded. 'Two are already sold.'

'But you know that I spoke to the university accommodation people,' she told him. 'They said they'd reinstate your houses on their lists.'

He shrugged. 'Yes, they told me. And thank you. But there will always be doubt about me here. Maybe only behind my back, but it will follow me around. Better I go home, make my mother happy.'

Although he smiled, his eyes – the same blue as the bare walls, she noticed – had a hurt, guarded look.

'So you'll accept my offer?' she asked.

He held out his hand and she took it, liking his dry, warm grasp. They shook on the deal, and then he followed her upstairs.

'If you want me to do any work before you move in, just let me know. I charge you a fair rate.'

'Thank you, yes, I may want some extra shelves and things.'

'He's in prison, the man you caught?' he asked abruptly.

'Danny Tooley. Yes. Awaiting trial. He's pleading guilty

to two of the murders, but he still won't actually admit to killing Polly Sinclair. We have clear-cut evidence, and he doesn't even really deny it, but I don't think he can bear to bring himself to say it aloud, not even to himself. Not yet, anyway. And maybe he never will.'

'But he wasn't the one in bed with Polly that morning?'

Grace could hear a strain of anxiety in Pawel's voice. 'No,' she said. 'That wasn't the man who killed her.'

'I can't forgive myself. I should have made sure she was all right.'

'If she was hurt that morning, then Matt Beeston is responsible, not you.'

He didn't look convinced. 'How are their families?'

'Not great. Maybe once the trial's over, it'll be a tiny bit easier and they'll find some kind of peace. I doubt it, though. I don't think the families ever truly recover.'

He nodded sympathetically, then moved to stand by the bedroom window, making out that he was checking the catch on the casement. 'I was very angry with you for a long time,' he said without turning around.

'I can imagine.' She didn't know what else to say. It didn't feel right to apologise, however unfair the consequences that had followed on from his arrest. The fall-out and detritus of a violent crime – like the occasional tattered yellow ribbon that still fluttered from trees or lamp posts around the campus – was perhaps never entirely effaced.

'You had to say those things to me,' he said, turning to face her. 'It was your job, but you didn't really believe any of it, did you?'

Grace thought of all the people – including Colin Pitman – who had congratulated her once Danny had been charged with all three murders, who had insisted they'd always trusted her judgement; Keith had been the only one she'd believed, and Lance the only one who truly meant it when he'd grinned and said he didn't mind admitting that he'd been wrong but that he didn't intend to make a habit of it. He'd also been the first to buy her a drink after she'd been made back up to DI. After everything she'd been through in Kent, the vindication had felt absolutely wonderful.

'Not for a moment,' she told Pawel with a smile. It was a good lie, a decent and respectful one, and as she uttered it, she realised that, deep down, despite his masculine pride and arrogance, she probably never really had thought of him as other than he was – a kind, honest, old-fashioned and hard-working guy.

He took a deep breath and exhaled joyously, most of the tension vanishing instantly from his face. Seeing the effect of her words, Grace smiled and held out her hand. Pawel ignored it. Instead he placed both hands lightly on her shoulders and kissed her formally on both cheeks.

At the front door, Grace turned back to look around once more at the light, open space that Pawel had created and that would soon be her new home. She would be happy here, she promised herself.

ACKNOWLEDGEMENTS

My original idea for this novel was hugely enriched by the ideas and experience of Jackie Malton, former DCI, story consultant, addiction counsellor and writer. I can't thank her enough for her generosity, wisdom and friendship – and for a great day out in Wivenhoe.

Several other people, from my brother to total strangers whom I accosted via Twitter, have also very generously given me the benefit of their expertise, and I would like to thank Allen Anscombe, Anthony Bateman, John Twomey, James Calnan, Josh Warwick, Geoff Ward, Mary Carter, Merle Nygate, Claire Baker and Camilla Grey. For writerly support there are none better than Elizabeth Buchan, N.J. Cooper and Laline Paull. All my characters are figments of my imagination and all errors entirely my own.

As ever, I would like to thank my wonderful and inspiring agent Sheila Crowley and her assistant Rebecca Ritchie at Curtis Brown, and Jane Wood, the most patient, kind and astute of editors, Katie Gordon, Margot Weale and all the rest of the great team at Quercus.